Praise for *The Dark Becomes Her*

"Lin has written a chilling and enthralling dive into Taiwanese mythology. Read it with all the lights on. Deliciously terrifying."
—Kat Cho, *New York Times* best-selling author of *Once Upon a K-Prom*

"A layered and emotional horror novel, viscerally told, where the weight of familial expectations takes on the fearful proportions of a monster and the bonds of love grow twisted and strange. Spine-tingling, pulse-stirring, and expertly crafted."
—Ava Reid, #1 *New York Times* best-selling author of *A Study in Drowning*

"*The Dark Becomes Her* is the best kind of horror story, drawing on vivid imagery and emotion to craft a story of sisterhood and spirits, of gods and family expectations, of the world of the dead and the (equally terrifying) world of adolescence—I couldn't put it down."
—Kate Alice Marshall, author of *Rules for Vanishing*

"Brimming with unsettling ghosts and haunting Taiwanese legends, this book will crawl under your skin and possess you."
—Rebecca Schaeffer, author of *Not Even Bones* and *Only Ashes Remain*

THE DARK BECOMES HER

Other books by Judy I. Lin

A Magic Steeped in Poison
A Venom Dark and Sweet
Song of the Six Realms

**More young adult stories
from Rick Riordan Presents**

Ballad & Dagger by Daniel José Older
The Last Canto of the Dead by Daniel José Older
A Drop of Venom by Sajni Patel
It Waits in the Forest by Sarah Dass

THE DARK BECOMES HER

JUDY I. LIN

HYPERION
Los Angeles   New York

First Edition, October 2024
1 3 5 7 9 10 8 6 4 2
FAC-004510-24200

Printed in the United States of America

This book is set in Maxime Pro/Monotype
Designed by Zareen H. Johnson
Stock images: ink 551435188/Shutterstock

Library of Congress Cataloging-in-Publication Data
Names: Lin, Judy I, author.
Title: The dark becomes her / Judy I. Lin.
Other titles: At head of title: Rick Riordan presents
Description: First edition. • Los Angeles ; New York : Disney/Hyperion, 2024. •
Audience: Ages 12–18. • Audience: Grades 7–9 • Summary: When a ghost from
the spirit world transforms her sister, Ruby Chen confronts the dark upheaval
in Vancouver's Chinatown as she enters into an ancient battle over the gateway
to the underworld as she attempts to save her sister and her community.
Identifiers: LCCN 2023058691 • ISBN 9781368099097
(hardcover) • ISBN 9781368099158 (ebook)
Subjects: CYAC: Sisters—Fiction. • Spirits—Fiction. • Vancouver
(B.C.)—Fiction. • Canada—Fiction. • Taiwanese—Canada—
Fiction. • Horror. • Horror fiction. • LCGFT: Novels.
Classification: LCC PZ7.1.L554 Dar 2024 • DDC [Fic]—dc23
LC record available at https://lccn.loc.gov/2023058691

Reinforced binding

Follow @ReadRiordan
Visit www.HyperionTeens.com

SUSTAINABLE FORESTRY INITIATIVE

Certified Sourcing

www.forests.org
SFI-01681

Logo Applies to Text Stock Only

For Mimi, the best sister ever
(You still owe me a bubble tea)

Please be aware there are content warnings for this book that some may be sensitive to. These involve descriptions of body horror and gore, descriptions involving the threat of and the occurrence of physical violence including mentions of self-harm, loss of parents (off page), and mentions of stigma against mental illness and substance use.

CONTENTS

Dark Magic in Chinatown

There is magic in this book. I can attest to this because I started reading *The Dark Becomes Her* one morning, thinking I would preview a couple of chapters, and by the time I looked up, it was evening and I had finished the book. I *never* read that fast.

Along the way, I encountered so many wonderful lines that I had actually stopped to *take notes*. Reader, I never take notes. Strange magic indeed that Judy I. Lin has conjured.

What is her secret—? A phoenix-feather wand? An eldritch book of spells? Nope. Turns out the author is just really good at creating believable characters within a terrifying story. And when I tell you this novel falls into the category of horror, I'm not just talking about the supernatural. Sure, there are nightmarish creatures lurking in the shadows. There are ghosts, demons, and mysteries that will chill your blood. But the greatest horrors Judy I. Lin conveys are the ways humans treat one another in their everyday lives, captured in this brilliant tale of second-generation Taiwanese immigrants in Vancouver, British Columbia.

Our hero, Ruby Chen, is haunted by visions. She sees strange shapes moving in the darkness, but she has learned not to talk about them. She has enough to worry about without her family thinking she is losing her mind. As the eldest daughter, Ruby is expecting to set a perfect example. She must excel at school, do all her extracurriculars, apply to the best colleges, and keep an eye on her younger sister, Tina, who increasingly resents Ruby's attempts to keep her on track. Her parents' expectations keep Ruby in an impossible situation—a pressure cooker of stress that many young readers will relate to. As Ruby puts it: "I feel like I'm breaking myself into pieces, again and again, none of the edges quite fitting right into the portrait of what they want me to be." The horrors of this story start long before we find out the truth about Ruby's visions. They are the horrors of disappointing your family, of being unable to follow your dreams, of leaving your friends behind and losing the friendship of a cherished sibling, or of something as simple and creepy as walking alone through a half-abandoned shopping mall at night.

And when the specters arise, taking our story to a whole new sinister level . . . well, I love the way Lin blends the quotidian horrors of being a modern teenager with ancient supernatural horrors drawn from Chinese folklore. Ruby finds herself racing to save her sister from a terrible fate, but it's only a magical extension of what any teenager fears: failing herself, failing her family, and losing her identity in the great unknown of the future. Our worst monsters don't look like monsters. As Ruby says after one chilling encounter: "The man who grabbed me looked like he could be my dad, an uncle, a teacher at my school, one of the security guards talking to my parents now. He could be any one of them. That was the most frightening part of all." In Ruby's world, there is no boundary between the supernatural and the natural. It is all part of the same dark tapestry.

But don't think that this story is all shadow and fright. It is also a tale of young love, heroism, and the resilience of community. You will be rooting for Ruby from the very first chapter, as she attempts to find her own path through the spirit realm and the gloomy streets of Vancouver's

Chinatown. There is music, tasty food, camaraderie, dancing, and laughter. You will want to stay in Ruby's world long after the book ends, even if it means facing those strange monsters you sometimes see out of the corner of your eye. As usual, Ruby says it best: "We're all phantoms, flitting in and out of each other's lives." I'm so glad I got to be a phantom, drifting through this wonderful story with the Chen family. I think you will be too!

Rick Riordan

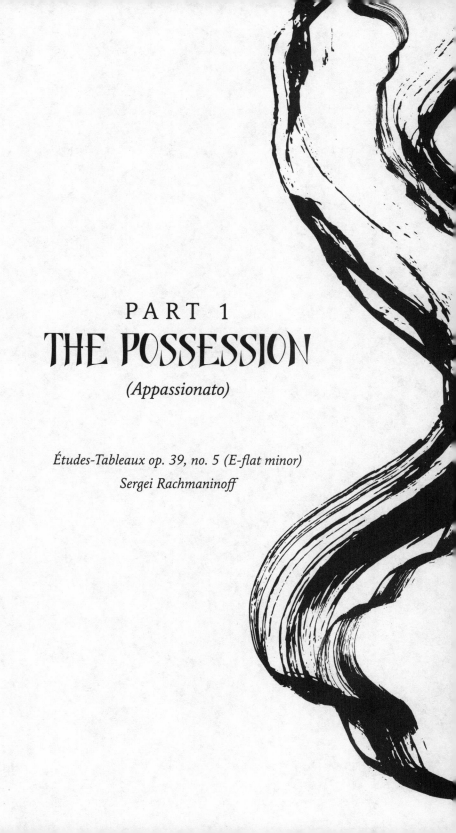

PART 1
THE POSSESSION
(Appassionato)

Études-Tableaux op. 39, no. 5 (E-flat minor)
Sergei Rachmaninoff

ONE

靈 心

(Soulful Heart)

The tick, tick, tick of the metronome drills the rhythm into my mind. I rest my hands lightly on the keys, the nervous expectation crawling across my shoulder blades like the legs of too many bugs skittering over skin. My teacher's attentive gaze bores a hole into the back of my head, waiting for me to begin. I take a deep breath and launch myself into the wild, feral tangle of notes that is one of Rachmaninoff's Études.

My right hand ascends into a discordant scale, while the left coaxes out an underlying melody that winds through those notes, like a beacon of light through the darkness. The music pulls me forward, until I emerge into a grand cathedral. I feel as if I'm surrounded by the ringing of bells, building and building until it echoes through the small studio. Finally, it erupts into the thunderous and triumphant wall of sound this piece is known for. I am filled with the thrilling grandeur, the overwhelming romance of it . . . then my left ring finger catches. It slips on the black key, and my other fingers follow, having lost the rhythm.

"Ruby! Keep going!" my teacher yells into my right ear, suddenly too close, clapping along with the metronome to force me to keep the pace, but it's no use. I fumble through the complicated fingerings, the notes crashing into one another until it all collapses. I sit there, at the center of the fiery ruin, the sound still ringing in my ears.

Disappointment slices its way through me. I clench my hands on my lap, resisting the urge to slam my fists onto the keys.

This is the piece that is supposed to prove to myself and to my parents that I'm better, that I can perform again. The one I've practiced so much that sometimes I wake up with my hands still twitching, with no reprieve from the music even in my dreams.

"You were doing okay until here." Mrs. Nguyen taps the tip of her silver pointer on the page—the black notes accompanied by the series of penciled-in fingerings, reminding me of how the sequence is supposed to flow.

"I can try it again," I say to her. "One more time."

"I think we're out of time for today," she tells me, and sets the pointer down on the edge of the piano. "You've made good progress on the other pieces, it's only this one that you're still . . . having trouble with."

I stay quiet and play with a frayed thread on my jacket. Somewhere above our heads, a fan whines as it starts spinning, as if sharing its own disapproval. I already know what my teacher will suggest next.

"You know, you don't have to do the Rachmaninoff," she says to me gently. "We can work on another piece instead. I'm fairly confident we can find a replacement for the program that will showcase your skills just as well."

But I don't want just any piece in the program. That feels like giving up. Like my parents were right, piano is only a hobby, something to put on my list of achievements so that I can move along the predetermined path of university degree, professional program, bright and shining future.

"I just need a few more weeks," I say, trying to sound confident, but it comes out shaky instead.

Mrs. Nguyen's lips purse, like she wants to say something, then she nods. "All right, we can give it another couple of weeks, but we have to decide on the program soon so that we can dedicate the rest of the year to completing your exam."

My stomach clenches, but I nod.

"I'll see you next week," she says, running a cloth over the surface of the keys. "Oh, and Ruby? I think you should talk to your sister about returning for her lessons, even if she only wants to scale back to once every two weeks. Seems like such a waste for her to stop now when she's almost ready for the next exam."

I pretend to be focused on slipping on my shoes so Mrs. Nguyen doesn't see my face.

"She's really busy at school," I mumble to the door. "My parents signed her up for tutoring. She doesn't have a lot of free time anymore."

"Right, right." Mrs. Nguyen sighs. "You're both at Westview now. Your education is important."

Tina and I started at Westview in January. It's a private school that promises a high university acceptance rate for all its graduates. A school that we would have had no chance entering if it wasn't for my mother's new job there. Something that she reminds us constantly we should be grateful for.

I say goodbye and scurry out the door before Mrs. Nguyen asks more questions about Tina's commitment to piano. The truth is, my sister almost wept tears of joy when my parents told her that she didn't have to take piano lessons anymore.

They don't want what happened to me to happen to her too.

—

The studio is tucked away on the second floor in a far corner of the mall, clustered together with a few offices that are only open during the day. They're all locked up at this hour, blinds drawn. There's only the dim light of the exit sign in the corner, and a single flood lamp that illuminates the hallway.

Creepy. I pull my bag closer to me, as if I could use it as a shield in case anything jumps out at me from the shadows. I hurry past the doors of the other businesses, until I'm at the glass railing that looks out over the hallway below, where there are more lights. Other people.

I don't remember this place being so eerie when I was a kid. Back when I had to attend Chinese school here, it was on Saturday mornings, in the daylight. Three years later, and the Pacific Dragon Mall has not been updated at all. The passage of time is even more obvious now with the peeling paint and broken tiles.

I check my watch and wince, quickening my steps and hurry down the main stairwell. It's already half past six, which means the bus should arrive in the next five minutes. If we miss that bus, then we'll have to wait in the shelter that always stinks of feet. I hope that Tina is paying attention to the time and waiting for me already, but I don't see her near the broken fountain or at the glass doors of the main entrance.

The rain is still coming down hard outside, turning the view of the street into gray, unrecognizable smears. In the foyer, crisscross strips of yellow light cut across the floor from the security gate that separates the sushi restaurant from the rest of the mall. The long glass window to my right runs along the opposite wall, covered with decals of silhouettes moving through a series of poses. A handstand with legs extended in a split, a backflip arcing through the air, a head tipped to one side peeking out from behind a fan.

Chinese characters are engraved on a wooden plaque above the window: 靈心舞蹈學院. The English name is printed on a red banner that hangs below the plaque: SOULFUL HEART DANCE ACADEMY. The door to the dance school is propped open with a cinder block, and bursts of laughter can be heard occasionally through it.

BAM! BAM! BAM! Someone slams their fists against the outer set of mall doors. I jump and turn to see figures waving frantically at me, gesturing for me to let them in for their last-minute errands. All the entrances to the mall are closed after six, and only stragglers like myself remain. I shrink into the shadows and pretend not to notice, but they rattle the doors harder. I feel a twinge of irritation at Tina for not being ready, but I shouldn't be surprised. She's not known for being on time.

I walk into the dance academy and immediately feel out of place. Glossy photographs line the hall: dancers in glittering costumes, positioned in elaborate formations, bodies twisted into poses that seem impossible to my eyes. Their bright, smiling faces forever captured by the camera. I try to pull back my shoulders and straighten out my terrible posture, which isn't helped by my long hours spent hunched over either a computer or a piano.

The waiting area is up ahead. There are girls perched on the arms of a black leather sofa or draped over the back, laughing. Boys are squeezed into the seat, side by side, dressed in white-and-yellow uniforms. The girls are dressed in matching pink-and-green jackets, colorful leggings. Tina has her back to me, and she leans over to whisper something into the ear of the boy sitting next to her. He looks up at her with a playful smile, reaching up to brush a curl away from her face.

This is not the side of my sister I typically see. On our way home she'll sit beside me on the bus, silently giggling at whatever she's talking about with her friends on the screen. When we get home, she'll usually disappear up to her room right after we walk in. When forced to be present during "family time," she'll hide behind a curtain of hair, thumbs always furiously typing away. Even Ma's threats to throw her phone out do not faze her.

"Tina!" I call out. "We have to go!" My voice comes out too sharp, too high, cutting through their conversation. I don't know why the dancers always make me nervous. They're so poised, confident, just like my sister is turning out to be.

Except it isn't my sister. A stranger turns and stares at me. *All* their eyes are suddenly on me, the room abruptly silent. Their expressions are unfriendly, varying from confusion to annoyance.

"She's not here," one of the girls finally tells me after a long pause. "She went home sick."

"Yeah, thanks," I mumble, and hurry back to the door, my face hot with embarrassment. I check my phone again to see if Tina sent me a message. My little brother's face, smeared with ice cream, beams at me from the screen. Nothing. Not even a *heading home* text to tell me she's already gone. A surge of resentment rises up inside me, bitterness at having to cover for her all the time and getting no consideration in return.

I glance at my watch. One more minute. If I run, I might be able to make it.

I rush down the hallway beside the dance studio, hitching the strap of my bag higher on my shoulder. The hallway is lit by a stretch of fluorescent lights, which casts a murky glow on the peeling floors. There are bathrooms back here, but they're dark and dingy and rarely cleaned, only to be used if you really can't hold it in anymore. Yellow crates line one wall, piled on top of one another haphazardly.

I'm in such a hurry, I don't notice until something crunches under my shoe.

I look down and gag when I lift up my foot. The crumpled body of a mouse, caught in a trap. Further mangled by the weight of my body crushing its hind legs. Smears of blood streak the floor beneath it. I kick it away from me, where it spins with the trap into the dark corner.

Gross.

The light flickers above my head. It takes me two tries, running into the bar, before the door pops open. The rain has slowed to a drizzle. The wet asphalt is a shiny path before me. My shoes splash in the growing puddles, and I'm ten steps into the alley when I see . . . the number 22 bus gliding out of sight.

Down the street, a siren wails, a shrill sound that only adds to my irritable mood. I look up at the darkening sky, and the ominous rumble of thunder in the distance. I retreat to the alcove, already knowing before I tug on the door that I'm locked out. Mouse blood and probably mouse guts on my shoe, my hair already damp and matted from the rain, having to wait for the bus because my sister didn't want to bother climbing one flight of stairs to let me know that she was leaving.

I don't think this day can get any worse.

TWO

長舌

(Long Tongue)

I only started working with Mrs. Nguyen this spring, when my old piano teacher retired. Twice a week, Tina and I walk from our school downtown to Chinatown. On Tuesdays, one of us would volunteer at Sunshine Manor, one of the handful of seniors homes in the neighborhood, playing cards or handing out cookies, while the other would be doing our "parent-approved" activity, then we would switch on Thursday. What used to be piano lessons for both of us has remained piano for me, and (as far as our parents know) math tutoring for Tina.

Except I caught her strolling out of the manor the first week back to school when I realized I accidentally grabbed her ID, and I followed her across the street. I watched her go into Soulful Heart, and that's when it all made sense. Why there was always loud music coming from her room through our shared wall, why she suddenly had a new group of friends at school I didn't recognize.

We had a huge fight that day, one of our worst, because I knew our parents would be furious if they ever found out. That she signed up for this hobby they saw as a complete waste of her time, using her math tutoring money to do so. She begged me not to tell, said that she would fit it all into our schedule somehow: school, volunteering, dance. . . .

The sky rumbles again, and a shadow falls over the alley, which suits my current mood.

She thinks I don't understand, but I do. I know what dance means to her. In junior high when she chose it as an elective, she glowed on the stage. She moved to the music naturally, conveying feelings and emotions that Mr. Brandt, our old piano teacher, never could get her to show. When I watched her performance at the end-of-year talent show, I understood then that piano was my instrument but that Tina's body was hers.

If only she had a passion for something else musical, anything else— any of the string instruments, the flute maybe, or even singing. All of that might have been acceptable. But not dance. Not when it was associated with skin tight costumes and makeup and drawing too much attention to how you look.

Not when our family motto is practically: *Don't stand out. Be like everyone else.*

I pull the hood of my jacket up over my head and step off the metal stairs into the alley to brave the rain, reminded of the argument I had with Tina last week while walking in this direction.

"I know how much you love dance," I told her then. "But think about it, a few more years, and you can move somewhere else. At university, you can be free. You can join any club you want! They want what's best for you."

Tina looked up at me, her eyes slightly red-rimmed.

"You know what?" she said softly. "You sound just like Ma."

It's the way she said it that felt like a knife straight to the heart. We're two sisters, born two years apart, our bond made even stronger when Denny was born eight years ago. He was premature and sick all the time, and we had to be helpful, to stay out of the way, to be *good girls.*

"Sometimes we have to do things that we don't want to do," I said, even though I knew that wasn't what she wanted to hear.

The question she asked me struck me like lightning, searing its way into my skull, and has remained there since. "Do you think you would be able to give up piano if they told you that you had to? That you had to wait two more years before you could play again?"

I didn't want to answer that question then, and I don't want to remember it now. It's a reminder that I was lucky, really lucky, that one of the activities they forced us to do ended up being something I loved. That if I chose anything else, I could have easily been forced to drop it. To let it go.

I thrive on approval. On doing things the "correct" way. Tina has never needed that.

"I know it's selfish." She turned away from me in the alley. I remember the hurt and frustration in her expression, the way she couldn't even meet my eyes. "But sometimes I wish you could feel what it's like to be me. I'm sick of always being compared to you. Sometimes I wish you weren't my sister."

My vision blurs at the memory, and I pull off my glasses to drag my sleeve over my eyes. I tell myself it's just the rain.

"Hehehehe." The giggle is awkward, high-pitched.

I jam my glasses back on my face, looking around. Someone is watching me, laughing at my misery. But there's no one there.

On my right, there's a chain-link fence that separates this alley from the one that runs along the building on the other side of this block. Through it, I can see a man dressed in yellow. He leans against the wall, smoking. But he's too far away to be the source of the giggle.

I quicken my pace to walk past the dumpster, where I'm certain someone is going to jump out at me, but there's no one there when I hurry past.

"Hehehe." The giggles continue. This time sounding like it's from above.

I should keep walking. I should just run for the road and not look back, but I can't. I look up, even as every part of me screams not to.

There's a figure crouched on the curved light pole above my head. Dark, stringy hair that falls down to the hands and feet wrapped around the metal. A dirty moss-green dress, dotted with small red flowers. She tips her head to one side as she leans over, peering down through the curtain of hair that falls over her face.

Not again.

She falls backward, black hair streaming toward the ground. She spins around the light pole, almost graceful, and lands on the ground before me.

She's not real.

Slowly, she stretches to her full height. Her proportions are all wrong. The limbs too long. The skin a greenish gray, the color of a corpse. The true horror though is her face. The deep, cavernous eyes that are all pupil, too shiny and fake. A long, drooping chin that stretches downward. A mouth pulled into a too-wide smile. Like a half-formed imitation of what a person should look like, done in clay.

All my life, I've seen things in the shadows. They cling to the walls of buildings, around the trunks of trees. I remember pointing them out to my parents in the park, on the street, long ago. My mother's lips tightened in embarrassment as she dragged me away by the wrist.

"Stop lying," she hissed into my ear, again and again. "Stop making things up. There's nothing there."

They took me to the optometrist and gave me glasses. I was told I was nearsighted and had bad astigmatism, just like my father. I still saw them, vaguely human-shaped figures that squirmed and shifted in the dark, but I learned to keep it to myself.

They've never bothered me. Never so much as raised a finger in my direction. For the most part, they've become just another part of the city.

Until now. For the first time, this...ghoul takes a step in my direction, staring directly at me like she can see me. Like she is here for *me*. Water drips from her eyelashes. Her tongue trails out of the corner of her mouth, like a fat, pink slug. It dangles much longer than a tongue should extend, swinging as she takes another step toward me. She's dragging her left foot, the toes pointed weirdly, as if someone popped her foot out and put it back on the wrong way.

Do something, Ruby! my mind screams at me. *Anything!*

I force myself to move, to veer slightly closer to the wall, holding my breath as I walk past it. To pretend like I see nothing, hear nothing, feel nothing. The street does not seem so far away. There are still cars passing in the distance. An image of perfect normalcy. I somehow convince myself the nightmare is contained only in this alley, and if I break free of it...it will prove it's all in my imagination. That I made it all up.

I make it past her. I don't look when I go by. With every step, I walk faster. The water from the puddles splashes up around my feet, sloshing between my toes. Until I'm near a run.

I jerk to a stop. My right foot catches on something, but the rest of my body keeps going. I fly forward, the wet pavement rising up to meet my face, and my hands reach out to catch myself. I bounce off the ground and land awkwardly on my side, pain shooting up my elbow.

I scramble to my hands and knees, but something is still caught around my leg. I look down, and there's a pink rope wound around my ankle, extending all the way back...down the length of the alley, and into the mouth of the ghoul with the melting face.

It's not a rope. It's a tongue. A *tongue* is touching me.

I choke back the revulsion that rises as I reach over and try to peel it off my skin. But it tightens around my leg, and then it jerks, unnaturally strong. I'm pulled backward, half of me lifting up in the air, then falling back down when I kick. My chin smashes into the ground, hard enough that my teeth crack against one another. I lie there, a little stunned.

They have *never* grabbed me like this. They've existed on the periphery of my life for so long that I've relegated them to something harmless, like stray cats appearing and disappearing.

I remember the man who was smoking in the alley. He might be able to help me, if only I can get his attention.

"Help!" I cry out, but it comes out as weak as a kitten's meow.

The tongue tightens again. I try to reach out, nails scrambling to find purchase in the slick pavement, as it drags me back. Inch by inch, I'm a fish being pulled in on the line, thrashing on the ground. I sob.

"Help!" I scream again as I'm dragged past the fence. I can't tell if the man in the yellow jacket is still there. I strain one arm in an attempt to hook my fingers on the chain links, but I'm too damn short. I'm going to get eaten. She's going to devour me in this back alley, and I'm going to be on a Missing poster. *Girl, sixteen, last seen in Chinatown...*

"Look here! 醜八怪!" The voice comes from the direction of the entrance of the alley. They sound like a boy. I lift my head as the footsteps grow closer. I've lost my glasses somewhere. They must have fallen off when I cracked my chin.

All I can see is a figure wearing a red hoodie and dark blue jeans. He waves his arms wildly above his head, shouting more insults in Mandarin, making fun of the ghoul's hideous appearance. Even though I must have been a sight to behold, one leg up in the air, I'm relieved someone noticed me.

He yells something I can't quite catch—Mandarin? or another language?—and gestures with his hand. Suddenly, the air around us changes. It's as if a spotlight flicked on overhead, illuminating the three of us. The light is different around his arms, a golden hue, as he moves them through the air in graceful, purposeful movements. Almost like the tai chi videos my dad likes to do in the mornings.

There's a growl in the air, one that makes all the hairs on the back of my neck stand up. Then the scent of something burning fills my nostrils, the spicy aroma of incense. Followed by a ferocious roar, a brilliant flash. So bright that I have to close my eyes.

An image of a tiger, launching itself in the air, burns onto the back of my eyelids. The sound of something landing heavily on the ground with a wet smack follows.

Hands grab my shoulders. They flip me onto my back. Someone is saying something, but it sounds like nonsense. In the distance, there's snarling, growling, the grinding of teeth tearing against flesh....I try to force my eyes open, but everything is too bright.

I fly upward, into the light.

THREE

茶旋風

(Bubble Madness)

When I'm back in my body, a ceiling fan spins above me. My head aches terribly, pain pulsing at my temple. It feels like someone jabbing a needle repeatedly into my skull. I roll onto my side and wince as my arm peels off the vinyl.

I was resting on a fuzzy pillow. A green cartoon frog with too-large eyes stares up at me, wearing red-striped suspenders. I could have sworn it winked at me. I hold it up in front of my face and squint. No, it's just a pillow, but the world turns a bit. I think I may throw up. Either that, or I'm dead.

"Here." There's a clink, and a mug is set on the table before me. I put my hands around the ceramic mug. The warmth sinks into my skin as I inhale the scent that rises. Who knew the afterlife would smell like jasmine tea? It's hot enough to burn my mouth, but goes down my throat in a soothing path, easing the headache ever so slightly.

"Oh, and this is yours, I think." Someone pushes my glasses toward me on the table. I quickly settle them on my nose, and the world finally comes into focus. Except there's a crack in the right lens. My parents will not be happy.

I glance around, taking in the space. It looks like a trendy café. There are posters on the wall, advertising various foods and drinks. Bowls filled with round mounds of colorful shaved ice topped with pieces of fresh fruit or brown sugar boba and drizzled with condensed milk. Fish-shaped taiyaki filled with red bean and mochi. Roasted oolong milk tea falling from the sky amid a shower of tea leaves. There's a counter at the back corner with the cash register and a glass case for desserts that's currently empty.

"You okay?" the girl says softly. "Do you feel like you're going to pass out again?"

I drag my gaze back to her. She doesn't even look real. Her hair is a bright blue, pinned up in a messy bun on her head. She's wearing an apron with a cartoon of a smiling bubble tea with arms and legs, spinning in the middle of a tornado.

BUBBLE MADNESS! the logo shouts in colorful, round letters.

"How...how did I get here?" The bubble-tea figure begins to swirl in my vision, and I squeeze my eyes shut. When I open them again, the art is still, but the girl looks even more concerned. She leans toward me like she's ready to catch me if I start to tip over.

"My coworker found you in the back alley. He thinks maybe you slipped and hit your head. He brought you in." She hesitates, before continuing. "Did...did someone attack you?"

I look down at my cup, not sure how to respond. How do I say *a monster dropped out of the sky and tried to eat me*, without sounding like I am absolutely deranged?

"You don't have to tell me if you don't want to," she says, still speaking in that slow, careful way. "But maybe I should call the police? They can get your statement or ... take you to the hospital to get looked at?"

"Oh. *Oh.*" I'm flustered too, when I finally realize what she means. "No, no, that's not what happened to me." But I'm grateful for her concern, even though she is a stranger. She seems relieved too and straightens, reaching for a mop leaning against the side of the booth.

I look at her name tag. "Delia ... can I talk to the guy who brought me in? I have to ask him some questions." *Did a glittering tiger actually explode out of his hands like some sort of firework display?*

"Shen?" She shrugs. "He's off shift now. Should be back to work on Saturday if you want to talk to him. He was just helping out tonight."

I slump. What did I actually see in that alley?

"You're welcome to stay for a bit longer if you want," Delia offers. "I'm just closing for the night." She turns to start mopping the floor again, and a sudden rush of panic fills me.

"Wait!" I stop her. "What time is it?"

She looks up at a clock on the wall. "Eight thirty."

I lost two hours. Two hours! A ringtone pierces the air. A familiar song—"Flight of the Bumblebee," assigned to my parents' landline. It's coming from my bag beside me. I dig it out and accept the call.

Before I can say anything, my mother's voice loudly carries across the line. Like she reached through space and time to punch me in the ear.

"Ruby! Where are you? Why are you not answering my calls?" I check the screen. Ten-plus missed calls and messages.

"I'm at the mall still," I say, mouth suddenly dry. Do I even tell my mother what happened tonight? She's always warning us to be careful. Bag clutched in front of us. Don't walk on the sketchy side of the street. Keep to well-lit places. You never know if anyone around you might have bad intentions.

"What are you still doing there?" The tone is already suspicious, which does not bode well for me when I get home.

"I lost track—"

Before I can finish my sentence, she yells so loudly that I drop the phone on the table, but I can still hear her clearly, as if she's standing right next to me. "Did you stop using your head? Sometimes you don't even think! How can your Baba and me trust you?"

I gingerly pick up the phone and ask softly, "Is Tina home?"

"Yes, Tina's home," she snaps. "She got a ride with a classmate. We don't even know them. How embarrassing!"

It's just like my mother to worry about how we might be perceived if we have to ask for someone's help.

"Baba's on the way to pick you up. Wait in front of the manor." The call disconnects.

I slowly get to my feet and bring the empty mug to the counter. Delia's pretending that she didn't overhear my conversation, but I'm sure she heard every word. I try to give her some money for the tea, and she pushes my coins away.

"Strict parents, huh?" She gives me a wry smile. "I understand. Be safe. I'll keep an eye on you from the window."

There are *strangers who are kind*, I think. Not like my mother's constant reminders of people who might want to take advantage of us. I pull my hood over my head and leave the café. I walk by the lit windows of the businesses on this side of the street that are still open, and the sight of it gives me comfort that I'm not alone. Tim Hortons. A Vietnamese restaurant. People eating inside. It's all normal again. Chinatown as it's always been.

I cross the street to stand under the bright lights that illuminate the path leading up to the manor.

Her words keep echoing in my head. *How can we trust you?* Something they've repeated many times before. My face burns again, even with the cool breeze. They told me this when my former piano teacher had suggested I apply for a special Young Artist program for the summer, intended for musicians who are serious about music and looking to attend music college. It wasn't even something that occurred to me until he mentioned it. The potential that I could go to university and study music, that I could keep playing piano. I put in an application as a whim, and when I received my invitation to audition, my parents had looked at me confused.

"Another program for piano?" my dad said, flipping to the tuition page, and making a face at the amount. "Why do you need this when you already take lessons?"

"What a waste of time!" my mother declared. "All kids think about these days is how to spend their parents' money."

With every word I felt something inside me crumple like a paper bag, and I got smaller and smaller.

"Hey! You can't stand there!" The door opens behind me, disrupting the memory. I realize that it must look like I'm lurking in the shadows, with my long black jacket and hood. I turn to explain, but whoever it was has already slammed the door shut.

I go and stand on the sidewalk, beside the bushes so that I can't be seen from the door. It doesn't take long for the SUV to pull up next to the curb. I open the back door and slip inside. My father glances at me in the rearview mirror and lets out a sigh. Again, I disappoint.

"Ruby," he says as he slips into that familiar tone he uses for our father-daughter "talks" in Mandarin. "You know that I'm busy with a project at work right now. I can't be at home very much, so I expect you to be good for your mother. To not cause so much trouble."

My father is an architect. His old firm shut down during the pandemic, and he struggled to find work. He was hired last year by a new firm in Chinatown, and he's been putting in lots of hours to make a good impression.

Something happened to me tonight, Baba. The words flop around inside my mouth, struggling to get out, but I can't seem to release them. *Something bad. It's happening again.* But what's the point of telling them when they won't even acknowledge something was wrong in the first place?

"I need you to be the older sister, the responsible one." The wipers swish across the windshield, and I feel myself sinking deeper and deeper into the leather of the seat. "Make good choices. You're supposed to be the example."

All I can think of is Tina's face when she told me: *I wish you weren't my sister.*

When we head into the house, my mother is waiting for me at the kitchen table. She gives me her teacher's stare, the one she reserves for her students who are especially bad. I already know what to expect. She'll tell me all that I've done wrong, but when I sit down and wait for her lecture, I feel a strange sense of relief.

Everything in the kitchen is practically the same as when we moved in here over a decade ago, and probably the same as when it was last renovated another decade earlier. The flower curtains. The plastic tablecloth over the wooden table. The overhead lights that turn everything a yellowish color. The linoleum floors that squeak when you roll the chairs over them. *Normal.*

Ma repeats what Baba already said. That I'm the example, the responsible one. They're spending so much money on me, putting me into Westview, giving me an advantage. I have to prove to them it's not all a waste.

"Look at this!" She waves a pamphlet in my face. "Hope Wu! If you only achieve a fraction of what she is able to do, I would be happy."

Hope's face beams from the face of the glossy magazine, with the tagline underneath *Westview alumni . . . where are they now?*

"Your glasses." She peers closer at me. "What happened to them?"

"I dropped them," I tell her. Sort of the truth.

She makes a tsking sound with her teeth. "You have to take better care of your things. Glasses are expensive. Especially with your eyes, being as bad as they are. Thankfully Tina and Denny don't have the same problem. It's all that time in front of the computer."

"I'm sorry," I say, because that's what she wants to hear, and that will end the lecture quicker than anything else I could say.

"All right," she finally says, waving me away. "Get ready for bed. You have school tomorrow."

I take my soggy bag and make my way up the stairs before she changes her mind. I can hear the murmur of my father's voice and envision him taking his glasses off and rubbing his eyes, while saying, *She's home safe. . . . That's all that matters. . . .*

I went to that Young Artist program audition anyway, in secret. A few months later, Mr. Brandt had requested my parents come in for a meeting with him—to announce that he was retiring, but that he was very proud of me as his student. He was so happy to let them know that I was waitlisted for the Young Artists program, and I should try to apply again next year. He was sure that I would get in the second time.

When we got home, my parents were furious that I disobeyed them, that I went ahead and applied anyway.

"I told you not to bother," Ma said. "And look, you didn't even get in! Do you think you are Hope Wu?"

"Try to focus your energy on something that actually matters," Baba told me, disappointment clear.

If the eldest sister of every Taiwanese family is supposed to be the example, all of us "examples" are compared to Hope—the Westview graduate who got into Yale and is on track now to get early acceptance into med school. A checklist of how to become the *Good Taiwanese Daughter.*

I didn't tell them then that I applied for that program to show them I am just as capable as Hope. That maybe they would understand how important piano is to me, how I lived and breathed and dreamed music. Maybe then they would finally be proud of me.

FOUR

疑惑

(Suspicions)

For some reason when I make my way upstairs, I remember the time when Ma took me and Tina to the children's carnival. Denny was just a baby then, not yet walking. I was supposed to keep an eye on Tina while Ma was changing Denny in the bathroom, but Tina ran away into the crowd, too fast for me to catch. I was torn between running after her or staying put, just like our mother had ordered us to do. I cried and cried while my mother frantically looked for Tina. She was eventually found in the lost children's booth, eating a Popsicle.

Ma was furious with me, even though I told her that Tina had run away from me. She just said I had to be responsible. That was what a big sister was supposed to be.

I pause outside of Tina's door. The light is still on in her room. I don't know why that memory is suddenly so strong. I can taste the saltiness of my tears on my tongue, how swollen my eyes felt after crying. There was

Tina, swinging her legs in the chair while the booth volunteer braided her hair. Maybe I should have been mad at Tina, but what remained was the sense of relief. The knowledge that she was safe.

I push the door open. Tina's sitting at her desk, in front of her computer.

"Don't you know how to knock?" She scowls when she notices me, slamming the lid of her laptop down. It would be an intimidating sight, except her hair is pulled back from her face with a pink bunny headband, one ear flopping down in front and the other sticking up.

I want to ask *Are you okay?* Instead, the words that come out are: "What happened to you today?"

Her lips purse. "I didn't feel good, so I came home." Even with the dim light in the room, I notice the shadows under her eyes. One leg is drawn up on her chair, while the other leg dangles off the seat.

I manage to swallow down the irritation and say gently: "Are you feeling better now?"

"I'm fine," she says, curt. "What happened to *you*?"

A dissonant chord crashes into my mind, rendering me momentarily frozen.

"Ma was mad. You should have heard her," she carries on without waiting for my answer. "Complaining about how we never listen to her anymore."

"I ended up talking with Mrs. Nguyen for a bit after," I tell her, the lie slipping out unintentionally. "I lost track of time."

"You don't have to lie to me." She sneers. My eyes snap to meet hers. Does she know about the ghoul? That drooping face... That long, long tongue... The misshapen figure taking one unsteady step toward me in the alley...

"I won't tell," she goes on, smug. "We both have our secrets." She's smiling like she knows something I don't. It grates at me, even though I'm fully aware she's trying to get on my nerves.

"I'm not lying!" My voice goes up, high-pitched.

"Sure," she drawls.

"Just because you have a secret doesn't mean that everybody else around you is hiding something!" My patience, already hanging on by a thread, snaps.

Tina jumps to her feet, surprisingly quick. She's in my face, staring me down. When did she get so tall? The light flickers overhead, probably from when she bumped against the table. I take a step back.

"Remember our deal," she whispers. "You stay out of my way, and I'll stay out of yours." There's something menacing about her glare, one arm raised as if she's about to hit me. Her lower lip trembles. The shadow passes, then she looks like she's about to cry.

"You're not going to be able to keep it up. Dance and school and all of this . . ." I say to her, feeling more concerned than threatened as I catch her wrist to stop her. "I told you before. It's going to be too much."

Tina snatches her arm out of my grasp and smiles at me, but it's more like a baring of teeth. "Why so serious? I was joking. I'll be fine."

She raises her hands between us and shoves me out the door. I stumble, catching myself on the wall so that I don't fall.

"I—" The door shuts in my face.

I stare at the sign that she hung on the door a few years ago. An art project we did together, her name done in pom-poms and Popsicle sticks. A trail of glitter dangles from the corner, peeling off. Back when we got along, she was eager for my attention, for me to help her position it so that she could hot-glue everything just the way she wanted it.

A lump rises in my throat. With Tina, I always have to be the peace-keeper when she butts heads with Ma. I have to make sure our mother stays calm, while reassuring Tina that half of those promised punishments are usually never doled out. Except now I think that Tina believes I am the enemy, conspiring with our parents against her.

Every day it feels like she's changing, turning into a stranger. Someone I don't recognize anymore.

In my bedroom, I undress, getting ready to jump in the shower after lying in the alley for god knows how long. A sharp pain runs up my elbow where the fabric brushes against it. I hold it up to my mirror to see where I scraped it against the road when I fell.

That feels real. Same with the ache in my jaw. Something happened to me tonight in the alley, but it may be closer to a hallucination than anything. I must have slipped on the staircase and fallen, bumping my head. Looked up through broken glasses and thought I saw something that didn't exist.

Maybe I should stay out of Tina's way like she's been telling me all this time. Look after myself instead. Maybe Tina is actually the brave one, and I'm the coward for letting our parents dictate everything I do.

I dig my hand through my desk drawer, pulling out my spare pair of glasses from last year and put them on. My prescription hasn't changed much, and that is when I notice something dark on my skin. I bend over and look at my bare legs. There's a red mark around my ankle. Like something wrapped around it, tightened, and pulled. A rope. Or a tongue.

I sit down heavily on my bed.

It did happen. The woman that tried to eat me. The boy in the alley. It was all real.

The next day, I'm at our breakfast table. After a night's rest, my mind seems a little clearer. It's hard to reconcile the nightmare of the ghoul with my brother splashing milk everywhere while trying to eat Frosted Flakes. All I know is this: The ghoul in the alley was different from my previous encounters. If you could even call them that, since the others all faded away to wherever they came from whenever someone actually living came too close. But the guy who shouted at her...he is proof that someone else saw that I saw. Except I didn't get a good look at him. Without my glasses, he is only a blur in my memory.

Tina clears her throat, returning me to the table.

"Ma, Baba," she says, addressing our parents in a way that is almost... demure. Not like her typical manner at all. Tina is rarely tentative about anything. "There is something I would like to ask."

"Yes?" Baba sets down his tablet where he was scrolling through the news, while Ma turns to look at her, expectant.

"Melody, my math tutor, she runs a study group after school a few days a week. Could I join her?" Tina asks. Melody. The girl who is helping her keep up the lie that she is studying math instead of putting all her time and energy into dance.

"Melody?" Baba looks to Ma, who is nodding her head, already inclined to agree.

"That's Mr. Lee's daughter," Ma explains. "She's a sweet girl. So helpful. She came highly recommended as a tutor from one of the teachers. Really took Tina under her wing, I heard."

"Ma! Stop talking about me with the other teachers!" Tina frowns, embarrassed—one of the unfortunate side effects of attending Westview with our mother as a teacher, even though she's all the way over on the Early Years campus.

Ma continues to butter her toast, not bothering to acknowledge Tina's protest.

"Oh, Mr. Lee! The one who gave Tina a ride home the other day!" Baba says with surprise.

"Who's that?" I ask, drawn into the conversation despite myself. Everything related to school has always been under my mother's purview. Baba usually keeps out of it, deferring to her education background. But to have someone stand out to the point that my father remembers him, there must be a reason.

"He's involved in a lot of the business associations around the city," Baba explains. "The owner of my firm knows him quite well. We were introduced before at an association dinner. Recognized me as Taiwanese."

"A Taiwanese family!" Ma is delighted.

That makes sense. My parents believe that if someone is Taiwanese, they are more trustworthy and dependable. They spoke fondly of the Taiwanese Association when they came here for university, even though many of those people have moved to other parts of the country now. That connection, that reminder of home, will always remain.

A part of me longs for that connection even as a part of me resists it, because it can be so stifling to always be aware of how you match up against others my age. How we're always scrutinized, compared, held up to impossible standards.

But for Tina, it means Melody is from a *Good Family*, so therefore she is trustworthy. Ma nods, giving her permission, and Tina runs upstairs to grab the rest of her things.

"She's really settling into Westview," Ma says before biting into her toast. "It was the right decision." Baba mumbles something, already back to scrolling the news on his tablet.

Even though they tried to keep it from us, I still overheard their murmured conversations last year as they debated whether Ma should take this job at Westview and whether they should move us from school midyear. Our opinions, of course, did not matter. I push my chair back and drop my plate into the sink, not wanting to hear Ma talk more about how well Tina is doing. How she's fitting in, making new friends. Because it will lead, inevitably, to reminding me of what I should be doing as well.

"Ruby," Ma calls out before I can escape up the stairs. "You should learn from your sister. Join a club. It's good for admissions. Show you're more well-rounded, not so antisocial all the time."

Spend too much time studying, I'm too bookish. Spend too much time practicing piano, I'm neglecting my studies. Now I'm too antisocial. I feel like I'm breaking myself into pieces, again and again, none of the edges quite fitting right into the portrait of what they want me to be.

When I get upstairs, Tina's door opens. She glares at me, her hair sleek and shiny, pulled back into a high ponytail. Just like all the dance girls. She brushes by me without saying a word. My stomach drops. I'm reminded of the question Tina asked, the one I'm too scared to answer. What if they ask me to give up piano someday? Would I be able to do it? Would it feel like chopping off my own hand?

FIVE

陰影

(Shadows)

A few days pass without incident. No ghouls leaping at me from around corners. No figures appearing more corporeal than they had been before. Tina meets me where she should after school, and we get home on time. We're used to pretending that everything is fine, even though our resentment simmers under the surface. I feel like I'm holding my breath, a rubber band pulled taut, already flinching from the inevitable sting.

But it's Tuesday again, and at the beginning of the lunch period, Tina waits for me at my locker, friends in tow. Even though we all wear the same uniforms at Westview, gray blazers over red shirts and gray skirts or pants, there are no rules on accessories. One girl wears bright pink glasses, while the other has dangly earrings—one side is bacon, while the other side is a sunny-side-up egg.

"I'll be at study group after school, so you don't have to wait for me here," Tina tells me. Is the study group actually real? Or is it another facade for dance practice? I don't bother asking. I'm more anxious about being back in the mall tonight. "You just have to be careful," I say, not wanting her to get caught, more on edge than I should be. "They're probably going to ask me again today at the manor when you're going to be back. If you get too many strikes, you're gone."

"I didn't ask you to cover for me." My sister's eyes narrow as her expression turns frosty. "I told you, I'll figure it out for myself. I'll make sure I'm ready to take the bus back home together."

I try to tell her that I'm only trying to help, but a whistle sounds behind me, high-pitched and mocking. *Someone's in trouble....* I whirl around, expecting one of her friends to be there, laughing. Except there's no one there along the row of lockers. The door to the classroom behind me is closed.

I turn back. Breakfast Earrings watches me with a brow raised, while Pink Glasses scrunches her face like I grew two heads.

I ignore them and ask Tina, "Did you hear that? Someone whistled." They all shake their heads.

"Maybe you're the one who needs to keep it together," my sister responds slowly. "I'll see you in the lobby of the mall tonight." She turns away, decision already made. The whistle made everything feel off-key, and I didn't have a good excuse to stop her.

"Your sister's weird," one of the girls says down the hall, not bothering to whisper even though I'm still within earshot.

After school, I put on my headphones when I line up for the bus that will take me toward Chinatown. The soothing sound of a Bach prelude and fugue accompanies the swaying of the bus, and the murmurs of the people around me slip away. One of my first memories is of classical music playing over the speakers. Baba, though he never played an instrument, likes to listen to piano as background music. I remember flipping through his CDs when I was really little, the excitement when

I was finally old enough to take them out of the cases and switch them. How the light would catch on the reflective surface, sending rainbow rings on the ceiling. When Tina would be spinning around, moving to the music, I'd lie there on a bed of pillows, just listening and taking it in.

The sound of the piano always conjures up a feeling of languid contentment. Like the feeling you get at the beginning of summer, when there's nowhere you need to be. There are people in the house somewhere, moving and doing their own thing, but you're warm and safe in the den lying on the couch that's so old your body sinks completely into it. When I play, it's the same sort of meditation, the music having that magic and power to transport me to somewhere else entirely.

There's only a light sprinkling of rain when the bus drops me off on the corner, turning away with a squeal of tires. I have some time before my lesson starts, and usually I would park myself at one of the food court tables to do my homework, but I don't have much to do tonight. I'm restless, out of sorts, missing Tina's silent presence. How pathetic, relying on my little sister for company.

A Rachmaninoff prelude plays over the headphones. One of Yuja Wang's renditions. When I first watched a performance by the Chinese concert pianist, she was not what I expected. Her hair was chopped short, black and jagged. She had on smoky winged eye shadow, black eyeliner. She strode out confidently to the grand piano, on black stiletto heels, wearing a tight yellow dress. She looked like she should be a rock star, a guitar slung over one shoulder, screaming into the microphone. Instead, she sat down at the piano bench and played the Prelude in G minor with perfect control—unleashing the wildness when it required it, pulling back with tender restraint where it slowed. She always wears glamorous outfits, covered with glitter and sequins, heels at least four inches high. I admire her virtuoso performances, her modern interpretations of the music, her carefree attitude. I may have had a little crush on her then and still do now.

I start walking deeper into the mall, to keep myself moving. To escape that nagging feeling I'll never catch up, that I'll continue to fall behind. On making new friends. On being able to perform the Études-Tableaux to Mrs. Nguyen's satisfaction. My shoes squeak a little on the waxed floor as I make my way around the fountain and the stairwell.

The first floor of the mall is in a figure eight. The loop at the entrance is the sushi restaurant, the dance studio, then the jewelry shop, all situated around the broken fountain and the curved stairs that lead up to the second floor. In the middle is the food court with the rows of tables, stalls on one side, and entrances to cafés on the other. There's one stall that offers steamed rice rolls, one that sells grilled kebab platters. Another has had a COMING SOON sign hanging in front of it for as long as I've been coming here. At the back are the gift shops—one for trinkets: good-luck charms, jade statues, and grinning Buddhas. Another is a store filled to the brim and spilling out to the corridor with racks of traditional clothing, qipao and hanfu of all colors and styles and sizes.

During the day, the restaurants and food court are frequented by office workers in the towers close by or seniors who live in the Chinatown apartments. Tourists who come to buy souvenirs and then pick up a drink to go. In the evening, though, most of the storefronts are shuttered.

I climb the back stairwell to the second level, where I emerge in a section with empty shop fronts. Red paper is taped to many of the doors with the Chinese character for *rent* and a phone number below for inquiries.

I circle around the landing to the other side and stop before the CLOSED sign for ABC Driving School. The banner draped across the glass promises: GUARANTEED TO PASS! There's a cardboard standee of an obviously photoshopped Chinese man wearing black-framed glasses. He gives a thumbs-up to passerby through the window, showing his too-white skin and white teeth. I peer through the window and see the reception desk in the same spot, the one long hallway that leads to the classrooms on either side. The green walls have been changed to a soft gray, but the navy-blue carpets are the same.

Years ago, this used to be the Chinese school that Tina and I attended because Ma was a teacher here. Every weekend we filed dutifully into the classrooms and sat in the narrow, uncomfortable wooden desks for three hours. I remembered Mrs. Yang with her thin bamboo stick. She liked to tap it against the whiteboard. Tap, tap, then the sudden slam as she whipped it in the air in front of our faces and struck the surface of our desks to make sure we were paying attention. I can still hear the sound of it whistling past my ear, and me, as I flinched away from the threat.

Beside it there is one more storefront, tucked into the back corner where the hallway curves in. There used to be an anime store here. The walls of the awkwardly angled space were plastered with posters of different shows: giant robots fighting monsters emerging from the ocean or girls striking cute poses in front of trains. The window displays had rows and rows of figurines of all shapes and sizes. There were mecha models ranging from a foot to four feet high. There were tiny Pokémon collectibles smaller than my thumb. But what we liked the most back then was the TV mounted by the door, where they would play various shows. All of us would crowd around the storefront while we waited for class to start. We stood there shoulder to shoulder, jostling each other for the best spot to see the screen.

The store is long gone now, as evident by the brown paper that has been plastered on the windows, hiding the contents of the unit from view. But light still shines faintly around the edges, where the paper doesn't fully cover all the corners. Someone left a light on. My ears pick up a noise coming from the unit. A familiar refrain, tugging at my ear. There must be someone back there still, staying late.

The tune pulls me forward, and I put my ear up to the door, straining to catch the rest. Another sound joins the music. Like someone humming along. There's a gap in the door where the paper isn't fully lined up. I peer in.

Inside, the floor is littered with paper. There's someone kneeling in front of the back wall. I don't know what they're doing. I can't see their hands, only that their figure casts a long, dark shadow that stretches out toward the ceiling. Something about the shadow catches my attention. It . . . ripples before my eyes, and yet the figure does not move. Slowly, bit by bit, the shadow straightens away from the body. An incomprehensible sight.

The music continues in the background, a low and throaty hum. I'm filled with a sense of dread. Maybe . . . I'm not supposed to be here. Before I can step away, the shadow lunges toward me, filling the entirety of the gap. One bloodshot eye meeting mine. Gray skin pulled taut over high cheekbones. The sound of someone panting, as if they've run a great distance, fills my ears.

I stumble back, but something has gotten ahold of me. *Through* the door. How is this possible? The shadow. Or whatever it is. Phantom fingers dig into my shoulders, pulling me closer. I try to push myself away, but it's so strong. It squeezes around my throat, closing tight, restricting my ability to breathe. . . .

"Hey!" a voice shouts behind me as a hand closes around my wrist. There's a whoosh, and the pressure that holds me suddenly lets go. I stumble back with a gasp. Beside me there are white sneakers, a swirl of what looks like gold confetti spiraling down toward the ground, which turns quickly into ash and . . . disappears. The storefront is dark. There are no lights anymore, and definitely no music.

I look up, wanting to thank the person who saved me, but the words die in my throat.

It's a boy around my age. Short hair with a slight curl at his forehead. Thick eyebrows. Serious eyes. He stares at me for a beat too long. A stranger who witnessed my bizarre behavior.

"You shouldn't be here," he says.

Something about his voice tugs at my memory. Lying on the pavement. Everything a blur. Except the flash of the tiger in the air. *That voice.*

"You...you're the guy from the alley..." I blurt out.

He frowns and takes a step back, hands up in the air. "I don't know what you're talking about, lady. I don't know you."

"Last Tuesday." I move toward him, trying to catch his sleeve. "You helped me."

"You've got the wrong person." His lip curls as he shoves his hands into his pockets. "There's construction back here. You're gonna get electrocuted."

I open my mouth to say something else, but someone calls my name on the other side of the landing. It's Ellie, the girl whose weekly lesson is before mine.

"Hi!" She waves, jumping up and down to make sure I see her. I hold up a finger to let her know to wait for me, but I turn back to see a figure quickly descend the stairwell.

He's already gone.

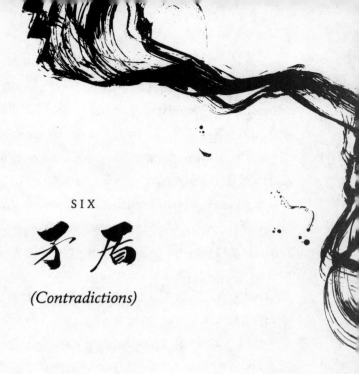

SIX

矛盾

(Contradictions)

Ellie is eager to meet me at the door to the piano studio, a pamphlet in hand. Her mother, Mrs. Kuo, is behind her and gives me a nod in greeting.

Ellie's an only child. I don't think her dad is around anymore, or at least, I've never seen him drop off or pick up Ellie at all in the past year we've shared a teacher. Often Ellie lets me in, checking to see if I'm lurking outside the door. We'll sit in the waiting area, and she'll show me her drawings while Mrs. Kuo asks Mrs. Nguyen clarifying questions about Ellie's lesson. It's different from my mother, whose involvement stops at making sure we have our butts planted on the piano bench. As long as it sounds like we were playing, she doesn't care what we're working on.

Ellie beams up at me and pushes the pamphlet into my hand before darting back to the safe space beside her mother.

"Ellie!" Mrs. Kuo scolds. "Speak to Ruby 姊姊 with your words, please!" She gives me an apologetic look as she nudges Ellie forward.

"Ruby 姊," Ellie squeaks, calling me big sister as is typical, even though we're not related. Just like I would call any woman Mrs. Kuo's age "auntie" in Chinese if addressing her directly. "Can you come?"

The flyer in my hand is for the Chinatown Mid-Autumn Festival. Cartoon dumplings smile under an equally happy, round moon with rosy pink cheeks. Sponsored by the Formosa Friendship Association. The name of the association sounds vaguely familiar, but I don't know why.

Mrs. Kuo tsks. "Ellie's art will be on display in Chinatown this weekend. She wanted to make sure you were invited."

"Thank you, Ellie!" I tell the little girl directly, even though she's clinging to her mother's leg again. "I'll try my best to come." She grins at me, in her adorable gap-toothed way.

"There you are, Ruby. I'm ready for you." Mrs. Nguyen is at the door now, gesturing for me to come in. Ellie and I wave goodbye as I follow Mrs. Nguyen inside.

Our lessons are usually in the biggest room in the back, which fits an upright piano and a small Yamaha baby grand. I run through the familiar routines of the warm-up on the grand piano to start. For the next hour, we work on technique and precision. The Bach has been a piece I've been working on for a while, and it is time to perfect the details, like ensuring one section sounds brighter and clearer or working on maintaining the tempo on a particularly challenging run. But it's the Romantic-era pieces that continue to frustrate me, the ones I desperately wanted to master. They're the type of music that asks you to draw out something deep from that well inside of yourself, to challenge the music head-on, force it to submit to your will or risk being consumed by it.

I finish the hour mentally exhausted, the tightness in my left shoulder twinging as it does occasionally to remind me that I'm still not fully relaxing into the music like I had hoped to by now. At the end of the lesson, Mrs. Nguyen brings up the question that I've been dreading.

"Have you given any thought to whether you're going to play at any festivals this upcoming year?" We spoke about it during the summer, when I told her I wasn't quite ready yet.

"Your mother told me from the beginning that your goal is to get your ARCT certificate, but I can feel your love for playing, and I wonder..." Her voice trails off. Ma wants the certificate because it's a tangible thing. A line on the college application to prove that I've met a certain achievement. But I don't care about that.

I used to love performing, but now the thought of playing in front of all those people makes my hands clammy, my heart race, and Mrs. Nguyen must have noticed my panic, because she pats my arm with sympathy.

"I know performance can be daunting for many, but I feel that you have real potential, Ruby. If you would like to pursue it." Mrs. Nguyen looks so sincere that it makes me want to tell her what I haven't had the courage to tell my parents yet. I want to try out for that Young Artist program again. I want to see if I do have that potential, that commitment to this dream always swirling around at the back of my mind. To study music for real.

"I... I'm not sure yet," I choke out, and my piano teacher's expression falls. She reaches for the pile of papers beside her, and taps it on the table.

"You can keep thinking about it," she tells me, not unkindly. "There's a deadline coming up for the Kiwanis Festival in the spring if you want to put your name in soon. Performing in front of people will really help with preparation for the diploma exam."

Frustration wells up inside me, and I resist the urge to snap at her. I want to perform at the festival, but I don't want to be trapped up there, frozen.

"There's also this banquet coming up at the end of the year. Here in Chinatown." Mrs. Nguyen hands me a card. SEEKING YOUTH PERFORMERS! "I heard about it from another music teacher. They're looking for talented young people to perform at the closing banquet for this festival. The proceeds are going back to the community."

"I'll take a look," I say, shoving it into my bag to be soon forgotten. I've been to Kiwanis before. It's ample opportunity for parents to brag to one another about whether their children won in their class or in their age group. But a no-name banquet? Forget it. My parents would tell me not to bother.

"See you next week." She gives it up for now, even though I know she wants to convince me to sign up.

I shuffle out of the studio, feeling lost. I tug my hair free from my ponytail, letting it fall loose on my shoulders, but it doesn't ease the pressure growing in my head. The knowledge that eventually I will have to play in front of strangers. My anxiety grows, expands, like the knotted hair I try to untangle with my fingers unsuccessfully. I imagine the hair winding its way around my organs, forcing itself up my throat, choking me from the inside out.

How can I even hope to become a musician if the thought of performing grips me with so much fear?

After Mr. Brandt said he was retiring, my mother was determined to find a teacher that would help me finish the final piano diploma so that all the money she spent on my piano lessons wouldn't go to waste. She used some of her connections to get me an audition in front of the Tanakas, a teaching couple famous for their eccentricities and unconventional methods, but also known for producing prodigies.

I attended one of their "workshops" for students as an audition. The first time I ever met them, I was told to play a piece that I was working on before a roomful of strangers. I chose a Mendelssohn piece, Song without Words in A flat major. I thought I played it well, as sweet and lyrical as it was intended to be. But after I finished playing, Mr. Tanaka turned to the students and told them to critique my performance.

I stood there and was eviscerated. I was ripped apart, from the tension in my body to my clawed hands to my stunted expression to my technical flaws. Each of the students were eager to offer their opinions, one after another. I could barely answer when Mrs. Tanaka asked me what other piece I was working on, and I sobbed as I fumbled my way through the Rachmaninoff. The tears still streamed down my face when they continued the critiques, and their words followed me to the curb when I called my parents to come and pick me up.

You're not ready for performance.

These workshops are for people who are dedicated.

You're better off with more . . . lenient instruction.

This isn't for you.

"That was absolutely embarrassing." My mother's face was red, furious, when she returned to the car after speaking with the Tanakas. Even when I tried to explain to her, she wouldn't listen. "What will I tell Ms. Shriver, who vouched for you?"

"You'll practice some more, and then we'll bring you back," Baba declared.

All my life, I've done what they wanted me to do. Got good grades. Played hours of piano. Took care of Denny and Tina when asked. I begged them to find another teacher for me. I tried to tell them I wasn't going back there, but they wouldn't listen. They were informed the Tanakas were the *best*, and they had already told all their friends it was only a matter of time before I was accepted. I wouldn't budge even after they tried to guilt me, then threatened to take away all my privileges.

It was my one act of rebellion. I was tired of being *good*. Good didn't mean that they paid attention to what I said. Good didn't mean they cared about me more than they cared about losing face in front of their friends. They yelled a lot. I cried a lot. I wasn't allowed to go out for most of the summer. Until one day I had enough of them not taking my refusal seriously, and I picked up Baba's cast-iron teapot from the shelf and threw it at the kitchen window. It punched a hole and sent a network of cracks throughout the entire pane. The wind blew in and filled the house, scattered all of Baba's papers stacked on the window seat to the floor. I screamed I wouldn't do it. I screamed I would give up piano and waste all their money. I screamed until I woke up somewhere else, my throat aching and my voice hoarse. I had cried so hard I lost sense of time. The only thing I remember was Denny's and Tina's horrified faces as they watched from the family room.

We never spoke about that day after. It was brushed under the rug, like any other argument. Pretend it never happened until it's true.

Soon after Ma took the job at Westview. It was easier to agree to move schools, even though I wanted to stay. I had "won" the fight about getting a different piano teacher, and I was too tired to argue about anything else.

I notice Tina sitting there on the edge of the broken fountain. She stares down at her feet, swinging them back and forth. *She's just a little kid*, I realize. My parents want to shape her too, force her into their expectations of what a Good Girl should be, and I can't have them do that. Squeeze her so tightly into a mold that she might shatter, just like our back kitchen window. Just like I did.

"Ready?" I speak up when I approach, and she jumps, startled.

"Yes, 姊," she says with a small smile, and then wrinkles her nose.

"Did you forget you were mad at me?" I can't help but tease her, even though I know the chances are fifty-fifty whether she'll be amused or bat me away.

She sticks out her tongue at me, then laughs. "I guess I'm not mad at you anymore." She gives me a hesitant one-armed hug, and I squeeze her shoulder in turn.

We ride the bus sitting side by side. Her head on my shoulder, dozing, while the buildings fly by, the setting sun reflecting against the windows of the towers of the Vancouver skyline. Everything forgiven.

SEVEN

惡夢

(Bad Dreams)

I stay up late into the night, working on an essay that's due next week. I'm accompanied by Debussy's delicate melodies, the rest of the house disappearing into the distance. There is *La fille aux cheveux de lin*, "The Girl with the Flaxen Hair," dancing dreamily in a field of flowers. Or *Clair de lune*, of songs sung under the moon, her light playing in the air and the water.

Months after everything settled, my parents eventually relented and said that I could even stop playing piano altogether if I wished. But I knew I wanted to keep going. I didn't want to lose all that hard work. I had previously attended Mrs. Nguyen's classes on Harmony and Music History, and her lessons always centered around a deep appreciation of musical foundations. She didn't want her students to just memorize the text and regurgitate it for the exam. She wanted the music to speak to us, and to use that connection to understand the influences that shaped the music composed during each era. It was similar to my old teacher's approach, and why I asked her if she had any openings at her studio. This time, I would play for myself. The pieces that I'm drawn to. I knew Mrs. Nguyen would understand that.

I am engrossed in my research for my essay, to the point that when I finally look up to check the time, it is already eleven. I pull off my headphones and stand up to roll my shoulders, stretch my arms above my head. There's a thumping under my feet, the sound of music traveling through the wall from Tina's room to mine—a more frequent occurrence ever since Tina started those lessons at the dance studio.

In our creaky old house, the top floor was once two bedrooms. The only renovation Ma and Baba ever did was to split the top floor into three rooms so that we had a guest room whenever our grandparents came to visit for a few months at a time. But we no longer have grandparents well enough to travel, so we all got our own rooms eventually. Mine and Tina's are the first rooms you encounter at the upper landing, the bathroom and Denny's room are farther down the hall.

My parents keep talking to me about trust. Trust that I am doing okay. Trust that I won't lash out, like I did before. But I wish I could tell them that trust goes both ways. They should trust that Tina and I are capable of figuring some things out for ourselves, that piano and dance are not distractions from school, that this is part of us becoming *well-rounded* people. Except I would never tell them how I really feel. In our house, we are the kids, and the parents are the parents. We should just accept what we are told.

I turn my light off and pull the blanket over me, rolling over to squish my cat pillow tight. The hollow *thump thump* next door is almost soothing, and I let it lull me to sleep.

—

I find myself back in the mall, below the cracked skylight. There is something peculiar about the quality of light that is coming down through the opening, casting a shadowy haze over the storefronts. As if smoke hangs low in the air, reminding me of when the wildfires burned last summer and ash fell from the sky.

Wherever I turn, I find myself back before the storefront with the strange music, the door now open just a crack. But instead of the beguiling song, whispers come from the darkness. I know I shouldn't listen. I know I should run as far away as I can, and yet that space still beckons.

I need to know what's inside.

I take one step, then another. I try to fight it, but my limbs jerk, out of my control. I keep moving forward, closer and closer. A violent force shoves me forward, and I fall, preparing to crash through the door. My hands touch a cold surface. Glass. Except when I open my eyes, a familiar face stares back at me.

The ghoul with her tangled hair, her green dress. I stare down at my dirty, bare feet. At the tongue hanging out from my mouth. I claw at my face and scream, but my reflection smiles eerily back at me. Her hot breath fogs the glass, and she cranes her neck back to unhinge her jaw as my head snaps back too. Her tongue, *my* tongue, wraps itself around my neck. I choke, kick in the air as it lifts me. I try to pry it off me, but it's too strong.

Terrible laughter fills the air around me. I strain against the pressure tightening around my throat, and look down to see her looking up at me, half in and half out of the mirror. Triumphant glee contained in the darkness of her eyes. I thrash, pull my arm back, and throw my fist toward her face with all my strength.

"Ow!" I look up into my brother's startled face.

"Denny?" I slam my hand on the switch for my bedside lamp, my room suddenly flooding with light.

Denny stands there with a petulant frown, and his hand over his cheek. "You bashed me!"

"How many times do I have to tell you? It's scary to wake up with your face right there!" The tempo of my heartbeat is too agitated, *staccato*. Because my bedroom is the closest to his, sometimes he ends up crawling into my bed instead of making it all the way down the stairs to our parents' room.

My little brother looks at me with wide, dark eyes as his lower lip juts out. He's on the verge of crying. I sigh and pull the hand away to take a look at his cheek. There is the tiniest little mark on the side of his face.

"I'm sorry," I tell him. "I had a nightmare."

"A nightmare?" His expression instantly softens. "Was it scary?"

I envision the contorted figure of the ghoul and shudder.

"Yeah," I admit. My brother understands. When he was younger, he used to wake up screaming from his nightmares. Now those night terrors seem to have passed, but the habit of him needing comfort in the middle of the night still remains. He talks about the shadows lurking on the walls, the beasts that bristle in the dark corners, the creaks of the house that sound like footsteps of monsters coming for him. . . .

I'm chilled at the thought that my brother might see the same things I do. Those misshapen forms existing on the edge of my peripheral vision. But I don't want to ask him. I don't want it to be true for both of us. I want him to be safe.

"I'll stay here and protect you," Denny whispers.

"Thanks, buddy." I lift up the covers, and he crawls in next to me, commandeers my cat pillow. I squish myself against the wall so we can share the whole blanket.

Even though sometimes I'm jarred awake by him shaking my arm, whispering about all the things he's afraid of, I still let him. Because he's my little brother. He needs me in a different way than Tina does. I listen to the sound of his breathing growing even, until he lets out the tiniest snores. That's when sleep takes me all the way until morning, and I don't have any more bad dreams.

"Pull your hood over your head! It's raining!" Ma scolds Denny as he opens the door and tries to rush out. She's always after us to keep our heads covered, because she's sure wet hair means we'll catch a cold.

The restaurant is hard to miss. The exterior is a soft pink with red awnings over the windows. We step through the doors into the bustling interior. This place is always packed on Saturday mornings, when it feels like everyone in Vancouver is here for dim sum. There are hundreds of seats. Round tables with lazy Susans that can seat six, ten, even twenty. Smaller tables tucked in wherever there is space. Almost every seat is filled, and the result is a sea of noise. The clinking of spoons against dishes, the sound of metal carts rolling by, people laughing and chatting.

It doesn't take long for us to get our table—the busy servers clean up immediately after customers leave so the next wave of diners can have their fill. We are crammed into a table in the corner. Denny wiggles about on his chair, gazing hopefully at all the carts that are still too far down the aisle.

"Not many of these places left anymore," my dad always laments every time he picks up the laminated menu. "Not like when I was a student."

"Once upon a time," Tina comments, and then looks at me. We roll our eyes before giggling to ourselves. Dim sum seems to always conjure up a feeling of nostalgia in Baba. He loves to talk about when he first moved to Canada in the '90s to attend university. Sometimes he'll listen to our suggestions to try a new restaurant down in Richmond, but he always grumpily wants to return to this place.

I'm an old man, he always tells us. *I like simple things. I don't need new creations, just familiar food.*

Ma knows what Baba likes, and she's already out of her seat, to ensure that we're not waiting too long to cover our table with various dishes.

"Ma!" Tina chastises, trying to get her to sit back down. "We can wait. You don't always have to go and harass the cart ladies!"

Ma, of course, just does her own thing and never listens. She's already talking to the older auntie responsible for the cart even though she's still a few tables away. Someone from another table is also trying to get the cart auntie's attention and shoots my mother a dirty look. Tina puts her hand up in front of her face, an expression of suffering, of being seen in public with our embarrassing family.

"Help me, Ruby." Ma gestures for me to clear the table, to move the napkins and plates as the stack of steamers are deposited in front of us. Steam curls up above the baskets, revealing glistening chicken feet in black-bean sauce, tender tripe in chili oil, and plump shrimp in translucent rice wrappers drizzled with sweet soy.

"I want the BBQ pork flakies," Denny demands, one hand already clutching a fork in preparation, waiting for his favorite dish.

"That'll come." Baba pats him on the shoulder.

Even with the mortification of Ma acting like the restaurant is her friend's home, all that embarrassment is chased away when we dig into our dishes. Tina is responsible for pouring soy sauce onto the little plates and mixing with red vinegar for dipping. Ma grabs a metal canister of red chili oil from an empty table that she prefers over the regular chili sauce. Dad makes sure our teacups are constantly filled with tea.

"Say hi to Mrs. Chen!" A little boy is pushed unwillingly to stand beside our table, his mom gesturing eagerly.

The boy mumbles a greeting, looking like he wishes the earth would swallow him whole.

"Oh, Mrs. Wei! Good to see you!" Ma puts on her teacher's voice as she smiles at the parent and then at her student. "Andy, how are you? Did you have a good lunch?"

Andy says something so quiet it's like the squeaking of an ant.

"Denny! You've grown so tall!" Mrs. Wei's attention moves on to the rest of the table.

Denny smiles with a mouth covered with pastry crumbs while Ma hastily gestures for me to wipe my brother's mouth with a napkin.

"These must be your 千金," she goes on, looking over me and Tina. The polite term to refer to girls as "a thousand pieces of gold" always sounds odd to me. Like daughters are something to be bought or sold. "We didn't see you at the Kiwanis Festival earlier this year! Andy was there for violin."

"Oh, the girls have been too busy." Ma shakes her head, not giving us a chance to speak. Not that we are supposed to. "IB classes, you know. Westview gives so much homework!"

I look down and shovel more rice in my mouth as they exchange more pleasantries that always sound like humble bragging. Of all the things that happen when parents get together, this is among the worst. It feels like a performance in itself, the way they always fall into this song and dance.

"If you're free later today, you should come to the Mid-Autumn Festival in Chinatown," Mrs. Wei continues, pulling an invite out of her purse and handing it to my mother. "Andy has an art piece in their Under Ten show. It would mean a lot to him to have his teacher see it. Right, Andy?"

Andy doesn't even respond. He's too busy watching a video about ducks with Denny on Baba's phone.

"Sure, if we have time." Ma gives that fake smile again. The one that stretches too wide.

"Well, we'll let you get back to your lunch! Andy!" Mrs. Wei finally leaves, and Ma's face snaps back to normal.

"I don't like seeing parents outside of work," Ma grumbles quietly to Baba when the Weis are out of earshot as she picks up her chopsticks again. "Always so tiring."

"Mama, Baba, can we go to this?" Tina holds up the pamphlet that Ma discarded on the table. It looks just like the one Ellie gave me.

"What is it?" Baba leans over and reads it out loud. "'The Formosa Friendship Association presents the Mid-Autumn Festival. Art show, crafts for kids, puppet theatre, lion dance, food stalls.'"

"Puppets!" Denny exclaims excitedly.

"What do you think?" Baba checks in with Ma, because she always has the final say.

"I have to go buy some groceries anyway." She nods. "Why not?"

"Yay!" Denny cheers, and even Tina shows a glimmer of interest.

"I'm hoping we can watch the lion dance at two," she says, and I can tell she's trying not to sound too excited, but I know it must be put on by her dance academy.

I feel a slight twinge of worry that she might run into someone who knows her. That someone might reveal her ruse. But Tina doesn't seem to care she's dancing too close to the sun. She's not afraid of getting burned.

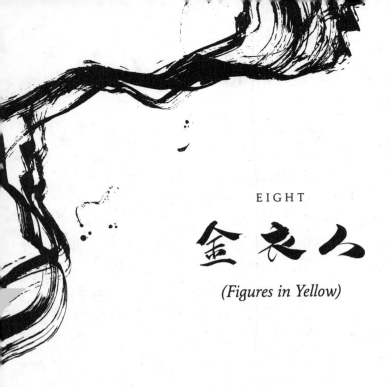

EIGHT

金衣人

(Figures in Yellow)

The rain stopped while we were eating, and the skies cleared to a soft blue by the time we left the restaurant, stomachs filled to bursting. Parts of Chinatown are blocked off for the festival, and we take a detour around the area to the parkade. Even though the streets are damp, there is a considerable crowd in the neighborhood. Families with kids holding balloons of cartoon characters walk by. Other passersby wave colorful fans printed with rainbow flowers. The atmosphere is festive, happy. There's the sound of music in the distance, someone singing Chinese opera, accompanied by the trills of a flute.

Tina and Denny walk hand in hand in front of us, eager to see everything the festival has to offer. My parents walk behind me, talking about something related to Baba's work. The entirety of the street in front of Pacific Dragon Mall is blocked off. There are tents set up on the sidewalk, staffed by people eager to give out free stuff: tote bags, pens, bookmarks. Baba collects everything eagerly, because he loves anything that is free.

There are stalls set up in the middle of the street as well. One is a bookstore, with children's books stacked on top of folding tables and a few rotating shelves. Another is a tent that sells art supplies, beside another tent that houses an assortment of art. I slow down when I notice the banner: ART CONTEST WINNERS! This must be the exhibit Ellie's mom and Mrs. Wei were talking about.

I find the Under Ten category, with the theme *What Home Means to Me.* Sponsored by the Association of Chinatown Merchants and Scotiabank. I find Ellie's name on one of the paintings and smile to myself. Two figures, her mom and herself in a polka-dot dress and braids, a black cat in her arms.

"It's Andy!" Denny gestures for Ma to come see. Ma snorts beside me but makes her way toward him, feigning excitement. Andy's drawing is of him playing violin, while his family claps beside him.

"We have to get to the stage, the lion dance is starting!" Tina is almost skipping with anticipation, which is rare to see during these family outings. I notice Ma and Baba exchange a different sort of glance, their initial surprise turning into approval. She practically drags us to the stage set up at the end of the street on a platform. The platform is flanked by tall metal structures, holding up the backdrop: a photograph of the corner of a curved temple roof with colorful carvings of green dragons with golden horns, against a too-bright blue sky.

There's text emblazoned across the top of the backdrop: WISHING YOU GREAT HAPPINESS AND GOOD FORTUNE FOR MID-AUTUMN!

An Asian man in a suit steps up to the microphone, waving at everyone for their attention.

"Today's lion dance is sponsored by the Formosa Friendship

Association! Let's welcome the Soulful Heart Dance Academy in their performance." He claps, and the crowd joins in.

A woman begins playing the harp to the right of the stage, the delicate plucking of the strings sending out a sweet tune that rises over the head of the audience. Five figures appear on the stage, dressed in hanfu in shades of soft blue and lavender with long, flowing sleeves. Their makeup glitters in the sunlight, butterfly wings blooming across their faces in vivid pinks and purples. They leap and spin, bodies forming graceful shapes, until they snap their wrists and the crowd gasps at the sight. Fans unfurl from their hands, fluttering in the air, like graceful birds flying to and fro across the stage. The music picks up in tempo then, the harp joined by the hollow sound of someone hitting a hand drum. The audience claps along with the beat, entranced by the performance. Too soon, it's over, and they leave the stage to thunderous applause.

But then there's the clash of cymbals as figures in yellow run up the stairs, holding two giant lion heads. The cheers around us grow louder. Next to me, Denny jumps up and down, thrilled at the spectacle. My excitement dies in my throat as a face suddenly pops into my mind. A man, who meets my eyes through the chain-linked fence, then looks away. That exact shade of yellow appears again in the distance when I'm dragged back into the alley.

Someone was watching me other than the boy in the red hoodie who rescued me. The memory conjured up by the sudden appearance of these men in their golden-yellow outfits, red hems at the neck and the wrists, red headbands around their brows.

Other figures in yellow appear from behind the stage, rolling large red drums before them. With a yell, they pull out sticks and cross them overhead, and then the drumming starts. The dancers on the stage stomp their feet to the rhythm. The crowd screams their enthusiasm and pushes forward toward the stage as both the lion heads are lifted.

I'm jostled by the sudden press of bodies, and I try to stand my ground in the wave.

The lions jump and sway, their too-large eyes with long lashes blinking, their rippling bodies in festive red and shiny silver thread. The lions fight, trying to be the first to snatch the red cabbage dangling above their heads from a pole. The jerky movements, the frenzy of drumming, the roar of the crowd . . . all of it makes my head dizzy.

I grab for Ma's arm to steady myself, but the arm is snatched out of my grasp. A strange woman looks down at me with disgust, annoyed. I open my mouth to apologize, but she's already swallowed up by the crowd. I look around, and there's nobody I recognize anywhere. I've somehow been pushed to the left of the stage. One of the lions casts a shadow across me, and it lunges in my direction, threatening to catch me between its massive jaws. I flinch downward, even as everyone around me laughs.

I turn away from the stage to try and find my family, but it's impossible to move in this crowd.

"Little girl . . ." a man whispers to my right. He flashes a mouth full of broken teeth, stained by tobacco. "Are you lost?" He spits on the ground, a red blob of something disgusting. He grabs for me, and I duck out of his reach, but then someone else pinches my shoulder. I back away, and I'm pushed again, thrust from one person to the next. Laughter surrounds me. Hands coming out of nowhere, belonging to no one. Flashes of yellow. Here, and there, then everywhere, whirling all around me. The drumbeats grow wilder, as fast as my racing heart.

A hand finally finds its target. Grips my arm hard enough to bruise.

"I remember you. . . ." He leers.

It's *him*. The man from the alley. The one who watched as I tried to crawl away from the ghoul. He's so close that I can see the large mole on his chin. He bends down over me, and I'm not sure what he's about to do.

"Leave her alone!" A slightly disheveled young guy with a backpack steps forward with a rolled-up newspaper, hitting the man who grabbed my arm.

The man with the mole releases me, surprised at this sudden onslaught. Newspaper guy thrusts his whole body between us. I shrink away from both of them, knowing that I should cry out for help, but I'm too afraid.

"I..." The man backs away, holding his hands up. "I'll...I'll see you again." He wiggles his fingers at me as he walks backward into the crowd. What does he mean he'll see me again? A chill cuts into me, a sense of dread the bright midafternoon sun cannot chase away.

"Yeah! Get the fuck outta here!" newspaper guy yells at him, then he turns back and looks at me with concern. "Are you—"

"Ruby!" Baba appears beside me suddenly. "Who is this person? Is he bothering you?" He turns to confront the man who helped me, no longer my usual mild-mannered father.

"What do you want?" he yells. "Get away from her!" Ma is there too, taking hold of my jacket and forcing me to step back.

"Wait!" I try to speak up, to tell them the young man with the backpack actually saved me from the man in yellow who was harassing me, but I'm pulled away.

"How many times do I have to tell you? Don't talk to people like *that*. He's probably a drunk or a drug addict," Ma declares loudly, drawing the attention of others around us. The young man receives a few dirty looks.

A terrible feeling washes over me. I shrink down and wish that I could disappear. I'm not brave enough to give him an apology, or even a second glance.

"I keep telling you girls that Chinatown is *dangerous*. It's crawling all over the place with those people," Ma lectures, one hand on Denny. Tina looks at us curiously, wanting to know what trouble I've gotten into now.

"He was trying to help me," I finally say, but my mother doesn't hear me. She's complaining to Baba about the terrible state of Chinatown, and how the city needs to clean up this mess.

I'm ready to go home after that encounter, but on the way to our car, someone calls out Baba's name from one of the booths. Enthusiastic introductions are made, and then a mention of the architecture firm that he works at, which means that this conversation will probably go on for a while. One of the volunteers at the booth asks Denny if he wants to make a fan, and I follow, half expecting Tina to be there too. Except she stays right beside Ma. I keep one eye on Denny while eavesdropping on the conversation with the adults, wondering why she's so interested.

But with Denny demanding that I help him fold his fan, I'm not able to catch too much of what they're talking about. Until Ma gestures for us to join them.

"This is my eldest daughter, Ruby, and my son, Denny." Baba is the one who introduces us, placing his hands on our shoulders. "Say hello to Mr. Lee."

"Ruby is our piano player," Ma says, a little too eagerly, sharing in a way that shows these are people she wants to impress.

The man in the suit extends his hand for me to shake first, and I realize he was the one who introduced the lion dancers. He's a distinguished-looking man, with salt-and-pepper hair, laugh lines in the corners of his eyes and mouth. His grip is firm and warm.

"My daughter, Melody, goes to Westview. You might know her?" he says, and I realize that it's *the* Mr. Lee that Baba had mentioned before. I nod, even though I can't recall Melody's face.

The woman beside him gives me a smile too, offering her hand for me to shake. She has on a dark green blazer and matching skirt. Pearls adorn her ears and circle her neck. She looks elegant, with her perfectly made-up face.

"I'm Mrs. Tsai," she introduces herself, and her voice is soft and gentle, like a teacher's voice. "I'm the director for the Soulful Heart Dance Academy." It takes every part of me not to react, and I force myself to keep my expression blank and pleasant. She is why Tina is hovering still, I understand now. To make sure she doesn't reveal too much about what Tina's been up to these past few months.

I force myself to smile.

"I've been trying to convince your parents to come join us at one of our Formosa Friendship Association events, and it looks like they might finally be interested!" Mrs. Tsai tells me and Tina. "We have youth groups too, so you can meet other Taiwanese kids!"

The thought of joining a group where I can meet more people for my parents to compare me to is less than thrilling, but Tina is already eagerly tugging on Baba's arm, knowing that he's the one who gives in to our requests more often than our mother does.

"We'll talk about it," Baba says, but he's also smiling.

"Wonderful!" Mrs. Tsai puts her hands together. "I look forward to it. I hope you've been enjoying the festival!"

"We loved all the performances, but we do need more security here in Chinatown." Ma purses her mouth. "Ruby was just attacked. Grabbed! Who knows what that man wanted with her."

"I wasn't—" I protest, but Mr. Lee waves over others dressed in security uniforms, very concerned, noting down the description of the man, ensuring that Ma's complaints are heard.

No one listens to me. It wasn't one of the visibly homeless people or the ones muttering to themselves who attacked me. The man who grabbed me looked like he could be my dad, an uncle, a teacher at my school, one of the security guards talking to my parents now. He could be any one of them. That was the most frightening part of all.

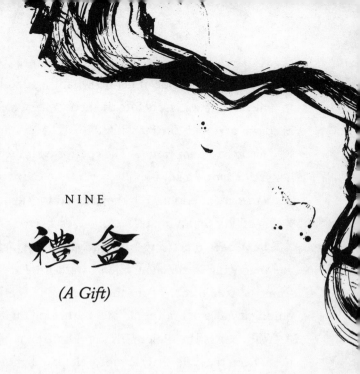

NINE

禮盒

(A Gift)

That night I nudge the door to Tina's room open, a tin of chocolate wafer rolls tucked under my arm. She's lying on her stomach with her laptop in front of her, the screen illuminating her face. She taps her fingers on the side of the keyboard, earbuds in, the tinny sound of music leaking out.

I dangle the wafer tin above her head, grabbing her attention.

"Hey, I gotta go, okay? Talk to you later," Tina quickly speaks into the microphone before shutting her laptop.

I drop the tin into her lap, and she twists off the lid with a squeal.

"Yum!" she says while munching on one of the rolls. "It's the good ones from Taiwan too."

"I hid this pack in the back of the pantry so Denny couldn't find it," I tell her. She chuckles and takes another, knowing that our little brother rummages for snacks at all times.

I sit down on the side of her bed, wanting to talk.

"The dancers we saw before the lion dance were really great," I say. "I liked the part with the fans a lot."

"That's the senior troupe! They perform all the time," Tina exclaims, her excitement already bubbling over from the first breath. "You have to get Vanessa's attention to be considered for them. Invitation only. We would all kill for an invite."

"You've been practicing lots," I say, my voice high and staccato. "I saw you practicing in the gym when I walked by at lunch. Are those girls from the studio too?" I try to sound excited rather than judgmental, pulling a wafer out of the tin and munching on it as well.

"Yeah, one of the senior girls said I have a lot of potential and picked me to be in the little-sister troupe." Her face lights up. "As long as I work hard, there's a chance I might get into the older troupes even though I don't have as much experience as some of the others. It's like a family, they said, we help each other."

"Wow, that's great!" I tell her, envious. Of being able to be on the team, part of a group where you're working toward the same thing. Like when I was in the school band at my old school—although now band has been removed from my schedule because it is not a "priority."

I tense, reminded that there is so much more I am supposed to do. The weight of grade eleven being "the final year where grades will matter on your university application"—my parents' constant reminder that I am running out of time. I rub the back of my neck, trying to loosen the knot there. I envy how easily Tina seems to flirt with being discovered, how she seems unfazed and unafraid.

"Weren't you scared today when Ma and Baba met Mrs. Tsai?" I ask. "She could have easily told them that you were taking a class there."

Tina smiles, a little mysterious. "Don't worry. It's all part of my plan. Mrs. Tsai understands."

"What do you mean, your plan?" Tina hinted at this before: a plan to get our parents to cooperate with her. But she shakes her head, refusing to share anything else. We used to split snacks late at night, just like this. Complain about our parents. Share our thoughts. We used to be close, but not anymore.

What is that phrase Ma likes to say? 熱臉貼冷屁股. *Don't put your warm face against a cold butt.* Don't suck up when you're not wanted. I need to stop obsessing over whatever Tina is up to. I have my own problems to deal with.

"Fine," I say, pretending like it doesn't bother me. "Keep your secrets." That's when I notice a small lantern on the shelf above her bed. A rainbow lotus, glowing as if lit from within.

"What this?" I reach for it, but she quickly rolls over and snatches it off the shelf before I can touch it.

"Don't," she says, cradling it like something precious. There's an odd quality to her voice, a slight growl at the back of her throat. "I don't want you to break it."

"Okay, whatever," I say, hopping off the bed and brushing the crumbs off my lap. "I'm going to get ready for bed."

"It's pretty though, right? I got it as a gift," she says softly, like she's talking to herself, her fingers running over the petals. The rainbow lights of the lotus are reflected in her dark eyes, stardust swirling in those depths. Like all her secrets, contained within.

Back in my room, my phone buzzes softly on my desk. I pick it up to check the notifications and notice messages from my friend Dawn. She was my closest friend at my old school, one of the few people I still keep in touch with after transferring to Westview.

Dawn: miss you lots. band isn't the same without you. new kids keep going off-tempo
Me: miss you too

I send her a few smiley faces blowing hearts. I've felt off-tempo for a few months now too. Trying to realign myself back to where I was supposed to be.

You just need to find your people, Dawn tried to reassure me a while back, but I still don't know where I fit in at Westview.

My thumbs hover on the keyboard, and I wonder if I should tell her about the strange things I've been seeing. I haven't told her about the ghoul, or the bruise that still circles my leg. Not to mention the encounter with that guy today in Chinatown. But I don't mention any of that.

Me: i'm still messing up the rachmaninoff...don't know if i'll ever get it
Dawn: you'll get it. you always do. just try not to get too in your head about it all

Her message is followed by a bunch of black hearts. I send her a goodnight, and as I brush my teeth, I wonder what my life would be like if I fought harder to stay in public school. If I would be happy with my old life, and Tina could be at Westview, building her new life. We'd each have our own space to figure out things for ourselves, and I wouldn't be so... *lonely.* My mind whispers that word to me, something I would never admit out loud. I scrunch all of that down into the darkness where I hide those thoughts, those insecurities, and crawl into bed.

—

Whatever Tina has planned with Mrs. Tsai, it arrives in the form of a Mid-Autumn gift box.

"Looks expensive," Ma comments approvingly when Baba takes it out after we finish eating dinner. He tells us Mr. Lee brought a bunch by his office that day as gifts.

We all gather around the kitchen table to see what it actually looks like. It comes in a purple bag, with a design of what appears to be a traditional carved-wood window, cut from paper to give a 3D effect. An origami bonsai tree sits before it, beside a tray with an origami teapot and two paper cups folded in geometric shapes. Beyond the window there is a dark blue sky dotted with tiny stars, a yellow moon in the corner, and the tiniest paper rabbit peeking out.

Ma pulls the container out, and it's an octagon in the exact shape of the window. The purple lid is printed with the same design as on the bag. The insert inside is a shimmery gold, and nestled within are five mooncakes, each in their own individual box of various colors. The flavors are printed on the lids of the boxes in gold.

"These are not traditional flavors for sure." Baba pushes his glasses up on his nose, peering down and reading them out. "Thai tea. Jasmine with dates. Osmanthus oolong. Hojicha with salted egg yolk. Coffee snow."

"There's an envelope." Denny pops up from under the table, purple envelope in hand, giving it to Ma.

"Grab some plates and forks for us, Ruby," Ma says while ripping open the envelope, eager to see what's inside. I follow her directions, taking out the dessert plates and the tiny forks.

"We've been invited to a party!" Ma looks up from the envelope, surprised, handing it over to Baba. "Which one shall we try first?" She's more eager to try the mooncakes while Baba looks over the invitation.

"A party? Where?" Tina asks, excited at the idea.

"Not a party for kids," Ma quickly corrects while taking out the black sesame cake. She lets Tina take a photo of the floral design before cutting it into five pieces, one for each of us to try. Each has an oozing center, flowing out on the plate.

"It's a fundraiser," Baba says. "A documentary on Taiwanese migratory birds, how fascinating!"

"That sounds boring," Denny declares, fork in hand. Tina chuckles. "Can we eat?" Ma gives us a nod.

Denny pops the small piece of mooncake into his mouth immediately, chewing happily. Tina slices off a corner and spears it with her fork, nibbling on the edges.

"我們 next Wednesday 晚上有空嗎?"

"...Maybe? 我看一下 schedule."

I cut into the mooncake with my own fork, half listening to my parents. Something on my plate moves, catching my attention. White shapes wiggling in and out of the black sesame filling. *Maggots.* I drop my fork onto the plate with a gasp. The clatter catches everyone's attention.

"Do you not like it?" Baba questions. I look down at the plate again, and the mooncake is back to normal again. No maggots. Nothing moving. Tina pops another section of the mooncake into her mouth, while Denny shows his teeth, black smears of sesame smeared across his lips and tongue. My stomach churns at the sight.

"You can have my piece," I mumble, pushing it toward Denny, who takes it eagerly.

What the hell is wrong with me?

The only one who notices something is weird is Tina. She watches me, and then smiles, a strange glint in her eye. Like she knows something I do not.

"But it's sooo good..." she says in a slow drawl, and takes her finger to pick up a crumb on my plate that Denny left behind, and licks it off.

Still staring at me, as if daring me to say something. My stomach flips. I push away from the table, envisioning the sight of maggots wriggling inside my guts, even though I didn't eat a single bite.

"I have to go to the bathroom," I mumble, and run upstairs. I only barely manage to shut and lock the door behind me before falling to my knees before the toilet. I retch, then everything I ate for dinner comes out, burning my mouth with acid. I rest my face against the cool porcelain of the bathtub, trying to catch my breath.

"Ruby?" Ma knocks frantically at the door, trying to open it. "What happened?"

"I'm fine," I call out, dragging my hand against my mouth. "Just not feeling good. I'll be out in a second." The lie makes me feel wretched, but who will believe me if I tell them what I saw?

TEN

怪味

(A Peculiar Scent)

"**What's that smell?**" Denny wrinkles his nose. His words come out all garbled, with his mouth wide open for me to inspect his teeth. I have to make sure he's brushing properly. Ma and Baba decided to go to that fundraiser tonight, so it's up to me to babysit my siblings to make sure they're doing their homework and getting to bed on time. "We must all make a good impression," he says when he told us, solemn, not in his usual joking manner. Ma grumbles a little at this, even as Baba tries to put a positive spin on it. About how attending these events will help him make connections for his job.

"And it's good for the girls," he continues. "A bit more independence." Ma turns away at this, as if not ready for the idea.

We have a decent enough night. All of us get along, which is a rarity in itself. Denny finishes his math homework with the promise of an episode of his robot show after dinner. I heat up leftovers: noodles Ma made yesterday with pork, cabbage, and carrots. I pull out the container that

68

has all the sauces, and we each take our pick. Me: hoisin. Tina: sriracha. Denny: ketchup...which both Tina and I make gagging noises at and tease him mercilessly about.

Tina goes upstairs to finish her homework in her room. I work on my assignment on the kitchen table to keep an eye on Denny, but even down here I can hear the sound of the bass through the ceiling. Probably more dance practice, like usual.

I noticed the smell earlier but thought it was coming from outside. As I lead Denny over to say good night to Tina though, we can smell it wafting around her door. Something sickly sweet, that I can almost taste at the back of my throat. Like incense, cloying and medicinal.

"Are you burning something in here?" I knock on the door before pushing it open, remembering the time last year when she snuck candles in her room and fell asleep and burned the edges of her curtains. Almost lit the entire house on fire.

"Hey!" Tina sits on the floor on her yoga mat. She turns to glare at us, scowling. The video continues to play behind her, the light bouncing off the ceiling. It's a woman demonstrating some sort of pose. A chant fills the air, slow and rhythmic, like the sound of the wood block, interspersed with chimes.

"You're...you're twisted like a pretzel," Denny declares, giggling.

"Not funny, brat!" Tina rolls onto her knees and throws a stuffed animal from her bed in his direction. It bops him on the head before falling to the floor.

"Ow!" Denny yelps, hiding behind me. "Who're you calling a brat? *You're* a brat, and you stink!" He pinches his nose with his fingers.

"Tina...we can't use candles in the house, you know that," I remind her, as gently as possible. "And you should apologize to Denny for bopping him."

"I'm not burning a candle!" Tina grabs something off her desk and throws it at me. It hits me on the leg and falls on the carpet. A little glass vial, with a label on it in Chinese. A character I can't understand. Underneath, in tiny letters, it says: ESSENCE OF CLARITY. Some sort of essential oil. That's why the smell is a bit familiar. A little like the traditional Chinese medicine stores that Baba would take us to when he needs to pick up packets for his high blood pressure and cholesterol. Ma used to make us drink them sometimes, the ingredients that look like dried twigs that she would cook down into a soup in a special pot. The taste made me want to throw up. Tina would never drink it, but I could be bribed to if given ice cream after.

"It's a diffuser, obviously." She scowls at me. "Now, will you two get out?" She snatches the glass vial out of Denny's grasp as he bends down to try and grab it, then places her hand on his shoulder, guiding him out. She glares at me over his mop of hair, gesturing for me to leave too with a thrust of her head.

Denny and I are left outside, staring at one another, bewildered at her animosity. Then he sneezes, and he starts giggling. I can't help but laugh too. He might be a baby sometimes, but he's still my little brother. He still looks up and listens to me . . . for now. Like Tina used to. He tucks his hand into mine to walk him to his room.

After tucking Denny in and turning on his night-light, I close the door gently and notice Tina's door is ajar again. I heard the water running earlier when I read Denny his nighttime story. The sound of music trickles out. She's still awake. I should say good night and apologize for bugging her when I know she wouldn't make the same mistake again. She was genuinely distraught last time when she burned her curtains; she even cried, promising she would be more careful from then on.

I push the door open with my shoulder, stepping into the room. That scent is even stronger this time, and the chanting louder. It sounds like muttering, the same syllables repeated over and over again, accompanied by that steady woodblock.

"I shouldn't assume you were burning candles again. I know you wouldn't forget. I was just worried." I extend the olive branch, voice low, as to not startle her.

Tina is now at her desk below the window. Her makeup mirror is to her left, only revealing half her face on the reflective surface. It's so dark in here, the only light in the room from the soft yellow beam of the desk lamp. It makes her look like she's floating in space. A girl glowing in the darkness.

"Whatever," she says, still sullen, face all scrunched up.

"I was only trying to make sure—"

"Yeah, you're checking up on me. Making sure that I'm doing what I'm supposed to do," she says, then her voice goes up again in that mocking lilt. "Report everything back to Ma, be their perfect daughter."

I feel a twinge of annoyance. "I said *sorry*," and it comes out sharper than I intended.

"I don't care," she says. Her fingers have stopped on the keyboard, but she still stares at her screen, refusing to face me. "Maybe you should get a life of your own instead of being so obsessed with mine and what I'm doing. You never think for yourself."

"Tina . . ." Her words sting, like she intends them to.

"Just shut up and get out!" Her voice rises up, high-pitched. The bruise on my ankle suddenly burns, as if fire licked my skin. I have to look down to check that nothing is touching me. The lights flicker at that moment, and I look back—for a second, even though she's looking straight ahead, her reflection in the mirror turns toward me.

What in the actual fuck?

"Get out!" she yells, her voice cracking, splitting into two. A growl. A shriek. Her shoulders rise up almost to her ears, her entire body trembling. With anger? Or something else?

The reflection in the mirror continues to stare at me. Not moving.

And then smiles.

Just like the man in Chinatown with the yellow uniform.

I'll see you again. His voice sounds in my head, crystal clear.

I stumble back into the hallway, in time to see her raise her hand and then the door slam shut. But she didn't get up out of the chair at all. *Impossible.*

I run into my room and shut the door. My pulse races like I ran around the track, my mind trying to make sense of it. I crawl under my covers and squeeze my eyes shut, force myself to take deep breaths. My sister's face floats before me. Her face whole. Her face split. Half of her laughing, while the other half has her part of the mouth open in a scream—a cry?

Sometime in the middle of the night, I hear the back door opening downstairs. My parents returning from their event. Their voices wash over me, bringing a sense of normalcy back into the house.

I convince myself it's all in my imagination. The stress, the pressure, the expectations. It's all getting to me. I'm the one who can't be trusted. The dark distorting my vision. My imagination making things up that aren't there.

I am safe. It's not real. I am safe. It's not real.

At school I try to pay attention to the lectures. Take notes on solving algebraic equations. Attempt to memorize the structures of the cell. But the feeling of unease continues to follow me, even as I try to shove it out of the way.

It was just a bad dream.

The rest of the week passes by, uneventful. Except the smell gets worse. The upper level of the house becomes permeated with that strange scent that only Denny and I seem to smell. I wake up in the morning to it stinging my nostrils. Tina continues to be on her best behavior. Washing the dishes, taking out the garbage without being asked. The music she plays has changed to a steady chant, a peculiar droning of syllables, repeated over and over. It doesn't seem to bother my parents when Tina reassures them it's for a school project.

After the weekend, I'm glad to be back at school, away from Tina's increasingly bizarre behaviors. When I started at Westview, I was coming in midyear, still trying to recover from the shock of pushing back on my parents' demands and succeeding. But in a way I didn't expect. I have more freedom now, and yet the pressure seems more present than ever. Keeping up with the classes, the increased number of assignments, community service, tentatively returning to piano. One misstep and it could all crash again. My hallucinations returning is proof that I am barely holding myself together.

I can't let anyone know, and yet I desperately want to find someone who might be able to understand.

One day I take my lunch out in the back to eat on one of the picnic tables in Westview's lone courtyard, which has a basketball court and the saddest little patch of grass.

There's a few girls I'm friendly with who are already out here, and they wave at me to join them. Showing me that I'm not a total social pariah. I sit down beside them and open up my dish of glass noodles. It's one of Ma's specialties, filled with cabbage and carrots, mushrooms and dried shrimp. Usually I would devour it, but I'm not feeling much of an appetite. They talk about one of the assignments they have coming up, a course I'm not in, so I don't have much to say. I take a bite and let my thoughts drift....

A shadow of something falls from the sky, like it flew off the roof of the building, hitting the cement before me with force—a mangled form of twisted limbs. I gasp, a bite of noodle going down the wrong way, and cough violently.

"Are you okay?" The girls all stare at me—concerned that I'm going to choke and die before them—instead of staring at the real horror. The figure on the pavement.

Keep it together, I tell myself. *It's not real.*

He landed without a sound, and then drags himself forward, leaving a bloody trail behind him. His neck is bent sideways, half of his face flattened from where he struck the ground. One of his eyes is gone, but the other turns in its socket, bright red with blood, looking up at me. His mouth opens, and all I see is bloody gums and broken teeth. One hand stretches out toward me, the angle of the elbow all wrong.

"Ruby?" another girl asks, and I force myself to turn to her, to pretend that everything is fine.

I clear my throat. "Choked on something," I mumble, taking a swig of my drink. The conversation resumes around me.

The door beside us opens, and I look up to see that boy again. The now-familiar red jacket he's shrugging on over his school uniform. He quickly descends the metal steps, not even glancing in our direction. When he walks by, he looks down, and ever so slightly, his mouth pulls back in a slight grimace. So quick that I almost miss it.

With a jolt, I realize he sees him too. The mangled body on the pavement. If he sees him, then that means it's not all in my head. It means that it is infinitely worse. It's all real. Everything that I'm seeing. What happened in the alley. What's happening with Tina.

I could keep on sitting here, pretend that nothing is wrong. Watch the boy with the red jacket walk away. I could smile with the girls like I don't see the guy grinning at me from the ground with his broken teeth.

But a sharp pain digs into my leg, reminding me that the bruise is there, and the sound of my sister's door slamming without her getting up.

I throw all the pieces of my lunch together, mutter the first excuse that jumps into my head. He's almost at the gate. I can feel my lunchmates' eyes, curious, burning into the back of my head as I hurry away.

ELEVEN

緣分

(Fate)

"Hey!" I yell. "Hey you!" He keeps walking, undoing the latch to the gate. I know he must hear me, and I walk faster, grabbing the gate as it swings back. He seems determined not to acknowledge me.

"Shen!" I call out the name that Delia told me. What I should have tried to call him back in the mall when we ran into each other again. He stops on the corner, the Don't Walk sign across the street flashing above his head like a warning. Finally, he looks back over his shoulder.

"What do you want?" he asks, tone decidedly unfriendly. As I draw closer to him, his expression changes like he smells something...bad, like a stench emanating from my body so putrid that he can't help but flinch.

I stop in front of him, suddenly struck with the realization that I have no idea what I'm doing. What I am supposed to say. How I should confront him. With him standing here now, it all floods back like a shock of cold water dumped on my head. The ghoul. The tongue. His blurry form. Light being shaped by his hands.

"You got my attention," he says coldly. "What exactly do you want from me?"

"I just want to know what happened in the alley. When you . . . saved me," I say, my voice coming out barely in a squeak. Not intimidating at all. Not like someone looking for answers.

I stand up straighter and force myself to stare at him in the eyes.

He gives an aggrieved sigh, rubbing his forehead with a knuckle. "I didn't *save* you," he says. "I found you in the alley. I don't want any trouble, so that's why I left you with Delia."

"That's not what I'm talking about, and you know it." I hate that I'm shaking a little.

"I acknowledge and appreciate your thanks." His voice drips with sarcasm, ready to dismiss me outright. I stare at him. It feels like we're having two completely different conversations. I'm not going to let him push me away this time.

"I want to know if you saw that figure in the alley. That woman." I raise my voice, stepping forward, more insistent now. Making myself bigger, pushing myself into his space.

"I didn't see anything." He takes a step back, eerily calm. "I found you, brought you in. Maybe you hit your head."

I look down, my hands clenching into fists at my side. Not knowing what I can do to make him listen to the truth. Except. I notice his fingers playing with the hem of his jacket. Something about that gesture makes me feel that he's nervous, that there's something to hide.

Impulsively, like I'm channeling someone else, another person reaching through me . . . I grab his wrist. Before he can react, I slide my other hand down his arm, pulling his sleeve back so that his forearm is exposed.

The tiger tattoo is brilliant against his skin. The fur a bright orange, with black stripes lined with red. Behind the tiger is a red flower, green leaves unfurling underneath. Vines and various vegetation writhe around it, almost like it would ripple on his skin with the breeze, bloom from his arms. He tries to pull back, but I hold on to him with all my strength, the truth inked onto his skin. It gained form in the alley to attack the ghoul... and saved me.

"Something happened that night!" I am not like this. I am never like this. But the fear makes me braver than usual. Fear for the darkness spreading under my skin. Fear for whatever it is my sister is changing into.

His eyes search my face. I dare him to lie to me again. Dare him to shake me off. Pretend that everything is normal.

"I have somewhere I have to be right now," he says, gently opening my fist. I snatch it out of his warm grasp. "But I'll be at Bubble Madness tonight. If you really want to know, you can come find me there."

My heart thuds at what I just accomplished. Something small, yet it feels like I'm taking a right step forward. I walk back to campus, feeling like I'm floating on air, my head spinning.

Tonight. Tonight. I'll finally have the answers.

The chill suits my mood as the cars fly past me, everyone leaving downtown at the same time, rushing to get home. Fall always comes slowly to Vancouver, in the swirling leaves piling up on the sidewalk and crunching under each step, in the slight crispness to the air. I walk past the futuristic high-rises towering above me, then the office buildings, and somewhere along the way, the neighborhood changes. A body slumps on the sidewalk. A police cruiser drives slowly past me down the street.

When Ama, my grandmother on Baba's side, was still alive and living with us, Baba would drop me and her off in Chinatown. I would go to Chinese school, and she would do her shopping at one of the grocers down the street. There are always boxes of fruits and vegetables out on the sidewalk for the other aunties and amas to pick through. There are still a few of those stores left open, but not as many as before. There are more people wandering the streets with a vacant look on their face, less tourists coming in and out of the storefronts. A store is here one day, then gone the next, something else taking its place, the cycle repeating over and over again.

Ma's warnings about being attacked, stabbed, kidnapped rang in my ears in the beginning, constant reminders of all the things that could go wrong. Except the more time I spend here, the more I realize how much the people on the streets are struggling with their own personal demons. They couldn't care less about us. We're all phantoms, flitting in and out of each other's lives.

I arrive at the street entrance of Bubble Madness. The bell above the entrance dings when I push open the door. This time I'm able to pay attention to the decor. There are shelves along the wall lined with plants, greenery draping downward from the pots. There's a cat sleeping by the front window, in a little section that is walled off from the rest of the café. Under the window seat there are board games tucked into the bench for anyone who wants to pull one out to play.

The rest of the space is equally inviting. I recognize the banquette along the side where I was given the tea to soothe my nerves. I hope that friendly girl is there again, so that it's not me facing off against Shen, who may have changed his mind since we last spoke.

"I'll be right with you." *He* stands behind the counter, stirring something in a cup.

"Sure," I mumble as I slide into a booth, not wanting his full attention just yet. The reality of what I am doing threatens to overwhelm me again. I am disrupting my sensible, regular, everyday life. I could keep taking the bus, learning the piano, keeping my head down and staying along the safe path, never straying. I'm throwing myself down this road to figure out something that may have an answer I don't want to hear.

"It's you!" Delia appears, giving me a genuine grin, like she's actually happy to see me. The sight of her makes that tightness in my chest ease a little.

"Hi," I say quietly.

"I told you she'd be back," she says over her shoulder. Shen approaches, impassive, arms crossed. They both have on the same Bubble Madness apron. He touches her shoulder and pulls her back for a moment, muttering something into her ear that doesn't sound too friendly. I can only catch bits and pieces of it. I recognize it as Taiwanese, having grown up in a house where my grandparents spoke it to us daily.

I hold back, not wanting to reveal yet that I know a little of what he's saying. In a city like Vancouver, either Mandarin or Cantonese is fairly common for people who look like us. But when it comes to Taiwanese, even back on the island not everyone is capable of speaking it. So here, an ocean away, it seems more like an anomaly to hear those familiar sounds.

Things that I've forgotten.

Things that still remain with me, after all this time.

They've turned to face each other now, arguing about what they should do. Him, terse and annoyed. Her, trying to convince him to listen, that he should be aware that things are changing in Chinatown, that he must see it too, and that I might be caught up in it.

"你需要鬥跤手!" she says. Something about helping.

I don't know if it's better to know they're Taiwanese, like me. It feels like a bad omen, like a wound being opened to the air, something hidden deep inside me revealed. I'm suddenly tired of pretending.

"Look," I say, then tell them in my broken Taiwanese, my tongue unaccustomed to the sound, "我聽有, okay?" *I can understand you.*

Then I return to what I'm comfortable with, my less broken but still stilted Mandarin. "I want to know what's going on. I don't know what sort of dangers you're referring to, but I'm seeing things, hearing things, I can't explain. Just tell me the truth." My voice crescendos until even passersby who walk past the doors leading into the mall turn to do a double take.

"See?" Delia arches a brow. "She's from Taiwan. 緣分." She stresses that last term, like that will finally convince him. *Fate.*

I look at him with my chin raised, challenging him. Fate dragged me here, and we'll see if it's unlucky or not.

He shakes his head, still unhappy, but unfolds his arms from his chest with a sigh. "Maybe it is 緣分. More likely it's my personal punishment from the gods."

TWELVE

陰陽眼

(The Sight)

Delia's not done yet, and she continues with a frown. "I'm not like you. I didn't swear an oath to"—she waves a hand in the air—"all of that. I only know what's right and what's wrong and this girl needs our help."

She looks at Shen, and he stares back. The two of them exchanging some sort of silent communication I can't understand. I could tell the two of them are bound by some sort of history. Friendship? Family? Or something else?

Shen considers this for another beat, then finally tips his head toward the door to the street. "If we're going to do this, then you'll have to help me. We'll close up. I don't want anyone overhearing this."

"Great." She flashes white teeth. Delia spins toward me, takes me by the shoulders, and guides me toward one of the booths. "You sit here. We'll be back in no time."

Shen goes to flip the OPEN sign to CLOSED. Delia pulls down the security gate that separates the store from the mall.

"What can I get you to drink?" Delia asks as Shen adjusts the blinds and dims the light in the space. She rolls up her sleeves, expression clear that she will not take no for an answer. "You're going to want a drink with what he's going to tell you."

"Fine, I'll have a jasmine milk tea with grass jelly." One of my favorite drink combinations, to make whatever truth he is going to offer easier to swallow. "Half-sweet and less ice, please."

"Coming right up," she says, stepping behind the counter, tying her hair back into a short ponytail.

Shen slides into the booth across from me, setting a book bag down on the table. I resist the urge to stare at him, instead focusing on his hands on the table. Long, slender fingers. Maybe even suitable for the piano. He pulls a coiled notebook out from the bag, setting it on the table between us.

"The woman you saw in the alley," he begins, picking up the book and flipping through, before landing on a page. A ghoulish figure looks back at me. She's not exactly the same as the one I saw, but fairly close. She still has the same bulging black eyes, the stretched-out face, the long, floppy tongue. "It's what we call a Hanged Spirit. 吊死鬼. Usually spirits don't linger long after they die. They're taken to where they're supposed to go by the wardens.

"And that boy who jumped from the roof of Westview . . . He's a 石榴鬼." When he sees my confused expression, he explains further. "石榴 is pomegranate . . . or in English we would call him a Split-Faced Spirit." I shudder, understanding. Pomegranates. His bloody teeth.

Another few pages are flipped, and then there are two figures drawn in charcoal, dressed in long robes like the judges from Ma's Chinese period dramas. One shaded dark, wearing a tall black hat. He's wide and stout, wielding a wooden placard and a curved sword. The other in white with deep circles for eyes, a white cap with wings drooping down beside his face. He's skeletal in appearance, gaunt and thin lipped. He holds a fan made of feathers in his hand, and from his other hand dangles long chains.

"These are the wardens," Shen explains, tapping the page with the back of his pen. "We call them 七爺八爺. Lord Seven and Lord Eight."

"They...take spirits to the afterlife?" I try to understand. Like the Grim Reaper.

"It's a disorienting process, dying. Souls can become confused when they are separated from the physical body. Some of them try to remain, wanting to return to their old life, refuse to go on," he continues. "But there are certain spirits that are...tethered. Their physical bodies die, and yet their soul remains in the place where they've died because of how they passed. A catastrophic event, often violent. They remain bound by the intensity of their fury, regret, or desire for vengeance. Usually they're harmless, bound to one place until a warden is able to find them and help them move on."

"But she attacked me," I say, voice trembling. "She wasn't harmless."

Shen frowns. "That was an anomaly, I have to admit. They usually are not powerful enough to attack anyone who has no connection to the afterlife."

My head spins with all this knowledge, and I'm not sure if I'm even able to understand him entirely.

"What does it mean...a connection to the afterlife?"

"Some are born with the ability to *see*," he says. "In English, we refer to it as the Sight, or in Chinese we call it 陰陽眼. Some people may call it a gift, but most see it as a curse. The energy of the living naturally repels the energy of the dead. If you exist between both worlds, well...many of the affected get sick easily, experience frequent nightmares."

The Sight. Is that what I have? The idea makes me feel slightly ill. Fortunately, Delia brings over our drinks then and slides my bubble tea in front of me. I poke my straw through and take a sip, grateful that I don't have to speak for now. Shen doesn't do the same, instead he regards me with even further scrutiny.

"You look . . . different from when I first met you. There's something not right." He gestures over my head. "I don't know what you've done, but . . ." He looks at me like I'm a specimen under a microscope, to be studied and dissected. I shrink under that gaze, like I'm being judged. Like I've brought this upon myself.

"Seriously?" Delia scoffs. "Are you going to blame her for being attacked?" I look up at her, grateful that she is standing up for me even though she doesn't know me.

"Tell him everything." She gives Shen a pointed look as she bumps his shoulder with her hip, getting him to move over so she can sit down. "I'll make sure he listens."

"I . . ." My voice comes out raspy from nervousness, and I clear my throat so I can speak. "I think I've seen them before, but I didn't know what they were. They always looked . . . blurry."

I tell them everything. How I've always been told to keep quiet about it, to never mention it so that I don't stand out. To fit in. That my parents didn't move all the way here to start a new life for us to waste their efforts. What I saw in the mall. The man that tried to grab me in the street. The smell wafting out of Tina's room. The weird chanting that seems to worm its way into my head. Her reflection. The more I talk, the more I feel like there will come a moment when they will laugh and tell me there is something wrong with me. But Shen's and Delia's expressions don't change.

"These figures that you're seeing. You say they're getting clearer?" His brow furrows as he taps his cheek with one finger. I nod. "And you're not feeling well sometimes?"

"Um...I don't know if this is relevant, but..." I reach down and roll up my pants so that they can see my leg. Delia winces when she sees it. Shen scoots out of the booth to get a closer look, and then kneels down before me.

"Can I?" he asks.

"Okay," I say, suddenly nervous, not sure what he's going to do.

He touches my skin, carefully pressing around the edges of the bruise.

"Does it hurt?" He inspects the other side of my leg, like a doctor would. His touch makes me shiver, and I shake my head in response.

"It's an...infection," he says softly, gently setting my leg back down. "Some part of the spirit made contact and left a part of its influence with you." He narrows his eyes, muttering to himself. "But I sent her away. Any lingering effects should have been removed."

"I think the elders should see this," Delia tells him. It makes me more nervous. *Elders? What elders? There are more people getting involved?*

"The elders aren't here," Shen says. "They're in San Francisco. They won't be back for two weeks, and we need more evidence before we bring her in."

"Even I know *that's* not normal." Delia gestures downward as I adjust my pant leg.

"Wait...wait..." I hold up my hands. "Can we back up for one second? Who are the elders? What does it mean...I'm *infected*?"

"It shouldn't even be possible, but there's something off about this whole thing." Shen pulls his drink off the table, and as he sips at it, he starts walking around the room.

"Don't mind him," Delia explains. "He does this when he's thinking."

After pacing down the café between tables a few times, he goes to one of the cupboards on the wall. The shelf is stocked with all sorts of items in jars. From this angle, they look like pieces of rock, crystals, beads, of all shapes and sizes, sorted by color. He pulls out a bracelet from one of the jars and brings it over. It looks like something my grandmother would wear. The beads are large and chunky, a deep, rich green.

I'm about to ask what this is when he drops it into my hand. The beads pulse with a strange sort of warmth. They feel . . . safe. I can't explain it. Only that holding the bracelet gives me a sense of comfort, like my favorite Schubert piano sonata. How the opening notes of that familiar melody conjure up a feeling of everything being right in the world.

"What is this?"

"It's a type of talisman," he explains. "Previously blessed by the gods. With symbols of protection carved into the beads." He points out the marks, etched into the stone. I hold the bracelet up to the light, and the markings are clearer, glowing faintly gold.

"I can sense there's something wrong about you, but I don't know how to remove the infection, and I don't know how to fix it." Shen frowns. "I hope the talisman will protect you until we can get you before the Head Elder. She'll be able to help you. She'll know what to do."

I let out a shaky breath. I still feel disoriented, turned upside down, but at least I'm doing something about it.

"Give me your phone," Delia demands, and I hand it to her. She scrolls through and finds the LINE app, which I use for group chats with my parents and our relatives in Taiwan. She quickly searches for a few contacts and adds them in.

"There's my contact info and Shen's info too," she says. "If anything happens, anything that doesn't feel right, message us."

With that ominous farewell, it's time for my piano lesson. Delia lifts the security gate to let me out into the mall. I walk down the hallway, feeling strange. Everything is the same, and yet everything has changed. I run my finger over the bracelet, and the weight of it makes me feel better again. I want answers, and they can't come soon enough.

THIRTEEN

信徒

(True Believer)

My lesson goes well, and Mrs. Nguyen is satisfied with my progress. Playing piano is more of a relief. It's easier to focus on the notes, to give my mind a momentary break from the chaos that is currently in my head. On my way home, I stop by our family's usual bubble tea café to pick up Tina's favorite order and one for Denny as well. On the bus, another girl sits down next to me, scrolling through videos on her phone. I look out the window instead as we wait at the intersection for the light to change.

There's a boy standing there, waiting for the cars to pass. The walk sign turns on. He steps forward, and a truck flies out of the alley, striking him. His body is spun into the wheels, disappearing underneath. I gasp, unable to help myself, as my hand flies to my mouth to mask the sound. Only the girl beside me notices, giving me an odd look, as she scoots a little farther away from me. My hand finds the bracelet again, clutching it so hard I can feel the shape of the beads dig into my palm. I remind myself of Shen's words.

They're tethered to our world because something horrific happened to them. I should feel sad for them instead of afraid.

Suddenly, the air in the bus feels too stuffy, making it hard to breathe. I gather my things and pull the cord, getting off two stops early. When I mutter "Excuse me" to the others in the aisle as I make my way to the door, I feel many eyes on me, even though I'm probably imagining it.

I gulp down the cool autumn air, trying to calm myself so my parents won't notice anything is wrong when I walk through the door. I force myself to smile and hug Denny when he runs over to see me. Baba can't help but nag a little about extra sugar when he notices the drinks, but he's appeased when I tell him that Denny's order is fruit.

I go up the stairs to give Tina her drink, keeping in mind that I should act normal. She's sitting cross-legged on her floor on her yoga mat, music blasting again from her speakers. She stares up at the now-familiar screensaver moving on her laptop screen. A swirling mass of symbols that spiral inward and outward, the inside that pulses like an eye. The twisting and turning of the shape makes my skin crawl, even though there's nothing about it that should be unsettling.

"What?" Her voice is a low rumble, like she senses me lurking at her door.

"I got you a drink." I place the drink with the bag next to her. "Strawberry milk with lychee jelly."

She reaches out and turns off the music, turning to face me. Her face stretches into a smile as she glances at the label.

"Less ice and double jelly, my favorite! Thanks!" She jabs the top with a red straw and takes a long sip.

"My friends told me about this new place in Richmond they want to take me to," she says. "They make their own pearls in rainbow colors, and each one is a different flavor."

"That sounds good," I say, happy that she sounds like Tina again. "Want to try mine?"

"Sure," she says, reaching up. "What is it?"

"Taro and grass jelly."

She takes a sip and makes a face. "It's too...taro-y. Not sweet enough." That's just like Tina. She's always had a sweet tooth.

I laugh. "It's supposed to be. They use fresh taro."

She bumps into the laptop when she sits back down, and the screensaver dissolves into a video of five girls dancing.

"What's this?" I ask.

"It's the song we're practicing for our first show." She reaches over and turns it back on. Five girls are dressed in alternating red and pink hanfu, dancing around a lady who sits in the middle strumming a zither. It's a lively tune, their figures graceful as they create beautiful shapes around the stage, the camera viewing them from all angles.

"It's so pretty," I say.

"Reminds me a bit of figure skating," Tina says. Skating is one of those "Canadian" things she was allowed to do when she was little, because Ma was friends with the instructor. But once Ma and the instructor had a falling-out, Tina was told to quit, and she was inconsolable. Her love of movement and dancing has always been there, even when she was six years old.

"I want to be part of something...something that's for me, nobody else," she says softly as she watches the video. "My teacher says I've got what it takes, but I need to put my whole heart and soul into it. I can catch up soon."

Now that we're older, and we know more of what other kids our age are able to do...it's easier to want. To want different than what our parents expect of us.

"Don't you feel like there's not enough time in a day?" She rubs her forehead. "That we're all running behind, trying to catch up?"

The girls in colorful outfits continue to flit across the stage, ribbons in their hair flying behind them. A pained expression ripples across Tina's face, something like longing.

"Mrs. Tsai says we only need to believe in ourselves. There's power in belief," she says as if she can speak it into being.

"Can she give you more hours in a day? I don't think so." I chuckle.

"Ha-ha," Tina says dryly, rolling her eyes. "You don't get it. She *knows* people. She has connections. They can literally grant wishes. They can make dreams come true."

"What do you mean, wishes?" I say, a quiet alarm bell going off in my head.

"It's a place you can go, a place called the Temple of Fortunate Tidings. If you're lucky enough to be admitted and you're a *True Believer*... then the god there will grant you your heart's desire," she says, suddenly fervent, her eyes shining with purpose.

"Let's say this place is real, and it grants you your heart's desire," I tell her, playing along, even if the idea already makes me uneasy. "What would you wish for?"

Tina looks down at her hands in her lap, like she's seriously contemplating my question. A sound starts up. Someone humming. For a moment, I wonder if Tina turned on the video again, but she hasn't moved at all. Then I realize the sound is coming from her.

My sister, who can't carry a tune to save her life. Humming a melody that I recognize as the chant that has been playing in her room for the past week.

Then she looks up at me, mouth stretching wide into a serene smile.

"It doesn't matter if you believe me or not." She smirks, and I get that sensation at the back of my neck again, the feeling that someone else is looking at me through her eyes, that my sister has changed. "You'll get to meet the Great Teacher soon." She puts her hands together then in front of her face and closes her eyes, bowing her head reverently. The humming returns, and my bracelet pulses against my skin.

"I . . . I'm going to go to bed," I tell her, not wanting to talk to her when she's acting like this. I don't understand half of what she's talking about. All this about "True Believers" and "Great Teachers." But I spent half of the afternoon discussing talismans and the energy of the living, which seems like nonsense too.

She doesn't respond. Not when I get up to my feet, or when I slowly shut the door behind me.

Denny complains about the music again, but when Baba reminds her to keep it down after Denny's bedtime, Tina just promises that she'll remember. She starts taking the later bus home by herself, reassuring Ma that she will stay with her friends Melody and Gina, both of whom have been "approved" by my parents because their parents are "respectable" since they are now socializing together at the Formosa Friendship Association.

My Rachmaninoff piece is getting off track again, my mind as tangled as the chords. I can't seem to bring myself to focus, the notes blurring on the page every time I try to work on it. My stomach pains are getting worse, my appetite slowly diminishing. Delia checks in with me each night, and I give her vague updates like *All is well, for now* . . . I should demand answers, about the spirits or the wardens and why the elders haven't gotten back to me yet, but those messages are typed and then deleted when Shen apologizes for the delay and asks me to be patient.

By the time I make it almost through another week, I'm a bundle of nerves and resentment. Why is it that I'm the only person who seems to notice that Tina is changing? I brood over this as I pull my textbooks for my afternoon's classes out from my locker.

"Hi." A face appears beside the door, making me jump. "Whoa, sorry!" It's Shen, holding up his hands once he realizes that he startled me.

"No, sorry, it's me," I sigh, pulling my books closer to my chest. "I'm . . ." I don't even know how to finish the sentence. Exhausted? Worried?

"Yeah, I get it," he says. He looks different dressed in his Westview uniform. Less prickly, but still unapproachable. We might have passed each other in these halls hundreds of times over the past few months and not known the other existed. Not known that he has the other life, that ability to send back spirits to where they should be.

The pause stretches on between us for too long, then he seems to catch on that I'm waiting for him to talk. "I . . . Delia asked me to check in on you. To make sure everything is okay."

"It's . . . fine," I tell him, and then cringe a little at how that came out. I hate that a part of me is disappointed the reason he's talking to me is because of Delia, but then I feel silly for thinking that, because I was the one who chased him down, forced him to tell me what he knows.

"Listen . . ." he says, dragging his hand through his hair, looking sheepish. "I don't have much experience helping people. It's always been my family. You came at a time when I wasn't prepared, and it was easier to tell you to go away instead of dealing with it. I'm sorry about that."

He sounds . . . sincere, genuine, and it changes my impression of him ever so slightly for the better.

"I appreciate it," I say, because I don't know what else to say. The awkwardness settles around us again as I shut the door to my locker and spin the lock. "I guess . . . I'll see you around?"

"Sure," he says, then holds up his phone, taps it. "Anytime, okay? Delia and the elders will take turns skinning me if anything happens to you."

He gives me a wry grin before heading down the hall. I stare after him for a moment longer, surprised he's actually being *nice*.

Until I feel eyes on me. I whirl around, half expecting to see no one again, but there are three girls standing there by the lockers. Two of the girls look away quickly, but I meet my sister's eyes. She seems perturbed by something, unhappy. I give her a little wave, and she tilts her head in acknowledgment before turning away to talk with her friends.

FOURTEEN

養老院

(The Manor)

Tina might hate volunteering here, but I don't mind the manor that much. The yellow walls are cheerful, painted in the borders with sunflowers. There are little details all around meant to make it more welcoming to Chinese seniors: one wall where red decorative knots are displayed—some appear to be shaped like butterflies, others flowers. On another wall there's a calligraphy scroll on which there is a good luck phrase bestowed upon the facility when it first opened eight years ago.

I let the cook in the kitchen know that I'm here, and she rolls out the snack cart for me. This is one of my jobs on Thursday afternoons—I make sure that I bring a snack to each of the residents and check whether they want to eat it in their room or if they want to join us in the common room for rec time.

There's a list of restrictions already waiting for me, though I've memorized most of them over the past few months. The wheels clack on the floor every couple of seconds as I push it down the hall. This is normal.

This is routine. Everything is as it should be. Nothing ever changes much in the manor, and I'm glad for it.

I knock on the doors of the rooms and call out today's offerings. Cut-up pears in juice, almond cookies, lukewarm tea or soy milk. There are ten residents down each of the three halls, and a few of them are still asleep, enjoying their afternoon nap. I fill up the water in their cups as quietly as possible so I don't disturb their rest. I leave one cookie for an uncle, who I know loves almond cookies and would be upset if he missed out. Some of the residents say hi to me as I wheel by, and tell me that they're excited to hear me play.

After making my way down each of the hallways, I return to the kitchen to grab more snacks, then make my way to the common room. There are two tables of seniors already playing mahjong. I can hear the clicking and clacking of the tiles even before I walk through the door. A man curses as one of the other ladies cackles and drops her row of tiles, sweeping the table triumphantly. I don't know much about how to play the game, other than the constant insults that fly back and forth as the tiles are shuffled together, their green backs facing skyward. They always offer to teach me, but whoever is in charge of me is usually quick to step in, telling them that they're not allowed to gamble with minors, even though they only ever play for nickels and dimes.

Cindy, the rec therapist, comes and greets me enthusiastically. "Are you going to play for us today?" She flashes me a grin.

"Yes, yes!" one of the aunties, Mrs. Sui, calls out from the mahjong table. Probably one of my biggest fans. As usual, she's bundled up in her wheelchair with a puffy vest and a scarf, since she hates the cold. She and her group of friends, who I call the Chorus of Aunties, love to listen to music. When I'm here, I play songs out of a "fake book," which has simplified melodies of songs from their era I improvise from so they can sing along. Like "Green Island Serenade" or "Remnants of an Old Love." Most of the songs have a Japanese flair because of Taiwan's history as a former Japanese colony. Or Cantonese golden hits like "Evening's Breeze" or "Winter's Romance." Here, it doesn't feel like a performance—I'm merely the accompaniment, which doesn't make me nervous.

I deliver the drinks to the aunties at their table and make sure everyone has their snacks while more residents trickle in at Cindy's invitation. There's the uncle who likes to sit by the window with the tree and often falls asleep with his head back, snoring. I put the bowl of pears in front of him. I notice another lady in the back corner, where the extra chairs are stacked. She faces the wall, not acknowledging anyone. Her eyes are closed, her head drooping, probably asleep. I put a cookie and a cup of soy milk next to her so she doesn't feel left out when she wakes up.

When it's time, I lift the lid off of the battered Kawai and flip through the songbook, waiting for them to pick which song I am going to play. While they squabble among themselves, I warm up quickly with one of Bach's prelude and fugues, which sounds better than playing a series of scales like I would normally do at home.

The singing starts soon after. I have to improvise with my left hand while keeping the melody for them to follow with the right, and my brain is kept busy with sight-reading the sheet music. The time passes by quickly, as the seniors sing and laugh and reminisce about the time when they first heard this song or that. I love listening to their stories too, imagining what their lives must have been like back in Hong Kong or Tainan. All the history they lived through.

After the singalong time is done, I help clean up the plates and put away the glasses. The Chorus of Aunties always make me stop and chat with them for a bit while they set up for another round of mahjong. Ms. Tang complains about the way Mrs. Wang shuffles the tiles and accuses her of pocketing one up her sleeve. Just another day at the manor.

"Hey, Ruby!" Cindy calls out to me from across the room, picking up a plate. "Who is this for?"

I turn and see she's still in the corner, standing right beside the lady that's sitting slumped, facing the wall. I stare, not understanding. She's *right there.*

I open my mouth to speak, but a hand grabs my arm. I look down at Mrs. Wang, and she gives me a slow shake of her head. Beside her, Mrs. Sui also looks at me, an expression of concern on her face.

"I . . . I must have made a mistake!" I call out to Cindy. "I thought there was someone there."

"Bring it here!" Mrs. Sui demands. "I want another cookie."

"Sure," Cindy says, bringing the plate over, suspecting nothing.

A chill runs down my spine. That woman still sits there. As real as anyone I've ever seen. Nowhere is safe.

"What's wrong with the lot of you?" Mr. Chu barks out. "Why did you stop shuffling?"

"Oh, hush, old man!" Mrs. Wang snaps. "Be patient for once in your life."

"Huh?" Mr. Chu is hard of hearing and returns to muttering over his tiles, completely unaware of what is happening with me and the Aunties. Mrs. Sui pats my arm, giving me a look of sympathy. "I think it might be time for you to go home, Ruby. It's getting dark."

They're always concerned about me taking the bus on time, keeping an eye on the clock, making sure that I'm getting home when it's light out. I always thought it's because they're like my parents, fretting about my safety, but now I realize . . . it might be because of something else.

"You can see her?" I lean down and whisper.

Mrs. Sui shakes her head and puts her finger to her lips. "Shh . . . not now. We won't talk about it while she's here."

While who is here? The woman in the corner? Or Cindy? Nothing makes sense anymore. The clicking of the mahjong tiles resumes, leaving me as confused as ever.

Tina spends the bus ride home chatting with another friend. Just as well, as it leaves me the time to brood with my own thoughts alone. When we get home, the house is filled with the smell of dumplings frying. Denny is so proud of himself, with flour in his hair and sticky fingers. He excitedly shows us his plate of dumplings that he made on his own. He makes us each promise that we will try one of his "specials," even as he whines that we missed all the work of making the dumplings.

The dumplings are delicious eaten hot off the pan, crispy around the edges and then juicy in the middle. We dip them in each of our personal sauces. I like mine with soy sauce, a little bit of black vinegar, and a drizzle of chili oil. Tina's is equal amounts of soy sauce and black vinegar. Baba puts a ton of fresh, chopped garlic in his soy-sauce-and-chili-oil blend. Ma likes soy sauce, sesame oil, and green onions, while Denny has the same, minus the green onions. We all agree Denny's creations are not that bad, though some of them are mostly dough and a smear of filling.

Baba is in a great mood tonight. He can't seem to stop smiling, and the mood is infectious. He takes out a bottle of sake that he saves for special occasions and pours some for him and Ma to share.

When Ma brings out a little cake covered with fruit that she bought from one of the Asian bakeries, we finally find out what's made him so happy.

"I signed a big contract today!" he tells us as he digs into his slice of cake. Ma reaches over and squeezes his hand, obviously proud.

"Great job, Baba!" Tina goes and gives him a hug, and Denny has to jump in as well, climbing onto his lap.

"It was a risk to join such a new firm, but it looks like it's finally working out," Baba says, face slightly red from the alcohol. He looks at Ma again, and then his voice quivers as he continues, as emotional as I've ever seen him. "When I moved here, I thought I would one day own my own business, and now it's a dream come true, and too bad Ba and Ma aren't able to see it."

Baba takes off his glasses and pinches the skin between his eyes, like he's trying not to cry. Ma rubs his back, and I can see she's emotional too. I get up to get Denny another slice of cake so that he doesn't disrupt their moment. Tina sits at the window seat, the cake still balanced on her knees, half-eaten.

"You good?" I ask.

She gives me a smug little smile. "Dreams do come true, do you see?"

"Sure," I say, not wanting to argue with her that it wasn't making a wish at some mysterious temple that made Baba's dreams come true. It was years of hard work. Years of working long hours at jobs where he wasn't treated very well, told he couldn't be promoted because of his accent. Tina was too little to remember those days, but I remember. I also know the word to describe it now: *discrimination*. It's why they sent us to public school instead of the Mandarin charter school, and for years didn't want us to join those Taiwanese youth groups. They wanted us to fit in, to speak English without an accent, so we would have different experiences than they did.

After I brush my teeth, Tina's waiting for me on my bed. I swallow the urge to snap at her, knowing that there's a reason she's lying there.

"That guy you were with today." She speaks up to the ceiling. "What's his name?"

"He's a classmate I have to do a project with," I tell her, the lie coming easy.

"Didn't look like that to me." Tina sits up, slowly, looking at me with that knowing smirk. "The two of you seem . . . close."

I yawn and turn to my dresser to pull out my pajamas, hoping she'll get the hint that I'm tired.

"Listen, it's getting late—" I start, but she's suddenly *there*, only a few inches from my face. I flinch as she jerks my arm between us, hard enough that I yelp.

"What is that?" she demands, shaking my arm. My sleeve slips down, revealing the bracelet.

My wrist begins to . . . glow. Tina stumbles back, snarling, the sound too animalistic to be coming out of the throat of my little sister.

"Did he give this to you?" she growls, voice still too low.

"No!" I choke out, struggling to maintain my composure. "I bought it because I thought it was pretty." But then a thought pops into my head. Shen had called it a talisman. A way of protection. I slip it off my wrist and hold it in my fingers, dangling it before her.

"Do you want to see it?" I ask, feigning innocence. "You can borrow it if you want."

"Get that . . . *away* from me!" Tina screeches, flipping backward, landing on all fours. Her back is raised, almost like a startled cat. Her head contorted at an unnatural angle.

I quickly slip the bracelet back on my wrist, pulling my sleeve over it so that it can't be seen anymore. Regretting that I even attempted this experiment.

Slowly, vertebra by vertebra, she unfolds from the floor to her feet. She takes one step backward, then another, her arms dangling limply at her sides, almost as if she can't control her movements. Like someone else is moving her body. Her eyes are still on my wrist, as if she's looking at a venomous snake, something that could reach out and bite her.

"You're up to something, Ruby," Tina murmurs, a dangerous glint in her eyes. She never calls me by my name. It's something my parents have never allowed. I'm always Big Sister or 姊姊, and the way she drawls out *Rubeeeeee* disturbs me just as much as her slow backward walk. "I'm going to figure out what it is."

There's a sudden gust of wind, and my door slams shut, leaving me alone in the dark.

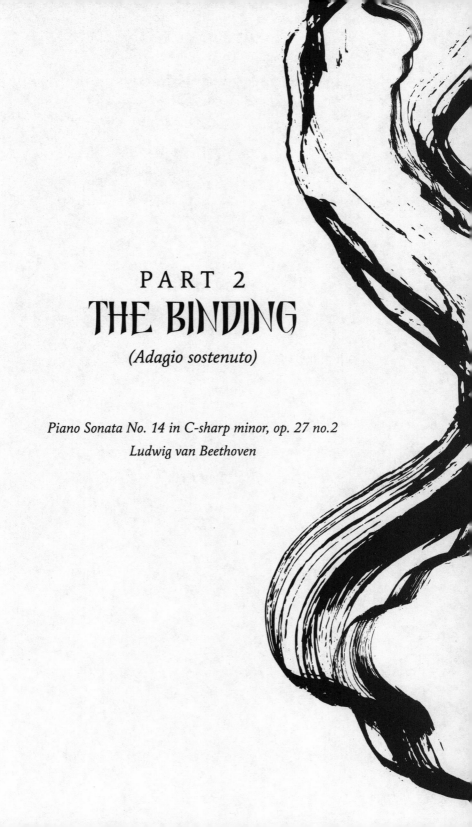

PART 2
THE BINDING
(Adagio sostenuto)

Piano Sonata No. 14 in C-sharp minor, op. 27 no.2
Ludwig van Beethoven

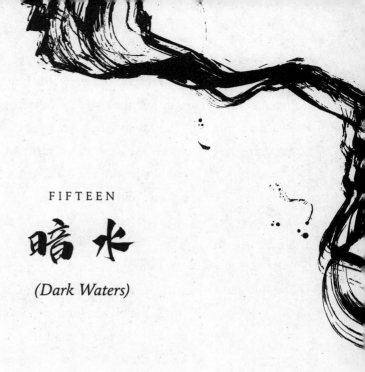

FIFTEEN

暗水

(Dark Waters)

After I realize that Tina isn't actually coming back, I decide that a bath will be the best way to soothe my nerves, to calm myself, and the best part: The bathroom door has a lock.

I turn both faucets and the water rushes into the tub, the sound loud in the small space. I pull off my clothes, humming a few bars of the Moonlight Sonata under my breath. The steam from the water fills the room, fogging the mirrors.

I sit on the toilet lid, looking forward to the hot water relaxing the tightness of my muscles. I stretch my neck to one side, then to the other. All the stress that I'm holding in my neck releasing with each crack and pop.

The water fills up to two-thirds of the way, just how I like it. I turn off the knobs and the pipes shut off with a clank. I ease my body into the tub slowly, the hot water stinging at first, but I feel myself relaxing. I lie back with a sigh. I think about the Moonlight Sonata again, allowing my arms to float, weightless in the water. My fingers move to the ghostly echoes of the notes in my head, darkly soothing. In Music History, we learned about how the Moonlight Sonata got its name, because a critic thought the piece sounded like a boat adrift in the moonlight. But I always thought it sounded more like a current, like the swift course of a mountain stream. Cold and tranquil, and then the countermelody is a slippery shape in the water, something wild and untamed slithering under the surface.

There's a sound above me that disrupts my concentration. A scratching, like nails being dragged across the wood. But not in the same room as me. It's coming from somewhere outside. *Scratch scratch, tap. Scratch scratch, tap.* I try to ignore it, but it continues, growing louder. I open my eyes and look up at the small window above my head. It's right at eye level if you stand up in the tub. Not low enough for any neighbors to see through, only to let a little light in during the day.

The sound doesn't stop, and now I'm worried. It could just be a branch that's tapping against the window, or it could be an animal trapped up there. Like the one time we found a raccoon in our attic.

It's probably nothing, but I have to check. I stand up, the water pouring off me, and I pull at the lever that opens the blinds. *It's only a branch.* The blinds lift, I squint because I don't have my glasses on, and then I see eyes staring back at me.

A face with a gray pallor. Eyes filled with darkness, only red pinpricks in the center. A mouth that seems to stretch wider and wider before my eyes, open in a cavernous scream.

I stumble back and slip, bash my elbow on the soap dish and land half sprawled in the tub, water sloshing out from the side.

There can't be anything there, I tell myself. *We're two stories up. There's nothing there.* But I'm not standing up to find out. My hand fumbles for the towel on the rack, then I look down to realize the water has turned black underneath me. Murky, tinged with green, thick with slime. Before I can comprehend it, a hand shoots out of the water and grabs the top of my head, pulls me face-first into the tub.

The water fills my nose and rushes into my mouth as I gasp for breath. I'm suspended in darkness, face down and thrashing. I can't touch the sides of the tub, which makes no sense. There should be lights overhead, and yet I can see nothing. The panic fills me quickly as I choke on the water, flailing in the dark. But a warmth grips my wrist, and a green light floods my vision. I'm pulled upward, and then flung out with force.

I land with a hard thud on the floor. The wood floor is cool against my face. Parts of my body ache from where they struck it. I roll onto my side, coughing, spewing up water. The only light in here is from outside, peeking through the shutters. Everything looks fuzzy, but there's the looming shadow of my bed, vague shape of my posters on the wall. I'm in my bedroom. Not the bathroom.

If I simply rolled out of bed, then why is everything wet? I push myself up on one wrist, wincing. It hurts. Everything hurts. My other hand lands in a puddle of water. Water drips from my hair, pooling beneath me. My clothes are soaked too.

I lift my arm, and my bracelet glows faintly green, illuminating the dark. Just like the light that shone beneath the water. I crawl over to my desk and fumble for my glasses, reach for my phone. With my phone in hand, I unlock the screen just as I hear skittering overhead. Like tiny claws running over wood. I catch movement in the corner of my eye, my curtain fluttering along the windowsill. A glimpse of a shadow behind the sheer curtain. I crouch down then, panting, afraid.

I press the flashlight button and point the beam toward the window. The light floods the room, illuminating the tiny forms. Shriveled bodies hang off my curtains, chittering as they try to avoid the light. One of them jumps down on my headboard while the other lands on top of my desk, scattering papers and pens to the floor. They look like . . . monkeys. Short black fur and red eyes, faces pink and wizened. They raise their spindly arms to cover their faces as the light hits them, screeching.

I scramble back, almost slipping again on the water on the floor. They jump up and down, flashing fangs, their shrieking reaching a feverish pitch, drilling into my ears. I count five in all. One of them picks up my pen and brandishes it like a knife, advancing toward me. While another jumps onto my bed, and another lands with a thud on the floor. They chatter at each other, beady eyes focused on me as they draw closer. I keep moving backward until my outstretched fingers brush against my door. My hand inches for the doorknob, ready to fling myself into the hallway.

But before I can escape, they scream. They launch themselves at me, like tiny torpedoes. One lands on my head and dangles off my hair while the second digs tiny claws into my shoulder. I rip the shoulder one off, throwing it against the wall. The one above me chitters, furious, and the rest begin to climb my legs. My scalp burns from the weight of the monkey pulling at my hair, and I yank it off me, throwing it to the floor. But then I scream when one of them sinks its fangs into my wrist. I drop my phone, batting at any one of them that I can reach.

There's a clatter as beads fall to the floor, bouncing everywhere. The cries of the monkeys reach a feverish pitch of excitement, somewhere beyond the beam of the phone flashlight. I jump to my feet and grab a clipboard from the wall with one hand to use as a weapon, slamming my other palm on the switch to turn on the overhead light. I stand there, trembling, ready to hit the next monkey that attacks me again.

But there's nothing.

Just smears of water on the floor. Beads scattered everywhere. I look under the bed, throw off the sheets and the pillows. Check my bookshelf, under the desk, open the doors to my closet. I pull out all the drawers of my desk, my dresser. Still nothing.

I get on my hands and knees and pick up each of the beads, putting them into an empty jar. I hold one, then another up to the light and notice that they have gone dark, murky. Some of them have streaks of black upon the surface, as if they were held up to a flame. Charred.

Delia and Shen told me I could contact them if anything were to happen. I think this qualifies as something fucking finally happening. It's time to send Shen a message. It takes me a few tries to even unlock my phone, my hands are shaking so bad. I take a photo of the beads and send it, along with one word:

Help.

SIXTEEN

家 族 史

(Family Histories)

Shen texted me to meet him at the café after school, so I put the jar with the beads in my backpack, keep it close with me all day. I don't even trust my locker. Every so often, I'm tempted to take it out. To look at it to make sure the beads have actually changed color, that it's not my own mind failing me.

It's Friday, but I have to come up with some sort of excuse to go into Chinatown. I message the family group chat that I'll be picking up some notes from Mrs. Nguyen. Lies upon lies, stacked up on one another, until I feel like I'm getting smothered by them.

The day passes by slowly, minutes trickling by. The exhaustion seeps into my bones, makes me jittery. I put on my headphones in the hallways to block out the sounds of the school. The song that trickles out from my headphones reminds me of the times Tina used to come into my room in the evenings. I would do homework while she read a book beside me.

Don't you ever get sick of listening to piano music? she would complain, and then put on one of her songs, perform the choreography from her imagination. The way she would pop out a hip or shimmy herself downward, show me a new move, and not care about how she looked. How she would throw herself on the floor, laughing, when she accidentally tripped or slipped. I can't remember the last time we did that. When she wanted to spend time with me.

I miss her, I realize.

I just want my sister back.

"Ruby!" A hand lands on my shoulder, disrupting my thoughts. I gasp, returning back to the sidewalk in front of the school. Not knowing if it is someone real or something from the shadows. I yank the headphones off my head, the music trailing away.

"I didn't know how else to get your attention." Shen has one hand up, like he's defending himself.

"Sorry," I murmur, and tap the headphones. "The noise-canceling is really good." No more whistles. No more whispers. I want to block everything out. All that *noise.*

"You . . . uh . . . you doing okay?" He steps closer and drops his voice, as other Westview students emerge from the gate and stream out onto the sidewalk. "You're not hurt, are you?"

I shake my head and hold up my wrist for him to see.

"A scratch," I say. He takes my arm carefully, fingers barely brushing my skin, so that he can see for himself.

"They shouldn't have been able to do that," he says, perturbed again. Someone bumps into him on the sidewalk, and he lets go of my arm, as if realizing where he is.

"Can I give you a ride? I have my car today. I just have to stop by the art studio to grab my project," he explains. "Can't cart it home safely on the bus. You have everything you need?" I nod.

We wait at the crosswalk and head to the building across the street, the same building as the Middle Years program. He has a key card for a separate entrance, and we head up a narrow stairwell to an open space on the third floor.

I realize this is where the giant windows are that can be seen from the outside, because this space is huge. There are large metal tables set up in one section, upon which there are all sorts of art installations. Pottery, papier-mâché creations, statues made from wire, half-carved sculptures, an intricate model of a house. In one corner there are easels stacked against the wall, some of them standing with partially finished works attached.

"Wow!" I exclaim, not sure where to look. My eyes are drawn up to the open ceiling, a crisscrossing network of ducts, fans spinning lazily overhead. "I didn't even know this existed."

"We call it the Loft," he tells me. "I guess it's sort of a secret space." Westview is known for its fine arts program, but I've never had affinity for any sort of art, so this has never been on my radar.

One of the students working at the table greets Shen with a wave, giving me a curious look before bending over his project again. Shen leads me to the section with the easels, and stops before one of the art pieces. It's a painting of a traditional temple, like the ones that I remember seeing on our previous visits to Taiwan. It's done in the style of what looks like Chinese ink painting, fluid brushstrokes, giving everything a wispy, dreamlike quality.

"You did this?" I ask him in disbelief, and then I remember he probably did those drawings in the sketch pad that he showed me before too.

"Yeah." A corner of his mouth lifts in amusement, then he shrugs, as if embarrassed, brushing it off. "It's what I do for fun."

"It's amazing." I can't help but gawk again. Noticing his delicate and deliberate use of color. Gold lettering on the plaque, red outlines on the roof tiles, a bit of teal on the scales of the dragons and red on the feathers of the phoenix. A large black censer stands in front of the open doorway of the temple, the tips of the incense sticks dotted red, the smoke winding its way up toward the gray-washed sky.

"Don't be fooled by that humble-artist act!" the boy who's still working at the table calls out. "It's how he impresses the girls."

I can't help but laugh, even as Shen picks up a paintbrush from an easel and whips it in his direction without hesitation. The boy ducks without missing a beat.

"Ignore him," Shen tells me. "Mark stuck his finger in wall sockets too many times. His brain occasionally short-circuits on its own." Mark sticks up two middle fingers in response. Shen then goes to this huge roll of brown paper on the wall and pulls a sheet off.

"Can I help you?" It feels weird to stand there and not do anything.

"Sure, if you want to grab that end." We spend the next few minutes wrapping the canvas with paper, and then with a layer of bubble wrap, before taping it up with more brown paper. He pulls a few more already-wrapped canvases from a rack, and we head out to the elevator to go down to the parkade.

"Are you also in grade eleven?" I ask while we slide the canvases in the back of his car, upright, and then balanced against each other against the back seat. "I've never seen you before we . . . met each other at the mall."

"What? Oh. I'm in a self-study program," he says. "I can take my pick of the prep courses and the Adult Learning classes in the evenings. It means I get more studio time during the day because they can't give us access to the Loft at night or the weekends. Can't leave us unsupervised or we might burn down the place." He flashes a grin to show that he's kidding.

"Ah, sorry." He opens the passenger door and reaches down to toss a crumpled paper bag into the back seat. "Wasn't expecting anyone."

"This is clean. My mom's car is a total disaster," I comment, thinking about the crumbs, shoes, spare clothes, and Denny's toys strewn everywhere. Baba always says it's like being inside a kid's backpack.

"Your parents are okay with you . . . doing your own thing?" I can't help but be envious. That would be a dream come true to me. To be trusted enough to have the freedom to make your own schedule. To do what you want. Even though we're the same age, his life seems so wildly different from mine. He's working at the bubble tea shop, driving on his own, working on his art when he wants. . . .

There's a long pause as he pulls into traffic, and for a moment I think he didn't hear me, but then he says, voice low: "My parents aren't around anymore. My sister's my guardian."

"I . . . I'm sorry," I stutter, stunned at this knowledge. I don't know what to say after that. To lose not only one parent, but both? Did he lose them at the same time? Was it a terrible accident? But all those questions seem intrusive, so I say nothing instead.

"It's all right." He clears his throat, then says lightly, "She has high expectations but gives me the space to figure things out. She's gone sometimes for her . . . job, so Delia steps in. She's kinda like a sister to me too."

That makes sense then, given the closeness that I've glimpsed, the easy way they talk with one another. Now I understand that they're practically family.

"Does Delia also go to Westview?" I ask.

"Nah, she went to King George. She graduated last year," he says. "Now she's taking courses at the university."

We settle into a companionable silence when we drive into Chinatown proper, which is busy as we head into the weekend. Grandmas walk by with their puffy vests, pulling little carts behind them with their groceries. A cluster of old men stands in front of a Chinese medicine store, arguing with each other. A bike zooms by and hops over a curb into our ath. Shen weaves expertly around the cyclist, narrowly missing him with the right bumper, even as the man shakes his fist at the car, yelling something we can't hear through the windows.

They're all *alive*, living out their own stories, their personal histories and tragedies. Just like the boy beside me, each of us carrying our own secrets. For some reason, it makes me feel less alone.

SEVENTEEN

詛咒

(Cursed)

"You can sit here." Shen gestures at the booth closest to the door a
we enter the café. "I'll be out in a second."

I slide into the booth, this place already becoming familiar to me
There's a textbook open on the table, and papers scattered around it
I glance at one of the pages: a syllabus for a course on Introduction to
Sociological Theory.

"Ruby!" Delia appears then, sitting down in the seat in front of me
flashing a quick smile in greeting. She gathers all the papers together
in a stack and puts them into her bag along with the textbook. "Too
much homework."

She then searches my face after everything is tidied away. "Are you . .
doing okay? I was worried about you most of the day."

"I'm . . . fine," I say, choking down the feelings that suddenly surface
at her sympathetic gaze. I want to tell her that I'm really not, that I'm

scared out of my mind . . . but the words freeze in my throat. Years of being told I was making things up have made me hesitant.

"Here." A drink appears before me, and a blue straw in a wrapper. I look at the label. It's the same drink I ordered before. Jasmine milk tea with grass jelly, half-sweet and less ice. *He remembered.* It's such a small gesture, but it makes the tightness in my chest ease ever so slightly.

"Thanks," I mumble, and I fish the beads out of my bag, placing them on the table. "They broke the bracelet. I'm sorry."

"Don't worry about the bracelet." Shen's gaze is suddenly intense as he sits down on the chair at the end of the booth. "Tell us everything."

Slowly, in bits and pieces, then growing more confident, I describe everything that's been happening to me. The mooncakes with the wriggling maggots. The reflection that moved on its own. The apparent telekinetic powers that my sister has developed. Then . . . the nightmare, being dragged into the bathtub, the vicious little creatures that attacked me. Shen notes everything down in his notebook, while Delia's expression gradually gets more and more worried.

Until I mention the wishes.

"Wait, wishes?" Delia exclaims, eyes bright with a curious gleam.

I nod, trying to remember. "She said there is a temple you can visit if you are accepted by their teacher. They apparently grant wishes." I can't help the skepticism that drips from my words, even as I know that everything I've seen so far has been impossible.

Delia's reaction surprises me. She jumps to her feet, looming over the table, appearing furious. For a moment, I think she's going to hit me, but instead she turns to Shen.

"I told you!" She chokes out the words. "They're back."

Shen's on his feet too, and he puts his hand on her shoulder. The two of them engage in their form of silent communication again as a wave of emotions ripples across her face, her initial fury fading into what looks like resignation. She makes her way out of the booth, shoulders drooping.

"I'm . . . I just need a minute," she says, already moving toward the kitchen. Shen takes a step in her direction, but she snaps. "*Don't* follow me. Talk to *her.*" Then she's gone.

I sit there throughout all this, wondering if I've done something wrong. Shen slides into her spot across from me, frowning, before he notices my face. "Hey, it's not your fault . . ." he says gently. "I never told you about how I met Delia. It's not my story to tell, but it was because she needed help from the guardians too." His mouth pulls into a thin line, like he rarely meets people for happy reasons.

"Has she encountered that temple Tina mentioned, then?" I ask, a little shaken. "Are they dangerous?"

"It's easier if I show you," Shen says, reaching for the jar of beads. He pulls out a bottle of water from his bag, followed by a thin sheet of yellow paper, the size of a bookmark. He folds it in half, sliding it into the bottle. He then opens the jar with the beads, pouring the beads into the water. Tendrils of black seep upward from the beads like ink, until the whole container is dark and murky. As if someone dipped a bunch of dirty paintbrushes in and swirled it around.

"Why is it doing that?" I ask.

Shen regards the murky bottle with narrowed eyes. "The markings on the beads repel anything with yin energy, and whatever it is in your sister probably reacted to that. . . ." Except he doesn't sound convinced. "A standard familiar. An animal spirit, like one of the ones that visited you. They shouldn't be able to touch the bracelet at all. They are formed out of pure yin energy. The charm should be enough to scatter them back to their source," he continues. "But if they're no longer spirits . . . if they're fed by the medium themselves and given an actual body . . ."

THE DARK BECOMES HER

He folds his arms in front of his chest, the perturbed expression returning to his face again.

"None of this is good." He follows that with a shake of his head. "It means the medium is stronger than I expected. I thought that maybe you or your sister had accidentally encountered something with yin energy and a bit of it brushed off on you, but..."

All these terms swirl around in my head like those beads in the bottle.

"Whoever sent the familiars knew the power of the bracelet, they recognized the protective charms and saw that the weakness is in the cord itself, not the beads. They knew how to remove the threat." He sighs. "I'm going to have to call *the boss*."

"The boss? Who's the boss?"

"The Head Elder." Shen picks up his phone and swipes through it, searching for a message, before setting it down again. There's a picture from an anime on his lock screen, two figures engaged in a fight, swords clashing between them. "Her flight lands tonight. There will be a gathering tomorrow and I'll bring it before the elders then."

"Can you tell me all this in plain, simple language?" I plead. He's so calm about it. "What does this all *mean*?"

"Someone has targeted your family," Shen says, with utmost seriousness. "You've been cursed."

I feel like I've been given a one-way ticket to Bizarroland. Curses. Animal spirits acting as familiars. Mediums. I grab the cartoon frog pillow beside me and squeeze it, as if that can give me a way to redirect the frustration rising inside me. The eyes of the frog bulge comically, and I don't know whether to laugh or to scream.

"I know this is a lot to take—" Shen begins, but I shake my head and talk over him.

"We're a normal family," I tell him, my mind struggling to comprehend all this. None of it makes sense. "My dad is an architect. My mom is a teacher. I feel like this is some sort of a joke. . . . Is this some sort of joke? Is there a camera filming us now?"

My voice quivers then, pleading, desperate for there to be a big reveal, a surprise. "Or you'll tell me that for the low price of four hundred ninety-nine dollars, you can make this problem go away . . . right? Right . . . ?" My words trail off as I can feel the tears bubbling up again to the surface, as he says nothing, only regards me with that sympathetic stare. Like that day in the Tanakas' studio, when the students watched me with disgust and embarrassment. At the girl who couldn't handle the pressure.

I'm crying then, putting my hands up to my face, but the tears continue to come, dripping out between my fingers.

"Shit," I hear him mutter, and he's gone. For a moment I wonder if he's left me alone, pathetic and sobbing in the café. But he's back not long after, a box of tissues in one hand. He pulls out a handful and offers them to me, averting his eyes from my disastrous appearance.

I use the tissues to blow my nose and wipe my face, then realize I cried all over the frog pillow too. I make an attempt to clean it up, but I smear everything around. He leans over and gently extracts the pillow from my hands.

"It's okay. Don't worry about him, Keroppi can be washed," he says, and for some reason thinking about the absurdity of Keroppi tumbling about in the washer makes me snort with laughter.

"I'm normally not like this," I tell Shen, somehow wanting him to understand.

He gives me that wry smile again. "I get it," he says. He slides the metal box beside him over between us on the table. "I have something that might help in the meantime."

EIGHTEEN

平安符

(Talismans)

I watch, curious, as he unlocks the box with a silver key that's hanging from a chain around his neck.

"Ta-da!" Shen says when he lifts the lid, as if performing a magic trick.
His grin tells me this performance is for my benefit, to lighten the mood.
I chuckle, appreciating his effort. The more time I spend with him, the
more I realize that maybe this is who he is *really*. Someone who is a bit
silly, but forced to be serious when oblivious girls like me crash into his life.

Inside that box is a stack of yellow papers the size of a bookmark. I
don't know what I was expecting, but not something this small. He
handles them reverently, carefully unwinding the red string that binds it
all together. I lean forward when he places them between us, examining
the symbols more closely. There are Chinese characters stacked on top
of one another, almost giving an illusion of a human figure, but done in
red ink. I've seen enough horror movies from Taiwan and Hong Kong
with Baba to know what these are. Another type of talisman.

"These are warding talismans," Shen confirms. "Put one above your window, one on the back of your door, and one behind your headboard. It'll prevent those creatures from entering your room or affecting your dreams."

I carefully put them inside my wallet pocket so that I don't accidentally rip or bend them. Even though these are just slight pieces of paper, I hope what he says is true. I need all the help I can get.

"Is there a way I can protect my little brother too?" I ask, worried about Denny.

"These are all I have, but I'll talk to the Head Elder," he says. "It's unfortunate that all of this started while she's away. The temple doesn't take transgressions like this lightly."

"Transgressions?" What an odd term.

"Use of animal familiars: forbidden. Making bargains with the deceased: forbidden. Attempting dream coercion: definitely forbidden." He ticks them off on his hand one by one. "The guardians will want to hear about this too."

"The guardians..." I remember he mentioned them earlier. "Are they like the wardens?"

"The wardens work for King Yanluo. He's in charge of the underworld," Shen says. "The guardians work for the gods."

"King Yanluo..." I repeat slowly. "You mean 閻羅王." The Lord of the Afterlife.

He smiles at me again. "It all sounds wild, right? Welcome to the club."

"Sorry, but your club sucks." The words slip out before I can stop them.

He doesn't seem bothered though. "There are no benefits. Terrible hours. Tons of ghosts. No promises of enlightenment." He ponders this. "Yeah, you're right. This club isn't worth it."

"At least you have bubble tea." I pick up my forgotten drink and salute him with it.

"That we do." He checks his watch. "That reminds me, I have to get back upstairs. I have people waiting for me." He locks the jar of beads into the box and puts it in his bag.

"They're waiting to kick your ass at Ping-Pong?" Delia returns then, eyes slightly red-rimmed, but she seems better now. Artist. Ping-Pong player. More things I'm learning about him.

"You know it," he sighs. Shen stands and meets my eyes. "Tomorrow, okay? I'll let you know." I nod. I'm left there with Delia, who looks a little sheepish.

"I ... I want to apologize for running away," Delia says to me then.

I shrug. "I ended up bawling my eyes out in front of Shen, so you're not the only one who fell apart today."

"I remember what it felt like," she says. "Finding out about ... all of this. This world existing alongside ours." Unknown, unseen, unheard.

"It's ... disorienting."

"Yup." She nods, reaching over to grab two brochures from a rack behind the booth. She holds them both up in front of me. Red and orange. "This is your life before, this is your life after." She starts folding them deftly, fingers flying, making creases until she joins the two together. A tiger appears in her hand.

"How did you do that?" I marvel as she places the animal in my palm. The red and the orange in a pattern.

"You learn to look at things a little differently," she says. "You'll adjust in time. C'mon, I want to show you something."

She tries to lead me to the hallway that goes out to the alley again, but I stop, not sure if I can continue. I've avoided that hallway ever since. It's still dim, and now there's a faintly menacing air. My heart rate speeds, a little faster. Delia stops and looks at me, giving me a reassuring pat on the arm.

"There's nothing out there anymore," she says. "That's what I want to show you. You'll see."

"You can see...them, then?" I still can't bring myself to call them what they are. Spirits. Ghosts. Whatever.

"The ones left behind?" Delia says, as if it should be a joke, but she's entirely serious. "No, I've never seen them, but I know they're out there." She pushes the door open and steps out into the alley, holding it open for me to walk through.

The alley is like it's always been, but now there's a stretch of the brick wall that has been painted white, and a black-and-white dragon writhes from one side to the other. Each scale is meticulously put in, the texture of the small horns upon its head, long whiskers trailing from its fanged mouth. The only color is in the blue orb that it holds between its claws, protectively.

"Beautiful, isn't it?" Delia says. "It took him a week to finish painting it."

I notice the square Chinese signature in the corner, like a stamp. The same mark on the artwork that I helped Shen move.

"Shen painted this?" I want to touch it, but I'm afraid of ruining it. I hope that it will remain here for a long time, even with all the reports of vandalism and graffiti in Chinatown. I hope people will recognize its beauty and not touch it.

"I think he felt responsible that something bad happened while the elders were away. Even though he's not the one in charge, it's still his family's temple, you know? The legacy his parents left behind for them."

"Oh," I say softly. I can't help but feel somewhat responsible too for being involved.

"There's so much here in Chinatown. Lots of history," Delia murmurs beside me, a wistfulness to her words. "So many memories, families passing through, but so much of it is forgotten and lost...." She sounds like Baba, reminiscing about how things used to be. Shen told me Delia has her own story to tell. Maybe one day she'll be comfortable enough to share it with me.

"Anyway, I wanted to show you this," Delia says. "To show you that there are people watching over us, protecting us. You don't have to feel alone. They saved me once, and I want to help in whatever way I can."

I nod. Delia wiggles her fingers in a wave and turns to walk back to the mall. I walk in the other direction, toward the main road. I glance back at the mural for a moment. Maybe it's only a trick of the light, but I could swear the dragon blinked. Did the orb spin too?

My phone buzzes in my pocket, and I jump. When I look back, the dragon stays still, just a lovely painting on the wall. Nothing more. And yet, it's as Delia says. Everything under a different light. Protectors watching over us.

Later that evening before bed, I pull out the talismans from my wallet. It felt different holding them in the café compared to seeing them in my bedroom, where everything looks normal.

I tape one talisman under a long poster of a scene from a Japanese garden above the window. The next one I put in the middle of the door, behind my red-and-gold wall calendar. It's the one we get for free from the bank, featuring zodiac animals and ads for different Asian businesses around the city. The last one I have to climb up on my bed to slap behind my headboard.

I wake up hours later; there's already a message in the group chat.

Shen: Bad dreams?
Me: nope. the cult paraphernalia was effective

Shen: Ha the talismans are working then, good

Shen: I spoke with The Boss. She'll meet you. Tuesday night

Delia: Inside jokes already? Cute!

Delia's message is followed by a cat with heart eyes. I grin, give Shen's message a thumbs-up, and put a side-eye cat into the chat before setting my phone down.

Denny has swimming lessons Saturday mornings, so he's already gone with Ma by the time I saunter downstairs to the kitchen table. Tina's door is closed. She's probably sleeping late, like she usually does. There's only Baba sitting there with a cup of coffee, glasses perched low on his nose, typing on his laptop. He raises his cup to me.

"Morning. You're the last one up," he says.

"Huh?" I check the clock. Nine thirty a.m. "Where's Tina?"

"She decided to go to the pool too. Meet some friends there," Baba says as he looks over his glasses at me. "Are you sleeping well? You look tired."

My good mood falters a little bit. I should be able to tell them everything. But I can't.

"Stressed. Lots of homework."

"Ah." He nods. "Grade eleven is a very important year, like your mother says. Have to keep those grades high."

Homework is always the Get Out of Jail Free card. It's the magic phrase to ease their worries, to let them believe they are helping to keep me on the right track. Good grades, good university. Nothing else matters. They remain unaware that their oldest daughter is seeing ghosts, and that their younger daughter is changing and turning into something different before their eyes.

They see what they want to see.

"Focus on what's important, right? No distractions," he says. "愛拼才會贏!" He pumps his fist in the air in encouragement. Some sort of Taiwanese phrase about working hard and winning at life. My grandfather used to say it too. I think it came from some popular song back in their day.

I force myself to smile at him.

"Ma left some congee on the stove for you if you want," he says. "I have to head into the office, so you'll be on your own this morning."

I eat my plain congee sprinkled with pork floss, chunks of spicy pickled radish, salty preserved cucumber, and crunchy peanuts. While I'm shoveling food into my mouth, my phone buzzes some more.

Shen: There's one more thing. we have the beads, but anything you can find related to the temple could help the elders figure out what it is we're dealing with

Me: got it

What better time to do that than with an empty house? I finish my breakfast and listen for the back door to open and close, the sign that Baba has exited the house. I go upstairs, tiptoeing, despite knowing that I'm alone. I grab Tina's door handle and turn, stepping in to see what awaits me there.

NINETEEN

辰下

(Under the Bed)

I ease the door shut behind me and survey the small space. Immediately my nose is assaulted by that pungent smell, smoky and medicinal. The wood blinds are pulled down over the windows, making the room feel even smaller and more oppressive. The gaps in the slats at least allow a little light in, so that I don't have to turn on the overhead lamp. Her covers are crumpled at the foot of the bed, half of Pudding Dog peering at me sadly from its wrinkled state.

I'm careful where I place my feet, to disturb as little as possible. The longer I stand in the room, the stronger the smell becomes. Almost like stepping into one of those herbalist shops in Chinatown, all the traditional Chinese medicine ingredients open to the air: dried flowers and fruit, roots and fungus. Then, underneath it all, a scent of sweetness. It reminds me of haw flakes, the thin pieces of "candy" that Ama used to give us to make those medicinal tonics more palatable. Every time I see them now, the taste of bitterness floods my mouth.

My attention is drawn to something new hanging on her wall. It appears to be an artistic calligraphy scroll, except . . . I frown at it. It looks like the talisman that Shen gave me, only on a bigger scale. I lift it off the hook on the wall, and then jump when I see what's behind it. She hung it over a poster of one of her favorite K-pop girl groups—all their faces are covered over with red marker.

I take a photo of the poster, then a photo of the scroll, before returning it to where it was on the wall. Then I notice the others. A picture of a sleepy ginger cat she's had forever, but now its mouth is drawn into a macabre grin with daggerlike teeth. A photo of our family from a trip to Lake Louise a few summers ago, now with scratches running across it, like she scraped at it with a knife.

Other decorations I haven't noticed before, since she's always so eager to get me out of her room. A sticker of a pink lotus up on her shelf. A pamphlet pinned up on the corkboard featuring a pair of floating, disembodied hands, holding a rainbow lotus in their palms. Underneath, there are the glowing red characters.

有求
A request offered

必應
An answer given

Something about the characters makes my skin prickle, my body reacting with an uncomfortable sensation that I could not explain. I take a photo of it too, as well as the list of events beside it. A line of cartoon kids, smiling happily, hands linked. Badminton. Ping-Pong. Mandarin lessons. Crochet animals. I unpin it from the board, and on the back: a logo of two hands shaking, the outline of Taiwan behind it. A collaboration between the Lower Mainland Taiwan Entrepreneurs and the Formosa Friendship Association. They seem to be everywhere these days.

My foot bumps against something, and I look down to see a box poking out from underneath Tina's bed. I crouch and pull it out. Something sloshes inside it. The box is filled with bottles of some type of drink.

"'Unsweetened High Mountain Taiwanese Oolong,'" I read aloud. Weird in itself, because Tina never drinks any sort of tea without adding a ton of sugar and milk to it. I take out a bottle and put everything else back the way I found it.

I look around again to see if I've missed anything, and then I notice that she's put a mirror up above her closet door, positioned toward her bed. I take a step closer to look up at it. There are symbols drawn in red, overlaid on my face, so my reflection appears as if I've been tattooed. I crane my neck back, trying to get a better look, my eyes drawn into those lines and whorls. There's something there in the loops and swirls, a message hidden within, if I just look at it for a moment longer. It's going to tell me everything. It's going to give me an explanation for all the mysteries, if only I can read it and comprehend it. It will tell me what's wrong with my sister, it'll tell me who is the true face behind whatever is influencing her. All those patterns have a meaning, a map pointing me in the right direction. . . .

"What are you doing?" Denny's voice snaps me out of it. The door is open behind him, and he stands right next to me, wide-eyed and too close.

I jump, almost tripping over the corner of Tina's bed.

"Denny! You scared me!" I scold, louder than I intended.

"You were ignoring me." He frowns. "You were staring at the ceiling. Being weird."

How long have I been standing here? I don't remember when I came in, but I had just finished breakfast, right?

"Did Tina come home with you?" I ask, remembering she went to the pool too.

"You're not supposed to be in here." He nods, understanding what I mean.

"I . . . I was looking for my shirt. Thought it might be in her closet," I mumble. I tuck the bottle of tea under my arm and take my brother's shoulders, guiding him toward the door. "But I couldn't find it. . . . Maybe it's still in the dirty laundry."

"She's not going to be happy . . ." Denny says in the singsong voice he uses when he tells our parents we're doing something wrong.

"She'll never know." I push him through the door, and hope that the bottle and the pictures are enough for Shen's elders.

"She already knows," he says, cryptic, glancing over his shoulder.

I stop him in the hallway, getting down to his level, making sure he knows how serious I am.

"Denny, what do you mean, she already knows?" I ask. "What did she say to you?" He looks up at me in that innocent way.

"There's Nice Tina, and then . . ." We both hear the door open downstairs. Denny is gone in a blink, into the bathroom without another word. I hurry into my room, quickly shutting the door behind me. I grab whatever I can find, a sweater, and wrap the bottle of tea in it, shoving it down in the bottom of my bag as quickly as I can.

What am I doing? I'm not so sure I know anymore.

TWENTY

心 願

(Heart's Desire)

Monday morning I drift through the halls of Westview, mind somewhere else entirely. The halls are decorated for fall, with fake leaves drooping from the doorframes and pumpkins everywhere. A more sanitized version of autumn. I miss my old school, where they went all out for Halloween. Every door would be decorated by the last week of September, with a giant werewolf statue dressed in the basketball jersey outside the gym, complete with headband and matching shorts. Here, decorations are probably frowned upon as a distraction from what we "should" be focused on.

I keep thinking about Tina. About understanding things from Tina's point of view. Maybe we're both trapped, tethered to our reality, just like those ghosts. My impossible dream of growing up to be like Yuja Wang—with her stunning performances and gorgeous costumes—the opposite of what Tina wants. She wants to be herself, and I want to be someone else.

During one of the breaks between classes, I text Delia.

Me: i know i should be patient, but i need to know

Me: why did you say not again when i mentioned the wishes?

Me: is my sister in danger?

Delia: It's easier if we talk in person. Do you want to go out for lunch?

Delia told me to wait for her by the front entrance. She roars up in a motorcycle, dressed all in black. Some of the other students stare, curious at her appearance.

"I have an extra helmet if you want to ride with me, or I can park and we can walk." I take the offered helmet, eager for us to talk. The only other time I've been on a motorcycle is when we visited Taiwan. Baba borrowed a scooter from one of our relatives for when we wanted to get around the city. The feeling of the wind in my hair as we sped down the street was both exhilarating and terrifying.

The traffic near the school is steady during the day, and Delia maneuvers us around the cars easily until we find a spot to park on the street.

"I got a craving for noodles, that all right?" she asks, and I nod. Even though there are people sitting outside waiting for a table on the benches, Delia strolls into the noodle shop like she knows someone. She waves at one of the servers, who puts us at a table in the back corner.

I don't know if I've ever been to this restaurant, though the decor seems familiar, like many Hong Kong–style cafés seem to follow. Glass-top tables, chopsticks and soup spoons and napkins in their holders you have to pull out yourself, laminated menus that are always a little sticky with pictures of the various noodle dishes. Another server brings over a silver pot of tea and two cups for us to pour on our own.

"The beef noodle here is excellent," Delia says, and then leans in, speaking conspiratorially. "The new chef is Taiwanese. But their shrimp wontons are really top-notch too. I've had them for years." I sneak glances at Delia while I look over the selections on the menu. She runs her fingers through her messy hair, trying to untangle the strands, still blue but slightly more faded now. I don't know anything about her except for her kindness, the way she helped me and spoke up for me, even though she didn't have to. I somehow knew even though my question about the wishes was intrusive, she wouldn't mind answering.

The server comes by again, speaking in the brusque way that those of auntie age usually do in these cafés, and we put in our orders. Delia pours us both tea in the cups and nudges one toward me. I put my hand around it, savoring the warmth.

"You're doing okay?" She looks at me over the steam of the cup, making her features waver as she blows gently on the surface to cool it.

Maybe it's the tea. Maybe it's the way I feel, unsettled and adrift. I crave some sort of reassurance, some sort of promise that everything will be fine. Which is why I messaged her. Because she survived whatever Shen alluded to. Whatever encounter she had.

"I don't want anything bad to happen to her," I say quietly. "She's my sister."

"Maybe you won't believe me, but I've been exactly where you are," Delia says. She leans forward on the table, huddling in on herself. "Someone I . . . cared about also came under the thrall of a temple."

Her gaze unfocuses then, as she speaks to somewhere above my head.

"Two years ago, I was a senior in high school, and my biggest worry was that I wouldn't get accepted into the same university as my girlfriend." Shen had said she graduated last year, so I thought she wasn't too much older than us, but whatever happened must have delayed her graduation somehow.

"She knew her parents wouldn't let her go to her dream university.

Not prestigious enough for what they envisioned for her. The plan was for us to move out east, get whatever scholarships we could, move away from here and from our parents'... reach. It would be just the two of us, taking on the world." Her voice remains light, as if she is speaking about someone else, and yet I can see her grip tighten on the napkin she is slowly crumpling in her hand.

"Hope came to me one day, excited. She said she found a wandering temple, one that traveled over from Taiwan. The god is supposed to be very..." Her forehead scrunches as she tries to find the word, snapping her finger each time as she struggles with the correct term. "Very... 靈... accurate? Prophetic? A true god. A powerful god.

"It wasn't something I understood very well." Delia shrugs. "My mom went to church. She didn't force me to believe, but I didn't learn a lot about the traditional gods and all that because of it. I wanted Hope to be happy though, and what was the harm? It sounded kind of cute... a place that grants wishes. The power of positive thinking.

"But she was... different after that. After she entered the temple. At first it was small things, like things she liked before, she didn't like anymore. Or the other way around. But soon she was obsessed with what she wanted, no matter how much she had to suffer for it, and no matter who else she hurt along the way."

"And what was it that she wanted?" I ask, even though I'm a little afraid of what Delia will say.

Two bowls of noodles are placed before us before she can answer.

"Eat first." She gestures, handing me a pair of chopsticks, the conversation interrupted for now.

A clear broth with wontons floating inside. I stir it with my chopsticks to find thin noodles underneath. Some green onions on top. A few pieces of bok choy. The scent that comes off the bowl makes my stomach growl, and I realize I barely ate anything this morning. Delia pushes a container of chili oil before me, and I drizzle a scoop over everything. The oil makes swirls on the broth, and for a moment I'm reminded of the mirror in Tina's room, feel myself falling in. . . .

I squeeze my eyes shut. *Stop it.* I quickly scoop up a wonton in my mouth and take a bite, burning my mouth in the process. I blow on the other half of the wonton, more careful this time, The wonton skins are thin, almost translucent, so that the pink of the plump shrimp can peek through. I slurp it up with some of the broth, which is a little sweet from the shrimp and not too salty.

"What happened to her?" I ask after I swallow, eager to know the rest of her story.

"She got what she wanted," Delia says simply. "She's studying neuro-science now at Yale, on track to get into medical school to study psychia-try. Living the dream of every Taiwanese immigrant parent."

I busy myself with scooping more wontons into a bowl. Contemplat-ing this. Could it just be that her girlfriend changed her mind? That she decided what her parents wanted for her was safe, that it was the way she should live her life?

Delia's expression turns hard. "I know what this sounds like. This is how most people react when I tell them about Hope and the temple. But I am telling you, as someone who spent almost every day with her, whatever she was before she left for school . . . she *was not Hope!*" She slams her hand on the table once, twice for emphasis, rattling our dishes.

She looks pained as she utters the next words: "When you are as close to someone as we were. When we spoke to each other about our dreams and our wishes. When she became something that we said we both despised . . ."

"You said though that she got what she wanted," I say. "What did she wish for?"

"She wanted her parents to accept her," Delia says.

Isn't that all we want in the end? What we all secretly wish for? For our parents to welcome us with open arms and say they're proud of us? But that's a sort of dream usually found in movies and shows. It's not the reality I will ever know. My parents care for us in the way they know how, which is to push us to excel, even if it will break our relationship in the process. Even if it will break me.

"But it wasn't her parents who changed. It was *her*. She morphed into a dutiful daughter. Obedient, meek, agreeable. Into someone I didn't even recognize."

They challenge us by pushing us down, tell us that we're not achieving our true potential. It works for some people like me, who will try my best to climb back up that scaffold, to achieve what I'm capable of. But Tina...the more you tell her to do something, the more she wants to do the opposite. The more she will fight back. Not like how she is now.

The noodles sit heavy in my stomach.

"I was forbidden from seeing her. I was an obstacle in the way of their daughter's glorious future." One corner of her lip turns upward, mocking herself. "And she didn't fight them. She didn't fight for me. For us. She let her parents send her away without a word.

"But I would be fine with that if I was only a distraction, a chance to rebel. Except I couldn't get over the fact that there is a temple out there peddling wishes. Wishes that changed the girl I loved, that could hurt others as well."

"So what did you do?" I whisper. Did she make a wish too?

"I went looking for the temple," Delia continues, braver than I would have been in her shoes. "I had a blurry photo that Hope had taken secretly. The storefront was an art studio, but the store itself, what was hidden in the back...all of it was gone."

I make my way through the rest of my noodles, contemplating this. I can tell from the determined way she spoke that she would have done anything to figure out the answer, no matter the cost, so that she could help the person she cared for.

"I started spending more time in Chinatown, asking around about this temple, trying to find out more about it. That was when I met Shen's family. They found me and . . . told me to stop looking."

That makes no sense to me. "Why would they do that? Aren't they supposed to be the good guys?"

"They told me that no good will come out of my investigation. They've been following the effects of the temple for a while, tracking them. . . ." She looks at me, serious. "There have always been people who try to take advantage of others. Scammers, liars stepping on other people to try and get ahead. Whatever the Temple of Wishes is, they're not that. They're *real*."

陰廟

(Dark Temple)

We finish paying for our food and end up back on the sidewalk in front of the restaurant. I don't want to let Delia go yet—there are so many more questions I have for her. So many more things I want to know.

"The temple that Tina mentioned, it was called the Temple of Fortunate Tidings," I tell her. "Is it the same?"

"They've shown up with many names," Delia says wryly. "Temple of Wishes. Temple of Good Fortune. Temple of Dreams. Promising their followers everything, and then resulting in nothing but ruin . . . for those who follow them *and* for those who get in their way. Shen's parents tried to warn me that anyone who gets close to the temple ends up getting hurt, but I didn't listen."

She shrugs, then drops the next bombshell on me. "The temple . . . hurt my mom, not long after that."

"Hurt her? What do you mean, hurt her?" I ask, alarmed.

"Here, walk with me." Delia gestures for me to follow her around the corner, glancing at the people walking by, like it's something she shouldn't be sharing.

"I could never prove it," she says, lips thinning to a grim line. "But she got into an accident. A bus hit her while she was on her way to work."

"I . . . I'm sorry," I say, once again awkward with my sympathy.

"After my mother was hurt, I wanted to give up. I dropped out of school. I didn't see a point anymore. I had wasted my life, chasing something dangerous, and for what? For a girl who didn't love me anymore." Delia's voice is soft as she recounts this. "But the guardians and their followers saved me. I owe everything to them. They were the ones who helped my mom get a bed in a facility that can take care of her, and gave me a job at the bubble tea shop while I figured out my life. Their duties were to support the guardians, not take care of some lost girl, but they tried to help me."

"Wait, who are the guardians again?" I know Shen mentioned them before, but it's all unclear. All the terms are jumbled up in my head.

"I guess there really is a lot to understand," Delia says, with a small smile. "But I'll try. . . ." She positions me so that a lamppost is between us.

"This lamppost is the doorway between the world of the living, where we are"—she raises her right hand and waves—"and the world of the dead." She lifts her left hand then and waves that hand too.

"The wardens exist on one side, the world of the dead." She gestures with the left.

"The domain of King Yanluo," I say, nodding.

"That's right." Delia grins. "And then the other side are the guardians. Both the wardens and the guardians are minor gods who serve the same function, to ensure that these two worlds do not cross." She puts her hands together, behind the lamppost, and then mimics an explosion.

"But honestly, I don't know what happens when the two worlds overlap, only that it's not good for either side," she says, poking her head around and making a face. She seems to be back to her cheery self again.

"I still—" I start to say, but Delia shakes her head, stopping me.

"I know Westview's schedule, and if we don't leave now you'll be late for the bell."

"I can skip—" I protest.

"No way," she says, then tries to soften it with an understanding smile. "I can't be held responsible for you skipping class."

We walk back to the motorcycle, and soon we're in front of Westview again. I hand my helmet back to Delia, who flips up the visor on her helmet and regards me steadily.

"In case I didn't make it clear: Whatever the temple is called now, whatever it's offering your sister, whatever it may offer you—it's not worth it," she says, as serious as I've ever seen her. "It preys on people's deepest desires. Have you ever heard of 陰廟?"

I shake my head. I only know the second part of the term, which means "temple."

"It refers to a temple that worships an unknown entity. When you offer something to them . . . who knows what you'll get back in return." With that warning, she snaps the visor in place, until I can only see myself on the reflective surface.

My pinched face, deep shadows under my eyes.

I look afraid.

I head to my classes in the afternoon, my head all muddled from what we talked about over lunch. My thoughts drift away from the confines of the classroom, to somewhere else entirely. It isn't until everyone starts packing up their books and lining up for the door that I realize I should be following.

"Where are we going?" I ask Anita, the Indian girl who is usually to my right in homeroom.

"We're meeting about the extended essay," Anita says, and then after she catches the expression of panic on my face, tries to reassure me. "Don't worry. We only have to give a tentative topic today. We don't have to decide on what we're actually writing about until later."

I vaguely remember this essay being mentioned at the beginning of the year, along with the threat of the upcoming university applications. One more thing to put on the list of to-dos. We sit in a circle of chairs in the big meeting room as one of the teachers goes through which teacher will mentor which topics. One thing I've had a hard time adjusting to in Westview is how focused they are on group projects, to learn "collaboration" and "personal engagement." Which is also my personal hell.

A part of me knows I'm the one to blame. For being antisocial. For not being able to talk to people. For putting all my focus and care and attention on the piano. But there are other people at school who excel at everything. Clarissa Oh, who plays the cello and is already doing summer co-ops getting experience at an engineering firm. Wesley Barrett, who won a citywide science competition for a software design and is working on a time-management app. Ma and Baba hope these excellent students will motivate and inspire me, yet they only make me feel like I'm falling further behind.

Everyone around me starts to pull their chairs purposefully toward their teacher-mentor, their topics probably already preselected the night after the extended essay was discussed. I shuffle around as one of the remaining stragglers, and finally decide on social studies. History seems like a safe avenue that I can cobble something interesting to say about, and I can always draw from my music history lessons as a last resort. If Ma knew the mental gymnastics I was contorting myself into in order to do the least amount of work possible, she'd scold me more than her most unruly student.

We settle in a circle around Ms. Choi. Everyone already has their notebooks on their lap, and I follow their example. She calls on someone across from me, and with dread I realize we have to give a brief summary of our chosen topic. My mind races as one by one my classmates describe their proposed essay topics. Some of them going into detail, their outline already prepared. I have absolutely nothing. I try to recall something of music history. Gregorian chants? The cantata? None of it sounds remotely interesting compared to everyone else's. Inside, I'm panicking.

"Ruby?" Ms. Choi asks, finally calling on me. "What are you considering for your essay?"

"Uh . . ." I fumble, the pause stretching longer and longer, until I blurt out the first thing I can think of. The one thing that has been on my mind all this time. "Chinatown?"

"Chinatown!" Ms. Choi exclaims with interest. "That's an area with many potential topics for research. What aspects of Chinatown are you thinking of looking into?"

"I'm not sure yet," I say slowly, trying to buy more time. "Maybe something to do with . . . Chinese seniors?"

"Huh." She nods. "There have been lots of articles in the paper recently about how Chinese seniors are being renovicted out of their apartments or not able to find housing at all. Much to explore there."

"My mom is on the Chinatown revitalization board," says Janet. She's in my homeroom, but I've only ever said a sentence or two to her before. "I can put you in touch with her." She's one of the girls who always seems put together. I vaguely recall she's part of Model UN or Debate Club or something that requires confidence speaking up in front of a crowd. Something I could never do.

"Excellent." Ms. Choi nods, approving. "How wonderful we're building connections with one another. That's what we hope for with these essay cohorts, that we can learn from each other and get to know our communities. I look forward to hearing more about this topic, Ruby and Janet."

"Thanks," I mumble in Janet's direction, relieved that I have some sort of passable topic so that the attention can be directed away from me for now.

After the session is done, Janet stops me in the hallway, and we exchange numbers.

"I'll send you more info." She's friendly about it, assuring me that she's happy to help. I just get too in my head about everything, like Dawn said. I wince, remembering what Tina said to me before. *Maybe you should get a life of your own.* Maybe she's right. I don't know how to think for myself, figure out what it is I really want.

But it isn't until I'm getting ready for my next class that I realize I've been so worried about whether those words are true or not, I never stopped to consider where those thoughts came from. Is it actually how she feels? Or something more sinister? Whatever this temple is, is it changing her personality, bit by bit . . . like what happened to Hope?

The worry follows me for the rest of the school day and all the way home.

That night during piano practice, the wild chords of the Rachmaninoff actually suit my dreary mood. I use my hands to channel the frustrations that I have building up inside me, the sounds escalating in complexity. In the quiet lulls, my mind is still working away at all the things Delia spoke to me about today. About the barrier between the living and the dead. About what's at risk if the boundary is broken. The notes of the Études-Tableaux fly from my fingers, chaotic in its fury, and yet seems less daunting to tackle now than everything else that's going on in my life.

When I'm at my laptop, I know I should be looking up talking points for my essay, but I return to the term Delia talked about today: 陰廟. The yin temples. It takes me a few tries, fumbling around with the keyboard, before finding the right characters for the search. The pages pop up. As I scroll down, I find that other translations refer to them with a more ominous name: "dark temples." A temple that may worship wandering spirits, calming restless souls, with the hope that providing regular offerings to them will keep them fed and contained so that they do not escalate and hurt the living.

The images are of small, ornate temples, found on the side of the road, nestled into the forest, on top of an apartment building. They remind me of the crosses erected here on the side of the highway for those who passed away in an accident. Different methods for the same purpose: a marker, a memorial, a shrine to the dead.

But one website lists a warning that sends chills down my spine: *You can offer the temple anything you want in exchange for what you desire, but dark tidings will follow those who renege on their promises. Woe to the ones who turn their backs on the restless spirits, for they will be devoured.*

TWENTY-TWO

行屍走肉

(The Walking Dead)

"I'm going to be spending more time in Chinatown for the next few weeks," I announce to the table while buttering my toast. Ma is upstairs getting Denny up, so it's the only the three of us right now.

"Mm-hmm," Baba mumbles through a mouthful of toast, checking his work emails.

"Why?" It's Tina that looks at me, and I can already sense her bristling suspicion.

"It's for my extended essay," I say. "I'm doing a paper on affordable housing for Chinatown seniors."

"Oh?" This gets Baba's interest. "I used to work on public-housing projects. You should have told me!"

"Boring." Tina sticks out her tongue and licks the jam off her toast, having already lost interest.

"I'll put you in touch with some of my old city-planning contacts," says Baba, nodding.

"You're spending more time in Chinatown?" Ma says from the stairs, having overheard our conversation. "You'll be careful? Avoid the street with all the homeless people? It's not safe out there."

"I know, Ma." I can't help the flash of irritation that surges through me at her anxious expression. All their worry about what could happen to us out there, when they don't see what is in front of them. Right here, right now. It makes me want to grab them by the shoulders, and yell, *Look!*

"Eww!" Denny giggles as he walks into the kitchen. Tina is grinning at him wide, raspberry jam smeared over her entire mouth like blood. She chases him around the kitchen, gnashing her teeth and growling. He shrieks, dodging her left and right. It reminds me of the bright red smile of the spirit who lives in that courtyard beside our school, the one with the mangled face like a smashed pomegranate.

I dump the rest of my breakfast in the garbage, my appetite gone.

Baba drops me and Tina off at school this morning because he's heading to Surrey to meet a client. Tina is already up the stairs and swallowed in a group of girls, all with their hair tied back in the same high ponytails with yellow scrunchies, chattering together excitedly.

The rest of the day passes, my classes uneventful. As the final bell approaches though, my stomach feels like it's being wrung from the inside out. Today I'll find out if the guardian elders will hear my case. I already decided earlier I can't sit around and wait anymore. I should go to Chinatown with my evidence in hand. Deliver it myself to show how serious I am.

Me: i have a meeting with a chinatown historian today. going to leave school early during the last period

Me: ma, can you give tina a ride to chinatown for her volunteering?
Tina: I don't feel good. I'm going home

That makes it even easier to hide what I'm going to be doing tonight. I make sure to take the bottle of tea with me. I brought it to school yesterday, wrapped in a sweater, and stuffed it in the back of my locker. It seems safer there than to leave it in my room.

There's one positive thing I can say about going to a fancy private school, I've decided. Back at my old school there was a complicated procedure where I had to get a permission slip signed or a parent has to call in so that you could leave. Here, the students are trusted to sign out ourselves if we need to go.

I don't bother waiting for the bus. It'll take the same amount of time to walk. I make my way through downtown, past all the condo towers of glass and steel, and the constant construction that never seems to end.

I catch movement sometimes. Suspect maybe I see a hand in the window, or a face through a grate, but then I blink and they're gone. Until I'm still not sure if I'm seeing ghosts or my mind is making things up.

Up ahead, the Millennium Gate looms over West Pender Street, welcoming everyone into Chinatown proper. Here is where Baba's memories start overlapping with mine, the way he always speaks about how this corner used to be a barbecue restaurant, or that shop was a place that would take your passport photos. Ama used to hold my hand when we walked together to visit her friends at one of the cafés. I sat at the tables next to her while they chatted over freshly steamed buns and plenty of hot tea. I always picked the buns that were shaped like rabbits, their backs colored the palest pink, with two red dots for their eyes. Inside, did they have red bean or custard? I can't remember anymore, and that café is gone too.

Someone brushes by me, pushing a cart full of empty cans. Baba's reminiscence of a disappearing Chinatown. *For every business that suc-ceeds, hundreds more fail,* he always told us.

But it's not only businesses that are closing, it's the residents being forced out too. Nowhere to go except for the streets. The news call them the Walking Dead roaming Vancouver's streets, without homes, with-out help. They wander the streets with vacant gazes or sit on the street corners, talking to no one. That man who helped me just a few blocks away during the celebration might have very well been one of them. The homeless, the neglected, the suffering. If there is a place in need of true gods, a Temple of Wishes to make all of their dreams come true...

I shake my head. I can't think like that, Delia warned me.

I push the door open into Bubble Madness, the bell jingling above my head. It's empty today. Even the cat isn't there sunning itself by the window. I walk up to the counter, hoping to peer into the kitchen, but there's no one there. I notice a small altar tucked into the corner on the floor. In front of the statue of the god there is a plate with a stack of tiny mandarin oranges. An incense holder. What do the owners of this shrine pray for? Protection from bad luck? Good fortune?

"Can I help you?" The voice that speaks up is not a familiar one. It's not Delia or Shen. It's a bored-looking guy who appears to be about university aged. He has shaggy bangs that fall halfway into his eyes. He's dressed all in black. Black sweater, black jeans. No Bubble Madness apron, though he surely works here. He reminds me of Badtz-maru, the sour-faced penguin that Denny loves.

"Ah...I'm meeting someone," I say. "I'll...wait for him outside."

I walk into the mall instead, suddenly embarrassed. I didn't even check in with Shen to know what time he'll be here. I assumed that he'll show up when I need him. I sit down at one of the tables in the food court and pull out my phone to text him.

Me: i searched tina's room. took pics. at the mall until you're ready

I put on my headphones and play one of my comfort listens, letting it drown out my anxiety. Rhapsody on a Theme of Paganini, the 18th variation, is often isolated for concert piano performances, and was my first introduction to Rachmaninoff's music. I can even remember when Mr. Brandt played it for me in his studio, the version performed by Vladimir Ashkenazy with the London Symphony Orchestra: the sweetness of the melody at the beginning, the simple strains on the piano, then it growing upon itself, building in intensity until the orchestra joins the piano like the crash of waves on the shore.

"I can see a deep appreciation for the music when you listen, Ruby," Mr. Brandt told me. "It's why I am willing to take you on as a student. It shows in your playing too. You truly love the music. I want to teach students who enjoy it, because once you get to a certain level, it's not only about practice and technicality anymore; there's a musicality that comes with being open to the music, to being receptive to hearing it and providing your own interpretation, eventually. It's something that I cannot teach. You have to figure it out for yourself."

It's directly contradictory to the reason why my parents wanted me to play the piano. The enjoyment should be secondary to being able to hold a certificate, to show that I am "well-rounded."

My playlist seems to understand how my mood turns, because the song that follows is discordant and disjointed. Chopin's Mazurka in A minor has an insistent, driving rhythm in the left hand and jangling trills in the right.

A shadow falls over my table, and I shriek, almost falling off my seat. I imagine ghouls with too-long arms, reaching down from the ceiling, tangled hair brushing against my face and slender fingers with extra joints trailing against my skin. . . .

"This her?" But it's only Badtz-maru from the café. He holds up a phone in front of my face. Shen peers at me from the screen.

"Ruby?" His face pixelates, warps, and then refocuses. His mouth moves, but it doesn't match with the sounds that are coming out.

"Yeah." I drag my fingers through my hair. "I'm here."

"I'm almost there." He sounds a little out of breath. Buildings are moving behind him.

"It's okay," I say automatically, because that's what I'm supposed to say, even though it's not okay. I drum my fingers nervously on the table beside me.

"I'll be there soon," Shen says. The screen goes dark, and then it's just me and the black-sweater man staring at each other.

"He's a good guy," the grumpy penguin informs me. "He'll help, if he's able."

I make a noise in response. Did Shen's family help him too?

"Never seen him quite so worried before though." He gives me a look, like he knows something I don't, before sauntering away.

I stare at his back as he disappears down the hall.

What is that *supposed to mean?*

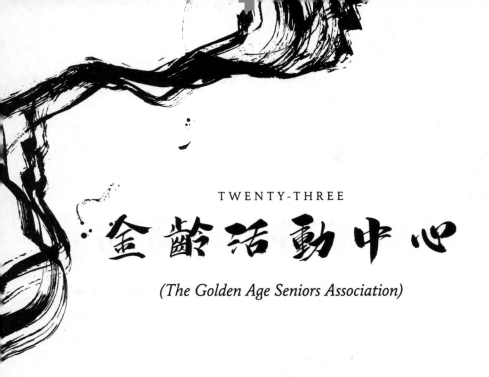

TWENTY-THREE

金齡活動中心

(The Golden Age Seniors Association)

After what feels like hours but was probably only ten minutes, Shen shows up. His hair is windblown, his tie loosened. I feel suddenly shy when he sits down across from me, reminded of how I reacted the last time we talked—sobbing and accusing him of lying to me.

"Before I left, I let them know you're already here," he says, brushing his hair away from his eyes, unaware of the inner turmoil that's brewing inside of me.

I reach down into my bag, hiding my red face under the table so he can't see it. After a few breaths, I finally straighten and slide the bottle across the table toward him, avoiding his eyes.

"I don't know if this is enough." My voice decides to tremble, betraying my nervousness. "But it's what I could find. Along with those photos I took. I sent those to you already."

"Yeah, I forwarded those on," he says, rolling up his sleeves to pick up the bottle, holding it with both hands. I can see the edge of the tattoo on his wrist. Definitely not something my parents would approve of, and I feel that twinge inside my chest. What would it be like if there was no Ma to tell me to make better choices, no Baba to remind me of everything at stake with my future?

Shen's face blurs before me again. *Oh no.* I try to hide it, but the tears well up, out of my control.

"Ah . . . hell," I hear him say, then a pack of tissues appears on the table in front of me. "I came prepared this time."

I take off my glasses and dab at my eyes with one of the tissues, my face really burning now.

"I don't even know why I'm crying," I blubber, and then wonder why I even bother trying to explain anymore. He already knows I'm a mess.

"I would say you're holding up fairly well," he says. I slide my glasses on, and he becomes clear again, just in time to see him take my hand into his, holding it between his palms.

"Remember, you were the one who found me, even though you were terrified. Hold on to that—hold on to that feeling, that strength," he continues softly. "You'll save your sister. Believe it. I believe it. I believe in *you*." My heart stutters a little. It's like he sees me, notices me, like I'm someone worth saving too.

There's a burst of laughter, a group of kids rushing by. I pull my hand away, and he clears his throat.

"I've seen quite a few people meet the guardians, willingly or unwillingly." He winces at the memory. "Sometimes there's a lot of screaming."

"I *am* screaming," I inform him. "You just can't hear it." He grins, even though the joke is bad.

"Well, I'll be there with you," Shen tells me. "Not that I'm useful at all, but—"

"I'm glad!" I blurt out. His grin deepens, and that's when I notice he has a small dimple on his left cheek. We stare at each other, the moment stretching on, too long, before his phone beeps. He glances down, and I snap back to reality.

He's helping you because of his family's responsibility to the guardians, I remind myself.

"She's ready for us," he says, and I'm on my feet immediately, clutching the strap of my book bag like it will save me.

Shen leads me up the stairs behind the broken fountain, to the second-story walkway, before stopping in front of the doors to the Golden Age Seniors Association.

"Wait." I pull at his sleeve to stop him. "You mean it's here? The temple to your guardians is here? *In* the mall?" It's been above us all along, another secret hidden within Chinatown.

I've walked past these doors before, dozens of times, on my way to my piano lessons. There is a full wall of glass, with the bottom half frosted. I can only catch a glimpse of the fluorescent lights. The name of the association is printed in red characters vertically beside the door, and then the English name in gold capital letters underneath, some of the letters having peeled off. Instead of THE GOLDEN AGE SENIORS ASSOCIATION, it is T E GOLD N AGE SEN R ASSO AT N.

"The mall has always been a gathering place," Shen says, matter-of-fact. "Why wouldn't a temple be here?"

A temple in my mind has always been a separate space. A building that stands out from the rest of the buildings on the block, with the traditional architecture of the sweeping curved roof, and the many carvings upon its pillars and adorning the rooftops. There should be stern-faced gold gods sitting on the altar in meditative poses, waiting for you to worship them.

I step inside behind him, tentative, unsure of what I will see. There are currently three tables set up, occupied by seniors. There is a very intense game of Chinese chess happening between two men close to the door. There are two other men in masks standing by the table, arguing with one another about the best upcoming move. The residents at the other two tables are playing mahjong. In an odd way, this does make sense. We used to go to temples with our grandparents, back when we visited years ago. Some of them had small courtyards in front, where there was a food stand with someone grilling sausage or someone else selling Popsicles from a cart. There were plastic stools everywhere, for people to sit down and eat their food or rest in the shade. There might be some seniors doing tai chi. A temple *is* a gathering place, I recognize now. Daily life flowing in and out of its gates. The gods are not closed behind the doors, but opened to them.

"Ruby! Ruby!" One of the ladies at the mahjong table waves. To my surprise, I recognize some of the faces from my Chorus of Aunties.

"What are you doing here?" I approach the table with surprise, feeling multiple parts of my life colliding at the moment. The manor. The mall. Shen.

"They finally fixed the elevator again," Mrs. Sui grumbles.

"You know A'Shen?" Mrs. Wang gives him a long look and then gives Mrs. Sui a sly grin. "How fun! Ruby's a nice girl. You best treat her well." She shakes her cane in his direction, threatening.

Shen sputters next to me as I shake my head.

"Mrs. Wang, Shen's helping me with something," I correct her. "You know...what happened, um, the last time I visited you."

"Ah." They both glance at the door in the back, suddenly serious. The joking air dissipates, as if sucked up quickly by the ceiling fan, and the thought of whatever is hidden behind those doors.

"Take care of her, A'Shen," Mrs. Sui says directly to Shen. "Keep her out of danger."

"I will, 姑婆." He nods. Shen and Mrs. Sui are related? He doesn't refer to her as Auntie, but as something else. One of the family terms that I can never quite remember.

Mrs. Sui must have sensed my nervousness. She scoots her wheelchair closer to me and reaches out to pat my hand.

"Shu-Ling is a good girl, just like you," she says, in her gravelly voice. "She will come up with a solution."

Mrs. Sui calling me a good girl makes me want to cry again. My mother's face flashes in mind, but I swallow those tears down because Shen is already leading me toward the double doors on the back wall.

There are posters taped to each of them. Door gods. One is tall and slim and dressed entirely in black, his tongue long and drooping from his face. He holds a fan in one hand and chains in another. With his tongue, he should have repulsed me like the Hanged Spirit, but he doesn't. He strikes a strong pose, and his uniform looks to be like what they wore in ancient times. The figure opposing him is dressed entirely in white, round and short. He holds a lantern and a flag in his hands. His face is dark and bristly. They appear to be fearsome protectors. *Wardens,* I understand now.

Shen pushes the doors open, and there are a set of curtains within, obscuring whatever is in the space beyond. He waits until I'm fully in that small area with the curtains before shutting the doors behind us. It's just the two of us in that tiny space, side by side. He gives me an encouraging nod and reaches out to part the curtains for me. But this reveals . . . a hallway. It looks like a storage space, two doors on either side. With each step, a feeling of anxiety creeps up my neck. Dread at what waits for me at the end.

We turn the corner, and the true space appears before us. There are red lanterns hanging from red rafters that cross the ceiling horizontally, decorated by elaborate wooden details of Chinese architecture. Hanging from one of the rafters is a large wooden plaque, stained a dark black, on which Chinese calligraphy is written in a flowing script, then etched in gold. If I had to guess what it said, it would be: *Illuminate, protect us.* Carvings of gold dragons crawl along the borders. Above the lanterns, the ceiling opens up further, so the eye is drawn upward. Slats of wood in a natural stain cover the roof, giving the space an open feel, instead of being dark and oppressive, considering there are no windows to be seen. I wonder if this is the heart that beats deep within the Pacific Dragon, if we are at the very center of the mall.

It takes me a moment to realize what I'm looking at directly in front of me, built into the wall. There is the partial roof of a traditional temple, with small gold lanterns hanging from the eaves, each of them decorated with red lettering, but too small for me to discern the characters. The altar below it is built from solid redwood, decorated with gold filigree, giving it an opulent air. The statues of the gods are set into small alcoves. Three in number. On the table below, there are plates of offerings: round yellow pears and large oranges, vases of flowers.

"You must be Ruby." A young woman emerges from the shadows, with a nod. "You've gotten yourself in a bit of trouble, I hear."

TWENTY-FOUR

控制

(Control)

The woman is taller than me, with short black hair, bangs swept across her forehead. She has on a gray mesh sweater, a black tank top underneath. Silver rings, six in number, glint in the light, starting from the tip of her left ear and then continuing downward. She also has a hoop piercing in her right eyebrow, capped with a red dot. When she smiles, the corner of her eyes pull up as well, and it makes me want to smile back. She doesn't look like she belongs to this place. She looks like she should be one of Delia's friends from university.

"I'm Shu-Ling," she introduces herself. She extends her hand, and I see rings on every finger—gold, silver, thin and heavy bands. Her touch is cold, and brief.

"In case you didn't know, Shen's my little brother." She reaches out and ruffles Shen's hair, and he slaps her hand away with a look that says *Take this seriously, please.* I can tell they're related by the shape of their eyes and the curve of their noses.

"We should get started," she says. Her voice is smoky, with a slight hint of an accent, just in the way her *rs* sound, that makes me speculate her first language isn't English.

The wall to our right is covered with floor-to-ceiling red curtains. There's a round table in the corner, chairs placed around it. Other chairs are stacked neatly against the far wall. Shen pulls out a chair and gestures for me to sit. I do and look around, waiting for the elder to appear. I wonder what they'll look like. If they'll be around my parents' age, if they'll be like one of the many professionals who walk down the streets of downtown with purposeful strides, heading somewhere important. Or if they'll be even older, maybe one of those seniors, hair gray, full of the wisdom of all the things they've seen.

"The Hanged Spirit, she touched you?" Shu-Ling sits down on a chair next to me. "Can you show me where?"

"Sure." I reach down and roll up my pant leg.

"I'm going to take a look at your leg, okay?" Without waiting for me to respond, she lifts my leg and places it on her knee, not caring about my shoe dirtying her jeans. I can feel her touch against the darkness on my leg, pressing gently.

"Um . . . when will the elder arrive?" I ask, tentative, as she pokes at the bruise with her fingernail, making me flinch. I'm not sure if this is yet another test, if I have to prove to another person that I'm in need of help.

"There's no other elder," she responds. "There's just me."

I can't control my reaction, jerking away. She straightens and curves up the corner of her lip slightly, amused at my response.

"I'm the head priestess," she says with a smirk. "Surprised?"

"Sorry," I say. "You're . . . not what I expected." I glance over at Shen, and he gives me a sheepish and slightly guilty look in return.

"Hey! It's not his fault." Shu-Ling reaches over and taps me on the forehead, forcing me to look at her again. "I make the rules. He doesn't tell people we're related. I don't want them bothering him because of temple-related stuff. Besides, when people get desperate enough to find me . . . they usually need all the help they can get." She raises one eyebrow, almost like a challenge. *Do you want to do this or not?*

Over her shoulder, Shen holds up his hands, joined together, reminding me of what he said earlier. *Remember that strength.*

"We can only help those who are willing," she adds, but not unkindly.

"I'm not afraid," I say to his sister. "Please. I need your help."

"Good choice." She pats my knee. "Don't worry though, I wouldn't have let you out of here without doing something about . . . *that.*" She waves at my leg with a grimace.

I look down at it again, even though I don't like to look too closely at what's spreading over my skin. It's still purplish blue, bruise-like, but the area surrounding it is angry, red, and continues to grow. As if there is something my body is trying to purge.

"Shen described for me what happened, but I want to hear it from you directly. Tell me everything, leave nothing out," she instructs.

I tell the story again, starting from when I first encountered the Hanged Spirit crouched on top of the streetlight. All the way to now, with the bottle that Shen hands over to her.

Shu-Ling raises the bottle and tips it sideways. The dark liquid moves from one side to the other. Her frown deepens as she traces her finger over the design on the label. Then she cracks open the lid, dips her finger in the liquid, and touches it to her tongue. *Ew.*

Her eyes narrow as she spins the lid closed. Shen and I watch her intently, waiting for the answer. She tips her head back instead and looks up at the ceiling. It's obvious that whatever realization she's had, it's nothing good.

"This is a . . ." She rubs her temples with her fingers. "Let me think of the best way to phrase this. It's a ward of containment and also a talisman of receiving. Whoever drinks this is more susceptible to influence, and it also affects the body's natural immunity to what would harm it." She snaps her fingers, gestures for Shen to come closer.

"Give me your notepad," she demands, and he fishes one out of his backpack.

Shu-Ling takes the offered pen as well and rips out a sheet of paper. She quickly draws a few lines, then connects several points. It reminds me of the characters on the talismans that I put up in my room, but not anything I can understand.

"This talisman was written on paper and then burned, and the ash poured inside the bottle, infusing the water with power," Shu-Ling explains, lifting up the sheet of paper, then taps her fingernail on the label. "This too is a 符; these lines seal the magic within the bottle so that it does not dissipate."

"What do you mean? What does it *do*?" I ask.

"Have you been drinking this?" she asks.

I shake my head. "I don't like drinking cold tea on its own. Tina also hates it, or I guess . . . used to."

"The living body naturally contains 陽氣, the life force, if you will. The opposite would be 陰氣, which could cause illness, death. In extremely simplistic terms, one repels the other. The living energy within your sister will want to force out anything that is from the other side, the ying energy," Shu-Ling says. "So whatever spirit is occupying your sister's body . . . they have to keep drinking this in order to stay in it. To keep the vessel hospitable."

"So if I stop her from drinking this, her body will eventually expel that ghost, that spirit, whatever, right?" It seems so obvious, though I'll have to figure out how to convince Tina to stop doing it. For her own good.

"You would think so, but nothing is ever that simple." Shu-Ling gives me a pitying look. "You have to understand that what is happening to your sister doesn't happen out of nowhere. A spirit has to be *invited* into a vessel. They cannot force their way in, possess a host, without the body being willing. There's a whole ritual that's involved to make it happen."

"You mean..." I finally say, almost forcing the words out. "You mean she chose this. She asked to be possessed."

"Depends on what the spirit offered her." Shu-Ling shrugs, like it's not anything surprising. "People have given up everything for what they thought they wanted."

"But what about me?" I exclaim, still not willing to accept that my sister *chose* this. "I didn't ask for anything. I've seen *them* for most of my life and tried to ignore it. I would never want a spirit inside of me, but they attacked me first."

"You...are a different case entirely." She regards me with curiosity, and I feel a prickling sense of scrutiny when she scans me from head to toe, like she wants to peel back my skin and see how I am on the inside. "My brother was right, you *have* been cursed. You were marked somehow when that spirit touched you. The wardens have already taken her away, or else I would have questioned her." She tsks, seemingly annoyed.

She stands up from her chair and then gestures for me to follow. I stand too, hesitant, as she approaches the altar. I can sense Shen behind me, keeping close. Directly in front of the altar, more details emerge from the wood. Burning suns and crescent moons, leaping fish and rippling serpents. The elaborate patterns continue on the embroidered robes of the statues, tigers clawing their way up their orange cloaks. The gods have faces carved from dark wood, peering out from under a traditional Chinese cap that has two wings that swoop skyward.

"We'll ask the guardian gods for their blessing first." Shu-Ling stands before them. "At the center is the Judge, the Keeper of the City. He controls the doorway into the Ying Realm, the afterlife, where ghosts must pass through for their souls to be purified and reborn again. His two generals accompany him. The General of the Dawn holds a fan in one hand and a book in the other; she is the one who documents all of your deeds, the good and the bad. The General of the Night wields the sword and the whip; he is the one who protects the living world from infiltrators—those who want to corrupt the spirits and those who desire to remain among the living"

Shu-Ling's voice takes on a reverent tone. "We are the Disciples of the 三將, the Three Guardians. Brought overseas to protect the community that has grown here in Vancouver. We work in the shadows to prevent the realms from spilling into each other."

Suddenly, it sounds like multiple people are speaking through her, like she is channeling the voices of many. "We settled, we thrived, one generation passing on to the next. We seek no glory, we seek no fortune; we remain steadfast in our role as representatives of the guardians and protectors of the living. Place your hands together and bow. The gods will hear you."

She brings her hands together palm to palm, fingers pointing straight up. Shen also puts his hands up, head already bowed, eyes closed, expression reverent. The gods regard me with their steady gaze, and I stand there, uncertain. Will they recognize me as a liar? Will they peer into the depths of my soul and realize that I do not know what I believe?

TWENTY-FIVE

法事

(The Ritual)

Shu-Ling must sense my uncertainty, because she turns to look at me.

"Are you afraid?" she asks.

"What if...what if I don't know who...or what to believe?" I say, tentative. Not wanting to be found unworthy, not knowing the consequences if they peer into my mind and find all the doubt there.

Shu-Ling nods and says, "Some things are true whether you believe in them or not." The words carry a similar reverberating quality in the air, just like before. As if an omen, ringing with its own power.

Then she follows it with a little smirk. "I got that from a movie I watched once. Sounds wise, right?"

I snort, and Shen makes a choking sound next to me. Some of the seriousness in the room dissipates, but Shu-Ling lifts an eyebrow, regarding me again with that steady gaze: *Are you ready for this or not?*

I mirror her pose, hands together, in front of my face. We turn back to the altar and stand before the gods. Shu-Ling bows, and we follow.

Please. Watch over my family. Protect my sister and my brother. Save them from whatever is after them.

With the acknowledgment of the gods complete, Shu-Ling places a hand on my elbow and guides me away from the altar.

"Help her, if anything happens," she instructs her brother, leaving me at his side.

"If what happens?" I look at her, but she's already facing the altar. I turn to Shen, worried now, but he gestures for me to look back at his sister. I'll have to place my trust in her, like I trusted Shen when I demanded to know the answers. I take a shaky breath and wait.

Shu-Ling bows her head before the statues again, lips mumbling something I can't understand. She tugs on a red cloth draped over a shelf beside the altar, revealing a chest of drawers. Her eyes close, but her lips still move. Her hand then slowly lifts in the air, birdlike, as she reaches over and slides one of the drawers open. The drawer is lined with gold cloth. From it, she pulls out a wooden sword, and then a red fabric pouch. The sword she fastens to her belt so that it rests along her right side, and then she hooks the pouch to her left hip. Her movements continue, deliberate, purposeful. The next drawer is opened, and a bell appears in her left hand, and in her right a coiled whip. When she lifts it up, I notice the handle is in the head of a snake, split into two colors: black and white.

"Ready?" she asks. For a moment I think she is speaking to me, but she's talking to Shen, who nods.

Shu-Ling begins to move before me in graceful, sweeping steps, like a dance. The bell rings in her hand, once, twice, a sweet sound, matching her movements. Two steps forward, one jump back. The bell chimes again, building each time, even though it is impossible: There is only one bell, and yet, the sound of multiple bells quiver in the air.

My leg begins to ache, then throb, in time with the ringing of the bells. Shu-Ling continues to perform her dance, feet moving in an elaborate pattern. My ankle starts to feel warm, then it begins to burn.

"Don't touch it." Shen guides me to remain standing even as I try to bend over to see what's happening. The pain grows stronger, and I gasp, but he steps behind me. He places his hands on my forearms, holding me still. I feel his steadying presence behind me. With a stomp of her foot, Shu-Ling stops before me. Her eyes are open in my direction, but she's looking through me, beyond me.

"聽好! 我叫你出來!" Her voice has joined the ringing of the bells, echoing as well, as if somehow it went into the bells and through the noise, magnified a hundredfold.

Listen! I'm telling you to get out!

The last two words repeat, again and again: 出來 出來 出來.

Get out . . . get out . . . getoutgetout . . .

The whip extends from Shu-Ling's hand, the rope uncoiling and falling to the floor. With a flick of her wrist, it snaps in the air before me. I flinch at the sharp sound. I'm afraid she'll use it on me. But Shen's hands strengthen me, keep me standing there, reminding me of what is at stake.

My sister.

Shu-Ling snaps the whip three times in succession, each time getting closer and closer to me.

"Sit. Down," she says, her voice deeper, sounding like someone else.

Shen lets me go, and I glance back at him, terrified he's leaving me alone to face her. But he slides a chair behind me so that I can sit. Shu-Ling regards me like a snake herself, not taking her eyes off of me as she slowly, deliberately, winds the length of the whip around her hand. She reaches out and taps the handle of the whip against my knee.

A scream wrenches its way out of my throat as soon as I land on the chair. It feels like someone dipped a red-hot knife into my leg. Tears well up in my eyes as I almost fall off from the pain. Shu-Ling places her hand on my shoulder and guides me back up. I manage to return to the seat, gritting my teeth as I attempt to breathe through the pain.

A hand finds mine, and I clutch it tightly.

Shu-Ling straightens away from me. "出來!" she commands again, this time more forceful, a shout, accompanied by a stomp on the ground.

A bright light flashes in the room. It stings my eyes, and I want to look away, but I force myself to open them. To *see*. The light illuminates Shu-Ling, until she glows with an otherworldly golden aura. She no longer wields the whip, but a sword is in her hand instead. She points it at something on the ground.

I gasp. There's a scorpion, impossibly large, partially inside my leg and partially out of it. It's about the size of a rat. I can only see its head and its pincers, which are a rich, deep red, but half of it disappears into my leg. It lifts its head and raises its pincers, menacing. My leg still throbs, but it's no longer that shooting, agonizing pain.

Shu-Ling darts forward, the sword a blur, as she pierces the body of the scorpion with her weapon. It makes a horrible hissing noise then as it thrashes, attempting to cut her with its sharp pincers, but the sword pins it in place. With her other hand, Shu-Ling pulls out a wooden amulet from the pouch and presses it against the head of the scorpion. Black smoke begins to emerge from its trembling form, as if it is burning from the inside out. She pulls the amulet back, and the scorpion moves with it, until it comes out of my ankle...bit by bit, finally landing on the floor with a sickening thud.

Shu-Ling gasps then, wiping away the beads of sweat on her brow. She picks up the scorpion by its tail and holds it at arm's length, where it dangles from her fist.

"What...what is that?" My ankle continues to burn.

"This is how you were marked," Shu-Ling says. She turns the scorpion to look at its underbelly, scrutinizing it with a frown. "The curse passed on to you when the Hanged Spirit touched you in the alley."

The scorpion, which was hanging limply, suddenly twists in her hand, swiping at her. Shu-Ling throws it down on the floor, where it turns and tries to scuttle its way toward me. But she's faster. She quickly brings the sword down, severing its head. Before my eyes, it stills, then disappears into black smoke. Leaving only a grimy red stain on the floor where it used to be.

"Too bad. I was hoping to collect it as a specimen." She sighs.

Shen coughs beside me, and I realize that I am still squeezing his hand.

"Thanks," I whisper, releasing my grasp, knowing that I probably hurt him with how tightly I gripped him. He kneels in front of me and helps guide up my pant leg, and we see the redness of my calf has already lightened considerably.

"It's faded," he reports to Shu-Ling, standing back up. The bruise itself is less purple, more mottled brown, as if healing before our eyes.

"The curse is...gone, then?" I ask.

"This type of dark magic always asks for a contribution, blood or flesh. That bit I removed from you will return to sender, and then they will reveal their true intentions. They always do, in time." A slow grin creeps up, and even though she's supposed to be the one to help me, there seems to be a part of her that delights in this thought a little too much.

"You mean you want to use my family as bait," I say flatly, understanding it very clearly now.

Shu-Ling doesn't disagree with my statement. "I've noticed in the past few months someone stirring up the spirits, causing trouble for the wardens, but I haven't been able to uncover the root of it, even with the help of the guardians." Her expression hardens. "I suspect it might be because I'm the youngest leader of all the guardian temples, and they believe my territory is the weakest, but I'm not going to let them get away with it. Not on my watch."

Then she shrugs. "We tugged on a very complicated thread, and we have to wait for the whole thing to unravel. It's going to be ... a little uncertain for you and your family for the next while, but don't worry. We'll be here." She says it so lightly, so matter-of-fact, as if she is commenting on the weather—an upcoming thunderstorm instead of something that can endanger our lives.

"I thought this would be it! Not put us in even more danger!" I react, frustration stinging my eyes.

"It's never as complex as one curse, one minion, one possession," Shu-Ling says. "Think of the enormity of the cost of everything they've done to your family so far. All those familiars, all those bottles with talismans inside, the spirit they sent to mark you. Would they commit all that effort without a greater purpose?"

"What's the next step, then?" I ask. "How do I save Tina?" That's all I care about. I have to focus on that, or I'm going to start screaming and never stop.

"The next part of the challenge is to weaken the influence of whatever has its hold on her, before it can fully take over, then find the right time to expel it. But I need to make a plan." Shen lays out the red cloth on top of the chest of drawers, and Shu-Ling hands him her items one by one. The whip, the bell, the pouch, the sword, are all laid out carefully.

"Delia told me that the wishes meant something," I tell her. "That this wandering temple had appeared here before. Is it true? What happened back then?"

"Back then, it was the Temple of Hopeful Desires," Shu-Ling says, expression darkening. "It ruined a lot of people's lives. Our parents died fighting them."

I wince, not knowing that this was tied to their own personal family history.

"But it probably has nothing to do with that temple at all." She shrugs, dismissive. "That temple was eliminated at the root. The threat contained. It's probably another restless spirit, willing to do anything to return to the living, and some hack they convinced to help them." Her attitude makes me bristle. Is she even taking this seriously at all?

"Don't worry." Shen steps between us as mediator. "The guardians will help us figure it out. They don't view transgressors in a kindly light."

Shu-Ling's eyes flash as her hand closes into a fist in front of her. "And if they dare to return to cause trouble again, I'll crush them."

TWENTY-SIX

大凶

(Great Misfortune)

In the meantime, I'm told to stick to my normal routines. Keep everything the same, maintain my regular schedule, so that whatever is inside Tina does not suspect what is going happen.

"You'll feel weak for a little while," Shu-Ling tells me. "The scorpion was formed from pure yin energy, and your body saw it as an infection it had to fight. Removing it will help, but it will have other aftereffects.

"You're going to continue to see the spirits, and they're going to be even clearer than before. You might even be able to hear them, sense their presence, but they shouldn't be able to hurt you. Just ignore them."

"But how do I protect my little brother? My parents? What if she hurts them?" I ask.

"You have to be patient," Shu-Ling says, and I can detect a slight annoyance to her voice now. "Trust us." She doesn't elaborate further, and I'm tired of being polite.

"Everything you talk about, you act like I should know it, but I don't. I never learned any of this while growing up. I was born here. I've only gone back a few times, and my family isn't religious. . . ." My voice trails off, my anger suddenly deflating out of me like a balloon as quickly as it came.

"I know nothing at all," I whisper under the weight of her impassive gaze.

"The guardians exist on the periphery of the living world," Shu-Ling says, ignoring my outburst. "Our role is to be unknowable, hidden from society. We'll share what you need to know. Nothing more. It's for your own safety. Shen, you'll see her out?" She disappears through a doorway hidden behind one of the curtains, then it's only the two of us again.

"She's usually like that," Shen tries to explain. "She doesn't mean it in a bad way."

"Comes in, does her flashy bit with the swords and stuff, then leaves behind a bunch of questions for everyone else?" I ask, and that gets a chuckle out of him.

"That sounds about right," he says. "Can I give you a ride home?"

"I have piano," I tell him, even though my head is filled with all the things I've seen today, so the lessons will probably be a disastrous one . . . again.

"You play?" He looks surprised, then impressed. "I've always wanted to learn an instrument, but it never made sense to me. It's like learning another language."

"The studio is just down here." I point down the length of the mall.

"We should talk . . . after. When are you done?" He's insistent, and makes me realize it must be important, whatever it is.

"Okay," I agree, knowing Tina won't be around to catch me with Shen. "I'm done at six thirty, and I need to be home by seven thirty."

"Great, I'll finish my shift then too."

—

Today's focus is Bach. I've been working on the French Suite in C minor for a few months, deceptive in its simplicity. My confidence in the Baroque selection is the best out of all my performance pieces. The suite is lively, with several movements to convey the feeling of a dance. I start the first movement after a warm-up, and the notes sparkle as they emerge from the piano. Mrs. Nguyen smiles beside me, her silver pointer still in her hand, but her foot taps, keeping that steady beat, as good as any metronome.

Light! Bright! Fingers up! I keep her instructions in mind as my fingers run through the notes. Her reminders are entangled with the history lessons my previous teacher gave me whenever we discussed the piece.

What does this mean? he would say. *Allemande?* He used to stand up beside his grand piano, the floorboards of his old house creaking under his feet as he performed the dance steps. *Imagine. A ballroom full of people dressed in their fanciest clothing. The way their hands would join, and come apart, as they spin and twirl, moving in an elegant configuration.*

I whirl through the dances, my mind lost elsewhere to the ballroom in my mind.

But the final movement is where the distractions begin to creep in. This movement always sounds off to me, like a puppet dancing with one of its strings cut, its movements lopsided. Tina's face comes to mind, speaking in the shadows of her room, her expression filled with devotion as she watches the dancers on the screen. I imagine her on the stage, spinning, jumping, her limbs guided by strings too. A vacant smile spreads across her face, stretching the corners of her mouth wide. Too wide...

My fingers stumble, collide with one another, and I force myself, through sheer muscle memory, to power through. But it only adds to the discord, the keys too slippery now. When I end, it's not with a flourish but a flop. I close my eyes, breath coming a little shallow.

"Sorry," I mumble. "I couldn't keep it going there at the end."

"We'll work on your endurance." Mrs. Nguyen does not seem to be bothered. "It's still in good shape. Now...shall we work on the Rachmaninoff again? How do you feel about it?"

"I'll...I'll try..." I gulp, already scared.

I open my binder to the music, dots on lines, treble and bass. I think back to what Shen said earlier. This is an entirely different language that I'm somehow able to decipher. Someone, years ago, heard this music in his mind and wrote it down in a way that those who came after him would be able to understand it. That I get to play it now, interpret it for myself, for others to hear, somehow seems like a sort of magic in itself.

Appassionato. Deeply emotional, with great passion.

My fingers rest lightly on the keys. I push everything out of mind, except for the lines of black and white, the reach of ten fingers. My two hands, capable of creating sounds soft and gentle or grand and booming. I take a deep breath, then let it all go. Unleash the discordance, the noise, the frustration, the anger, the resentment. I make myself feel all the ugliness of my feelings, all the emotions I've been forced to hide. Because they never listen. Tina and I have been doing the equivalent of shouting at the top of our lungs, but they don't hear us.

Fear, crashing into the anger. The bells tolling overhead, an omen, a warning. The sense of something building, that I'm waiting for a terrible thing to finally happen.

I imagine myself exploding outward, the noise thundering through me and all around me, filling the room, until...I retreat back into my body. My left leg quivers. That spot on my right ankle still aches. My eyes are watering again, and I don't know why.

"Ruby..." Mrs. Nguyen is there in front of me, spinning me to face her. She smiles down at me, holding my hands, her mouth pulled wide in a grin. "Ruby! That was beautiful and passionate and brave. Whatever it was you channeled, whatever conjured this feeling of desperate, deep emotions—that is what you need every time! This is your breakthrough! Remember this. How it made you feel. *Appassionato!*"

I don't know whether to laugh or cry at the realization. I've finally found what motivates me.

It's fear.

Shen waits for me in the hall outside the studio, leaning against the door of one of the empty offices. He's changed out of his Westview uniform. Now he's dressed all in black: a black baseball cap on his head, a black hoodie with a cartoon of a black bear on it, waving a flag that says "Made in Taiwan." The sight of it makes me chuckle. He looks like one of those boys Ma always warns me about, pulling me close every time we have to walk by one of them on the street. She always believes they are "up to no good," the ones who loiter outside stores and paint graffiti and have no future. But then there's his mural of the dragon in the back alley, the art in his notebook. He's so much more than I ever expected. We never should have met, and yet...

He approaches me with a hesitant smile. "I've heard music around here a lot," he says with wonder. "But I always thought it was coming from a speaker."

"I think this studio only opened this year," I tell him as we make our way to the stairs. "That's why I started spending time at the mall."

"That was you playing, right?" he asks.

I nod.

"Wow."

I shrug, but I'm secretly pleased he seems impressed by that.

"Ruby! Ruby! Come here!" Mrs. Sui is at the door of the Senior Centre. She gestures at me frantically, looking upset. Mrs. Wang is there too, frowning, sitting on the seat of her four-wheeled walker. Shen and I hurry over, worried someone has gotten hurt. The two of them are bundled up, like they're ready to go outside. Mrs. Wang wears a puffy red vest, and Mrs. Sui has on a thick wool jacket, along with a black bucket hat that has red flowers embroidered over the front.

"姑婆, shouldn't the volunteers be taking you back to the manor?" Shen asks.

"We were waiting for them," Mrs. Sui says. "But Mrs. Wang wanted to ask the gods a question."

I notice then Mrs. Wang's hands are cupped around something.

"I only wanted to ask for their blessings for Ruby," Mrs. Wang says, opening her hands anxiously. She's holding what looks like two crescent-shaped pieces made from wood, painted red. "Look."

She holds the wood pieces in her hands and brings them up to her forehead, eyes closed as she murmurs. A prayer? A request? Then she shakes them in between her hands, like she's rolling die. Once, twice, three times, before letting the pieces fall to the floor below. They land with a clatter, the "raised" portion of the pieces face up, with the flat sides on the floor. Mrs. Wang leans over to scoop them up and deposits them in her hands again. She lets go, and the pieces land again with the flat side down. Shen's expression is stony now instead of curious, and when the pieces fall a third time, the exact same way . . . he frowns at the pieces on the floor as if they've personally wronged him.

"Over and over again," Mrs. Sui mutters. "So many times in a row."

"What does it mean?" I ask, not wanting to interrupt their ritual, not knowing why the three of them are suddenly so gloomy. Like something precious has fallen and shattered in front of them on the ground, irrevocably broken.

"It's bad." Mrs. Wang shakes her head now. "Really, really bad.

"土地公 is giving us a warning," she says, somber, calling out the god by name. The Earth God, the protector of the people. A guardian in his own right, I suppose. They all turn to look at the shrine that's inside the Senior Centre. They're supposed to bring in good fortune to businesses, watching over the owners and the patrons. When I was little, I always thought these tiny houses were adorable.

Shen takes the pieces from the older woman's hand and shows them to me.

"When we ask questions to the gods, they answer through these." He turns the pieces so that the raised and curved side faces up. "This is the yin side, and the other is the yang."

"When you have both yin sides up, it means the gods say 'no' or 'disagree' or . . ." He hesitates then, like he knows I won't like what he will say next.

"大凶!" Mrs. Sui declares, a phrase I do not recognize, shaking her head slowly again. I look to Shen for an explanation.

"It means 'great misfortune,'" he sighs.

"Are you ready to go?" Two of the staff members of the manor approach us, having come up the stairs, wearing matching reflective vests. Mrs. Wang purses her mouth. They fall quiet, not wanting to discuss the gods in front of them.

"I'm serious, A'Shen!" Mrs. Sui tsks. "You take care of her!"

Shen nods. "I'm trying, 姑婆." We watch as Mrs. Sui is wheeled away, Mrs. Wang assisted by the other volunteer. She gives me one more worried look over her shoulder before they turn down the hall that will take them to the elevator.

"Let's go," Shen says, shoving his hands into his pockets, looking decidedly unhappy.

"Wait, you're not going to talk to me about this? About what it means?" I ask.

"Let's go for a drive. I think better when I'm driving." He pulls out his keys. I follow him, certain that whatever he shares with me won't be anything good. Again.

TWENTY-SEVEN

夜驚

(Night Terrors)

We descend down into the depths of the parkade below the mall. He tosses his stuff into the back seat, and gestures for my backpack too. When he slides into the driver's seat beside me, his hair lifts a bit from static. I resist the urge to reach out and smooth it down.

Even though this is the second time I've been in his car, this is the first time I wish it could be a more...momentous occasion. Like the songs and the books tell you, when you finally get to go for a ride with a crush. When you're nervously expecting how the date will go, if he'll finally tell you how he feels. But he's not a guy that I'm on a date with. He's just a boy who had the misfortune of being there when I was attacked.

Shen turns on the car and it starts blasting loud rock music, but instead of lyrics in English, the vocals are in Taiwanese.

"Sorry," he apologizes, and turns it down.

"I kind of like it," I tell him. "Don't turn it off."

"Really?" He hesitates, then turns it back up.

"My dad loves Wu Bai," I explain. The Taiwanese rock star was popular in the nineties when Baba was a teenager, and his CDs were the cherished ones he brought with him to Canada. He's continued to listen to his music since. This song has a similar style.

The drums kick in when we leave the parkade, then it goes to a funny sort of tune that makes me chuckle. We listen to the song for a bit, but then it's done, and I can't put it off any longer.

"Should we be worried about what Mrs. Sui said?" I ask. "The 'great misfortune'?"

"I wouldn't be too worried," he says. He doesn't appear as bothered by it as I am. "The gods can be cryptic in their responses. The interpretation is an art."

"It looked ominous to me," I say, not entirely convinced.

"It means you were right to seek help. Shu-Ling can manage it." Shadows and light cut his face from the buildings going by as the car slides up the ramp and then down the street. It's raining again, typical of Vancouver weather. The wipers swish softly across the glass.

"You said that Shu-Ling would be able to explain it, but she didn't . . . not really," I say, my head still full of questions.

"Oh yeah." He coughs. "Um . . . She is *very* good at what she does. You don't have to worry about that. But she's not what people expect in that sort of role, typically. Most people come around in time."

"Not that they have much of a choice." The words slip out. He's too easy to talk to.

Shen snorts. "Yeah, that's true."

"How did your sister get into this . . . job anyway?" I watch the lights of downtown go by, the city lit up and glittering in the night.

"It's a family calling," he says. "My parents were both responsible for the temple, together. After they passed, the responsibility went to Shu-Ling, as the oldest."

I feel that pinch inside my chest again, the reminder of his loss.

"They died two years ago, when Shu-Ling was nineteen and I was fif-teen." He smirks to himself. "I'm sure she didn't ask to be saddled with a little shithead like me, but she transferred back here, took care of me. I could have gone to one of my uncles, but I'm glad she came back for me."

"It must have been hard," I murmur.

"We survived, but it took Shu-Ling a while to accept her role." He turns the car smoothly as we pass over the bridge that takes us over the water, and then we're turning into a parking lot that overlooks the marina. The water sparkles in the distance, dancing with the lights above. He turns off the engine but leaves the heat on. It hums a little in the background while we talk.

"Shu-Ling's finishing her degree during the day. Does her temple duties in the evenings," he tells me, arms folded over his chest. "My parents had the town house, the bubble tea shop, and those who were in our community, who my parents have helped before . . . They came together and helped us."

"How exactly does it . . . work? Shu-Ling's role?" I ask.

"The guardians are gods. They cannot walk among the living. Shu-Ling talks to them and conveys their messages through visions and dreams. Sometimes, they even speak through her."

That deep, authoritative voice that she spoke with during the ritual. I shudder at the thought.

"How do you fit into all of this then?" I wonder. "It seems like you're part of the temple too."

"I help Shu-Ling with whatever she needs. Whether it's preparing her tools, or drawing her talismans," he says.

"You draw the talismans?" I don't know why that surprises me, know-ing his artistic abilities.

"Shu-Ling is terrible at drawing." He grins, then is serious again. "She's the only one who is capable of infusing the talismans with real power, but because of her training with the guardians, she's taught me a few things too. I can mark unruly spirits for the wardens to find, and in turn, they gave me this to protect me." He gestures to his arm.

"Why are there so many of them out there still, if the wardens are bringing them to where they should be?" I ask.

"They try to wait for them to pass on," he says. "Seven days is a typical length of time, but some spirits linger for longer than that. Most of them need time to process and let go, and they're usually not difficult to find, because they're tethered."

"Unless someone frees them," I say.

"There are some spirits that draw power from the darker forces that still linger in the world of the living. They somehow sever that bond, or convince someone to break it for them," he explains. "These spirits usually grow more malevolent the longer they are left unchecked."

My mind is a jumble of knowledge, new terms and strange beliefs. I take a deep breath and let it out, allow the weight of all that he told me to sink in.

"Am I talking too much?" He runs his hand through his hair, brushing strands out of his eyes. "I can stop."

"No, no." I shake my head. "I want to know. I want to learn."

"There will be some form of retaliation when they realize what happened. You'll have to be careful."

"I don't even know who *they* are," I mutter, and he puts his hand on my arm. I can feel the warmth of his grasp through my sleeve. He's so . . . close.

"I know sometimes what Shu-Ling says doesn't make sense, but there's always a reason why. I—" His voice catches, and I'm suddenly super aware of the sound of my heart beating too quickly in my chest. "I don't want you to get hurt, okay?"

I look up and meet his eyes. He looks worried. Like he genuinely cares. "Okay," I say softly in return when I see how serious he is.

Shen glances at the clock then and clears his throat. "Looks like our time is up. I better get you home."

We drive home with the Taiwanese music playing in the background, each of us lost to our own thoughts. I have him drop me off a block away so my parents won't catch a glimpse of him. The horror of me being in the same car as a boy.

"If you need anything, let me know?" he reminds me again through the lowered window. I nod, give him a thumbs-up. He waves and then drives away into the night.

I catch movement down the street, in my peripheral vision. I have the feeling of being watched, as if someone is peering at me from behind a bush. But when I look closer, it's just the wind blowing through the leaves. I'm growing more paranoid by the day.

I turn my face up to the light rain. It feels cool on my skin. Shen is different, not what I expected. And neither is Shu-Ling, or Delia, but it feels like my world is changing, just like Delia said. My world *is* expanding— for good or for bad, I'm learning all the same. I shove my hands into my pockets to keep them warm and make my way home.

That night, I've almost drifted off when I hear the door creak open, letting in a bit of light from the hallway.

"Ruby?" Ma whispers. "I cut some fruit. Are you hungry?"

I pretend to be asleep, lying as still as possible. She tiptoes in and checks on me with a brief touch of the back of her hand to my forehead. For a moment, I imagine rolling over and grabbing her arm. Telling her everything.

I've been so worried about Tina.

I think something awful is about to happen.

But the moment passes when she pulls the blanket over me, covering me up better, and leaves, shutting the door behind her with a click of finality. I'm left alone again, with only Beethoven for company. The bad dreams and sneaking around have exerted a toll, and I fall asleep somewhere around the third movement of another one of his sonatas, the music still trailing from my headphones.

A sound startles me awake from the midst of my dreaming. The room is too hot, the air stuffy and uncomfortable. Something hard presses against my face, leaving an indentation in my skin. I touch it and realize I fell asleep with the headphones still on my head, muffling the sounds from the rest of the house. *What woke me up, then?* I pull my headphones off and roll over.

A face looms out of the darkness. A pale smear with no discernible features, floating in the dark without a body. Its mouth moves above me, a void that could stretch and envelop me inside its widening chasm. One that could swallow me whole.

I scream and push it away from me, throw myself sideways onto my bedroom floor. I scrabble backward like a crab, reaching up on my desk for my glasses, the other hand raised to protect myself from whatever is coming for me in the dark. The room comes into focus as my eyes adjust, and the floating head turns into my brother's slight form.

"Denny?" I manage to croak out, my throat dry and mouth parched from being open when I was asleep.

He stands there, not moving. His face still slack and expressionless. His eyes gleam, pinpoints in the dark; they gaze somewhere in my direction, vacant and unseeing. In his hands there are pieces of yellow paper, ripped apart into tiny shreds.

"Why did you do that?" I look over at my door, half-open, and see that the calendar has been pulled off too. Tossed to the other side of the room. Denny wasn't tall enough to reach where I taped the talisman, and he carried his stool over from the bathroom so that he was able to reach it.

Denny doesn't respond. I grab him by the arm, frightened by the way he is so silent. Usually he talks your ear off, always getting into something, forever playful. I carefully extract the pieces of the talisman from his hands, placing them into my desk drawer, picking up the few stragglers that have fallen to the floor. Somehow he knew the talisman was there, that I hid it behind the calendar, and someone sent him to remove it, knowing that it protects me from anything that wants to enter this way. From whatever it is that lives on the other side of my wall.

I pick up Denny and put him on the bed, tucking the blankets around us. My door has no lock—none of ours do—so I put my chair behind it, so that if it opens in the middle of the night, I'll be able to hear.

He lies there next to me, still. His eyes slowly close, but I stay wide-awake, keeping watch for any intruders, until my alarm goes off.

TWENTY-EIGHT

蔡阿嬸

(Mrs. Tsai)

In the morning, I resist the urge to run into Tina's room to shake her, to tell her to stop what she's doing to our brother, what she's doing to herself.... I have Shu-Ling's warning in mind: *Be patient.* Tina stays home because she's still not feeling well, and I catch a ride with Ma. She's in a particular mood this morning, face pinched as she hurries Denny to the car. He's dawdling as always, distracted by something in the alley. She sharply calls out to him to get in.

Denny puts on his headphones to listen to music, and that gives me a chance to talk to my mother. Without the risk of Tina being close by, overhearing my conversation, and then accusing me yet again of sticking my nose in where I don't belong.

"Ma, does Tina seem...different to you?" I ask, broaching the topic tentatively, wondering what she's noticed lately. Or if she's noticed anything at all.

"Different? You mean her getting sick?"

"No..." Then I decide to come out and say it. "Different, like not herself. Like she's changed." The noises in the middle of the night. The weird things turning up in Tina's room. The chanting that plays nonstop from her computer.

"Not herself?" Ma huffs as she turns her head to check for traffic coming behind us before changing lanes. She's always been a nervous driver, so I don't know why I thought it was a good idea to talk about this with her right now. I regret it. "The two of you always cause my blood pressure to go up. Constantly trying my patience. Your Auntie Tseng always warned me. Teenage girls, they're going to cause you so much grief, and I tell her all the time—my girls are good girls, they listen, they do their work, but now I'm not so sure."

I sigh. Sometimes when I talk to my parents, it reminds me again that they don't quite understand what I'm saying. We're both speaking English, and yet, there's a gulf between us, a distance that is as far as the ocean between here and Taiwan.

"Maybe I should have signed you up for those Taiwanese youth activities, instead of just Chinese school," Ma continues, still talking away, oblivious to how I've turned away from her. "I wanted to make sure you fit in, learn Canadian culture, but look what happens now! You and Tina become so westernized, distracted by all these ideas rotting your brain."

"We're going to be late, Ma," I say as we pull into the school parking lot. I hurry out the door, and it shuts behind us with finality.

It looks like I'm still on my own.

In the afternoon, even though I could have gone home with Ma and Denny, I retreat to the library during our extended essay period. I ask the librarian, Ms. Yang, for materials we have in our small library on

Vancouver's Chinatown. She is happy to oblige but says that I would have more luck in the public library or even the UBC library, which has more academic texts. She tells me about an exhibit there that tracks the entrance of Chinese immigrants into Canada in the 1880s, capturing it all with documents and photographs. The first group of immigrants came here as laborers to work on building the railroads all the way across Canada or were miners and part of the Gold Rush, then they settled to try and make a life here afterward, despite the policies that restricted where they could work and what sort of businesses they could own. The groups of immigrants that came in later waves had different restrictions placed upon their entry. They had to prove they had enough funds to start up their own businesses or enough money to pay for higher education.

My parents brought with them their own complicated feelings about China, which they passed on to me—they recognize we are ethnically Chinese, and yet with our own distinct Taiwanese identities from my ancestors moving to Taiwan many, many generations ago. Though the current conflict seems very far away.

I don't know if it was ever in their plans to stay in Canada after they came here for university. I don't think I've ever asked. I realize, the sad thing is, I spend all this time thinking about how everyone I encounter has their own stories and their own histories, but what do I really know about my own history? About my parents' history? They never shared that with us. And we never asked.

I take my time walking home instead of taking the bus, telling myself it's because I want to stretch my legs, and not admitting it's really because I don't want to face Tina. When I'm finally home, I take off my shoes at the door and then stop. Something's different. The lights are on in the dining room—the room where our piano lives, and where the lights are *never* on unless I'm practicing.

We have guests over. All their faces turn to me when I walk past them in the hallway.

"Come here, Ruby," Ma calls out, and I pad over in my socks. "You remember Mrs. Tsai?" she says. "She's here for a visit."

"Hello, Auntie." I duck my head.

"好乖." Mrs. Tsai nods at me, smiling, praising me with a term that is more for obedient children than teenagers. But I force myself to smile back.

"Ma, what's happening?" Tina appears on the stairs. She looks as confused as I feel.

"Ah, Tina, Mrs. Tsai is here." Ma waves her down. "Come and say hello."

"How are you feeling, Tina? Your parents tell me you're not feeling well today," Mrs. Tsai says warmly, looking up at her.

"Director Tsai!" Tina exclaims, suddenly conscious of her pajamas. "Just a moment please, let me get changed." She turns and runs up the stairs.

"While we wait for her, Mrs. Tsai was kind enough to bring us some pastries," Ma tells me. "Ruby, could you bring some plates from the kitchen?"

I go into the kitchen and hesitate when I open the cupboard: the regular white Corelle plates with the dark blue flower borders, or the special pale blue ceramic plates for guests? I can hear the murmur of their voices through the wall, but I can't distinguish their words. I pull down the stack of pretty plates, figuring I can't go wrong with that.

"Also a knife, Ruby!" Ma calls out. "And some forks too."

I bring a handful of the small dessert forks and set them down on the dining room table.

The box of pastries has a festive design on them, red and gold. There are six of them inside, individually wrapped. Ma has already taken one out and unwraps it, the plastic crinkling, and slides it out onto one of the plates. It's golden and round, flaking around the edges, about the size of my palm.

"This bakery is in Richmond; they have the best wife cakes. The ones with the black sesame on top are filled with black sesame and winter melon," Mrs. Tsai says. "The ones with black and white sesame on top are filled with red bean and winter melon."

"Then we'll have to try both." Ma smiles, taking out the other flavor as well and cutting them into quarters.

"Wife cake?" I ask, not sure if I've tried this before.

"老婆餅," Baba says. "You've had them before. We usually call them sweetheart pastries. Your uncle brings them all the time from Taichung." Uncle David is Ma's brother, our only real "uncle" and the youngest out of all of our relatives of our parents' generation. Tina loves him because he has a tendency to buy us tons of sweets when we visit.

"None for me, thank you, but I will take more tea." Mrs. Tsai picks up her cup. "This is delicious."

Baba's face lights up, because he always complains that no one has his palate and appreciation for tea. He eagerly pours her another cup. "It's a red oolong...from Taiwan, of course. Can you taste the honey finish?"

Mrs. Tsai nods, smiles as she takes another sip. The steam fogs her glasses, obscuring her eyes, giving her a vaguely sinister air. Ma gives me a plate and tells me to go give it to Denny, and I get up from the table eagerly. Tina runs down the stairs and past me in the hallway, dressed in T-shirt and jeans, her hair braided. Denny's sitting in the den at his Lego table, and he cheers when he notices me come over. He shoves one of the pieces into his mouth and then chews with his mouth wide open.

"Gross." I make a face. "Can you eat with your mouth closed?" Denny puts his hand in front of his mouth and giggles. Even though I want to sit there with my little brother in the den and play with Legos, I know I'm expected to return to the dining room table.

"Like I was saying," I hear Mrs. Tsai say when I return, "the team at Soulful Heart believes in Tina's potential. We think she's very talented, Mr. and Mrs. Chen. She shows a great aptitude for dance. She understands the movements of her body, she exhibits dedication and focus, but most importantly—she is passionate about it. That is something you cannot teach."

My stomach drops. Here it is. Tina's secret finally revealed.

"Tina is smart." Ma looks unimpressed. I can tell from the way the side of her cheek twitches that she's holding back her anger to save face in front of Mrs. Tsai. "She does not have much time for other activities."

I can't see Tina's face, since her head is hanging low, like she wishes she could sink into the earth and disappear.

"I understand," Mrs. Tsai says smoothly. "You've been told that the best path to getting into a good university is through Westview, and padding up the résumé with activities like music, volunteering. But we all know children like that. They're all pushed to excel the same way, and now none of them stand out.

"Dance though." Mrs. Tsai leans in, hands together, focused. She looks at Ma and then at Baba, acknowledging them in turn. "Soulful Heart does not perform just any type of dance. We have a lion-and-dragon dance troupe. We have Classical Chinese, we have Modern Interpretative, but we always add cultural elements. We incorporate the beauty of our culture, acknowledge our traditions, remember our history." Her voice is earnest, just like a teacher's. She's a Person of Authority, so that makes my parents more likely to listen to anything she has to say.

If Mrs. Tsai isn't able to convince my parents to let Tina dance, then no one will be able to.

TWENTY-NINE

同鄉會

(The Formosa Friendship Association)

Mrs. Tsai came prepared, because she reaches down into her bag and pulls out a folder. She places a few glossy sheets on the table, lays them out for everyone to see.

These are pamphlets, with professional photos of dancers as their backgrounds, done artistically, just like the photos the studio has hanging up on their walls. Girls in sparkling sequin costumes, makeup, floating across the stage with their arms outstretched. In one picture, a girl is photographed up close, her hands framing her face, her gaze turned skyward. Stars done in silver glitter trail from the corner of her eyes, and stars dangle from her fingers like constellations. *The Sky Maidens*, the caption beneath says. On another one, a girl floats downward from the ceiling, suspended by a thin wire. Red wispy gauze surrounds her like fire. In her hands she holds two white fans, one above her head, one at her hip. Her pose is strong, fierce, like these fans are capable of cutting you. She looks like a warrior out of some sort of wuxia epic. The type that Ma likes to watch with assassins and swordplay and tragic romances.

All the photographs are dazzling to the eye. Baba picks one up where a row of young girls stand, their graceful necks like swans, curved to one side. They all beam at the camera, like they're ready to burst from being filled with happiness.

"This looks expensive," Baba says, tone dismissive. "All the costumes, the time spent practicing." He shakes his head slowly.

Tina looks up, mouth opening in an O, about to protest, but Mrs. Tsai places her hand on hers. Silencing her.

"We completely understand the worries that parents have about the time and monetary commitment of dance, and that's why we have sponsors in the community who are eager to support the next generation," she says, unfazed.

Mrs. Tsai raises her hand and begins ticking off points. "We also have a carpool list, parents who are willing to take dancers from Westview to Chinatown and then drop them off back home. We have fundraisers where you can contribute time to gain points to reduce some of the fees for the costumes or the recitals."

"I don't know...." Ma says, exchanging glances with Baba, more uncertain.

"Here is a list of our alumni, many of the names you may recognize from our community." Mrs. Tsai pulls out even more pamphlets. This time of smiling young people, dressed in outfits related to their professions.

"We ensure our students are taken care of. We have many older dancers who are still local, who are attending UBC or Simon Fraser, and they are always willing to set up coffee meets to talk about university applications or career goals." Mrs. Tsai pushes up her glasses, still smiling. It's a practiced, well-rehearsed speech. I can see why she's the director. She's probably made this same pitch to hundreds of other families, convinced parents to let their children join the dance academy.

"Stanford?" Baba leans forward, one of the quotes catching his eye, interested now. Always tempted by the lure of prestigious universities or the Ivy League. That promising future.

"Yes, Stanford." Mrs. Tsai has another list prepared, knowing her hooks are in now. "Stanford, Harvard. My daughter, Hope, she's been at Yale now for two years, and I have it on very good authority that dance enriched her portfolio, made her stand out among the rest." Ma's eyes widen at this, even though I know she's holding back, trying to appear like that doesn't tempt her as much as it does.

"What do you think?" Baba mutters to Ma.

"One more thing that I need to mention before you make your decision." Mrs. Tsai leans in and goes for the kill. "I talked about scholarships before. We have one that is sponsored by the Formosa Friendship Association that is specifically for Taiwanese Canadian dancers. I think Tina would be perfect for this, and I'd like to put her name—"

There's a clatter. I dropped my fork on the table. Having automatically reacted to the mention of that association again.

"Sorry," I whisper when their eyes all turn to me.

Mrs. Tsai switches to Mandarin then; some of the phrases are familiar to me, while others go by too quickly for me to track. But Ma nods, seemingly in agreement, then chuckles at the next thing Mrs. Tsai says. They're catching up, sharing information about the few friends they have in common. Vancouver is a big place, but the Taiwanese community is small, and though we've never been officially part of those groups, my parents' social circles definitely overlap with Mrs. Tsai's.

In the end, Ma and Baba agree to an invitation offered by Mrs. Tsai:

tickets for all of us to attend one of their upcoming recitals in November. To see one of the performances for ourselves.

They're all smiling. Tina looks pleased, all of it falling into place, just like she said. I keep the smile on my face even though inside, I'm trembling. I hold Denny back as we all crowd around the door to say goodbye. An example of a nice Taiwanese family.

There's nothing to see here, nothing to hide.

Denny is immediately sent upstairs to brush his teeth so that he will be out of the way when the eruption finally comes.

"What is she talking about, Tina?" Ma's wrath crashes down upon us like thunder before Mrs. Tsai's headlights even leave our street. She hates any sort of surprise, especially when it comes to people within the community. The importance of keeping face. "How long have you been doing this 'dance'?" She says that word like it's something to be ashamed of.

"I..." Tina lowers her head. "I'm sorry, Ma. There is no excuse."

This isn't her! I want to shout at her, at our parents. When has Tina ever looked down instead of snapping back? When has she ever shown regret for something she's done? She's always forged forward, strained against the rules and restrictions they bind her with. Always acted first and then dealt with the consequences later.

"After everything we've done. So many years your father and me worked hard, made sure you got into the best school, made sure you are given all the opportunities," Ma scolds. "Moving across the world. For you. For you and your sister and your brother. This is what you do. This is how you *disappoint* us." A speech that would have cut me to pieces, reduced me to tears. I brace myself for the shouting that should soon follow. My sister will jut out her chin and raise her voice, say something that will cause our mother to raise her voice in turn.

"I know I shouldn't have done it," Tina says, shrinking, appearing like the very picture of apology. "I didn't mean to keep it from you."

"What?" Ma looks taken aback, unsure of how to react when she was initially expecting a fight. Tina should already be stomping her way toward the stairs right now. Ma would warn her not to slam the door, and the sound of the door slamming would shake the whole house.

"I knew it was wrong, so that's why I asked Mrs. Tsai to come to our house to talk with you," Tina continues, in that quiet way that sends another ripple of discomfort through me. "She said that she will try to help in any way she can."

"How would dance help you more than piano?" Baba finally speaks up. I can sense the underlying current of frustration in his voice, a slight vibrato. "How would standing around flailing your arms and legs on the stage contribute to anything? Remember what I always tell you? 頭腦簡單，四肢發達!" It's a phrase that Baba loves to throw around. There's an equivalent phrase in English too; I looked it up. *All brawn, no brains.* They believe that anything that takes time away from studying is a distraction.

"Look though!" Tina points at one of the pamphlets left on the table. A smiling girl, dressed in a striped white blouse and a gray pencil skirt, holding a clipboard. Behind her "professional" look, there's a photo of her dressed in traditional hanfu, complete with flowing sleeves adorned with embroidery, her hair pinned up with gold pins. She poses elegantly with a fan dangling from her fingers, expression serene. "This is Mrs. Tsai's daughter, Hope. She's Taiwanese, just like us. She's going to be at that performance next month. You can go and meet her and talk to her. She's the one that got into Yale. Neuroscience!"

"Let me see," I demand, forcing myself to look. I don't know why I never connected the dots. Mrs. Tsai. *Hope* Wu. I never made that connection because Mrs. Tsai still has her maiden name. This is the Hope who attended Westview. Under her photo there is a caption: *Soulful Heart changed my life! They helped me Dream Big. With their assistance, I fulfilled all of my dreams, with much more to come!* It all makes sense. Yale. Dance. Dreams. Wishes. This is Delia's Hope.

"You know something about this?" Ma's attention turns to me then, laser sharp, and I immediately regret throwing myself into the fray. I should have just stayed back and let them sort it out.

"I . . . I . . ." I can't find the words to say everything that I want to say.

Tina jumps in. "She was only trying to help. She didn't mean to hide it from you." She defends me in a way that would set off Ma's ire, a redirection of her anger. Since I'm the one who should make sure my little sister is doing what she is supposed to.

"Ruby." It's my name, but filled with the weight of all their expectations.

"I know lying is bad, but she was protecting me." With every word, Tina buries me deeper.

"Lying! Both of you!" That sets off Baba's ire as well. He hates lying, sees it as a shortcut, sometimes even worse than the original transgression.

"We should be honest." Tina stands up straighter, her eyes gleaming with an understanding of what she is doing. I stand there and struggle with the urge to slap my hand over her mouth before she makes it worse, and yet I know that if I do it I will look even more guilty. "She said that she could help me with my shifts at the manor, said that I should use my math-tutoring fee for dance instead until I could get a scholarship." She looks so wide-eyed, innocent, like she didn't know what she was doing, until I led her astray.

My mouth drops open.

"I didn't—" I try to protest, but it's too late.

"閉嘴!" Baba's hand slaps the table. His order makes me obey, snapping my mouth shut. "You...you..." He points his finger in my direction. He's so furious he can't even get the words out. Tina, or whatever is inside Tina, has them twisted around her little finger.

"What an absolute disappointment." Baba shakes his head. Huffing. "You're better than this. Both of you." The sinking feeling drags me down, until I feel about an inch high. Ma places a hand on his shoulder, a subtle reminder for him to calm.

"The two of you go up and get ready for bed," Ma says firmly. "In the morning we'll talk. About all of this. After your Baba and me decide what we will do with you."

Ma's anger is the initial strike of the match, a brief flash of orange flame before it quickly burns out, her frustration easily soothed by a sharp word, a swift reprimand. Baba's anger is slow and simmering, then it suddenly flares up and burns everything down into ash. His fury doesn't peak very often, but when it does, it's best to get out of the way.

Tina runs up the stairs, her feet pounding the wood. I grab my backpack from the foyer first, all my thoughts jangling loudly and competing with each other in my head. I don't want to look at her. Anger. Disgust. Shame. Guilt. All of it vying for space inside me. When I finally make it to the landing, I see Tina standing beside Denny in our shared bathroom, whispering something to him. They make faces in the mirror. Denny growls. I don't like the sight of his little face contorting into something ugly and ferocious. I don't like how she meets my eyes in the reflection... and smiles smugly, like she's already won.

THIRTY

交替

(The Binding)

I want to keep Tina away from Denny. To protect him. I'm afraid of her and whatever she is preparing for.

"Did you remember to floss, Denny? I'll help you." I force my way into that tiny bathroom, squeezing in between Tina and Denny. My little brother groans but hands me his floss. Tina has moved out of the way and stands in the hallway, watching me through the mirror again.

"You should go before Ma comes up to check on us," I tell her, pulling floss out of the spool.

"Whatever you're planning," she says to me, coldly amused, "it won't be enough."

I say nothing, bending down instead to give the floss to Denny so she can't see my face in the mirror any longer. I choke down everything that I want to say to her. *Be patient*, I remind myself. If she knows what I'm up to, there's a chance she might be able to stop me. I won't let her.

"What?" Denny turns his head, but with his fingers in his mouth, it comes out garbled. I pretend to be extremely interested in pointing out bits of sesame between his teeth. By the time I straighten up, the hallway is empty, and her door is shut.

"Brush your teeth really good," I warn him. "Or else Baba will come up and check on you."

He nods his head quickly, agreeable to avoiding Baba's lectures on the health of his teeth. How easy it must be to be eight years old, with the faith that our parents know everything there is to know about the world. That they are our protectors, the definitive boundary between us and the scary world outside. But he doesn't know the scary thing isn't out there. It's here. Inside the house.

My night is once again broken into slivers, restless dreams. I don't know if it's because of the loss of that talisman or everything that's happened today. I keep thinking there are shadows under my door, cast by figures that scurry back and forth, their feet too small to be human. I dream of eyes that watch me through the small gaps alongside the door and underneath, red and moist, spinning in their sockets.

Breakfast is a terse affair, with Baba sent up to wrangle Denny into getting ready, while the two of us face Ma across the table. Like we are sitting before the judge, awaiting the verdict. She lays out the rules for us and makes it clear there is no room for disagreement or negotiation.

"Since the next season of dance lessons has been paid up, you will attend those lessons until January," Ma says to Tina. "I have already confirmed with Mr. Lee that your study sessions are genuine, so at least you did not lie about that. Mr. Lee has offered to drop you off at our house after study group on Tuesdays and Wednesdays." Tina's lower lip juts out in a pout, slowly sinking into her chair after every restriction.

"And you…" Our mother's gaze slides to me. "Since Melody also attends dance classes Thursday evenings, Mr. Lee has kindly offered to take both of you home as well. No loitering, no lingering, no stopping *anywhere* along the way. Do you hear me?"

I nod.

"Do you both hear me?"

"Yes, Ma," we murmur. Already knowing what will be at risk if we do not. Our already-limited freedoms narrowing. The restrictions that we have accepted as a matter of course as kids growing up in a Taiwanese household. *No sleepovers. No parties. No friends who are too wild, too out-spoken. No friends who have bad grades. No friends who are bad influences. No boys, not as friends, and especially not as boyfriends. No. No. No.*

When Ma gets up to get ready to take us to school, Tina lets out a breath beside me in a whoosh. I can't even look at her. A part of me is still reeling from what she told them last night. She lied so that she could keep dancing, made sure that I was involved in her deception, so that if our ship sinks then she will drag me down with her. She tries to talk to me, but I get as far away from her as possible. Too afraid the next words that come out of my mouth will be something I'll regret.

By the time we arrive at school, I've calmed down a little. It feels better now that one of Tina's secrets is revealed. If I'm watching her, then I have an excuse, that I'm "keeping an eye on her," like our parents asked us to. I never paid much attention before, but I'm starting to recognize some of the dancers from Soulful Heart. It doesn't help that there seems to be an aura about them. Girls who are confident in their skin, confident with the way attention follows them, as if they are surrounded by a shining circle.

A week passes, then two, as we adjust to the new routine. We exist in a weird space, like we're trapped in the stillness of a snow globe, only waiting for one shake before we're tumbling through a violent blizzard.

Tina keeps her promises to our parents, and I do too . . . sort of. Even though I stumbled into my research topic, I find myself interested in what it's unearthed. I talk to Delia and Shen on a regular basis, sometimes in the group chat, sometimes separately.

I see Tina flit in the midst of their crowd, laughing and chatting. More at ease with her friends than she has ever been at home. Tina once told me our parents don't care if we're happy or not. I scoffed at that before. At that pessimism. Our parents love us; they want what's best for us. We are the reason they stayed in Canada, because they want that better future for us. But then I think back to all the folk tales they taught us in Chinese school: students who kept reading through a crack in the wall by moonlight, scholars who burned themselves with a candle to stay awake so they could continue to study, people who kept grueling schedules to pass the final exams. In comparison, we're always told we have it easy, even as our parents whittle away everything that doesn't fit their mold of what a perfect daughter should be, no matter how much it hurts us to have part of ourselves cut away. They tell us it's for the best.

There's a bang on the locker next to me, startling me out of my contemplations. It's three of Tina's friends, evident by their matching high ponytails.

"Stop following her," one of the girls say to me accusingly. She's taller than me, which, to be honest, is not a huge feat since I'm only five foot four. The other two stand behind her, arms folded, trying to look intimidating. But it's the intensity of this girl standing before me, dedicated to protecting Tina from *me*, that startles a laugh out of my mouth.

"I'm her sister," I tell her. "What do you think I'm going to do to her?"

That seems to confuse them. Whether it's me readily admitting to following her, or if they thought by sheer numbers they would be able to intimidate me to back away. Maybe I would have before I knew all the things I've learned the past few weeks. About what waits for us after death, and how we might remain trapped on this earth, reliving our last, tormented moments if we're unlucky enough to suffer a grisly, gruesome end.

These girls with their pretty faces and their sleek hair and their long limbs. They're the ones who don't quite seem real now. What if some sort of darkness exists behind their eyes too? What if someone else is looking out from those eyes?

"This is ridiculous." I push past them, not caring if I bump into one with my shoulder. She yelps, stepping aside as I make my determined way to Tina. She's at her locker, talking to a guy I don't recognize.

"Excuse me," I interrupt. "Family emergency." I take Tina's arm and pull her away before she can say anything else.

I check the science lab at the end of the hall. It's currently quiet and empty. I push Tina in and shut the door. The lab benches are all cleaned, waiting for the next class to enter. A good place for us to have a private conversation.

"Whatever is going on with you, you're scaring Denny." I drop her arm and face her. "You have to stop. He's having night terrors again."

"What do you mean, 姊姊?" she says sweetly, a mocking lilt to her tone. I don't buy the act. The sudden obedient nature. *Yes, Ma. Yes, Baba.* My sister is bold and funny and dramatic and loud. Not the way she is now.

"It's not worth it, whatever you're doing to yourself," I say, still hoping to talk some sense into her, while pretending I don't know what's going on. "Staying up late at night, practicing for hours and hours. In the end, something is going to give. You can do whatever you want to yourself, but you can't keep Denny up too. Telling stories or making him watch you practice or putting things in his head."

"What is it you think I'm doing?" Her eyes darken as she regards me. "What could I possibly do to him? To that...little...*monkey*?" She licks her lips, knowing that I know what she means. Then she smiles, mouth stretching too wide. The whites slowly seep out of her eyes until they turn into shiny black orbs. Something moves inside them, writhing impossibly. Beside her, the glass doors of a cabinet begin to rattle, at first quietly, then louder and louder, until it is cacophonous. All the beakers and containers within vibrate as well, until they begin to ring with a piercing sound that drills directly into my ears. My hands fly to the side of my head, trying to protect my eardrums from that incessant noise.

The back of the shelves are mirrored, reflecting Tina from different angles: snarling, laughing, screaming.

"You went into my room and you took something from me," she growls, the voice coming from deep within her throat. Her hand flies out and tightens around my arm. She moved so fast, too fast for me to even see. Her hand burns against mine; her skin is so hot, like she's burning up from within.

"Why?" she demands, still in that ringing, terrifying voice. "Who is helping you?"

I try to pull away, but she turns her wrist, forcing my arm up between us. She's impossibly strong, even as I use my other hand to try and push her away, but she doesn't budge.

"Stop it!" I shout, then transition to begging as she keeps up the pressure, to the point where I have to turn with her or risk snapping my arm. "Tina! Please!"

"You want to keep him safe? Your precious, precious brother?" She hisses. "You stay away from us. Otherwise, there is a lot I can do to him.

He might find himself on the roof one day. Maybe he'll even believe he can *fly*."

Her other hand flies to my neck, fingers digging into the tender spots there, the pain reminding me of how fragile my throat is. She means every word. Every threat. Tina loves Denny. Dotes on him, just as much as I do. She would never harm him. Unless... Her grip tightens further, making me gasp.

The light clicks on above us, and immediately, Tina blinks. The black retreats from her eyes, and her expression turns to normal. Her face smooths back into a smile, like slipping on a mask. She's a teenage girl again.

"Something you need, girls?" It's Ms. Lo, the chemistry teacher, looking at us. "What are you doing here, standing in the dark?"

"We were...talking. We're done!" I stumble out of there, my heart beating so fast, my neck still aching.

That is no longer my sister. Whatever is inside her must have taken over completely. Just like Delia warned.

PART 3
THE SHOWDOWN
(Allegro Agitato)

Fantaisie-Impromptu, op. 66 (C-sharp minor)
Frédéric Chopin

THIRTY-ONE

暗 路

(Dark Roads)

I need air. I need to get out of this place. The walls seem to shift and move before me, like they're closing in. I hurry down the hallway, Tina's horrible face looming in my mind, the deep voice ringing in my ear. I think someone calls out my name from a distance, but I ignore them.

I'm almost at a run when I hit the door. It flies open, the impact reverberating through my wrists, and I hurry down the stairs. I stop on the bare patch of grass, realizing it's the courtyard I usually avoid. The pomegranate spirit lies there on the ground. I quicken my pace to walk past him.

"Heh heh heh heh..." I hear him chuckle as I go by, like he's speaking right into my ear. "Not long now..."

I don't know where I'm going, only that I'm not able to stay here any longer. I place my hand on the latch for the gate, and someone puts their hand on my arm.

I do cry out then, high and thin pitched. It's my sister and her friends, coming back to finish what they started. Hands fly to my shoulders, and a worried face comes into view. It's Shen.

"Ruby!" His eyes are wide as he takes in my near-hysterical state. "I've been yelling at you to stop, but you didn't hear me. What happened?"

The adrenaline that kept me going, sent me running, empties out of me in a rush. My knees buckle, and I half collapse against the fence, letting it catch my weight. I try to suck in air, but my breathing comes too fast and shallow. Stars dance in my eyes.

"Breathe....Just breathe....Follow me...." Shen is suddenly right next to me, holding me up, his hand finding mine. I listen to his instructions, feel his breath skimming my cheek, his gaze holding me steady. Keeping me tethered to the ground, even though the rest of me wants to float away. The tingling feeling slowly fades from my hands and feet, until bit by bit, I'm back.

He guides me through the gate and down the sidewalk. He doesn't let me go, even as he finds a bench for us to sit on, and I settle myself on it.

"She..." I gulp, then try again. "She threatened me." I tell him of the darkness that flooded Tina's eyes. Of her threat to throw Denny off our house after luring him up there. I feel myself starting to shake again, my mind unable to control my body.

I don't know if he saw the terror in my eyes or if he sensed that I needed it, but he pulls me close until my head is resting on his shoulder, my cheek pressed against his chest. He wraps his arms around me, strong and steady. I close my eyes and let myself sink in. Focus on the roughness of the fabric against my face. The smell of his jacket, something sharp and a little spicy. He's...safe.

My peace is interrupted by a buzzing noise coming from his jacket, and he slowly pulls away.

"Sorry," he murmurs against my hair as he reaches into his pocket, even though I'm the one who should be sorry, having what I think was a panic attack in front of him.

There's a sudden chill in the air; the wind picks up, blowing my hair across my face. The clouds above us threaten snow. I sit up and try to breathe and settle my racing heart while he answers his phone.

"I'm with her," he says. "Something's happened." He shifts beside me, arm brushing against my shoulder.

"Yeah, I'll ask her." Shen lifts his phone away from his face and looks at me. "Shu-Ling wants to invite you over to our place for dinner tonight. She has an idea and wants to hear what you think. Do you have time?"

I have volunteering tonight. But I think the aunties will understand if I take a break from playing classic songs for them for one night. I nod, and he turns back to the phone.

"She'll be there," he informs Shu-Ling. "Well, text me the list. We'll pick it up on the way. Sure. See you later." He puts the phone back in his pocket, and it's just the two of us together again. Sitting on the bench. A lazy snowflake drifts down and lands on his hair, then another.

Snow in Vancouver usually doesn't start until December. It's early this year. I reach off and brush a snowflake off his hair, absentmindedly. It isn't until I've done it that I realize maybe I shouldn't have. My hand stops midair, and he traps me with his gaze. I should say something, but the silence between us stretches on. I envision myself leaning over, closing the distance between us. Touching my lips to his. My heart beats a little faster, but for a different reason entirely.

But his eyes narrow as he tugs my sleeve down, exposing my wrist. There's redness there, the shadow of a bruise already forming on my skin. Yet another physical mark on me.

"Who did this?" he demands. "Was it her?" He looks upset, more shaken than I've ever seen him.

"It must have happened when she grabbed me," I say, examining my wrist more closely.

"Dammit." He shakes his head. "This shouldn't have happened. We'll tell Shu-Ling tonight, that we need a solution." My heart skips again when he says *we*. I like the sound of it. Like we're doing this together.

"Thank you," I say softly. "I don't know if I ever told you this before, but if I have, I'll say it again. Thank you for helping me."

"Don't thank me yet," he says. "I haven't done anything. The problem hasn't been resolved."

"It's enough that you believe there's a threat. That you're taking me seriously," I say, with as much earnestness as I can muster so he can understand how I feel.

"Of course I believe you!" he says, loud enough that a crow in the tree beside us squawks and flies away with a swift flutter of wings, making both of us jump and then laugh at ourselves. I like seeing that dimple in his cheek again. I like it when he doesn't have to be so serious.

"I . . . I wish we could have met for different reasons," I tell him.

"Ah, um . . ." He scratches his head. "I don't know if our paths would have ever crossed. I don't really meet anyone outside of the Loft or through the temple."

"Right," I sigh. "That makes sense."

"Not that, uh, not that I didn't want to meet you, or anything like that . . ." He stumbles over his words a little. At least he is honest. A part of me cringes, having imagined that he would have wanted to get to know me even if circumstances were different.

"I get it." I hop off the bench, trying to brush away the disappointment. "Well, soon you won't have to babysit me anymore." I hope, anyway. As long as Tina doesn't try to kill me again.

"Wait, Ruby!" He gets to his feet too and catches my arm. "I don't mean it in that way. I mean, I'm not so good with people in general, but you're different. I like spending time with *you*."

He looks so earnest, I can't help but tease him a little. "Well, that makes sense, considering you were raised in a cult."

He grins. "Right, right..." And the tension in the air is gone, just like that. Carried away by the wind. We're okay again.

I check my phone, and third period is already almost over. I should go back for the last period, but I really don't want to.

"What time do we have to get to your place to meet Shu-Ling?" I ask.

"She's already home. She wants us to pick up a few things in Chinatown on the way there, ingredients for dinner."

"Do you want to go now?" I blurt out.

"Don't you have class?" he asks, puzzled.

"My sister almost killed me," I tell him. "Learning about 'the mitochondria, the powerhouse of the cell' is the last thing I want to focus on." The bell rings in the distance. We'll have ten minutes to grab our stuff and leave.

"Sure." He nods. "Meet you back here in ten and we'll go?"

Shen and I walk side by side as we make our way to Chinatown. A few people glance at our uniforms when they walk by, probably wondering why two high schoolers are strolling on the street in the middle of the school day.

There are a few times when I stop, hesitate when I think I've noticed something. An arm coming out of a grate set against the side of a building. A face peering at us from behind glass and then passing all the way through, a floating head leering at us as we hurry by. What Shu-Ling warned me about is frighteningly real. As each day passes, those spirits that linger in our realm are clearer. They seem to notice me too, because I can feel them watching me, even from a distance. That sensation prickling against my skin, a warning.

Shen must sense my discomfort, because he steps closer to me as we keep walking down the street. "You get used to them after a while," he says, keeping his voice low. "They'll try and talk to you, to get your attention, especially once they figure out you can hear them. The best thing to do is to learn to ignore them."

"There . . . there are so many more of them than I expected," I murmur, even though I've seen them before. It's not quite like this.

"After the ritual Shu-Ling performed, you're walking around with a 'Look at Me!' sign on your head, because you're new," he explains. "The ones that have been stuck here for a while . . . they recognize us."

A bearded man dressed in a long, worn jacket and fingerless gloves staggers out from the alley, nearly knocking me over. Shen pulls me back as the man grumbles at me, swinging his arm in my direction. He shakes his fist at both of us when Shen blocks him from reaching me, then shuffles away to jaywalk across the street.

"Stay close," Shen says softly. Another group passes us on the sidewalk, this time a cluster of women with iced drinks in hand, sunglasses perched on their heads. Tourists, I think, with the way they chatter excitedly about their evening plans, oblivious to the people around them. We're forced to step into a small alcove to avoid being trampled. I'm tucked into his side, his arm around my shoulders. I should shrug his arm off, see it as a friendly gesture, but instead I stay here for a moment longer. *I wish we could have met for a different reason.* The thought from earlier resurfaces again, even stronger now. *Would you see me differently then?*

"Sometimes it helps me to be around people, the energy of the living and all," he says in that steady, careful way. As if knowing that I am close to running away or leaning in. "This okay?" He gently squeezes my shoulder.

I nod and then, to hide my nervousness, joke: "Lucky me. Is this the special treatment you give all the girls?"

"Didn't you see all these girls lining up on the street for me?" Shen chuckles, and we start walking again. It takes us a few steps to get our strides to match. "I should be advising you that for the next little bit, you shouldn't be wandering about in too many places with yin energy."

We're back to the serious topic again, and yet with his arm around me, the warmth of his body next to mine . . . I feel calmer, a little less afraid.

"Where are places with yin energy?" I ask.

We turn the corner onto one of the main intersections of Chinatown. It's busier here. A police car goes by, lights flashing. We pass one of the grocery shops, with some of their produce out on tables on the sidewalk, cardboard signs with the prices on them sticking out of each box. Shen looks down at me when we wait to cross the street, eyes still crinkling in the corner with amusement.

"Graveyards, hospitals, and the like." He grins. "I'm guessing you won't usually be wandering those places after dark."

"Graveyard trespasser, that's me." I snort. "I'll keep that in mind."

"若無行暗路, 袂去拄著鬼," he tells me.

"What does that mean? My Taiwanese is really bad."

"I thought you said you speak Taiwanese," he teases, the dimple in his cheek peeking out again.

"How else could I have convinced you to listen?" I give him the voice that I usually reserve for scolding Denny, and his grin deepens.

"My mom used to tell me this all the time." He repeats the phrase again, slower. "Directly translated it means 'If you avoid walking down dark roads, then you won't meet many ghosts.'"

I consider this, still a little confused at how to interpret it.

"It's an old saying. . . ." His brow furrows as he searches for the right words. "If you don't do 虧心事, guilty things, then you'll be free from the burden of your past coming back to bite you."

He pulls me into another alcove, out of the way of all the people crowding the streets, looking to get home after work and school. It's a side entrance to a bookstore, its windows all boarded up.

His expression is serious again. "I can understand why you want to protect your sister and your brother. I want to take care of my sister too, so she can keep us safe. Shu-Ling walks those dark roads on purpose so that the rest of us don't have to."

The noise of the people passing by, the traffic in the street... all of it fades away when his hand slides down my back, pulling me closer, until I'm standing in a circle of his arms. It's not fair for a guy to have lashes so long, to have cheekbones so high, to have a smile that leaves me longing for all the things out of my reach.

"I meant what I said earlier," he murmurs, long lashes skimming his cheeks. "It's different with you. . . ."

I'm about to ask him what he means by that, but he leans over and brushes his lips against mine before I can say another word.

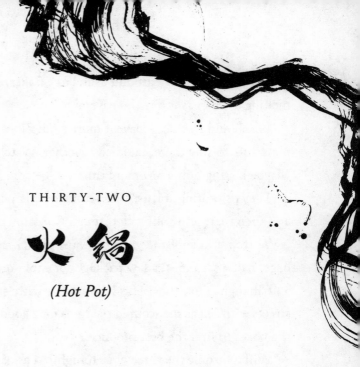

THIRTY-TWO

火锅

(Hot Pot)

The kiss starts out tentative. Just a brief touch of his lips to mine. He pulls back then and looks at me, a question in his eyes. I'm the one who closes the distance between us this time. This kiss deepens, as my hands find their way to his arms, seeking out something solid to hold on to.

I've only kissed two people before. Both times in Gordy Kitchener's basement at his birthday party when we played spin the bottle. Kissing Keith Lam was like kissing a cold fish. He tasted like the root beer he just had a sip of. Kissing Angela Olson left my head spinning and confused. She wore strawberry ChapStick, and her hair tickled my nose after. But this kiss with Shen is something entirely different, achingly sweet....

We finally break apart, and his hand slips into my mine, as naturally as if he's always been there. He brings my hand up and kisses the back of it, like he's checking to make sure I'm real.

"I've wanted to do that for a while," he says, voice feather soft, looking away shyly. I squeeze his hand to let him know that I feel the same way.

The snow comes down around us in large flakes, swirling in the air, but melting as soon as it hits the pavement.

"We should go...?" I leave it more a question, even though a part of me wants to stay there, huddled together. Watching the people go by. Maybe kissing him a few more times, to be sure it was real.

"They're waiting for us." He scrolls on his phone to find the note, and then we resume our trek through Chinatown again, hand in hand.

We stop at one of the grocery stores to pick up a head of napa cabbage, half a taro root, a few packages of enoki mushrooms, both white and Shanghai bok choy. This I'm familiar with: strolling through these streets with Ma as she scoured the signs for a good deal, picking through the boxes to find the best produce.

"Will it be only the three of us tonight?" I ask Shen while we stand in line at the seafood counter. I watch a lobster make its way slowly across the bottom of the tank.

"I think Delia will be there too," he says.

As if we summoned her, a familiar voice calls out, "Hey, you two! Ruby! Shen!" It's Delia, holding a freezer bag under one arm, a backpack slung over the other shoulder.

"說曹操, 曹操就到," Shen comments with amusement at her coincidental appearance. She gives him a one-armed hug and reaches over to give me a hug as well.

"Your hair!" I exclaim. She's dyed it black and cut it into a bob. It doesn't stand out as much as it used to, but it still suits her. She shakes her head and laughs as her bangs fall across her eyes.

"I'm still getting used to it," she says, then her gaze goes down to our joined hands. "I see that other things have changed too." She gives Shen an exaggerated wink.

"Ha ha," Shen says dryly as he turns to pay for our order. Delia quickly grabs me by the arm and ushers me toward the front of the store.

"I knew it!" she whispers excitedly, like this is the best news she's ever heard. "I knew there was something going on between the two of you. I could see the sparks from a mile away. Why didn't you tell me?"

"It . . ." I gesture in the air. "It kinda just happened."

"I love it for you." Delia nods. "You'll be good for him. I can tell."

I feel my face warm a little at her declaration. "I don't even know what we are yet."

"You'll figure it out," she says. I wish I could feel the same confidence, but I'm happy all the same.

Shu-Ling greets us from the kitchen when we enter, rinsing vegetables in the sink. She's dressed in a baggy black T-shirt and gray sweatpants, her hair tied back. Along with the row of rings in her ear, she has jade studs in her earlobes today. She looks like any other college student that I take the bus with every day, still not like my imagined persona of a "head priestess" at all.

I look around, curious what their place looks like, not sure what to even expect. At the far end of the apartment there is a huge wall of windows looking out over the street. In the living room sits a black sofa with cheerful plants on a wood shelf mounted to the wall above it. On the other wall there's a window and a bookshelf crammed full of books, a TV hanging between them above an electric fireplace. I notice we have the same wall calendar on the door. The one with the red-and-gold art of Chinese zodiac animals and the ads for sponsored businesses running along the bottom.

We deposit our bags onto the free space on the kitchen island and begin the process of setting everything up for hot pot. I help wash, rinse, and cut up the napa cabbage into smaller pieces while Delia dumps out an assortment of colorful fish balls, egg and fish dumplings of various shapes and sizes, and tempura sticks, separating them onto different plates.

I can't think of the last time I was with a group of friends like this. Maybe a party at Dawn's house, a while ago. But the invitations from my old friends to hang out have slowed to a stop, probably because I keep telling them I'm too busy, that I don't have the time.

I'm nervous initially, being in their apartment for the first time. If Shu-Ling will start grilling me with more questions, or they will launch into uncomfortable revelations about what's expected of me soon. Like I would have to perform animal sacrifices or chop off my foot to save my sister. All sorts of wild speculation flies through my head, but after a few minutes, it feels like I'm visiting a cousin's house instead.

I find out Shu-Ling is in the last year of her pharmacy degree, that the three of them like playing badminton together on the weekends, and she has lots of gossip on the teachers at Westview. Her humor is sarcastic and witty; it definitely runs in the family. It's a room filled with conversation and laughter, and I'm content to mostly listen.

By the time we sit down around the table, my stomach is hungry from the sight of everything tumbling about in the pot. Half of the pot is red with a spicy soup base, while the other one is a rich, milky color. Our glasses are filled up again with fizzy Apple Sidra from the yellow bottle or sweet milky tea.

Delia watches as Shen puts a few pieces of pork and beef into my bowl, half filled with fluffy white rice, along with some of the cuttlefish balls and egg dumplings that I like, then nudges Shu-Ling with her elbow. "Look at him, trying his best to make a good impression. Cute, isn't it?"

I almost choke on my sip of Apple Sidra at her casual commentary.

"Oh? What? Did you see something today?" Shu-Ling asks, with exaggerated curiosity.

Shen gives Delia a pointed look, which she immediately ignores. "I followed them for a while in Chinatown while they were shopping. They were . . . especially close." She winks.

"I didn't know you were being so creepy." Shen flicks a few pieces of green onion at her, which Delia knocks aside with her arm, laughing.

"Hey! You're making a mess." But she lifts up her bowl, still giggling all the way as she scoops up more rice.

"It's none of your business," Shen declares. "Ruby and I are . . . hanging out." He glances at me, and I nod. That seems safe and ambiguous, but secretly I'm thrilled he didn't declare us as *just friends*.

"Mmm, I suppose I did tell you to keep an eye on her." Shu-Ling lifts one brow. "I didn't know you would take it so literally."

"Stop . . ." Shen groans, scooping up some prawns from the pot. They emerge pink and plump, ready to be eaten.

"We'll stop if you peel prawns for us," Delia quickly declares, and Shu-Ling nods, enthusiastically. They look toward me, and I have to laugh as well, saying everything but saying nothing. Shen grumbles but begins his work, and Delia gestures for me to eat more.

I remember what Dawn always used to say to me: *Take a chance.* If I ever remember to tell her what's going on with me, I bet she will be shocked and delighted. I make a mental note to text her when I get back home. To check in with her too. I don't want to lose her friendship.

I eat until I'm close to bursting, and then the table is cleared. I try to help with the dishes, but Shu-Ling says to stack them all in the sink. She sets out a platter of fruit. Apples, dragon fruit, Asian pears piled high. My mother would approve. She's always on us to eat fruit after dinner to facilitate gut health. I experience a sudden flash of nervousness, thinking about what Ma would do to me if she finds out I'm not where I'm supposed to be tonight. My hand searches for Shen's under the table, and he looks over, surprised, but rubs his thumb over my knuckles, giving me a smile. Even though he doesn't know the worry I have inside me, that tiny gesture is enough for me to remember that I have help. That I'm not alone.

Delia brings her backpack over and pulls out a thick binder. She tosses it on the table, where it lands with a loud thud. A few slips of paper slide out from the top where they had escaped the paper clips. It looks like we're wrapping up the fun and moving on now to the actual topic of the evening.

"Well, you asked me to bring this," Delia says to Shu-Ling. "Want to tell me why?"

THIRTY-THREE

壽德公

(The God of Good Deeds)

Shu-Ling flips through the pages, as if looking for something in particular. The three of us wait, while she pierces another piece of apple with the tiny fork, until Delia rolls her eyes.

"Typical Shu-Ling behavior—always telling everyone to be patient, but operating on an entirely different plane than the rest of us," she comments, more for my benefit, I think. "We're here, you see." Delia holds one hand up and then raises her other hand a foot above it. "She's here. Our high priestess." But she's obviously joking.

"Hush," Shu-Ling says absentmindedly, unbothered by Delia's impatience, until she stops on one page. "Here." She spins the binder around so that it's the right side up for me, pointing at it with her fork.

"This is a map of Chinatown, a few years ago," Shu-Ling explains. "All of these pages that follow are articles, interviews, transcripts that Delia collected about strange occurrences that have happened here. In this three-block radius."

The end of her fork touches a shoe store. "The owner of this shop was a father of five. He won a lottery, said it was thanks to a temple that he made an offering to so he could continue running his store. Business was pretty good after that because of the publicity. A few months later, he took his whole family on a lake vacation. Something he had promised them for years. His entire family died in a boat accident, and he was the sole survivor."

The next shop she points out is a bakery. "This store opened because a young baker won a prestigious competition. With the winnings and community support, she was able to open a shop."

She flips to a page where there is an article of a darkened husk of a building. She reads the headline aloud: "'A dream gone up in flames. Tragedy strikes over Thanksgiving weekend as an accidental fire results in loss of two prominent Chinatown seniors and heartbreak for Vancouver bakery.'"

Then another, the initial happy headline of "'Talented student wins prestigious international dance competition, accepts scholarship to renowned university.'" Followed by the grim headline in black capital letters: "'Murder-suicide of beloved family doctor rocks tight-knit Taiwanese community.'" This one I've heard of, because of how horrified my parents were, since the doctor was a friend of a friend who treated many people they know.

I'm dreading the next one as Shu-Ling returns to the map, listing shops again and again. Telling their stories of success that end with horrific headlines.

Each featured family experienced amazing luck and then terrible misfortune due to circumstances out of their control. It all seemed to happen in the span of a year. Eight stories. Eight tragedies. But other than the Chinatown connection, a few of them have one thing in common: the mention of a temple that they attributed their good fortune to. A temple that helped all their dreams come true. Shu-Ling nods at Delia, who picks up the story after that.

"I never had a chance to tell you what happened after Hope left the city. I started asking around about that temple. Interviewing those who have visited it and discovering this strange pattern. How was it possible for these people to have their dreams come true, only to have their lives crushed in the worst way?" Delia waves at the binder. "I talked about this to everyone who was willing to listen, but no one cared. They all thought I was losing it.

"But... Mr. and Mrs. Chang believed me." Her face softens. "They found me at the hospital right after my mother's accident. They told me they would look into it, investigate what happened. I desperately wanted their help, because even though they didn't promise me that they would be able to bring Hope back, I knew something was wrong in Chinatown after what happened to my mother. I knew that there was evil here, hunting folks in plain sight, preying on their hopes and their wishes."

I reach over and place my hand on her shoulder, because she looks like she is hurting.

Delia nods at me, voice trembling a little, before continuing: "Shu-Ling came and met me, not long after that. To tell me the news. The temple was stopped, but her parents gave their lives to stop them."

"It was a demon who pretended he was a god. He called himself 壽德公, or the God of Good Deeds," Shu-Ling informs me. The name seems to ring in the air between us, bringing with it a sense of ominous dread.

"This is the Great Balance," she continues softly. "Where there are gods, there are forces of evil working against them. And in this case, the demon was able to grow stronger from the suffering of its victims. He was able to feed on 惡意, the darkness that cycles within human hearts. Sadness. Pain. Anger. With the power he gained, he lured malevolent spirits to work for him as his lieutenants. To bring him more victims with the promise of all that they craved: *resurrection*."

"Coming back to the living from the dead? Wouldn't that mean the realms would cross and bad things would happen?" Even with my very simplistic understanding, I know this is something forbidden.

Shu-Ling nods. "In their selfish pursuit, they do not care they are destroying the world they so desperately want to return to. That is the lure and the lie of true evil. If the realms are ever joined, restless spirits will overwhelm the living world looking for hosts. Demons will cause chaos and darkness on earth. He imagined himself as the king of this dark future."

She flips back to that original map of Chinatown, pointing out the symbol that is formed when the eight stores are connected. Black lines are drawn throughout the streets, the location at the very center circled with a furious scribble.

"The Bagua Formation is typically used in feng shui and fortune-telling, but he used the suffering of the families as sacrifices. Blood offered and then spilled. He would absorb the yin energy that enters the doorway, becoming impossibly powerful."

"Our parents closed the door and stopped him before he could complete his ritual. Forced him back to where he came from," Shen says.

"But lately the rumors of unrest are growing. Something doesn't feel right. The spirits seem to be getting bolder, influenced by whatever dark energy has been steadily building in Vancouver. That's why I was in San Francisco, consulting with another guardian temple to see if they're experiencing the same thing in their territories."

"Do you think it's another demon who wants to open that doorway again?" I ask.

"The beads you gave me confirmed it. They were broken by demonic influence." Shu-Ling nods. "The spirit that possessed Tina must be one of the demon's new lieutenants, and I'm hoping that by expelling it from her, we can track down its master.

"But..." She pauses. "I don't think you're going to like how I'm going to do it."

"What are you going to do?" My voice quivers a little, but I still ask.

"If we are going to find answers, then we need to speak to the spirit possessing Tina," Shu-Ling tells me. "We need to perform a similar ritual to what I performed with you, but she won't be willing. You'll have to get her to the mall, and we'll have to find a way to corner her alone."

This sounds absolutely bonkers, right? Kidnapping Tina. Forcing a ritual. Expelling whatever it is inside her. The three of them remain quiet, waiting for me to process this.

"I need to know...what happens if we leave her? If we do nothing at all?"

"A host cannot hold a spirit forever. The body will literally tear itself apart from the negative effects of the yin energy. Best-case scenario? The spirit becomes bored of her and finds another host. Worst-case scenario? They use her body until it's too weak, and then they kill her."

"Wow," I exhale. "Not much of a choice."

"We should do this sooner than later before it results in any sort of permanent damage," Shu-Ling says. "Time is unfortunately not on our side. When is the next time she will be at Chinatown?"

"Well, tonight," I start. Shu-Ling shakes her head. Too soon. "Oh, and Saturday night!" I reach into my bag and pull out the pamphlet for the Winter Recital, and along with it...the glossy brochure featuring Hope.

Delia takes it before I can stop her and stares down at the picture of the brightly smiling girl, color suddenly flooding into her cheeks like I just struck her.

"I...um...I heard she's coming back this weekend too," I tell her. Delia looks pained at the news, but it would be worse if she is in the mall that day and Hope suddenly appears. Keeping that from her so she can't prepare herself for that possibility seems too cruel.

"Can I...can I take this?" Delia asks shakily, and starts folding it, putting it into her bag before I can even respond.

"Delia?" There's a note of warning to Shu-Ling's voice. "That road leads nowhere. You of all people should know it."

"I know," Delia says, a strange light in her eyes, and I wonder if I've made a mistake in revealing the pamphlet.

But the rest of the discussion is about Shu-Ling's plan. Saturday night, I'm responsible for bringing Tina to the bubble tea café after the performance. I'll give her a drink that Shu-Ling will prep, with a talisman hidden inside, like those bottles of tea Tina has in her room.

"I'll make sure the drink will work. You focus on getting her there."

Saturday. A purpose. A task. To save Tina. I can do this.

Delia and Shen walk me out to the lobby, with Shen offering me a ride back to the mall to meet Tina, pretending that I've been at the manor all this time. But when I check my phone, I see a message from Ma. Tina's already home. She didn't feel well during practice, so Mrs. Tsai gave her a ride. I'm supposed to get home by myself. I no longer have to feel a twinge of my usual guilt now that our parents know what she's actually up to, so that is one bright spot that shines through all this mess.

"Wait, you volunteer at the manor? You never told me that; you mean you know Shen's great-aunt?" Delia's eyes look like they're about to bug out of her head.

"I play piano for them once a week, that's all," I say, not knowing why this is such a big deal.

"Mrs. Sui and Mrs. Wang are elders in their own right! They were followers of the guardians ever since they moved over from Taiwan. They're two of the few remaining elders after the temple...split." She gives Shen a guilty look, as if she's said something she's not supposed to.

"After my parents died, many of the senior temple members wanted to move elsewhere," Shen adds. "They said that too much has happened in Chinatown. A bloody history. They wanted a fresh start. But Shu-Ling refused. She said Chinatown needed us more than ever. Many of the members moved away and joined other chapters. They thought that we would collapse . . . but we didn't." He looks like how he appeared when I first met him. Serious. Determined.

"This is the prime example of 緣分," Delia says, fervent again. "There's a reason why all of this is happening. Why *you* came to Chinatown. Why *your* sister made the wish. Why *you* volunteered at the manor. Why it was Shen who came across you in the alley, and not anyone else . . ."

"I don't know if I like that," I say with a frown. "It makes me feel . . . helpless. Like there's nothing I can do except wait for the inevitable to come."

"Or you can look at it another way. Everything happens for a reason," Delia says. "We might struggle against it, fight to go against the tide, but sometimes all we have to do is . . . float. Let the current take us where it will. We'll end up where we should be in the end."

THIRTY-FOUR

安心

(Inner Peace)

The snow is coming down heavy when the car emerges from the underground parkade. Shen turns on the wipers, and the snow leaves smears on the windshield, softening the world into blurry colors. The song that plays in the background is a croony Mandopop ballad, a man singing about how even though the sunset is beautiful it will inevitably end. It conjures up the feelings of helplessness that the night ended up making me feel, that maybe there is nothing I could have done to stop what is happening to Tina, to me.

"Worried?" Shen asks when we've been driving for a few minutes and I haven't said anything in that time. His hand finds mine in the dark, interlocks our fingers together.

"That obvious?" I joke, but really I didn't feel much like laughing.

"My sister is a ... complicated person," he says. "She's always known that the gods might call upon her sometime in her life, but none of us

232

expected it to happen so soon. She took that responsibility on her shoulders without a single complaint. Even though she tries to play it off like she doesn't care, she cares more than anyone will ever know."

I should believe that Shu-Ling will try her best to help me, but what Delia said about fate still makes me nervous. As we make our way down Main Street and we get closer and closer to my house, the more that feeling of dread continues to smother me, until I find it difficult to breathe again.

"Can you . . . can you take me somewhere?" I ask him. "Somewhere quiet. Where we can sit for a little while."

He glances over at me. "You doing okay?"

"I don't want to go home," I whisper, even though it feels like I'm admitting that I'm weak.

"All right." He doesn't ask any other questions and makes a U-turn at the next intersection, going south instead. The music plays on, the same man singing sentimentally about a notebook and about how he realized there was nothing happy about his relationship with his lover, and tries to convince himself to let her go. Not long after, Shen pulls into the parking lot of a neighborhood park. It's quiet now, because of the weather. There's a playground structure in the distance. A cluster of trees. He turns off the engine but keeps the heater going, humming in the background. The guitar starts up, wailing, and the two of us look at each other, then we start laughing.

"It's a little much, isn't it?" he admits, and I nod. "He's one of Shu-Ling's favorite singers. She drove the car earlier today."

"Sure, I believe you," I tell him. "You don't have to hide your secret love for Taiwanese heartbreak songs."

Shen chuckles and shakes his head, then turns and reaches for his backpack behind his seat.

"Before I forget again," he says. "Shu-Ling gave me this earlier, but I forgot to give it to you at school. I have a few more talismans. For your door and for your brother's room. She says to keep your door locked at night. That's when you're most at risk of being influenced."

I make a face. "Do you think my parents would let me lock the door, ever?" He nods, understanding what it's like to live with traditional parents, then I feel a small stab of guilt too. Here I am, complaining about my parents when he doesn't have his anymore.

"I . . . Sorry." I fumble for the words, feeling bad for bringing this up again.

"It's fine," he says, then the corner of his lips curves up, the shadow of a smile. "It's funny, but I think I'd give up anything to have my mom lecture me again about staying up too late. About keeping my room clean. About spending too much time on my art." It's my turn then to find his hand in the dark, to hold it tight.

"Come here," he whispers, his gaze suddenly making me feel warm, and pulls me close, so that I'm nestled up against him. I wonder if he'll kiss me again, but he leans his head against mine. The snowflakes begin to collect on the windshield, the windows starting to fog. We're in this small, intimate space hidden from the world, just the two of us. Every once in a while, the wipers wipe the snow away again, and the lights reappear, misty and surreal.

"All I do now is try my best not to tarnish their memory," Shen says, breath stirring my hair. "I've seen the aftereffects of what happens when evil infiltrates the world of the living. I don't want that to happen to your family."

"I have one more thing for you," he says after a few moments of us sitting in cozy silence. "This isn't from Shu-Ling. It's from me." He holds it up in front of my face. A jade pendant dangling from a red string.

"I know the bracelet broke, so here's something that's easier to hide.

More difficult for someone to grab," he says, dropping it in my hand. There's an etching of a character in the middle.

The character for safety or peace. It gives me a good feeling when I touch it, like the bracelet did before.

"It's a protective charm," he says. "Usually you can ask for a blessing, a paper talisman like the one for your room or a pouch, but I like the feel of the jade. This one belonged to my mother."

"I can't—" I start, but he shakes his head, cutting me off. He pulls out a pendant that he's hidden under his collar.

"I already have one," he says, voice serious, like he's not taking no for an answer. "She wouldn't forgive me if she knew I didn't help you in all the ways I know. You can give it back to me after all this is over."

Just a loan. That's not so bad. I try to put it on but can't seem to loosen the knot. Shen watches me fumble with it for a few moments before taking it from my hands, chuckling. He loosens the knot and then lifts it up, gestures for me to lower my head. He slides the necklace down slowly, and I feel his touch trail around my ear and run down my neck.

"Turn around?" he says. I turn quickly, so he doesn't see the way my face suddenly warms up.

"Your hair," he says, and I reach back to lift my hair out of the way, our fingers brushing.

He adjusts the knot so that the pendant slides up. "Good?"

"Perfect." I let my hair fall and turn back, too aware of my pulse, beating fast. "We'll match." And then I immediately feel silly for saying it, the way he makes me feel clumsy and awkward and unsure.

"We will." He leans forward and kisses me, soft and sweet. Before he pulls away, he reaches out and carefully smooths down the collar of my shirt, hiding the necklace from view. Later on he drives me home. I slide out of the car, emerging into the winter night. The chill feels good against my too-warm face. My shoes slip a little on the sidewalk, leave footprints in the accumulating white. Before I go into my house, I turn and look back. He's still there, waiting to make sure I'm safe. I smile to myself, even as I walk through the door. Carrying this secret inside. A feeling only for me to know.

THIRTY-FIVE

白雪

(White Snow)

"The Soulful Heart recital is this afternoon," Tina announces Saturday morning. I know the unspoken question there. *Will Ma and Baba take us?*

"I have to be in the office for a bit this morning," Baba says.

"Again?" Ma voices her displeasure. "This is the third weekend in a row!"

"Only for an hour to file some papers," Baba says quickly, trying to explain. "I'll finish as fast as I can. In time for the recital." He looks to Ma to see what the verdict will be.

"I talked with Auntie Valerie," Ma says, referring to one of her friends. "Asked around about this program. She says that it's a reputable one." To my parents there are considerations on the hierarchy of people whose opinions we trust. Those from a Taiwanese background with higher professional standings are among the most trustworthy. Then it's a complicated network depending on your age, relationship, profession, until we reach the people at the very bottom: the kids. I can talk to them until my lips are blue, but it will not play an iota into their considerations until someone else in a higher threshold says the very same thing.

"Maybe we'll go and see what all the fuss is about," Baba says, nodding. Tina shrieks excitedly and high-fives Denny, then bustles around the kitchen helping with the dishes. Being on her very best behavior all morning.

The voices still come on the other side of my bedroom wall. Sometimes laughing, sometimes weeping. Too many voices. Smells that continue to permeate from her room when I walk past her door. But my parents brush it all away. They keep seeing what they want to see.

I stay in my room to work on my essay, even though it's more *Investigations into Demonic Influence on Vancouver's Chinatown* than *The Changing Landscape of Low-Income Chinese Seniors' Housing Availability*. I already searched for the name Shu-Ling gave me when I came home from hot pot: 壽德公, *The God of Good Deeds*. It didn't come up with very much. An obscure page somewhere listed it under a header of a *type* of god: 有應公, *The God that Answers*—usually nameless and homeless, with no ancestor shrines set up to worship them, they're instead considered restless spirits who are appeased with generic offerings after unexplainable phenomena. Hauntings. Supernatural activity. Curses.

Often they're sought out by people who are desperate, who have been turned away from other, more legitimate temples because what they seek is not salvation from evil, but the kind of dark promises that only evil can make. These websites come with a warning: Beware of offerings to these nameless, faceless gods because you don't know who might answer your request.

I think about the people who have nowhere to turn. The people who come up again and again in my research into Chinatowns. Chinese Canadians once congregated here because it was difficult for them to find homes and jobs elsewhere. They came together and found strength in numbers, in helping each other. Sharing common goals. The various benevolent associations started as a way for people to build community, to help transition the immigrants as they settled into life in a new country. The Formosa Friendship Association is just another variation on that.

Except now, many people would rather set aside our past difficulties and challenges and replace them with a shiny and sanitized version of history and call that progress. So many dreams and hopes, so many stories, forgotten. It makes me feel small and insignificant, like a pebble in a stream.

"Ruby!" Ma calls up the stairs, disrupting my focus. "It's time to get ready for the recital!"

I change into something more presentable than pajamas, then we're off to the recital at Soulful Heart. We find parking on the street and walk over to the mall. Tina chatters animatedly beside Baba on the short walk, so excited she's almost vibrating. Denny slips his hand into mine and slides on the icy sidewalk, laughing when I pull him up.

"It seems like she's settled in well at the new school. Making lots of friends, right, Ruby?" Ma says, walking beside me, watching Tina up ahead. "After all that crying and protesting about switching schools." It sounds like she wants me to validate her choice, that in the end, it was a good idea for her to take the teaching job at Westview, to move us both away.

"Yeah, I'm sure," I mumble, the safest answer. "She has lots of friends now."

"What about you? Are you liking Westview?" *Oh no. A follow-up question.*

"I like our new school!" Denny chirps, saving me. "Everyone is nice."

"That's 'cause you're nice." I reach over and ruffle his hair. "And your teacher loves you." Because Denny is friendly and clever and eager to help.

"Yeah." He accepts this view of the world without hesitation.

"Westview definitely has nicer equipment." I manage to say something positive. *And cute boys*, my mind interjects helpfully, but I don't share that.

Ma nods, satisfied with this answer.

"At first I wasn't sure about the influences of those Westview girls, but after Mrs. Tsai's visit..." Ma gestures. "Dancing being able to help get you to Yale and Harvard. Imagine that!"

"Everyone is good at different things," I say.

Ma frowns, disagreeing. "Sure, sure, but some things are better than others. If your sister decided to do hip-hop with her stomach showing and shorts, shaking her butt, your father will have a heart attack and then she will have to live with the memory of his death forever."

"It's only a costume," I say, resisting the urge to roll my eyes. "They're performers."

"You get used to things, and then you wear them every day," Ma argues back. "Like that dress you wanted to get for last year's recital. With that long slit along the side. What would everyone *think*?"

"We're here," I say, not wanting to get into an argument about the validity of dance costumes. Or be reminded of the beautiful green dress that I almost bought last year for the year-end recital, which made me feel pretty with the way it moved.

"Baba says there's going to be food there," Denny whispers at me conspiratorially when we walk through the doors. I hide a giggle behind my hand. My family does love a chance at free food.

There's a sign hanging on the main door. MALL CLOSED AT 3 FOR PRIVATE EVENT, USE SIDE ENTRANCES FOR STREET-SIDE BUSINESSES. I didn't even think it was possible to shut down the entire mall for that. When we walk into the lobby, I can't help but let out a gasp. The entire space has been transformed. A stage has been set up beside the fountain, which has been decorated with twinkle lights and draped with flowers. Black backdrops hang on either side of the stage, obscuring the view of the other businesses so that it doesn't even seem like the mall any longer.

A series of photographs on stands for display highlight the members of the troupe, all dressed in traditional white hanfu. Their long sleeves are embroidered with blue patterns. The photographs follow a progression, twirling, bowing, leaping, until the final photograph shows a woman with her arm extended upward, sleeve rippling overhead, her face caught in a moment of artful yearning.

Behind these photos there is a section with black cocktail tables, where smartly dressed people are mingling and chatting with one another. The banner is hung over the doorway into Soulful Heart: WELCOME TO THE WINTER SERIES, then the title of the performance follows:

白雪紛飛
White Snow, Wildly Dancing

"Welcome, welcome." Mrs. Tsai appears from nowhere, greeting us with arms wide. Her smile wide. "I'm so pleased you were able to make it."

"Tina! Tina!" We're surrounded by a circle of girls. All of them beaming with too-white teeth and similar wide smiles. They're followed by older women dressed in white blouses and floral skirts. The girls are in light green, ruffles at their shoulders and wrists. To my surprise, my mother and sister also match them. They must have coordinated earlier. The feeling hits me in a cold rush. *You don't fit in.*

"This is Amy Liu," Mrs. Tsai introduces one of the women, only distinguishable to me from the others at this moment by her small gold hoop earrings. "She's one of our dance teachers of the younger troupes."

"I'm going to sit with my friends!" Tina flutters her fingers in our direction and fades into the crowd of girls, arm in arm.

"Welcome, Mr. and Mrs. Chen!" Amy beams at us, then bends down to my little brother. "And this must be Denny!"

My brother clutches my hand and clings to me, tighter.

"Denny!" Ma's voice goes high as she tries to nudge him forward. "Say hi!"

"Hi," Denny says in a whisper, not quite like his usual friendly self.

Amy doesn't seem bothered by this. She straightens and gestures for us to follow her. "Come grab some appetizers before they're gone."

"Stop it! Be friendly!" Ma hisses through her teeth before following Amy with a smile, Baba right behind her. Denny stays back, not so eager for food as he was before. He gestures for me to lean in closer.

"She smells like Tina," Denny whispers in my ear, then wrinkles his nose. "Yuck."

I don't like it. Does that mean Amy is a part of them too? My guard is up, sweeping my gaze across the crowd of people, searching for anything that might stand out as strange.

"Stay close to me tonight, okay?" I put my arm around him as we trail after our parents. My finger reaching compulsively to touch the pendant through my shirt, to make sure it's still there.

Amy shows us to a table in the corner, with a glittering RESERVED sign sitting in front of it. There's a waiter dressed in black and white who stamps our hands to permit us access to the spread of food.

"For our VIP guests." She grins, glasses in hand, filled with something fizzy and pink. She hands them to Ma and Baba, who look pleased with this special treatment.

There's tuna served in green porcelain spoons, topped with slivers of cucumber, and black and white sesame seeds. Slices of beef on a cracker drizzled with garlic sauce, accompanied by slender tendrils of green onion. Tempura shrimp, smothered with red gochujang sauce. Everything in tiny portions. Not to mention trays of fresh fruit and veggies. A stack of shrimp tails quickly collects on Denny's plate.

While we eat, I furtively text the group chat.

Me: at the lobby, about to go in for the performance
Delia: Getting there now.

I scan the room, but I don't see a familiar face. There are too many people now, waiting for the performance to begin.

Shen: What? You're not supposed to be here
Delia: I just want to see her.
Shen: Delia, don't
Shen: ...
Shen: Delia???

THIRTY-SIX

紛飛

(Wildly Dancing)

A bell dings, and the announcement sounds overhead. "Please make your way into the studio. The show will begin shortly." My parents come to collect us, and I have to put my phone away. I look around, nervous, trying to see if I can catch sight of where Delia is. I don't know what she is planning. She was agreeable yesterday when we talked about the plan. To keep a lookout for us, because it takes time to prep the talisman, to put it into the drink. She didn't mention anything else. I should never have told her that Hope's in town.

We walk slowly through the double doors and down the hallway, where the lights have been dimmed. In the waiting area, colorful streamers spiral down from the ceiling, sparkling in the lights, creating an optical illusion of spinning. I've never been past the receiving room, but we are ushered into the main studio. Light wood floors polished to a shine. Along the length of one wall there are red curtains, and the other wall has floor-to-ceiling mirrors.

We're seated in the back row, and I'm glad we're not in the front, because we don't have to stare at our own reflections so clearly on the opposing wall. I stop Denny from bouncing on the seats, even as he looks around, curious.

"Where's Tina?" Baba asks as Ma consults the program that we are handed when we entered the space. "Where is she going to sit?"

"We have a seat with the junior troupe for her," Amy says cheerily. "She'll be here soon! It will be a wonderful performance. She can't wait to share it with you." Amy goes off to take care of her other responsibilities, and all there is to do is wait. I want to take out my phone, to see if Delia's texted back, but Ma puts her hand on mine, shaking her head.

I look up and around to see there is also a balcony space up top, a catwalk around the entirety of the studio, so there can be an audience watching from above as well. Figures are filling up those seats, but I can't tell what they look like from here, the lights too bright from up ahead.

The lights dim and the bell rings again. "One minute until the start of the show..." the disembodied voice announces. That's when I notice there are tables draped in black in front of the mirrors. Three women file in, clad in black floor-length dresses. Sequins adorn their costumes, trailing from their high necklines down their arms, shimmering silver in the light. One of them holds what looks like a pipa.

"A long guitar!" Denny whispers excitedly beside me, even as Ma shushes him.

Another woman pulls off the table covering and unveils an instrument on a beautiful black-and-gold stand with a series of strings. In her hand, she holds thin, red-tipped mallets. She strikes the strings in series, listening. Tuning, I assume. The woman in the back stands before a large drum, and the long stand to her right holds a series of gongs of varying sizes.

I manage to take out my phone again, sneak a photo of the performers to send to Dawn, because I know she would be interested in that particular unique mallet instrument. No updates from Delia. She must be somewhere in this room. The lights are fully dim now as Mrs. Tsai appears under the spotlight in the corner, standing behind a podium.

"I want to start by thanking you all for joining us here today. Whether this is your first time at Soulful Heart or if you have been here many times in the past, we welcome you." She bows, and a light scattering of applause follows from the audience. "I am so happy to celebrate with you on this day, the first anniversary of the opening of our studio here in the Pacific Dragon Mall. As the director of Soulful Heart, I am so proud to be part of such a vibrant community here in Chinatown, and to support the artistic pursuits of the younger generations." The applause is louder this time, echoing in the room.

"Tonight, we are pleased to present to you this intimate performance for our studio family first, as we unveil our winter series: White Snow, Wildly Dancing. We have partnered with the Ribbon Ensemble to perform the accompanying music, showcasing traditional Chinese instruments...." With a loud whirring noise, a projection screen emerges in front of the mirrors. The shadows of the musicians stretch out along the wall, then the music begins, as the projector casts the shapes of a stretch of mountains behind them.

The sweet tones of the string instrument fills the space, the sound amplified by a microphone. The dancers then sweep in from the other side of the room behind another set of swinging curtains. They're dressed in white, like the photos in the displays outside, delicate blue embroidery adorning the hems.

Admittedly, I still know nothing about dance, but I can admire their performance. The control of their bodies to move in sync to the music, to be able to bend themselves in various poses, all sorts of ways that would be impossible for me. They form crescent moons and wind-blown trees, their sleeves rippling in the air similar to the northern lights that dance across the sky. The gong sounds, parting the wave of dancers, then the drumbeat accompanies the sound of their footsteps as they exit the stage.

"Tina! She's there!" Baba whispers, gesturing at the stage. For someone who doesn't care much for dance, he seems happy to see her. The row of dancers in the front shed their jackets as they stand from their seats to join the performance. Their hair has been styled, pulled back away from the face and pinned to one side. They must have coordinated it all while we were eating. Ma's expression is conflicted, watching with pursed lips, but Baba leans over and whispers something in her ear that I can't hear. She nods in understanding, her frown relaxing for the moment with whatever he said.

Tina is part of the line of dancers in green, and they weave into a complicated formation with the dancers in white, who have returned to join them on the floor. They come together, and then apart, one group moving clockwise, and the other opposing them. I can see Tina in the midst of it all, keeping up with the complex pattern, turning her head this way and that, maintaining the precise movements of her hands and feet. I can see the intensity of her focus as she moves. From the center, a girl emerges, lifted on the hands of the other dancers, shedding the outer layer of her costume and emerging in blue. A white owl mask covers the upper half of her face and her lips are curved into a smile below. They set her down on the stage as the other dancers depart. The rest of the music fades, until only the steady beat of a wood block remains.

The clinking of a small cymbal joins it then, as the other dancers quickly disappear into the edges of the room, melting into the shadows. Her movements are slow in the beginning. She takes deliberate steps forward, crouching, as if looking for something. The spotlight follows her, and on the projection screen, stars seem to dance above her. Then her head snaps back as the pipa strums a lively tune; a shooting star swoops overhead, disappearing. Her body arcs as she throws herself upward, defying gravity. The audience gasps, then she's off, accompanied by the sprightly sounds of all the instruments joined together.

She flings her mask off and looks up, the light catching her face. I recognize her, even though we've never met.

It's Hope.

Hope dances with the entirety of her body, from her face to her fingers to the tips of her toes. The corners of her eyes lift, her expression joyous as she throws herself into the choreography. She flies through the air, feet barely touching the ground. The percussionist of the ensemble pulls out finger cymbals, and accompanies her lively steps. The audience catches on, clapping to the beat. Hope spins, her sleeves swirling around her so that she is in the center of a whirlwind. In the final, breathless moment, she falls backward and catches herself with one hand, then sinks to the ground as the final run finishes on the pipa with a flourish. The studio fills with applause and whistles.

One of the dancers emerges from the sidelines to help her up, and then they all line up in two rows. The troupe in green in the front, obviously younger than the dancers in white in the back. All of them beaming at the successful performance, Tina included. They bow, together, drinking in the additional applause. Mrs. Tsai appears again to announce a brief intermission, and the spotlight moves around the room.

As the lights slowly turn on, I look around for Delia again, and even check in the balconies to see if she might have gone up there. But I realize with a seeping sense of dread that the balconies are empty. There are no chairs up there. There are no people coming down the stairs. Then who are the people I saw filling up that space? Who are those figures watching the performance alongside us?

"That was wonderful," Baba exclaims excitedly while they enter the line for more drinks. Ma dabs at the corner of her eye with a tissue.

"Mama?" Denny questions. "Are you crying?"

"I'm fine," she says, eyes red-rimmed as she looks down at him with a strained smile. "Just reminded that I used to dance once."

"What?" I exclaim, too loud, enough that the people waiting before us in line turn around to give us a curious look. I lower my voice, but I can't help but ask: "You used to dance?" Ma has always been the most vocal about her dislike of dancing. How it leads nowhere in life, an excuse for attention-seeking people to look at them.

"It was ballroom dancing," Baba says to us, grinning at this shared secret. "She took me a few times to her dance club, but I couldn't keep up."

"Psh." Ma slaps his arm, dismissive. "It was so long ago, I forgot about it!"

"I want more fruit." Denny tugs on her arm, and Ma leads him away, leaving me to stew on this topic alone.

I check my phone. Still no message from Delia.

Me: i went into the performance and i think spirits were watching. is that normal?

Shen: The mall has always been a gathering place for spirits because of the temple. They're drawn to the yin energy that seeps through the doorway

"Did you see? Did you see?" Tina comes up, eyes shining. Her makeup still glittering at the corners of her eyes. She's so lively and excited that I can't help feel that twinge in my heart.

"It was quite the performance," Baba acknowledges. "Quite the production. Very impressive." Tina's expression falls a little. It's just like our father to comment on the quality of how something appears, rather than pay attention to her and how she performed. Baba turns to speak with a man who greets him with familiarity, and Tina is pulled away by her friends again.

I end up standing in the corner, scrolling on my phone while furtively glancing everywhere to see if Delia is around.

Me: i don't see her
Shen: Keep looking

The five-minute warning before the show resumes is announced as someone rests their hands on my shoulders.

"Boo," she whispers into my ear, making me jump a mile.

I turn around, and it's Delia, standing there grinning like she just won the lottery.

THIRTY-SEVEN

山海

(Crossing Mountains and Seas)

"Where the hell have you been?" I can't help but burst out, annoyed with her for disappearing like that.

"Don't be mad," she says, not bothered at all. She grabs my arm and leads me to the other side of the room. Away from where the others are clustered around the food and drinks. "I was doing some reconnaissance."

"Are you going to try and talk to her?" I ask. That girl who danced in the studio with a brilliant smile, who once shattered Delia's heart into a million pieces.

"She seemed . . . happy," Delia says, averting her gaze. "That's enough for me. I'm only here to make sure the Temple of Hopeful Desires hasn't returned under another form. I don't want anyone else to get hurt like my family, like Shen's family." Her lips pull into a thin, harsh line.

"And did it come back?" I have to know. "Where is it?"

"I heard the Temple of Fortunate Tidings is *here*. Somewhere in the mall. Can you believe that it's been under our feet all along?" Delia licks her lips, her eyes shining. "I have to see it for myself. See if it's how I imagined it. Maybe I'll even make a wish." She speaks loud enough that someone near us glances over. I half lead, half pull her behind the black curtain so we are hidden from view.

"Didn't Shu-Ling tell you to leave it alone?" I remind her, though part of me is still reeling from the revelation. How can the temple be here? But only a moment later, I realize that it makes sense. All of Tina's dreams, all her desires, they're wrapped around the dance studio. That's where she met the "True Believers." Soulful Heart. The Temple of Fortunate Tidings. They're all linked together. Hiding in plain sight. So close to the guardians.

"I know Shu-Ling and Shen want to protect me." Delia pulls her arm out of my grasp. "They don't want me chasing ghosts. I've spent so much time afterward, getting accepted to university, working on my degree. But I've met so many people in Chinatown while working on my research here, met the aftereffects of the temple rippling through it all."

"What are you saying?" I ask, uneasy.

"It's no longer about *me*. It's about people like you, people like your sister. Families being ripped apart," Delia says, insistent now. "I'm the one who doesn't have anything to lose, so it's my responsibility to end it all."

I feel a sudden chill even though the space is warm, shielded from the winter cold.

"Delia..." I say helplessly, trying to hold her back, but she slips away from me. *Oh no.* I follow her, quick on her heels.

"You're stronger than you know, Ruby. Remember that. I'll see you later," she says, with a finality that makes me nervous, before stepping through the curtain. I'm about to go after her, but Ma is suddenly there, taking a firm grip on my shoulder.

"Who are you talking to, Ruby?" Ma says, Denny in tow. "The show is about to start."

"Just a friend..." I turn back, but Delia is gone. I have to let Shen know.

We return to our seats in the studio. I think I catch a glimpse of her at the other end of the room, which eases the worry inside me a little. Will she do something rash? Like rush to Hope while she is performing, fall to her knees and declare her love for her? Beg her to keep her promises? I don't think so. That doesn't seem like something she would do, even though I haven't known her for very long at all. She said so herself—she's gotten therapy, she's working on putting the past behind. But the way she spoke about the temple...that look on her face...

The light dims as the second half of the show begins. I try not to look up, because if I do, I'll see those humanlike shapes again, leaning over the balcony. Their faces obscured by shadows.

The drums are struck lightly as the feet of the dancers pound to a new beat. Five figures rush into the studio, yellow jackets on, each of them wearing frightening masks of red and black. Large eyes that bulge out of their sockets, wispy black hair decorated with bells that trail down the sides of their faces, comically huge ears with a gold ring dangling from each. They growl and shape their hands into claws, leaning into the performance.

They remind me of the man that grabbed me on the street, and I hate that the memory resurfaces, leaving a sick feeling at the bottom of my stomach. The lithe bodies of the dancers form spiderlike shapes as they crawl on the ground, forcing their limbs into disjointed postures. As the drumbeat of the song progresses into a frenzy, they approach the audience, causing many of them to shriek when they get too near. I don't like their movements, the unnatural way they skitter across the floor. I'm glad when the performance is done, and Mrs. Tsai comes up to close out the session. All the dancers then stand and join hands for a final bow, and I look at all the men, wondering if I can see the one who threatened me, but I don't find him there.

When we file up to leave the studio, there is a bottleneck at the door. Too many people shaking hands, talking to each other. Someone bumps into me, and we step away from each other, apologizing.

"You dropped this." Another audience member picks up a white card at my feet and hands it to me. Before I can tell him it's not mine, he's already gone. I stare at the card in my hand.

There's a large red square stamp that acts as a logo, the character 緣. My breath catches in my throat as I read THE TEMPLE OF FORTUNATE TIDINGS below it in plain black capital letters, then tucked underneath: BLESSINGS. GUIDANCE. GOOD FORTUNE. There's no phone number, web page, social media. Nothing to show how to contact them. I flip it over and there is an address. A date and a time. Tomorrow. Four p.m.

Even though I didn't seek it out, the temple has found me.

"姊, c'mon!" Denny whines, tugging at my arm when I don't move. But I forget all about the card and the temple when I see Delia at the end of the room, talking to someone in a yellow jacket from the studio. I start in her direction, determined to stop her from doing whatever it is she is planning on doing. But my parents are all smiles as they stop me. They're with a man I recognize, Melody's dad—Mr. Lee.

"Hello again, Ruby," he says. He has on a black jacket over a white shirt, with a tie that has lucky cats on it, and extremely shiny black shoes. I force a smile on my face as I say hi, even though I want to spin around and find Delia.

"What did you think of the performance? Melody tells me that they rehearsed many, many times to ensure they got it right," Mr. Lee says.

Melody comes up beside him, beaming, as he places his arm around her shoulder. I see Tina standing there beside Ma as well, and I know she probably wishes for the same sort of acknowledgment from our parents. But they're not the physically affectionate type.

I glance over my shoulder. Delia is now surrounded by three men wearing those yellow jackets. The sight of them makes me nervous. I don't like it. I need to get over there, talk to her, make sure she's okay.

"Mr. Lee is talking to you." Baba places his hand on my shoulder, forcing me back to the conversation.

"Melody also plays piano. She has your piano teacher, Mrs. Nguyen," Mr. Lee tells me. "There's a great opportunity coming up tomorrow. A concert in the Chinese garden, music provided for the attendees as they participate in various activities. We had a stellar lineup, but one of our performers got sick. If you are available though, we'd love to have you involved. It's for a good cause. A fundraiser."

"I can't," I immediately say, a burrowing feeling in my gut as I flash back to the last time I played for an audience. I haven't prepared for this performance—for any performance. I already told Dawn I would visit her at the conservatory tomorrow.

"Ruby!" Ma reprimands, but then gives Mr. Lee a smile. "Sorry, give us a moment please while I discuss this with my daughter.

"This is a big deal," she tells me. "Mr. Lee sponsors a lot of art programs in the city, and he's also a board member at Westview. He has a lot of connections. To scholarships, other opportunities."

"I promised Dawn I would see her play tomorrow," I tell her.

"Dawn will understand," she says with a scowl.

"And I don't want to," I tell her. "I don't want to perform."

"What's the point of all of those lessons, then?" Ma says, furious. "What's the point of paying thousands and thousands of dollars of our well-earned money? Those hours your Baba works away, traveling to all those places, me taking jobs that I don't want, so you and Tina and Denny can have the best opportunities? This is how you repay us?"

I can't help the sudden anger that rises inside me, the one that retorts: "You don't even care if I never perform as long as I get my diploma. That's all you want me to do, so I can put it on my university applications, because your friends or whatever said that most people never make it to the ARCT level before they graduate high school. That's what you told me to do. Now you're going to force me to perform?"

"It's not even a big deal. You'll play one of the pieces you've been working on for your diploma anyway, as practice." Ma's eyes flash, angry that I'm using her own words against her. "You will do this tomorrow and you will do it with a smile, and one day you'll tell me '謝謝, 親愛的媽媽 for making the right decision for me.'" She places her hands on my shoulders and physically walks me back to face Mr. Lee, talking over my head as she confirms my attendance. Ignoring how her "Thank you, dear mother" comment made me bristle. Tina watches all of this, gleeful, enjoying the show.

But I don't care about Mr. Lee and the performance and whatever good it will do for my future. I'm worried about Delia now. I look back toward the room again, but there's no one there anymore. None of the dancers in the yellow jackets. Only the drawn curtains. The empty chairs.

Mr. Lee leaves with Melody. I stand there, with a bad feeling growing inside me. I'm sure Delia hasn't left the studio; I've had my eye on the exit the entire time. There must be another way out, somewhere that the dancers emerged from earlier. But when I pull the curtain back, there's nothing.

I hear whispers above my head, and when I look up, I can see ghostly forms standing there on the balcony, watching me with eyes that glint back in the dark. Shen told me that I shouldn't talk to them, but I'm too worried about Delia to care.

"What happened to her?" I shake the curtain to get their attention. They grow larger before my eyes, a darkness stretching and stretching above me, bending over the edge of the balcony to loom overhead. Is it one spirit? Or maybe more? Their bodies contorted all together, twisted and misshapen. Their features are blurred, partially obscured by wavy black hair that hangs like a curtain over their faces. Glimpses of things that writhe and catch the light at certain angles, sights that no one should ever see: the movement of too many eyes blinking, snakelike tongues flicking out from cavernous red mouths...

"Miss! Please don't touch that!" One of the studio staff hurries over to stop me. Before I step away, I can hear them whisper above me, voices overlapping: *"They took her.... They took her down...."*

THIRTY-EIGHT

障眼法

(Smoke and Mirrors)

I'm so distracted by Delia's appearance and what the spirits said that we are on the sidewalk before I remember what I'm supposed to do.

"Wait!" I call out to my family up ahead, waving a coupon in hand. "I have a free coupon for this bubble tea place in the mall. Let's grab a few drinks to celebrate. It's on me." I got the coupon knowing that my parents hate to turn down a good deal.

Ma and Baba exchange glances, and then Baba offers: "Why don't I go grab the car, and you can all go to the shop since it's snowing so much. I'll bring it around so you don't have to walk in the snow." Even more snow came down while we were watching the performance, making the street slippery. Sirens sound somewhere in the distance.

"Let's get out of the snow. Quickly, Ruby!" Ma hurries us, having already brushed off the fight we had earlier, like nothing had happened. We traipse forward, our little crew fighting against the wind that lashes against our faces and our bodies.

We crowd into the café, stomping our feet and wiping our wet shoes on the carpet.

"Welcome!" a voice calls out from behind the counter. "We'll be right with you." It sounds like Shu-Ling.

"This is cute," Tina says, looking around. There isn't anybody else here in the café, probably due to the weather. It's warm and cozy in here, the heater humming beside us.

Ma chooses a table close to the window, and we settle in on the white chairs.

"Sometimes there's a cat that sits there." I point out the window seat to Denny, where there's currently an empty cat bed and some blankets with toys on it.

"A cat? Where?" Denny peers excitedly into the space, looking for her.

"Sorry, the cat is off today," a familiar person says behind me. Shen sets down the laminated menus, smiling at me. I grab one of the menus, looking down, suddenly nervous. It feels strange to see him here and have my family here too. The two sides of my life have always been kept separate from each other until now. I don't know what to do, how to act, so I stay quiet.

"Aww…" Denny pouts, disappointed. "We'll have to come back!"

"She's usually here during the day when it's sunny and her mom brings her," he says. "I'll give you a few minutes to decide what you want to order."

"Ruby!" Ma whispers. "The coupon! Check to make sure it's still good."

I'm about to open my mouth and protest that I know it's still good because I was given it yesterday, but then I realize this is the perfect opportunity for me to go talk to Shen. I push back my chair, and it scrapes against the floor with a loud screech, making me wince.

"I'll go check," I say quickly, and then head up to the counter.

"Hi," he says softly, and there's a warmth reserved in those eyes, just for me. "Shu-Ling's in the back. She's ready." She told me yesterday it's better for her to stay hidden, because most of the spirits in Chinatown know her by face or by name because of her association with the guardians and the wardens. Whatever is inside Tina may get spooked and run if she's seen. It makes me feel better though, knowing that she's here. The only wrench in our plans . . . Delia.

"Have you heard from Delia?" I ask, keeping my voice low so that my family doesn't overhear.

"No." He shakes his head. "She hasn't been answering my messages."

"I told you about the spirits in the studio," I tell him. "I talked to one of them."

His eyes widen, knowing that this is what they warned me against. I expect him to be annoyed I went against his sister's suggestion, but he seems curious instead. "What did they say?"

"She said that Delia was taken down," I say. "What does that even mean? She disappeared somewhere."

"I'll keep trying to reach her," he murmurs.

"姊姊!" Denny is calling out from across the café. "We're ready to order! You're taking so long!"

"And I'm ready for you!" Shen responds with a wave, then looks at me with a slight smile. "Your little brother is funny." I think Denny would get along really well with Shen. I can imagine them hanging out, having the best time together. Drawing. Listening to music. My heart squeezes at the thought. Not that my parents would ever permit it, with boys as one of those taboo things on the unacceptable list.

I return to the table with him, and Ma orders for us, even as Denny changes his mind again and again, wavering on whether he wants rainbow jelly or popping brown-sugar boba.

"How about this?" Shen tells him. "I'll give you both if you really want it."

"Can I?" Denny looks at Ma excitedly, and she nods.

"It'll take a few minutes, but I'll get started on these right away," Shen tells Ma, polite.

"Wait," Ma stops him, and for a moment of panic, I wonder if she knows. If she is able to deduce, with the way that we look at each other, that there is something going on between us. She gestures up at the art on the wall. "I quite like these. Do you have a card for the artist?"

Shen stutters for a moment, glancing up at the colorful portraits in square black frames, looking embarrassed, like a deer caught in the headlights. "Um, I drew these. I'm the artist."

"You are?" Ma exclaims, surprised. "You're quite talented. Are these from Peking opera?"

"No, they're called the 八家將." He mentions the term in Taiwanese. "A Taiwanese temple procession."

"You're from Taiwan?" She looks even more delighted now. "I thought you might be!"

"Taiwan! Taiwan! We're from there too!" Denny kicks his feet, also excited.

"Yes, we are," Ma says, slipping naturally into Mandarin. "How wonderful."

"Anyway, I'm going to go make the drinks now." He holds up the notepad and meets my eyes briefly, sharing my amusement, before walking away.

"Just look at the detail." Ma stands up, peering closer at the portraits, still focused on them.

"Who is that guy? You spent a lot of time talking with him," Tina says slyly. "He's cute, Ma—don't you think?"

"He goes to our school," I say, keeping my voice flat and boring, revealing nothing. "He's in the same grade as me . . . I think."

"What a nice boy. So friendly. He's only in high school?" Ma shakes her head, sitting back down. "Such a surprise how talented young people are now."

I sit there, a little on edge, waiting to see what will happen. They said for me to get Tina here, but what will happen when she drinks whatever Shu-Ling is preparing? How will they get her alone? There are so many questions, and nothing I can do, except to sit and wait. As is evident from the events of the past few weeks, I am terrible at waiting.

I set up a game of Jenga with Denny to distract me, while Ma keeps looking at the art and Tina scrolls on her phone. Eventually, the drinks arrive. We put Baba's and Ma's drinks in a bag, while Denny and Tina quickly jab their straws through the tops of theirs.

"I'm going to go pay," I tell them, and go to the counter again, where Shen is busy trying to look busy, wiping the counter. I watch him pretend to enter the drinks in the till, while talking to me.

"What's going to happen?" I ask anxiously, wanting to know how Shu-Ling is going to question Tina. How can she talk to her while my mother is watching our every move?

"Patience," Shu-Ling chimes in, appearing suddenly pushing a mop and a bucket and heading back toward the bathrooms.

"Tina?" I hear Ma say behind me, and then Tina's hurrying toward the bathrooms as well, her hand up, clutching her stomach. I look back at Ma and Denny, and Ma waves a hand for me to go help her, frowning.

"Go," Shen says, voice low. "I'll be here if you need me."

I put my hand on the bathroom door, pushing it open, half-afraid of what I will see. Tina kneels on the floor in front of the toilet, Shu-Ling behind her. There's something ominous about the sight. Shu-Ling's expression is harsh as she looks down at my sister's slight form, lip curled with disgust. At that moment, I'm scared of her. Scared of what she's going to do. Then her eyes snap up and she says sharply, "Come inside and close the door."

I slip through quickly, following her instructions. Tina's hands clutch the side of the toilet as she dry heaves, her whole body shaking. She turns her head then to look at me when the door clicks shut, through a mess of tangled hair that has come loose from her braid, one eye glaring accusingly in my direction.

"What...did...you...do...to...me?" she snarls, hatred contorting her expression so that she is unrecognizable, even as she turns back again and gags. Then a rush of dark liquid floods out of her mouth, splattering in the bowl and on the ground beside her. She chokes, thrusting her head back, then falls forward again, throwing up even more. My stomach turns at this sight, at the sour and sickly smell that starts to fill the small space. The light above our heads is a decorative chandelier, shaped like a birdcage, and the bulbs within begin to pulse, as if they are at risk of shattering over us.

But then there's a yelp, and I turn back to see Shu-Ling has pulled Tina up by her hair. Her expression is cold as she raises her other hand, a yellow talisman between her fingers. Tina looks up at her, black smeared over her mouth, tears streaming down her face, her makeup running, a truly pitiful sight.

"Please..." she begs, reaching her hand out toward me. "She's going to hurt me.... Stop her...."

I don't know what to do. I take a step forward, uncertain. But Shu-Ling brings her arm down and places the talisman on Tina's forehead. Tina's eyes roll into the back of her head and turn milky white, as her mouth opens in a silent scream. The crystals on the chandelier overhead begin to tremble, clinking against one another, and then the light fixture starts to sway violently. Shadows waver along the wall, like long fingers scratching at the ceiling. The air quivers with a strange quality, and it feels like all my hair is standing up at once, from the top of my head to the tiny hairs on my arms.

"出來!" Shu-Ling commands whatever is inside her to get out.

Tina falls to the ground, convulsing, her arms straight beside her body, fingers splayed. Her eyes still white, her tongue drooping out of the side of her mouth. A curl of gray smoke emerges from between her lips. It forms itself into a face that only has impressions for eyes and a mouth open in an angry roar. It twists and turns in the air, growing larger and larger, its mouth stretching open, as if trying to eat us whole.

"Got you!" Shu-Ling grins, another talisman in her hand. She holds it up in front of the floating head, which recoils, but Shu-Ling slaps the paper on its cheek. A howl surrounds us, and I clap my hands over my ears to try to block out that terrible noise. The head begins to fly chaotically now, zigzagging through the air, before throwing itself into the mirror with a resounding crack.

THIRTY-NINE

許願

(Wishes)

The mirror splits before my eyes. The cracks spreading and moving, stretching across the entirety of the surface. I don't think, I scramble forward and grab Tina by the shoulders, drag her toward the door until my back hits the wall. I throw my arm around her, protecting her face and my own as the mirror falls off the wall and strikes the floor with a resounding crash. Glass flies everywhere, a million daggers, and I feel pieces of it slice into my exposed arms and face.

When everything quiets. I'm left holding Tina in my arms. Her head lolls to one side, her eyes closed. Her face isn't contorted into that vicious, pained expression anymore. She looks . . . peaceful.

"Is it . . . gone?" I whisper, afraid that if I talk too loud whatever that thing is might come back.

Shu-Ling nods, carefully getting to her feet, glass crunching under her shoes.

There's a pounding on the door above my head, causing me to start.

"Ruby? Are you okay? What's going on in there?" Ma yells through the door, trying the doorknob, but she can't open it because of the weight of our bodies leaning against it.

I meet Shu-Ling's eyes and mouth, *Let me explain.* She nods, understanding that I have to tell my mother in a particular way.

"We're right here," I call out. "Just a second."

Shu-Ling helps me carefully move Tina to the other corner, in a section without much glass, and then I slowly get up from the ground. I open the door to my mother's horrified face, Shen close behind her. His mouth drops open when he sees the bathroom. It must have looked worse than even he expected, considering he knows what we were up to.

"What happened?" Ma manages to gasp.

I cobble together a story in those few moments. About how I saw Tina barge in while Shu-Ling was mopping the floor. She tried to warn her, but Tina slipped and banged her head on the sink. Hard enough that the sink hit the mirror above it, which loosened, falling onto the floor and breaking into a thousand pieces. How Shu-Ling and I barely managed to pull her away so that the mirror didn't land on her, and how she must have passed out in the process.

Ma still seems to be in disbelief. Denny pokes his head in too, wondering what's going on. I yell at her to get him away from all the glass where he could get hurt, while Shu-Ling gets Shen to help her lift Tina out of the bathroom. He tells me where I can pull a blanket out of the cupboard. I spread that over one of the booths, and they carry her over.

"You're bleeding," Shen tells me, carrying over a first-aid kit.

"I'm fine," I try to protest, but he leads me to sit at one of the tables. I look down at my arm and see streaks of blood, and Shen dabs at my cheek and my throat gently with a towel.

That's how Baba comes in and finds us. Shen bandaging my wounds,

Shu-Ling sweeping up the glass in the hall, Tina lying in the booth, unconscious.

"What happened here?" he demands. "Why are both of my daughters hurt? My wife's explanation doesn't make any sense!" Ma probably took Denny out to the car to get Baba to come in and deal with the rest.

It's Shu-Ling who comes over and bows, speaking to him in Mandarin, in a calm and steady manner. Baba's frown goes from furious to puzzled to nodding when she continues her explanation. He turns to me then and asks, "Is this true?"

But we hear a groan coming from the booth, and I knock Shen's arm aside to hurry over to Tina. She tries to push himself up to sitting, moaning a little still as I help her up. I have a feeling of déjà vu. I've woken up there before, in that very booth. Wondering about what I witnessed, not knowing how much my life would change.

"姊姊..." she whispers weakly. It's the way she utters those syllables, how she calls me older sister, that makes me know this is Tina. This is not that thing that used to occupy her. I squeeze her hand so tightly that she squeaks out in protest.

In the end, Baba is appeased when both Shu-Ling and Shen bow in apology, offering free drinks for our family for a year in compensation for this accident that's happened in their store. Even as Tina weakly protests that she was the one who went into the bathroom without paying attention to her surroundings. I help Tina to the car, and she clutches at me like she doesn't want to let me go. Ma and Baba argue in the front of the car about whether they should take her to the emergency room, while Tina tries to tell them that she's fine, she just wants to go home and sleep.

After we get home and tuck Tina in, Ma reminds me to find an outfit for tomorrow. The performance is the furthest thing from my mind, but I flip through my closet, feeling bitter that they still want me to do this show. But then I remember how Shen told me to hold on to my strength. How I found the courage to track him down and confront him to find out what was happening with my sister. How Delia's last words to me before she left were to remind me I am stronger than I know. I can get through this performance, to prove to myself that I am better than the Tanakas and their miserable workshops, that I can perform and do a damn fine job of it.

Shen sends me a message, checking in, make sure that I'm not too shaken up after what happened. He tells me they still haven't heard from Delia, which makes me feel sick.

Shen: She'll turn up, I'm sure of it
Shen: Sometimes she gets like this. Disappears for a few days, says she needs to clear her mind, comes back rested

But I still can't shake the feeling that something is wrong.

I wake in the middle of the night, with the sense of immense pressure on my chest. In my dream I was being buried alive. One by one, I could feel the weight of each stone placed upon me, and there was nothing I could do but wait for the darkness to descend, for the breath to slowly be choked out of my body. . . .

Now awake, features come slowly into focus as my eyes adjust to the dark. It's Tina. Did nothing change? Is she going to try and kill me in my sleep again?

I open my mouth to scream, but she quickly claps her hand over it so the sound comes out muffled, using her knee to press down my arm to keep me in place.

"Shhh..." she whispers, eyes darting here and there. "They're listening. We have to be quiet." At the sound of Tina's hollow voice and her bizarre words, I still. It doesn't make sense, but it also doesn't seem like she's about to kill me, so I force myself to settle down and breathe. She peels her sweaty palm carefully away from my face and climbs off me until I gasp, relieved that I'm no longer carrying her entire weight balanced on my torso.

"Sorry," Tina gulps beside me with a sob. "I've been so scared."

Something rustles outside my door, and we both jump as we wait for whatever it is to come through. But there's nothing. I wait for a moment longer, then slowly sit up. Tina follows suit, so that we're both sitting cross-legged, face-to-face.

"What's happening, Tina?" I ask, reaching for her hands. "You have to tell me."

"They were... in my head all the time," she says. "Always whispering at the back of my mind. Telling me of all the ways that I could get what I wanted, if I just did what they said."

"Do you hear them now?" I ask, aware that they could still be here. Listening. She shakes her head slowly.

"Where did they come from?" I press further, eager to know.

"They said that it was an initiation," she says, pulling her hands back to wrap around her body, shrinking in upon herself. "In order to actually become part of the troupe, we had to go into this... temple. There was a wall, with, like, hundreds of these little plaques. And a huge statue in the corner, but half of it was covered by a black cloth. It gave me the creeps." She shudders.

"What did they actually make you do? Did you... make a wish?" This would confirm everything, that the wish is where it started, that the temple is still around. Everything that Delia was worried about. It's all true.

"They taught us to bow before the statue in the corner and warned us that she could hear our every thought and see our every dream. We had to offer up our deepest desire to her, and if she found us worthy, then she would take care of the rest." Her voice quivers. "I was scared. We all were, so we wrote down our desires on the back of the plaques. On the front, we wrote our names and then they pricked our thumbs, made us put our print on there in blood."

Scaring young and impressionable girls into dark rituals. Despicable.

"Where is it? The actual temple itself? Do you know?" My hand clenches into a fist. Will she confirm my suspicions?

She shakes her head. "It's somewhere in the mall, I'm sure, but they blindfolded us. Made us put our hands on the person in front of us and then forced us to walk. I remember there were a few stairs, maybe one or two flights?"

That doesn't help. I sigh. Unless I go and wander each floor of the mall, try to open every door. What if it's as well hidden as the guardians' temple? A door inside of a door?

"But I did overhear something," Tina whispers. "All I know is that something big is happening tomorrow. They've been talking about it, preparing for it all this time."

"What is it they're working on?" I ask, grasping on to this eagerly. If there is something that I can give to Shu-Ling, maybe this time she will take it seriously and bring it all the way up to the guardians, request assistance from the gods.

"I don't know!" she cries.

The sound of chattering, screeching fills the air. *The monkeys are back.* The shadows on the windowsill, their little figures banging on the glass. But the talisman seems to have done its job. Not letting them back in. Tina weeps, rocking back and forth on the bed, moaning to herself again. I can't keep pushing her like this. I help her lie down and pull the covers over her. Her tears soak into the front of my pajamas as I stroke her hair, telling her that she's safe, that it's okay, that nothing is going to hurt her now.

I only hope that I'm right.

FORTY

焦慮不安

(Haunted)

In the morning, I try my best to piece together for Shen everything Tina told me.

Me: temple is linked to soulful heart somehow
Me: tina said that they've been planning this for a long time
Shen: Shit. I'll tell Shu-Ling
Me: it's all happening together. fate, like delia said, but not in the way she expected. fhe temple, luring people in again with false promises. hope returning to vancouver. delia being taken...
Shen: We still don't know if Delia was taken
Shen: But you're right, it's too many coincidences in a row
Shen: I should have made Shu-Ling pay attention

I clean up my room in an attempt to ease my nerves. When I fold my jacket, a piece of paper flutters out of the pocket and lands on the floor.

I pick it up and see the card for the Temple of Fortunate Tidings. In the chaos of last night, I forgot all about it. It's slightly bent in the corners, but the smudged red seal seems to be an ominous warning. A bad sign. *Something is going to happen tonight.* I take a photo of it and send it to Shen, the back and the front.

Shen: Tonight? Where???
Me: it doesn't say where, only a time

I check it again and again. I hold it up to the light. Dampen it with a bit of water. As if it will reveal a secret, hidden message, for those clever enough to decipher it. But there's nothing. Even holding for too long though, gives me a bad feeling. I rip it up into pieces finally and throw it into the trash. It's a lure, a trap, that's what Delia's binder said.

Shen: Stay away from the mall for now. Just in case
Shen: Until we figure out what's going on

Ma calls me then for breakfast, and I have to spend the morning with her figuring out what pieces I'm going to play for the performance.

My hair is curled into waves that fall below my shoulders. I wear a black dress that leaves my shoulders bare, but I have a lacy maroon shawl that I can wrap around my shoulders to keep warm. Ma applies the lightest makeup that she deems tolerable, eye shadow to my eyelids, a bit of blush to my cheeks, and a light pink lip gloss.

Tina is quiet through all this, eating her oatmeal, lost in her thoughts. Except for a cut on her hand and a small bruise on her chin, she seems to have emerged from yesterday's incident relatively unscathed. Physically, at least.

"Do you want to stay home?" Baba offers, a rarity these days for him to permit one of us to skip out on "family bonding" activities. Tina refuses, a flicker of worry on her face that I understand. She doesn't want to be left home alone. Who knows what could still be lingering in our house? Who is still watching her?

We pile into the car to head downtown to the Dr. Sun Yat-Sen Chinese Garden. My parents refer to Dr. Sun as "國父," the Father of the Republic, because he is acknowledged as one of the influential leaders who led the revolution against the Qing Dynasty, and formed the Republic of China as the leader of the Nationalist Party. The members of that government eventually lost the civil war and then moved to Taiwan, where the resultant effects are still felt to this day. Though the rule of the Nationalist Party has not always been the best for the people of Taiwan, Dr. Sun is regarded in mostly a favorable light as an idealist, a philosopher, a leader of the people. That he once visited the gardens in Vancouver himself is what my parents talk about on the drive there, a bit of history I didn't know.

When we walk through the doors, the white walls provide a barrier between the gardens and the bustle of the city. They remove all the cars and the noise and the people, so I can almost pretend that I've been transported back to what China once was. Despite the snow, yellow, red, and gold leaves still remain on most of the trees or have fallen in drifts in the pond and on the sides of the paths.

The sound of the piano trickles out from one of the rooms down the hall. At the entrance there is a poster of the event: AN AFTERNOON OF TRANQUIL MUSIC & REFLECTION. FUNDRAISER FOR THE OWNERS OF SUNDAY RICE BOWL. SPONSORED BY THE FORMOSA FRIENDSHIP ASSOCIATION. There is an image of a smiling family. Happy Asian parents, two kids in their best clothes: a girl wearing a red polka-dot dress, a red bow in her hair, while the boy is in a white shirt with a gray polka-dot bow tie.

"I heard about what happened." Ma tsks. "Such a sad story. The res-taurant was doing really well, even won an award for the best curry rice bowl in the city. The father is from Taiwan, the mother from Japan. I had been meaning to go there and try the curry. But there was a fire in the store. The little boy died, the little girl got smoke-inhalation dam-age in her lungs and is still undergoing treatment. Both parents were burned badly. What a tragedy." She shakes her head.

"I know, it truly is tragic what happened to them." Mrs. Tsai is sud-denly there. "That's why we must all come together in support."

She puts a hand on my arm and says, with great seriousness, "Thank you, Ruby, for your help. We appreciate you filling in for us. I promise it will be very low-key."

I pull my face up in a smile. Tina clings to me a little and has to let go when Mrs. Tsai leads me away. She looks so small and sad as I'm walking down the hall, that I almost turn and run back to her, but I'm pulled into another room and handed off to a smiling woman who calls herself Mrs. Lin. There are other musicians here too. A boy who's about Denny's age, tuning his violin. Another girl in a long, floaty dress, play-ing a flute. They all seem happy to be here, to be part of the program. The opposite of how I feel.

"Can I get you anything, Ruby? Snacks? Drinks?" Mrs. Lin offers, but I shake my head.

I stare at the calligraphy on the wall while I wait for my turn. I feel like I should be nervous, I should have that feeling that I'm going to throw up, like I've done in my previous attempts at performing, but I'm strangely calm. I know the pieces. I am certain of it. I know that I am able to play them, and I know that I am able to perform them well. It's all the pressure, the expectations weighing on me, that tears me up inside and out. But I reach for the pendant at my throat, thinking of the letter hidden there: *peace.* A feeling of serenity drifts over me. I look at the fluid brushstrokes, thinking about how Shen once referred to calligraphy as meditation, a way to look within.

I don't play piano to impress teachers, to have something to list on the résumé, for my parents to brag about my achievements with their friends. I play piano for me, because of how the music makes me feel, how it unravels all my worries and anxieties, throws them out for the audience to hear. For them to experience. To accept me as I am. Flaws and all.

"Hehehehe . . ." Suddenly, I hear giggles from behind the shelves in the room. Eyes watching me somewhere up above. "She thinks she's safe . . . but it's almost time. . . ."

I shudder but stay focused on what I'm about to do. I also have to trust that Shu-Ling is going to communicate with the guardians. Tell them about what is happening. Have them save Chinatown from the dark force of the temple. Protect girls like Tina.

"It's your turn, Ruby!" Mrs. Tsai waves at me from the door. I walk out, standing tall. I don't look back.

The performance is in a lovely room with folding doors that can keep out the chill or be opened to the garden. I can still see the view of the garden if I turn my head, and the people walking by, pausing with drinks in hand, to listen to my performance. I pretend that I am at the manor, performing for the Chorus of Aunties. Mrs. Sui and Mrs. Wang sitting at the very front seats, waiting to hear me finally play a piece for them.

I close my eyes, and even though I had prepared myself to play the Moonlight Sonata, it's the Rachmaninoff that pours out of my hands. The Rachmaninoff that starts as a steady wave, moving forward, pulling back, building and building upon itself. I move to the sound of the music, the rich and dark chords, let it flow through my body. I imagine myself as a channel, for the emotions that course through me as I work through this piece. The gentle lull in the middle, that rumbling current that still ripples under the surface.

Again and again, relentless in its power, the sound swoops through my hands, dragging out what is hidden in the deep. It comes back, rising, more powerful each time, my hands flying across the keys. I become the ocean, sometimes gentle and calm, an illusion of safety, but other times I break through and nothing can hold me back. When I finish playing, I can feel myself sweating a little from the exertion, something inside me trembling as the last notes fade away.

The audience applauds, and I stand and bow, resisting the urge to wipe my hands on my dress.

"Wonderful, wonderful." Mr. Lee goes up to the microphone and thanks everyone in the audience for attending, along with a speech of appreciation for the performers.

I hurry away to stand beside my family, eager to be out of the eyes of the audience. I survived. I played one of the more challenging songs in my repertoire. A sense of relief flows through me as I think about my performance—how I did it without panicking, without my stomach in turmoil, without thinking about the Tanakas and their harsh criticisms, and I steady myself against Denny, who looks up at me and smiles.

Suddenly, my mother grasps my arm, making happy noises of excitement, disrupting my inner dialogue. I had zoned out from the speech, but all the eyes of the audience have turned to me. Everyone is clapping. I'm confused.

"They're giving you a scholarship, Ruby!" Ma shakes my arm. They're all watching me for a reaction. The applause continues. I plaster what must look like the fakest grin on my face as I approach the microphone.

"The Formosa Friendship Association and the Sunrise Foundation are pleased to present this cheque to you in support of our brilliant future generations!" Mr. Lee pumps my hand several times, grinning, while handing me a large cheque to hold. I stand there beside him while cameras flash. The name Sunrise Foundation sounding vaguely familiar in my head—maybe something Delia mentioned? I feel a pang of worry as my thoughts drift to where she could be, but before I know it, the event is over and other parents come by to offer my parents their congratulations, their mouths forming similar praises and platitudes, until they all run together. Many of their children stand sullenly behind them, looking like they wish they could be anywhere else but here.

Mrs. Tsai is there again, shaking my hand as well. I finally look down at the cheque. Five thousand dollars. A good start to my university fund. I should be grateful.

"Aren't you happy you agreed to do this, Ruby?" Baba nudges me, beaming. "To think you almost turned down this opportunity!" Another thing they can add to their list of things to hold above my head and tell me that every decision they make for me is for the best.

The excitement at conquering my fear of performance sits sour in my stomach.

I almost laugh when Mrs. Tsai's next words are to tell us to join her in Soulful Heart Studio so we can sign some papers and she can give us the real cheque, and to invite us to the fundraising dinner.

Held at the Pacific Dragon Mall.

FORTY-ONE

夢 想

(Dreams)

I could make a run for it right now. Hand my parents the cheque, tell them I'm going to the bathroom, then walk out the front door and head home. They would be angry. Furious with me. But it's not like I haven't dealt with that before. Except Tina and Denny stand there, waiting for me, while my parents are already halfway down the hall toward the exit, following Mrs. Tsai's lead. Tina looks like she's about to be sick as she clings tightly to Denny's hand. Denny looks back at me, unsuspecting and innocent.

"Ruby! Let's not keep Mrs. Tsai waiting!" Ma chides me from a distance.

If I run away, what will happen to my brother and sister?

"Do you remember what you said last night?" I ask Tina quietly as we make our way down the hall. "That something is happening today?"

Tina shakes her head, wide-eyed and confused.

"Did I talk to you last night?" she asks. "I don't remember.... I just woke up in your bed."

I bite my lip to hold back a swear. How much does Tina remember of what happened to her? While we're waiting at the intersection for the light to change, I call out to my parents.

"I don't think Tina's feeling well," I tell them. Tina leans on me, swaying on her feet. A helpful act? Or something else?

"It won't take long, I promise," Mrs. Tsai reassures my parents, not even acknowledging Tina. "We'll sign some papers, and then we'll be done."

Too soon we are already at the door to the mall. The same sign is up, about the mall being closed for a private event. Mrs. Tsai has to call for someone to come and let us in. A man in yellow quickly appears at the door, and there are a few more of them waiting inside, bowing for us like we are revered guests. The sight of them makes me nervous, and I no longer care about acceptable excuses—I want to grab my family and run. But the doors shut and lock behind us, and it's too late.

"These young men are part of our lion-and-dragon dance troupes," Mrs. Tsai explains to my parents, gesturing to the men wearing matching yellow headbands and yellow pants.

We walk down the hallway that leads into the studio, but this time the eyes on the photographs seem to be following our every move. Tina walks so closely next to me, I almost trip over her feet.

"Maybe Denny and Tina can wait in the kids' space while we finish up," Mrs. Tsai says. In the corner there is a table with chairs, a shelf filled with books and art supplies. I didn't notice it yesterday, with the studio filled with people. Now the quiet is almost deafening, pressing around us from all directions.

"We'll wait here," Tina says quickly, leading Denny away.

"Please, come in." Mrs. Tsai opens the door to what looks like a conference room. A huge table takes up the space, with office chairs all around it. There's a flat-screen TV mounted to the wall. Ma and Baba take their seats. Mrs. Tsai takes the cheque away from me and leans it against the wall, gestures for me to sit as well. I perch on the edge of one of the rolling chairs, ready to get this done with and go home.

"Help yourself." Mrs. Tsai pushes forward a few water bottles already on the table. The room is warm, the heater rumbling in the corner on full blast, circulating hot air in the small room.

"Oh, thank you. I am a bit parched." Baba opens a bottle and drinks it. Ma follows as well. I realize too late when I look at the bottle that I recognize the label. It's the lotus symbol. The same bottles as the ones in Tina's room. The same one that Shu-Ling said made someone more susceptible to influence.

Mrs. Tsai watches me, a small smile curving her lips. She knows that I know. The room suddenly feels like it's closing in, the space folding in upon itself. I should have asked Tina where she got the bottles from after we broke her free from the possession. I should have been smarter, and now, even after knowing the connection between the dark temple and the dance studio, I still walked straight into this trap. Since Mrs. Tsai is the director, there is no way it could have operated without her knowing. They're not going to let Tina go.

"At Soulful Heart, we see our students as family," she explains. "We are committed to supporting them in every aspect of their lives, ensuring they do their very best." It's similar to the speech she gave us at our dining room table, promising access to everything, yet she never mentioned the true price.

"But what do you get out of this?" I burst out, unable to stay quiet any longer. The reality of what Tina told me before hitting me now. Each piece on the Wall of Wishes has the name of a girl. How many girls are walking around out there, carrying something else inside them—something evil?

"Ruby!" Ma chastises, embarrassed that I would dare speak up against an elder.

"No, no." Mrs. Tsai shakes her head. "It's a great question, isn't it? What do we get out of helping our students? Well, our board members strongly believe in supporting the next generation. We encourage good behaviors. The right behaviors." The light above our heads dims, and the flat-screen TV on the wall flickers on. But her hands still remain on the table in plain sight. She didn't reach for anything or press a button. She didn't move at all, and yet . . .

"What?" I manage to sputter, but my parents both turn their heads obediently toward the screen, unbothered by this whole display. The drinks are still in their hands.

"Stop drinking that!" I knock the bottle out of Ma's hand. It falls on the table, spilling its contents across the surface. She doesn't react. She doesn't stand up and look for paper towels to wipe it clean, apologizing profusely for my outburst. She sits there with a blank look, eyes unfocused.

"You could have a bright future ahead of you, 陳小姐," Mrs. Tsai continues as if I haven't done anything, that infuriating expression of mild amusement still present. "It only takes a little bit of sacrifice. Listening to your parents and to your elders. Not associating with people of 'questionable influence.'"

I remain standing, hands on the table. She must know everything. The guardians. My requests for their help. The battle hidden within Chinatown. What if I just make a run for it? Push through the doors, grab Tina and Denny, and get out of here?

"We've been interested in your association with the followers of the guardians," Mrs. Tsai says. The screen changes behind her, showing an image of the altar hidden inside the Golden Age Seniors Association. Three statues with offerings before it. The camera zooms out then, panning across the entirety of the room, and stops on two figures standing in the middle of the space.

There's a woman dressed in a long red robe, wearing a high black hat. Between her index and middle fingers, she holds a talisman lit with a white flame, but she doesn't seem to be burned by it. She waves it in the air, her lips moving as she continues her purposeful steps, just like Shu-Ling did for me when she removed the darkness on my ankle. A man stands to the left of the altar, periodically ringing the heavy-looking gold bell in his hand. The video pixelates and then refocuses.

"This is Mr. and Mrs. Chang. You are familiar with their children, Shu-Ling and Kai-Shen." She speaks in that bland voice. "Two years ago, they died, part of a senseless and futile struggle, and now Shu-Ling continues on this course. Change is coming for them, a new order."

"And Delia . . ." When the video flickers, I see Mrs. Tsai's face ripple, like the TV screen. Only for a moment. Enough for me to wonder if I really saw it or not. "Delia . . . sticking her nose where she doesn't belong." The video changes to one of me standing outside the school. Delia handing me the helmet, me climbing onto the back of the motorcycle.

"Why were you filming me?" I gasp, shocked at my appearance on the screen. Even though I know they can't hear or see me now, I look toward my parents almost involuntarily, knowing that they will disapprove. Still, they sit there silent, not reacting to anything that Mrs. Tsai is speaking about.

"It's all for your own good, don't you understand? Our dream of a different life than the one we came from." Her red lips pull away from her teeth, snarling. "All of you girls. Don't you know how much we sacrificed, coming over here, giving you all of the opportunities in the world, only for you to waste them?"

How many times have I heard the same thing before from my parents? That they came here to start a new life, to give us the best education, the best opportunities. For that, we should always follow what they say.

"But here we have to deal with young delinquents like Delia." Her scowl deepens. "These children who are permitted to run amok without proper supervision, dragging people from good families down with them, ruining their futures." Delia told me it was just her and her mother, having to fend for herself most nights when she was old enough because her mother had to work two jobs to make ends meet.

"Delia loved Hope," I say quietly. "All they wanted was a different sort of life than the one you imagined for them. Is that so wrong?"

"What does she know at seventeen?" she scoffs in return. "You think that you will marry the first person who pays you any attention. Some girl who is probably just a phase, ruining your life . . . for what?"

"There's nothing wrong with liking girls," I retort, trying to defend Delia, a complicated tangle of emotions surging in my chest. I haven't had crushes on many people in my life, but sometimes it's girls and sometimes it's boys. A realization that I've always kept to myself, afraid of reactions like these. Another way to disappoint my parents.

"Of course you would say that, when you're guilty of it yourself. Too busy kissing the same delinquents." A strange light comes on in her eyes as the screen behind her changes yet again. This time to Chinatown. The video zooming in on Shen . . . and me, standing in the bookstore alcove. Him lowering his head and kissing me. Someone filming us from across the street. My stomach recoils at the thought of someone following us, watching us. My hand finds its way to my chest, to the bump under my shirt, the pendant that's still there.

"You think that pendant will help you?" She tilts her head to one side, as if amused. "Why don't you take it out? Hold it. See for yourself if it works."

She already knows that it's there. Shen said that it will protect me, and perhaps it will do its job now. Tentatively, I reach down for the pendant, pulling it out of my shirt. When my hand closes around the jade, the world shifts. Like a candle being blown out, Mrs. Tsai's face melts away.

FORTY-TWO

(A Request Made)

Behind her face is a corpse. Half of her skin has peeled away, her eye sockets empty, her nose gone. Her mouth is just grinning teeth. It never occurred to me that she too could be a vessel. I scream, pushing myself away from the table, sitting down heavily on the chair with wheels. It rolls back a few feet before bumping against the wall.

I'm crying now as I throw myself at Ma's arm, trying to pull her back. I dig my fingers into her shoulder, trying to wake her up, yelling beside her ear, "Wake up, Ma! Wake up! What's wrong with you? This is messed up! You can both see that this is messed up, can't you?"

"Ruby..." Mrs. Tsai says, voice gentle. "They can't hear you." When I look back at her again, she's returned to normal. The same as she's always looked. Like an elegantly dressed lady who works in an office, like a classmate's mother, like one of Ma's friends who I have to call "Auntie."

"What did you do to them?" I'm standing between my parents now, my head racing with all the possibilities of what I could do. Somewhere in the distance, I think I hear the sound of a gong. The clock on the wall behind them continues to tick. It's four o'clock.

"There's our signal. The show's about to start." Mrs. Tsai grins again, that macabre expression. "Hope will understand everything I've done for her, like you will understand what your parents have done for you."

I throw myself at the door and pull it open. I run down the hallway, screaming for Tina and Denny. I know I have to get them out of here, get help. If I can find my way up to the second level, then maybe I will be able to talk to Shu-Ling. She can bring the guardians to save us. She has to.

But the play area is empty. I run down the front hallway to the studio doors and pull at the handle, but it doesn't budge. I slam my fist on the wall, crying out, hoping someone will hear me when they walk by. The doors rattle, and the locks hold. Footsteps sound at the end of the hall. Two young men in their lion dance costumes turn the corner, advancing toward me with their eerily blank expressions. They grab me by my arms, even though I yell at them to get off of me. I push them away, try to kick, but it's no use. I'm too weak and they're too strong.

"Where did you take my brother?" I scream. "Where's my sister?"

Mrs. Tsai stands at the doorway of the conference room and watches as I'm pulled past her. My parents also stand behind her, their expressions mirroring the same vacant stares of the men beside me.

At the end of the hallway, they open a door and push me through. It's a back stairwell, no windows. Concrete steps leading upward and down. One of them retrieves a piece of fabric hanging from a hook on the wall and pulls it over my face.

"No . . ." I beg, terrified that I'm not able to see anything now. "Please . . . Let me go."

They push against my back, and I stumble forward as they half guide, half drag me down the stairs. My feet keep catching on the steps, and they lift my arms with bruising grips when I fall. The floor changes beneath my feet when we squeeze through a doorway, from the roughness of concrete to what feels like the slipperiness of tile.

The heavy scent of incense invades my nostrils, fills my mouth and throat under the covering. I'm spun around, disoriented as hands roughly grab and tug the fabric off my head, yanking some strands of hair out along the way. Someone pushes me forward, and I fall, catching myself on my hands and knees. I look up and turn my head slowly. I notice that the lower part of the wall is covered with a long red curtain. A strange decorating choice. It isn't until I tip my head back that I notice what is hanging on the upper half of the wall. Rows upon rows of wooden plaques, dangling from red strings. Just like Tina described.

The Wall of Wishes.

Somewhere in the distance, a phone rings. But I can't see anyone else in here with me, other than the two men who brought me here. They're still standing there stiffly, hands folded before them. Watchful guards. I look down the other length of the room but can't see an exit, only shelves running along the wall. On top of which sit items of various shapes, but all wrapped in black fabric and tied with red string, and it is impossible to see what is underneath.

On the floor before the wall there is a pile of bags. A peculiar assortment. A violin case. A backpack. A duffel bag. Another mound of what appears to be clothing is beside it. There's a purple windbreaker, a dark blue hoodie with the yellow UBC logo. But before I can dwell on it for long, someone answers the insistent ring of the phone. A man's voice. Too muffled for me to understand what he is saying, but the voice gets louder, and I realize that he's getting closer. Until there's a rustling at the end of the room. A curtain slides open to reveal a doorway, and a man steps through.

Salt-and-pepper hair. A black polo shirt and black pants. He turns off the phone and slips it into his pocket. He stands above me as my mouth drops open in shock because I know who he is.

"Hello, Ruby," he says in his smooth, radio-announcer voice.

Mr. Lee. Melody's father.

I don't understand what he is doing here before the Wall of Wishes. My brain cannot make the connection. I knew that he was part of one of the many Chinatown business associations and had some connection with the Taiwanese community too. But what does he have to do with Soulful Heart or the temple hidden underneath it?

"I understand all of this must be very overwhelming," he says. My hand fumbles for the pendant, closing around it, trying to see if his face hides something monstrous underneath, like Mrs. Tsai. But his face remains the same. Unchanged.

He reaches out for me, and I flinch away from his fingers, but hands are suddenly on my shoulder, holding me still. With one hand, he lifts the pendant out of my shirt and looks down at me, brow slightly furrowed, then he nods in recognition.

"Ah . . . this won't help you," he says, and with a sharp tug, the string snaps, the pendant falling into his hand.

"That's mine!" I protest, trying to snatch it back, even as he straightens away from me and examines the pendant closer.

"Actually, this belongs to my family," Mr. Lee tells me. "This was my sister's pendant."

"That's a lie!" I raise my voice, even though I probably shouldn't in my precarious position.

"You got this from my nephew, did you not?" He lifts a brow. "A'Shen?" I must have looked baffled again, because he laughs.

"This belonged to my sister, Evelyn Lee." He dangles the pendant above me for a few moments before slipping it into his pants pocket. "Though most people know her as Mrs. Chang. Mother of Shu-Ling and Kai-Shen."

"But they follow the guardians." There must be something I'm not understanding. Some way for this all to make sense, if only I can see it. "They fought the Temple of Wishes."

"The Temple of Hopeful Desires," Mr. Lee corrects me. "They fought against the demon who called himself the God of Good Deeds and got themselves killed in the process. But my sister and her husband were always foolish and weak, never understanding the bigger picture." His lips curl in disgust.

"What do you mean?" I whisper, the sense of danger growing now rapidly. "Did you have something to do with their deaths?"

"No, I was foolish too. Still believed in the cause of the guardians." He smiles then, and I did not know why I once thought he was kind. "All that has to change now. The start of a new order." He snaps his fingers.

I look over my shoulder to see more figures in yellow, dragging another person between them. She's thrown forward and lands on her side at Mr. Lee's feet. Another girl. One of the performers from the garden. She looks up at the man, terrified. Her hands are bound behind her, but still, she kicks and struggles, trying to break free. Her screams are muffled by the gag in her mouth.

"You are so blessed that you will play a part in the grand ritual." Mrs. Tsai's voice sounds behind me as she walks around us and ends up beside Mr. Lee. He takes her hand between his and pats it, looks at her with affection as she regards him in turn. "We will bring fortune and prosperity again to those who deserve it, and our enemies . . . well, they will deserve their fate too."

"What ritual?" I manage to gasp.

The sound of the gong rings again, and this time it feels like we are inside it. The room seems to tremble with the sound, and I have to cover my ears with my hands to try and stop that ringing.

"It's time for the second sacrifice," Mr. Lee announces. He grabs the girl at his feet and pulls her up, even as she kicks and thrashes.

"The gods will stop you! You can't do this!" I plead, trying to stop them from doing whatever they are going to do to that poor girl.

"Oh, there are plenty of gods watching us, don't you worry." Mrs. Tsai pulls out a sharp knife the length of her forearm. It glints in the light as she points it in the direction of the wall of shelves and their mysterious objects. "But they won't be able to hear you. No one is coming to help you. Just like no one is coming to help *her*."

Before I can even react, Mr. Lee pulls back the head of the girl by the hair, baring her throat. With one quick slash, Mrs. Tsai cuts her throat open. Blood spills all the way down the front of her body as she convulses. The awful sound of her choking. She falls to her knees, hands clutching at her neck, as her blood pools beneath her legs.

I turn my head at the sputtering, groaning noises she makes as she takes her final breaths. I can't look at her. Sobs rise up in my throat at the horror of what's in front of me. They murdered her, and I know I'm next.

The ground rumbles beneath our feet, like an earthquake. The ringing of the gong finally stops.

"The next door opens!" Mr. Lee exclaims, and then he begins to chant. The other figures in the room step close, joining him.

I witness the blood on the floor before my feet moving, joining together into large droplets, and then rising into the air. A spiral of blood, spinning above them, reminding me of those decorations hanging from the ceiling in the studio. An optical illusion, except this one actually moves, making its way toward the corner. Where it falls upon a large shape draped under black cloth.

A statue, Tina mentioned last night.

Under my gaze, the cloth twitches.

"Don't you want to know what happened to Delia?" Mrs. Tsai is suddenly before me, crouching down. Her cold hand grips my chin as she turns my face to look at her. At her gleeful expression. Then she forces my head to turn, to look down, as she pulls up one of the jackets to reveal...

Delia's face. Her eyes are still open, giving her a faint look of surprise. But there's a gash at her neck. The front of her white shirt soaked in blood. She's dead too. Mrs. Tsai lets go of me and steps away, joining her voice to the chants as I collapse, hands flying to my mouth as I hold back my screams. *They're dead.* I rock back and forth on my knees. *They're all dead.*

"Psst..." a voice whispers to my left, coming from behind the lower curtains. "Psst... Ruby!"

FORTY-THREE

必 應

(A Response Given)

I look over to the wall only to see a face emerge from the fabric. Delia's face. Even while her body is lying there in plain sight. I gasp, and she quickly shushes me with a finger to her lips, crawling out from the space underneath the curtains where she was hiding.

"We don't have much time while they're performing the rest of the ritual," she whispers. "Only Mr. Lee can fully see and hear me, but they will definitely see you move, so you'll have to move quick."

"But..." I have so many questions. She shakes her head.

"We'll have time to talk... after. But right now, I'm going to need you to follow my directions very carefully," she tells me, as serious as I've ever seen her. "You're going to need to reach into the pocket of my jacket. The inner pocket."

I stare at her, scared of what she will ask me to do. Then my gaze slides to her body. To her still-open eyes staring up at the ceiling.

"Pretend I'm sleeping. Pay attention!" Delia snaps her fingers in front of my face, startling me to focus on the task at hand. I reach in. Her body is still warm, and her shirt slightly damp and sticky. That's her blood. My fingers are covered with it. My vision starts to blur, my head growing dizzy. I squeeze my eyes shut and try to recall what she said. Pretend she's only sleeping.

I find her pocket, and then inside it, something small and smooth. A lighter.

"Good." Ghost Delia nods. I slip it into my own jacket pocket. "My bag is in that pile. The duffel bag with the cat boba key chain."

I spot the colorful key chain quickly, and I slowly creep toward it, even as I'm certain I will be discovered in the next second. I slide the zipper open with the pull, trying not to make a noise.

"There's a jar inside, wrapped in some clothes. Pull it out. *Carefully.*" Her instructions are a clear warning. I tug at the jar, but it's weighed down by the other bags on top of it, and I have to try and maneuver it out. Slowly, inch by inch, I'm able to ease it away from the bundle.

When it's in my hands, I dare to glance at the chanters again. The blood spiral has disappeared. Instead, there is a symbol glowing above the large statue in the corner they now surround. Tendrils of red and gold, like blood vessels, spreading across the white ceiling tiles. They still haven't noticed me.

"What should I do?" I whisper at Delia. The jar is cold to the touch. It's sealed with a lid, but there is a bit of cloth sticking out on top. Liquid sloshes about at the bottom.

"Use the lighter and light the cloth, then throw it at the wall," Delia says, raising her arm to point at the Wall of Wishes. She looks up at the rows of wooden plaques, face twisted in pain. "The cause of so many people's suffering."

I can see through her fully transparent hand to the wall beyond, and that fills me with a sudden, quiet rage. All those girls who didn't know what they were a part of.

"Do it now!" Her gaze meets mine in understanding as she nods. "Before it's too late!"

I fumble for the lighter, use my thumb to start the flame while staggering to my feet. Time seems to slow, as if I am watching myself from a distance, bringing the flame to the wick.

"What's she doing?" Mrs. Tsai shrieks, finally noticing me. "Stop her!"

The liquid sloshes to the other side of the jar as I shift my weight, bringing my arm back. I'm praying now, begging to whatever god is able to hear me, whatever god might still be listening. The jar flies out of my hand and hits the wall just as a body hits mine, and we fall toward the ground in a tangle of limbs.

The jar shatters above me, sending a shower of glass toward the ground. The fire erupts overhead with a sudden whoosh. There is the sound of screaming, and I roll over to see one of the men in yellow burning. His hair, his back, are all covered with orange flames. The curtains below catch fire as well. Everything is wood, fabric. Fuel for the eager flames. I kick against the floor as I scramble back, away from the man, who continues to scream.

"Go to the door! Now!" Delia is suddenly before me, gesturing frantically, yelling in my face to get up. There's a door beyond that curtain. The one that Mr. Lee passed through earlier. There are more screams behind me as I jump to my feet and run for it.

My fingers grasp the curtain and pull, only for something to yank me back. There's another man in yellow behind me, but he's burning too. There's fire in his eyes, in his open mouth. He's burning up from the *inside out*. The fire has grown big enough to cover the wall and the flames are licking the ceiling. He drags me back toward the inferno, while Mr. Lee struggles with a fire extinguisher to try to calm the flames.

I grab on to shelves on the wall, but my hands slip. One of the items on the shelf comes away. It's solid, and it has weight. I swing with all my might and it cracks against the side of his head. He falls sideways. I tuck whatever it is under my arm like a football and turn to run through the curtains and the door.

"Down this way!" Delia floats ahead of me as I kick the door shut behind us. We're running down a back hallway, the lights turning on by motion sensor, clicking loudly as we pass them.

There's something smeared across the left lens of my glasses, making it difficult to see. I try to swipe at it as I continue to run. The light at the end of the hall begins to flash, pulsing a warning red. Delia disappears through the door, and I fly through it a moment later.

It's another stairwell.

"I'm up here!" she calls out, already up the flight of stairs, not constrained by a body and gravity. I follow her, panting all the way, wishing desperately that I were in better shape than I am now.

But in the distance I hear footsteps and more yelling. They've entered the stairwell too. I run faster as I follow Delia into another hallway of back doors.

"Here!" Delia points. The door in front of us is marked GOLDEN AGE. I try the doorknob, but it rattles in my hand. I knock on the door, then begin to pound it, as I can hear more people advancing up the stairwell.

I pound the door harder and yell: "Shen!" Delia, with a look of determination upon her face, runs for the door and disappears through it. I catch a whiff of smoke, the acrid taste running down the back of my throat.

The door flies open, and Shen is there. He pulls me through and locks the door behind me. I'm here. I'm finally safe. Shen leads me to a chair and I half slide, half collapse into it. My legs quivering like jelly.

"Ruby, what happened?" Mrs. Sui rolls up in her wheelchair.

"Ai-ya, ai-ya." Mrs. Wang shakes her head, looking distraught.

"When I saw Delia, I thought..." Shen's voice cracks, his face pale. I reach out and grip his hand. He squeezes my hand back, hard.

"They performed some sort of ritual, beneath the dance studio," I tell him—this boy I've gotten to know, grown to trust over the past few weeks, who would believe me no matter what sort of fantastical thing I'm saying now. "They killed Delia, and another girl, and they were going to kill me too."

"怎麼會這樣..." Mrs. Sui wrings her hands in her lap.

"Truly, a touching scene." Delia waves frantically at the door. "But they're coming!" The door slams; whoever it is on the other side seems to have thrown their entire weight into it. Then, harder this time, the frame bulging from the force.

Shen goes to the file cabinet beside the door, and I join him. With a horrific screech of metal scraping against the floor, we manage to push the cabinet to block the doorway.

"What did they tell you?" he tosses over his shoulder while he goes to pulls the security gate shut, locking it with a key, then secures the glass doors.

Above us, the lights flicker. All of us look up at the same time. The thumping against the door has stopped, but there's a sudden whine, like something powering down. The lights flicker again in the Senior Centre and remain on, but the lights outside in the mall darken to an ominous shade of red. Emergency lights.

"They used me as part of a blood sacrifice. The blood was collected into a statue and formed a sort of symbol," Delia finally responds, with her arms folded over her chest. Speaking of her murder like it was nothing. She tries to grab a notebook, but her hand passes through it. She gives a grunt of frustration before gesturing for me to pick it up. I follow her finger as she points, outlining the symbol that she saw.

"Where the hell is Shu-Ling? What is she doing?" Delia demands when the drawing is done.

"She's in there." Shen thrusts his thumb toward the doors that lead to the guardian altar. "Trying to get a message to the gods."

The double doors swing open, and Shu-Ling appears. Still dressed in what I've come to recognize as her usual outfit: baggy sweater, jeans. Except for the talisman she's still holding in her hand between two fingers, pointed skyward. A tendril of smoke lifts toward the ceiling.

Shu-Ling notices me then, and her gaze lands on Delia. Her eyes only widen slightly in an expression of shock, followed by sadness.

"Well, shit," she exclaims. "No wonder I can't get through." She blows out the flame of the talisman, then thrusts it into a glass of water that's in her other hand.

Shu-Ling frowns at Delia, then turns her head, scanning the room, like she's looking for something.

"Something stinks here," she says, pointing to the bundle that rolled out of my arms when I staggered into the room. I pick it up, but it suddenly wiggles in my grasp, like it's alive. It falls out of my hand and unrolls itself as it lands on the floor, revealing what is inside.

It's . . . a statue. About one foot high, like the size of the god statue that sits in the corner of the Senior Centre. 土地公. Except . . . there are jagged edges to it, like someone has taken an ax to it and hacked pieces off. Shu-Ling kneels down before it and pulls out her snake-head whip from her belt. She nudges it so that the statue rolls onto its back.

"Ah!" Mrs. Wang yelps as if someone pushed her, and Shen is there to steady her so that she does not slide onto the ground. But we all find ourselves returning back to stare at what she reacted so strongly to. Because the statue has no head. Someone chopped it off entirely. The neck is blackened, burned, and the rest of it scorched, as if it was held in a flame.

"Desecrated," Shu-Ling says with disgust. "Headless, unable to communicate with the heavens. Removed his hands and feet so he can not call for help. Corrupted it with ashes from a murdered corpse. It's an empty vessel now...to hold whatever disgusting, foul thing that they wish to call forth."

"Remember when you asked me how bound spirits could leave the place where they are bound?" Shen tells me softly. "This is one of the ways."

"They have many of them, lined up against the wall," I tell Shu-Ling, trying to remember. "Ten, maybe twenty of them?"

"They've damned themselves many times over," Mrs. Sui declares. "Even the most forgiving god would never accept them in their presence now."

"They're not welcoming gods," Shu-Ling says, voice severe. "They're welcoming something else entirely."

The speaker crackles overhead, an announcement forthcoming.

"Please make your way down to the lobby in an orderly fashion. This is not a drill," Mr. Lee's voice says in Mandarin, lightly amused, like this is all a great joke to him. "I repeat, this is not a drill." Then, a pronounced pause before he says: "Shu-Ling. Kai-Shen. I'm talking to you."

Shen frowns. "That sounds like..."

"It's your uncle," Delia says flatly. "He's the one who murdered me."

FORTY-FOUR

(Door Gods)

"Uncle Tim?" Shen doesn't seem to believe it. "But...why? He wants nothing to do with the guardians. He broke ties with us when we refused to move the temple out of Chinatown."

"Your Uncle Timothy has always been ambitious," Mrs. Sui says, eyes wide. "As the eldest son, he expected to be the one chosen as the next head priest. Sadly, it would not surprise me to see him take matters into his own hands."

"We should have seen it," Mrs. Wang says, remorseful. "But there are not many of us left now."

"Delia...Delia smuggled a Molotov cocktail in," I try to explain, struggling with the tears that are coming up again. "We destroyed the Wall of Wishes. That should have weakened them...right? The fire-fighters will be coming soon?" I'm talking now more to comfort myself than to find the answers. I need to know that help is coming.

"Since I'm not able to get a message out of this place, then I doubt anyone will be able to physically enter unless the entirety of the mall crashes down and takes us with it," Shu-Ling says. She turns to Delia and then bows, bending fully at the waist, rising up after to regard the younger woman with great sincerity. No longer the flippant woman I initially met. "I am sorry I did not listen to your warnings. I failed in my duty to protect you and to protect the people in Chinatown."

Delia looks taken aback at this, before finding the careful response. "They're planning something, that's all I know. I overheard them talking about it in the room. You'll have to stop them, whatever it is."

Shu-Ling's expression turns grim. "I suspect they want to finish what the God of Good Deeds started all those years ago. To rip open the barrier between worlds. For there to be hell on earth."

"We should go and see what they want, then." Shu-Ling sighs. She kneels before Mrs. Sui and takes her hands. "姑婆, you'll stay here until it's safe?"

Mrs. Sui pats her arm and says sadly: "戇囡仔…戇囡仔…姑婆 is too old and weak to help you. . . ." Even with my poor Taiwanese, I understand what it means. *Foolish child.*

"What you asked us to finish for your earlier is on the table." Mrs. Wang points to the long table in the middle of the room with a shaky hand.

"Thank you, Auntie." Shen helps her back to her walker, where she sits down heavily, sighing as well.

"Ruby, roll up the statue for me," Mrs. Sui instructs. "Be careful not to touch it with your bare hands. If there is nothing else we can do, we can at least clean this foul thing up."

I follow her directions, kneeling down to fold the cloth over the statue before rolling it up back into a bundle again.

"Can you help them into the temple?" Shu-Ling directs me while she bends over the table with Shen, looking over whatever the Aunties prepared for them. I push Mrs. Sui inside to where the statues of the gods still sit. But this time, the curtain along the other wall has been fully pulled open, and I gape at the marvelous art that was hidden behind it.

The entirety of the wall is covered with a mural. I recognize Mazu, the Goddess of the Sea, revered in Taiwan. She wears the equivalent of the crown of an empress, and her robes are red, flowing into the water and turning into rippling waves behind her. Beside her are her disciples, the One Who Sees a Thousand Miles and the One Who Hears the Wind, each with comically large features of their special abilities—all painted in a very familiar art style. This is Shen's work.

Mrs. Sui turns toward the wall and bows reverently. "Even though we are followers of the guardians, they are her generals. It is Mazu's divine will that protected us from Taiwan all the way to Canada. She still watches over all of us. You'll see. Believe in her."

I still feel that nagging doubt that I experienced before. The question that I asked Shu-Ling: *What if I don't believe?*

"You'll stay here with 姑婆 and Mrs. Wang," Shen tells me as he enters the room with Mrs. Wang, pulling over a padded chair for her to sit on. "It's safer here."

"What do you mean?" I challenge him. "I'm going with you. My family's down there."

Shen shakes his head, opening his mouth to argue some more, but Shu-Ling appears behind him.

"She's coming," she says, handing him what looks to be a sling bag and one for me as well. "We need all the hands we have."

"I'll do whatever you need me to do," I tell him, hoping I sound more confident than I feel. He looks down at me intently, like he wants to say something else, but then he blinks and the moment is lost.

"Just...be careful." He finally turns and walks back to the main room, with me following. The Aunties call out worried goodbyes as Shu-Ling shuts the doors. She bites her finger open and then draws a symbol on the door with her blood, between the two portraits of the gods. The blood seems to glow and then disappear into the wood. Blood, again. Similar to the ritual that I witnessed before.

"Blood is life," Shu-Ling tells me, as if she can sense my revulsion. "It's a wonder in itself that we are able to live at all, because it is so easy for us to die."

Is this one of her quotes of "wisdom" that she got from a movie? Or something she learned from the gods?

Shen brings over a green robe, which she shrugs on, then Shu-Ling ties her hair into a tight ponytail. She fastens the same items that she used from previous rituals onto her belt. The sword. The bell. The whip.

Shen pulls out a stack of talismans and tells me, "You have a matching set in your pack. These react to yin energy."

He holds up one stack, secured with a green rubber band. "The green set stuns spirits. The blue set blows up whichever part of them you put them on."

I check in my pack and pull them out, holding each of them in turn to confirm. "Stun. Explode." He nods. Even though we have these talismans for our use, it still feels inadequate. Not knowing what to expect. Not knowing what is out there waiting for us.

"Delia," Shu-Ling calls. The ghostly girl is currently leaning against the wall. "See if there is a way out. Anywhere." Delia nods and then disappears through the security screen.

"A way out . . ." Shen begins to pace, circling around the table. "There has to be a way we can get the message through." Shu-Ling stands still, massaging her forehead like that will conjure up an answer.

There's another rumble. This time even more violent. Hard enough that I stumble and have to catch myself against the wall.

"He found a third sacrifice." Shu-Ling's eyes snap open. She turns to the door of the temple. "I'm going to do this." Whatever choice she is making, it looks like a difficult one.

"Are you sure?" Shen asks, hesitant, as she raises her arms. "This will leave the temple unprotected."

"If he truly found a way to open the door, the temple is the least of our worries!" she snaps at him, then bites her other finger too. The pictures of the door gods stare at her balefully. She touches the door gods with her fingers at the same time, leaving a smear of blood on each of their foreheads.

The speaker crackles again.

"You're about to miss the show." It's Mrs. Tsai this time, her voice high and mocking. "I promise you, it will be spectacular."

The drawings of the door gods begin to blur—then to my amazement, they step off of the wall, lengthening before my eyes. They're thin, just like the paper they emerged from. Their features flat. They move in a strange fashion, shuffling forward, having to move their bodies in exaggerated ways due to their 2D nature. They swing their arms almost comically, their weapons raised in their "hands."

"Let's go," Shu-Ling says, striding toward the door, the paper soldiers following her in their lumbering fashion. Shen is behind them, and I'm the one who brings up the rear. Afraid of what we will find waiting for us in the mall.

The dim red light continues to flash, slow and steady, giving the already worn-down mall a sinister air. I hear music in the distance, coming from somewhere downstairs, in the direction of the lobby. Loud popping, like firecrackers being lit. A celebration.

We approach the railing and peer down at what lies below. From this perspective, I can see an audience, sitting in the folding chairs before the empty stage. With shock, I spot my parents in the third row. Those same, eerie placid smiles plastered on their faces. Denny sits beside them too, more still than my brother has ever been in his life. Fully controlled by whatever evil force it is that has them all in its grasp.

The sound of the firecrackers stops, replaced by the sound of drums, beating slow and steady. When we arrive at the base of the stairs, that's when I see the other figures lurking in the shadows. Small shapes peeking around the pillars. Silhouettes of all heights and shapes, standing there, watchful, farther into the mall. Every part of me screams, knowing that they are not among the living.

Finally, a figure emerges from that crowd, finding her way onto the stage, followed by ten young girls.

"Our honored guests!" Mrs. Tsai calls out toward us, arms open in greeting, while the children form a long line. They have the same blank, empty expressions. Staring out toward the audience, seeing nothing. I recognize Tina among them, and I take a big, involuntary step toward her, but Shen pulls me back. He shakes his head beside me, warning me to be careful.

Shu-Ling approaches the stage, standing there under the lights, looking up at Mrs. Tsai without fear.

"Why are you doing this?" Shu-Ling asks. "You're involving children. The innocent. They don't know what they're asking for."

"Two years ago, my daughter made a selfish decision that broke our family apart. She was going to follow Delia to god knows where," Mrs. Tsai says coldly. "But then she changed her mind. We thought she finally came to her senses, started following our recommendations...."

That's when her voice breaks, with the memory. "We were so happy... returning from Europe after Hope won that competition. Then the God of Good Deeds came to claim his prize. We were like puppets, under his control. He made us . . . watch as my daughter picked up the gun and shot her brother, her father, then turned the gun on me. He laughed and said we deserved it."

The competition. The murder-suicide. Not only a headline, but a living, breathing example standing before us. Except I'm not sure if Mrs. Tsai is fully alive anymore.

"If I remember correctly," Shu-Ling says with barely suppressed fury, "my parents came in and saved your life as well as your daughter's life. You should at least be grateful you're still alive. Not all of his victims were so lucky."

"Lucky?" Mrs. Tsai's face contorts, expression turning feral. "Your guardians came too late! My daughter should have been the one who died. Not my son. Not my husband. They're the innocent ones, but the guardians couldn't bring them back. . . ."

"Your daughter may have made the wish, but did you ever consider that you may have pushed her to make that desperate choice? That you might be part of the problem?" Shu-Ling doesn't flinch from the woman's accusations. "Demons are drawn to families with the most potential for suffering. All of that rage, despair, sorrow . . . it tastes like candy to them."

"You don't know anything about my family!" Mrs. Tsai strides forward, hands clenched into fists at her sides, and spits in Shu-Ling's face. "What does Hope know about suffering? We gave her everything."

Shu-Ling reaches up and wipes the glob of spit running down her cheek, unaffected by Mrs. Tsai's anger.

"I can only help those who are willing to accept my help," she says, voice steady. "If you are unwilling to see reason, then there's nothing else I can do."

"All of you girls are the same. Ungrateful, foolish . . ." Mrs. Tsai raises her arm, about to hit her.

"Now...now...let's talk about this." The curtain at the back of the stage parts, and Mr. Lee steps out. He's dressed in a robe just like Shu-Ling's. Except his is a deep crimson. He holds a large gold bell in his hand, face stretching into a wide grin. "Sorry I'm late."

FORTY-FIVE

最後的表演

(The Final Performance)

"**You should have** stepped aside when you had the opportunity," Mr. Lee addresses his niece with distaste from the stage, looking down at her, the type of admonishment from an elder that always made me feel small. "I would have ensured you were taken care of. You and Kai-Shen. How powerful we would have been—the Chang and the Lee lines!"

"We had a sacred duty to protect the borders between the realms," Shu-Ling replies. "Whatever you've done is destroying everything they've built."

"Once, I believed in all of that nonsense," Mr. Lee says, then turns his smile to the woman beside him. "But Joyce showed me a better way. She helped me see how I should have been respected, listened to. Now you will see what we have been able to accomplish with Hope."

"It might be too late for her, but it's not too late for you, Uncle. Listen—" Shu-Ling argues, but Mr. Lee waves his hand, dismissive.

"Who needs the gods? There are others with greater powers than them." Mr. Lee lifts his arm. "You'll see soon enough." He rings the bell, and the sound quivers in the air, with the same peculiar quality as the gong, growing louder and louder, expanding outward. He continues to ring the bell, matching the rhythm of their steps around the edge of the stage. Then, the piercing screech of an erhu, the bow scraping against the strings in a painful sound that causes us all to flinch, before it begins a happy melody.

The girls behind them begin to dance. Their feet move, stamping on the wooden stage, making it rattle under their feet. Shu-Ling watches this with a thoughtful expression, her hand at her belt, waiting to choose a weapon.

The ten of them raise their arms over their heads and sway, like the wind blowing through the trees, then join hands, forming a circle. They spin around, the song still bright and energetic, as their faces stretch out in the same smiles, showing rows of white teeth.

They look like how robots would imitate the dance of children. Macabre and surreal. Then they all stop at once.

The floor in the center of the stage, in the middle of the circle, parts, as someone emerges from underneath. A figure sitting cross-legged, a long black veil draped over their head and falling to their knees. Just like the statue before the Wall of Wishes. Slender fingers lift the fabric slowly, revealing her face as she levitates from the ground.

It's Hope. Mrs. Tsai's daughter. The girl Delia still loves, after all this time. Her empty eyes look out from her expressionless face. Like no one's home. She straightens her legs, eerily graceful as she continues to rise, until her feet touch the stage. The veil slips down behind her to drift to the floor.

The erhu's song begins to play again, and the dance continues. The feet of the girls striking the stage with a frenzied beat.

Shu-Ling chooses the whip then. It snaps from her hand with a fierce clapping sound as it strikes the floor beside her, but Mr. Lee sees it and whistles. Two spirits fly out from the watching crowd, wailing. Black nails, sharp as daggers, extend from their outstretched fingers, aiming for her face. Shu-Ling jumps back, nimbly, fingers finding a talisman from a pouch, while her whip snakes back, winding itself around the leg of one of the spirits. The spirit is flung through the air with a howl, while another gets a talisman to the face and screams. Its head explodes into ash. Just like Shen said it would.

Mr. Lee's expression darkens, his amusement gone.

"Kill them!" he yells over the sound of the dance. "Whoever succeeds will gain a new body!"

The spirits squirm and thrash in the back, eager for this promised prize. Some of them launch themselves at Shu-Ling, while others advance toward me and Shen.

Shen rolls up his sleeve and runs his hand over his tattoo. The tiger appears again from his skin, its golden form landing nimbly on the stairs beside us. It begins snapping at any of the spirits that come too close, taking off a hand or a foot in the process.

There are snarls behind us, dark forms appearing on the landing.

"Use the talismans!" Shen calls out, turning me so that we stand back-to-back. I look up the stairs while he looks below. The tiger leaps up the stairs and begins to fight the spirits who are attempting to descend upon us while the paper soldiers stand guard at the foot of the stairs.

With shaky hands, I fumble for the talismans, choosing the blue ones. Explosions sound good right about now. I risk a glance over at the stage. I can still see Tina among them, dancing in a frenzy. The shrieks of the spirits build and build, a growing cacophony. One of them comes too close, and I slap the talisman on an outstretched limb, clawing toward my face. Half of it explodes in a shower of gold sparks, and the remainder of it falls into ash. I draw out another talisman, ready to face the next threat.

There are so many. So many. I don't know if we have enough talismans to hold them off.

The beat of the music seems to speed up as we fight. There's a rustling noise, growing louder and louder, and then . . . the music stops.

"It's time!" Mr. Lee yells, voice reverberating in the air. The spirits fall silent. All at once. The shadows retreat, beaten back by a peculiar glow that has formed above the stage. It's a portal of dazzling blue, almost too bright to regard directly.

"Oh no . . ." Shen says beside me, and it is then I understand the spirits are only a distraction. Whatever horror is coming . . . this is only the beginning. The girls wait under the portal, their faces turned upward, eyes reflecting back that strange blue light. Hope extends her arms, rising from the center. She's glowing too. As she lifts up, the other girls drop in unison to kneel in a circle around her. Mrs. Tsai and Mr. Lee drop to their knees too, bowing to whatever is within Hope.

She hangs there like an angel, then her body snaps, bending backward in an arc. Her head is thrown back too, arms and legs splayed out, convulsing as something . . . breaks free from her chest. A head, first, the shoulders coming after it, until it unfolds out of Hope's body like a butterfly emerging from a cocoon. A woman.

Hope falls down to the stage when the feet at last emerge, collapsing onto her side. Her eyes remain open, unseeing. Three lines of black blood trickle out from her nostrils and slightly parted mouth. The woman above her has her eyes closed. Her lips are gray. Her skin is pale with a bluish tinge, like the skin of a corpse. Her tangled black hair spills over her shoulders in riotous waves. She has on a long red dress, which further contrasts with her unhealthy pallor. Dark lines run down her arms like too-prominent blood vessels, and they seem to writhe on her skin, forming symbols that seem almost decipherable, and then they change. . . .

What I thought were scars along her cheekbones are eyes too, blinking open to reveal the black pools behind them. She opens her mouth, and a clicking, crackling sound can be heard, her jawbone shifting from side to side as she moves the bones of her face like no one human ever should.

Two sets of arms, extending from her ribs, unfold from the side of her body, palms up. She lowers slowly, bare feet landing lightly on the stage. The portal above her head flickers and then disappears from view. She turns and regards the girls kneeling around her. Beautiful and regal and terrifying, all at the same time.

"Who among you called me?" she calls out in Mandarin. Her voice is higher than I expected, followed by a faint echo, like she's speaking from a different plane entirely.

"We are your servants, Great Goddess Juyan." Mr. Lee crawls on his hands and knees to bow at the edge of the circle. "We offer you ten willing bodies for your selection. Pick from among them the vessel with which you will walk upon the earth. The rest . . . you can feast upon—their flesh or their suffering."

"Hmm." She looks down at the girls, then gestures for them to rise. The girls slowly stand and look upon her with adoration, as if she is the most wonderful thing they have ever seen. It sickens me to see it.

Juyan regards each of them in turn, all her eyes spinning, hands reaching out to touch a chin or run her finger through their hair. The demon then stops before my sister. Tina smiles up at her, docile and compliant. Juyan reaches out and cups her face. Her sharpened gray nails stroke Tina's cheek. She closes her eyes. Tendrils of black emerge from Tina's eyes, and Juyan inhales them into her nostrils, as if savoring the scent.

"This one . . . this one has good flavor. So much anger, so much pain . . ." She sighs, rocking back. "She tastes the best of all."

"No!" I yell from the stairs, not even caring what she is, how easily she could crush me. I already understand that if she chooses Tina to be her vessel, then I will truly lose my sister forever. I'm certain of it. I run down the stairs, even as Shen tries to stop me, but I slip past him. The paper soldiers try to stop me too, but they are partially shredded now with the attacks from the demons, and their symbols do nothing to me.

It's Shu-Ling who stops me with a crack of her whip, flying in the air, close enough to my face that it would have struck me if I hadn't stopped in my tracks. The demon turns to look at us, eyes grazing over me from head to toe.

"You can't have her!" I shout, even as I realize how weak and pathetic I sound, with only my words to hurl at her. "She's not yours!"

"Impudent child!" Mrs. Tsai snaps at me before hurrying over. "Goddess, forgive us. There are those who are unwilling to bow to your great power. Destroy them."

The demon Juyan slips her hands off of my sister's face and turns fully to regard us from the stage. I find myself cowering below her, terrified of that fearsome appearance and the weight of that attention. While Shu-Ling wields her whip above her head, in her other hand she draws the wooden sword and holds it in front of both of us protectively. She's confident, unafraid.

There's a rustle to our right and left, the paper soldiers making their way forward too. Shen adds his steady presence with a hand on my back. He mentioned the dark roads his sister and his family walk down, but I never fully understood what it meant until now.

"The almighty wardens?" Juyan's eyes roll in their sockets as she laughs, raspy and amused. "This is what you have been reduced to? Sheets of paper, puppets in the hands of the guardians?"

Then the amusement sweeps away as quickly as the winter wind clears the snow, leaving only an icy expanse, a chill to her words. "Which one of you shall I feed upon first?" She takes one step forward.

"Wait for us to bring them to you, Glorious One!" Mr. Lee scurries forward in supplication, snapping his fingers. Figures in yellow emerge next to the stage. I see them now for what they are—possessed soldiers. They seem eager to drag us over as the final sacrifice.

Shu-Ling chuckles, drawing the demon's ire.

"Did you think your bravado would impress me?" Juyan sneers. "Will you continue to laugh when I feast on your still-beating heart?"

"I would give up my life to ensure you never walk upon this earth." Shu-Ling's voice rings out clearly over the din of the eager servants, waiting for their master's instructions to unleash their violence. "But demons are all the same. Unable to see the lies that are in front of them."

"*She* is the one uttering lies!" Mrs. Tsai says, frantic. "Do not listen—"

One slender arm darts out and closes around her throat, lifting her up, kicking and choking.

"Silence," Juyan hisses, then redirects her attention to Shu-Ling. "What lies?"

"They call themselves your faithful servants, but you don't know the full extent of their *offering*." From her pouch, Shu-Ling slowly draws out a vial.

"Stop her!" Mr. Lee roars, and the figures in yellow quickly surround us. One of them makes quick work of the paper wardens, ripping them apart with their bare hands. They saved these men for this. To ensure that we will be compliant, brought up to the stage as willing sacrifices. But Shu-Ling throws the vial onto the wooden stage before they reach her, and it shatters and releases gold sparks into the air.

FORTY-SIX

厲祭

(The Sacrifice)

The sparks remind me of Shen's tiger, which has long disappeared. They rise up and dance, spreading along the stage, burning with a transparent flame, but there is no heat—only a symbol that emerges. The same one that was formed from the blood of the three sacrifices. The one Delia made me draw.

"The temple is directly underneath us," I whisper. Golden threads emerge, rising to the skylight. They form a boundary, a golden cage.

"It's the Bagua," Shen says, calling the symbol for what it is.

"*You...dare?*" Juyan's voice rises, as an impossible wind picks up. It lifts the hair of the demon, rippling wild black waves above her, and lightning flashes in her eyes. She drops Mrs. Tsai back onto her knees, where she clutches her throat, gasping for air.

"No...please..." Mr. Lee drops down to the floor, lowering his forehead to the stage. "It's not...it's not what you think."

"It's exactly what you think," Shu-Ling says, calm and steady, even as the figures in yellow grab her arms, pull them back. "They want to trap you, bind you, so you can be controlled to do their bidding."

"It is a doorway." Mrs. Tsai folds herself in half, chokes out her words. "It's a way to bring more of your lieutenants from hell. A way for you to set up your own kingdom, here among the living!"

Juyan takes a purposeful stride forward, sweeping two girls aside as she reaches out and touches the barrier. It sends out another cascade of golden sparks, and she pulls back, hissing.

"Go." She gestures, and all the children stand, obedient, forming a single row behind her. Leaving only the prostrate forms of Mr. Lee and Mrs. Tsai in the middle of the stage.

"Look at me!" Juyan commands. Mrs. Tsai's shoulders tremble while Mr. Lee looks fearful for the first time. Juyan's upper arms join together in prayer at her chest. Then she lifts her lower set of arms as well, placing her hands on their heads. Like she's about to offering them a blessing.

There's the feeling of electricity in the air, like the taste of the rain before a storm. Then...the heads burst. A shower of blood arcs above the stage, dripping down the edge and splattering onto the floor before our feet. Mrs. Tsai's body falls sideways, sliding off, landing into the fountain with a plop. While Mr. Lee lands on his side, blood dripping from what remains of his neck.

The pressure on our arms cease as the figures in yellow who were holding us back all let go.

The demon Juyan lifts her many hands to the air, catching the droplets as they splatter upon her skin. She raises one hand to her lips, almost delicate, and licks her finger, slowly, an expression of almost ecstasy on her face.

"Soon! Soon we will feast!" the spirits yowl.

"I've forgotten how good it tastes," she says, continuing to lick the blood from where it splattered against her skin. "But now...who among you will free me?" She reaches out and grabs one of the girls. *Tina.*

I scream, but Shen grabs the strap of my pack. Pulling me close to him. I can feel him shaking beside me.

"Patience," he reminds me, whispering into my ear. I'm about to turn on him and tell him what I think about him and his sister and his *patience*, when—

"Wait!" Shu-Ling nimbly vaults onto the stage, passing through the still-shimmering barrier like it is nothing. "I have a bargain for you."

Juyan regards her with her head tipped and a decidedly unfriendly stare. "What other treachery will you offer me? Let me tell you there is no other option. Free me, and the rest of the children can go. Or else you can watch me eat them, one by one."

"Leave them alone," Shu-Ling says. "You require a better vessel. Someone with the knowledge to escape from here. I will help you. If you let them go." She places the whip at her feet, takes off the pouches, lays them down as well.

"No, you can't!" It's Shen who protests now, realizing what his sister is offering. "You can't! She's going to be too powerful."

"Stay back!" Shu-Ling snaps, holding her hand up to stop him. She pulls the sword out and holds it up to her palm, slices it open, with only a slight frown to indicate that it hurts when it cuts into her flesh. Blood wells up, darkly red, as she lifts it up toward the demon, tossing the sword off the stage, where it lands in the bloody fountain.

The demon licks her lips. "Interesting."

"Taste my blood." Shu-Ling holds up her hand. "You'll know that it has the power of a conduit to the guardians. The Sight. The ability to wield yin energy. You will have no better vessel than me."

"Hmm." The demon lowers her head beside Shu-Ling's and sniffs, her breath stirring her hair. She then pulls back, dips her finger into the blood, digging her nail into the wound, grinning all the way while Shu-Ling grimaces. Finally, she lifts it up to her mouth and tastes it, nodding with satisfaction when she confirms it is good. "You speak the truth. You and I, we will do great things."

"Let them go first, and then you can have me." Shu-Ling does not cower, even as the demon regards her with a thoughtful expression. Without breaking their gaze, the demon nods again, and then the girls turn and walk obediently down the stairs, single file. They join the audience, sitting down cross-legged upon the floor. Waiting.

With her lower arms, Juyan grabs Shu-Ling around the waist and lifts her up into the air. With her upper hands, she holds Shu-Ling's head still. They stare at each other for a long, drawn-out moment. The air is suddenly filled with the sound of indecipherable whispers, slowly building. The whispers join together, becoming many, many voices, muttering a guttural chant.

Blackness fills the whites of Shu-Ling's eyes as her mouth drops open, and from its depths emerges a terrible scream. Her body thrashes violently, still hanging in the air. My ears ring from the sound of the screams, as the chants turn into furious howls.

Someone else *is* screaming too, alongside her.

I think it's me.

"Ruby! Ruby!" Someone is yelling my name, trying to get my attention. My ears still ring with an odd noise. Black tendrils emerge from Juyan's body, piercing Shu-Ling all over, until she's enveloped in it, and I can't see her anymore.

What did Shu-Ling call it once? 惡意 . . . *all the darkness within human hearts.* That's what she is filling her with. Somehow, I could hear her voice still. Echoing inside of my skull. My memories? Or something else?

My mind fragments, as there is only so much a person is able to endure without succumbing to terror. Dances by girls to call forth a demon. Shimmering strands of mystical gold crisscrossing the ceiling like spider-webs. A woman with too many eyes and limbs. The explosion of heads, like watermelons. Blood raining from the sky . . .

"You cannot let her off the stage." Somehow Delia is there, speaking urgently to Shen and to me. Shen shakes me once, shakes me twice. He's the one still yelling my name. Behind him, Shu-Ling emerges again from the black. Eyes closed, face serene.

Delia's words are slow, running through my mind like molasses, trailing through my fingers, sticky and difficult to comprehend.

"If we cannot contain her, more horrors will come. . . ."

Shu-Ling's eyes snap open, and something unearthly looks out. The darkness has filled her eyes entirely, but there is a red ring that outlines where her iris should be. She slowly moves her head forward, neck crack-ing as she rolls it in a circle. Her fingers bend backward, unnaturally, bones crunching with strange sounds as her joints adjust and pop into place. Her hands curl back into fists.

Shen reaches into the fountain and pulls out the dripping sword. His jaw is set with grim determination. He climbs the stairs beside the stage. The fountain seems to bubble behind him.

Blood is life. Shu-Ling's voice echoes in my mind. What she once said to me. *It's so easy for us to die.*

Shu-Ling lifts her hand and holds it up before her face, regarding it with that alien curiosity.

My blood is the conduit.

"She thought she could bargain with me." Juyan speaks with Shu-Ling's face, but the voice that comes out is not Shu-Ling's. It's deeper, more calculating. "But now who will stop me from keeping up my end of the bargain?"

Shen lifts the sword above his head, a talisman in the other hand, advancing upon his sister. Ready to strike her down.

"Kill them!" the demon screams from Shu-Ling's mouth. "Kill them both, and you can have your pick of all of the waiting bodies here. You can return to the world of the living again! I promise you blood! I promise you life!"

The spirits shriek in triumph and rush toward us in a frenzy. My hand reaches for the talismans again pulling them out. I slam the first against the eager spirit reaching for me with their too-long arms. I expect it to explode, but instead it freezes before me.

Shit. I picked the wrong one. Another spirit tries to grab for me, and the talisman stuns it too. It seems to have formed a boundary, the spirits now having to crawl over each other to reach me. But there are too many of them, gnashing their teeth, snarling, all of them wishing for my death.

"Get in the barrier!" Delia yells at me from the stairwell. "Help Shen! Keep her in there! They're coming!"

Who's coming?

I scramble up the stairs just as a spirit's hand closes around my ankle and tries to pull me down. I look back and kick at it, ripping another talisman out and slamming it on its head. It explodes in another shower of sparks, letting me go. I crawl inside the barrier and see more spirits throw themselves against the boundary, but they're not able to get in. They shriek, furious that they're not able to reach me. My arms are covered in scratches and bruises. There's a line of pain running down my shoulder.

Beside me, there's a strangled cry. I leap to my feet, only to see that Shu-Ling is holding Shen captive by his right wrist, the sword landing with a clatter on the floor. Shen's left arm hangs down at his side, limp and useless. Even from here, I can see the angle is wrong, like his arm has been twisted out of its socket. Talismans flutter down toward the ground around him, useless. She smiles down at him and grips another finger, bending it back until it snaps. He screams again. The pain is evident upon his face, having already suffered so much.

"How will you draw your pitiful symbols now?" The demon laughs. She drops him, and he lands on his knees, jarring his arm. He falls onto his side, tears running down his face. I can see the bone of his forearm protruding from his elbow, and bitter bile rushes into my mouth.

"First, I'm going to eat your uncle's heart," the demon says, grinning down at him. She raises her foot and kicks him right at his broken shoulder. He falls onto his side, groaning. "Then I'm going to eat the heart of your little girlfriend." Her gaze flickers to me, her enjoyment evident, confident that there is nowhere else I can go, with the spirits waiting outside the boundary to kill me.

"Then, finally, I'm going to eat your heart. I'm going to savor every bite of your suffering while your sister screams inside of me, knowing that she chose this for you. Her *precious little brother*." She utters those final words with joyous delight.

"The sword, Ruby!" I hear Delia calling from a distance, but everything outside the boundary seems muffled, far away. I reach down and pick it up. It's still damp and warm from Shen's hand. I don't know how to wield it, but I'm going to have to. I'm the only one now.

Shu-Ling turns and crouches over the body of her uncle. She plunges her hand into his chest and pulls out the heart. She brings it to her mouth and begins to eat, taking big, ravenous bites, ripping and tearing into the flesh with her teeth. I pick up a handful of talismans, half expecting they will be useless against her, but I have to try.

She looks at me expectantly when I lift the sword with a cry, her bloody mouth open in a vicious grin. Her fingers lengthen, nails sharp like claws. I throw the talismans in her face. She swipes at me, and I drop down, her fingers catching in my hair, but with both hands joined around the hilt of the sword, I thrust it into her foot, throwing the entirety of my weight upon it, piercing it in the center.

I feel it go through, and I use all my strength to push it farther, as it sinks deeper still.

This is it. Will it hold her?

FORTY-SEVEN

開光

(Eyes Open)

Shu-Ling howls above me as her hands find my hair, dragging me backward, until my head is on fire with the pain. She throws me as hard as she can, and I fly in an arc, landing with my back against the fake stone mountain behind the pool. I feel something crack as I slide down to fall onto the stairs underneath. The pain shoots up my thigh, and every time I shift, it sends another jolt of agony through my body.

"You think you can stop me?" Even from this vantage point, I can see Shu-Ling with her hand gripped tight upon the hilt of the sword. She pulls it upward, inch by inch, straining with the exertion. Smoke seeps from her hand, like it's burning her skin, but she doesn't seem to feel the pain.

Is it too late? The strength slowly seeps out of me, and I shut my eyes, ready to be ripped apart by the waiting spirits.

Suddenly, my face is drenched with water, my eyes snapping open again at the shock of the cold. I look up to see something rise out of the fountain. A man dressed in gleaming red armor, a huge sword strapped to his back. I watch him step out of the fountain and stand on the floor of the mall, the water mysteriously disappearing the moment he sets foot on the tile.

In his arm, he cradles a headless statue. But all the blackness has been cleaned off of it. I can see the vibrant color of the statue's robes, even though its hands and its feet are still missing. The man looks down at me sternly, and I stare at him, not knowing what he wants, before he slips the statue into my arms. He pulls his sword out of the sheath and then begins a complicated formation, as another symbol rises into the air above his head. Bagua, again, but the markings inside the shape are different this time. Just like his statue. *The Night General.*

A sound comes from above, and two more figures descend from overhead. One, a woman, dressed in robes of blue green. She holds a fan made of peacock feathers in one hand, and in the other, a book. Those are the tools of the General of the Dawn. The final man has dark brows and severe eyes. He wears a black robe embroidered with gold designs, and on his head is a hat with two pieces that come out from either side like wings. An official's hat. *The Judge.*

I can't help the gasp of relief that comes out of my mouth. The guardians are here. The gods have finally found us.

"No!" Shu-Ling stares at them in disbelief, Mr. Lee's blood still dripping from her chin. "No! Not when I'm so close." She turns to run, but the man in the red armor leaps in the air, and a whip snakes out of his hand as it wraps itself around Shu-Ling's body and sends her crashing down on the stage.

Using her fingers, she draws a symbol in the air, and it explodes outward, catching the the Night General on the shoulder. He twists to avoid it, but the whip follows him, loosening its grip on Shu-Ling. She jumps nimbly to her feet and off the stage with a grin, the golden cage no longer able to hold her.

"Who will join me?" she calls. "We will fight back against the tyranny of the guardians!" The spirits are a mass of teeth and claws and limbs. They roar as they descend upon waiting generals, who are a whirlwind as they counter the attack.

Shu-Ling makes her way through her silent audience and toward the exit, intent on her freedom. But something ripples on the glass of the doors. One face emerges, another next to it. A tall, thin figure, dressed in white, with skeletal features. A short, stout man with bulging eyes and a bristly beard. She falls back into a fighting stance.

"You shouldn't be here!" Shu-Ling screams, hands already busy drawing more shapes in the air. She throws them at the wardens, but they absorb the sparks, rendering them useless. Chains appear in the hand of the shorter warden, clinking as they fall to the ground. The taller warden wields a slender sword, as the two of them advance upon Shu-Ling. *Lord Seven and Lord Eight.*

Her arms drop to her sides as they push her to her knees. She does not try to struggle or flee any longer. She instead glares at them balefully as they wind the chains around her torso, hissing all sorts of vile things.

The air is filled with the sound of wailing as the guardians quickly dispatch the spirits that tried to fight them. Many of them, realizing the tide of the battle has turned, try to fly to the skylight to bang on the glass or rattle the exit doors. But whatever boundaries prevented Shu-Ling from making contact with the outside world before seem to still be capable of keeping the spirits locked in.

I keep an eye on Shen as I'm sitting there, watching the chaos unfold around me. Every time I shift my weight, my leg spasms painfully, so there is nowhere I can go. As yet another spirit cries as they are taken in by one of the guardians, Shen finally moves, groaning. His eyes blink open. He tries to sit up and yelps when he jostles his broken arm, only managing to flop himself to a half sitting position.

"I don't think you should move," I tell him.

He turns his head to look at me and then winces when he attempts a smile. Half of his face is already puffy and bruising.

"Probably good advice," he says. "How are you doing?"

"I've been better." I nod, the relief rushing through me with the knowledge he's still alive, then I add: "I think my leg is broken."

Delia appears at the other end of the stage. She bends down to check on someone, and I can see the tenderness in her expression. In the way she reaches out to try and touch them, but her hand passes through. Something pained crosses her face. Regret? But then she stands up and makes her way toward us.

"Wow, you're in a sorry state," Delia comments as she plops herself down between us, addressing Shen. He cranes his head to try and say something to her, but then winces at the pain.

"What do you think the afterlife is like?" She meets my eyes then. "Do you think there will be cats?"

"What are you talking about?" I glance at her. "You're ... you're coming back." Then I remember her body beneath the Wall of Wishes. All the blood spiraling to the statue. The fire that burned there ... Is there a body she can return to? What if this means she's actually gone?

"I'm dead, remember? With a capital D." She makes a slicing motion across her throat, then, more serious, she pulls her legs toward her and folds her arms on her knees. She still has that gray pallor.

The three of us fall quiet for a few minutes while watching the guardians capture more spirits above and around us. As unreal as any action movie.

"I'm ready for what comes next," Delia says slowly, appearing slightly faded now. "If you see Hope, and she remembers me . . . take care of her, okay?"

"We will," Shen tells her. I nod, already feeling the tears welling up, because even though I've known her for only a short while, she's made me feel accepted as a friend.

"Thanks." Delia grins. "Also, there's a cookie tin in the cupboard above my fridge. It's blue. There's a bunch of sewing stuff in there, but underneath it all is a few hundred dollars. My emergency stash. The two of you go on a date. Somewhere nice."

Shen and I both sputter, shocked that she's bringing this up at the most awkward time.

"Promise me! Don't cheap out." Delia remains insistent. "Ruby can pick. Go to one of those fancy places by the waterfront. You pay for it all." She looks down at Shen, trying to appear stern.

"Yeah, okay," Shen finally agrees, meeting my eyes. Something warm rises in my chest. At whatever this is between us, new and forming. Or it could be internal bleeding. Who knows. I start to giggle and then start half coughing, half wheezing.

"If you survive this far only to choke to death, I'll drag you out of the afterlife myself," Delia threatens. I chuckle again then, genuinely this time, trying to stop myself from sobbing. "And don't forget to feed Rabbit."

"Gods," Shen groans, exasperated. "What else are you going to add onto your list?"

"Rabbit? You have a rabbit?" I ask, confused.

"It's the calico cat that's as round as a Swiss roll," Shen tells me. "The one that she brings to the café all the time."

"Hey! She's big-boned! You take that back or else I'll break your other fingers," Delia threatens with a laugh. I can hear sirens over the commotion of the battle. In the distance through the entry doors, red and blue lights appear. The police, the ambulance, the firefighters, they're here.

There are muffled shouts, people calling out, but they seem very far away. It feels like I'm floating away from the world. The sight of those lights remind me it's almost Christmas. Tina's favorite holiday. I should tell Baba to put up the lights.

FORTY-EIGHT

使命

(The Call)

I wake in a hospital room. The sound of something beeping beside me. I ache all over, my throat dry and parched. I don't have my glasses on, so everything is a blur. I can see, sort of, one leg poking out of my hospital gown, the other leg encased in a cast and propped up on a pillow. My right arm is hooked up to an IV. I stare at my hand and try to wiggle my fingers, but I can't. I tell my left hand to move, but it doesn't. It lies there, limp.

A sudden rush of panic floods my body. The fear that I will remain here, forever, trapped in my own mind. I open my mouth to scream, and then the hospital room disappears in a flash of blinding light. So brilliant I have to close my eyes. When I struggle to open my eyes again, there are three forms before me. Three figures, I think, though it's hard to tell with the light. They turn to me, and I'm flooded with the sense of peace. An understanding that they do not wish me harm.

"Chen Jing-xian." One of the figures calls out my Chinese name. A man's voice. A teacher's voice. Speaking in crisp Mandarin, forcing me to feel like I should stand at attention. "Also known as Ruby."

"Present," I croak out, and then I'm immediately mortified. All those years of getting drilled in Chinese school, the response automatic.

"You've put yourself in harm's way to protect your family and others around you." Another voice speaks, this time a woman's. "Along with Chang Kai-Shen, Sun Xin-di." *Shen, Delia...*

"Are they... are they okay?" I ask, even though I'm afraid to know. Where is Delia now? Has she moved on to the afterlife? Was it like what she expected? My heart clenches at the thought. Will I ever see her again?

"You have a choice to make, Ruby," the woman continues softly. She pronounces my name in a funny way, in two drawn-out syllables, like many of my relatives often do back home. Roo-bee. But what she says next takes away my urge to laugh. "Chang Shu-Ling sacrificed herself to save others, and we will work to make sure that sacrifice is not in vain."

"Can you save her?" I find myself pleading. She's lost so much. Taken on a role that nobody should have to fulfill unwillingly, and yet she tried her best to maintain her parents' legacy. "Can you expel that demon out of her?"

"We can try." Another man joins the conversation, this voice is younger, warmer. Honey-toned. "And here is where you have a decision to make. An important choice."

I stay quiet. I don't know how I can do whatever it is that they will ask of me. I'm just a girl.

"That's where you are wrong," the woman says. Like she is able to read my mind. "Everyone is capable of making a choice. Young, old. All that matters is doing something, even when you're afraid." They look at each other, like they're consulting with one another, before the first man speaks again.

"We have asked for an exception from Mazu, the Sacred Mother—a glimpse into what is to come," he explains. "Juyan's appearance is only the beginning. There's been unrest in hell. War looms. We cannot hold it back any longer."

"But...that has never been the concern of the living," the honey-voiced man speaks up. "You can go back to your old life. Like the rest of your family. Wake up knowing that there's been a terrible accident, with spotty memory and the knowledge that something exists out there, always out of reach."

"What...what's the other option?" I venture, even as I am scared of what they will say.

"And that is why I had faith in you, Ruby, all along!" the woman exclaims. "This was your trial. I've watched your struggle, but when picking between the known and the unknown, you choose to keep going. You have passed beyond our expectations."

Fate, Delia told me. Too many coincidences for it to be accidental.

"One conduit is no longer enough for the coming war. We ask you to join the others, to become the embodiment of the guardians. We will be Three on earth yet again, to face the coming threat," the teacher man explains. "Shen is one. Delia is the other. You could be the third."

"What do you choose?" the honey-voiced man asks.

"Are you willing?" the woman says, eager.

I'm afraid of what comes next. I've always been afraid. But I don't want to sit idle any longer, without a purpose. I don't know if I can return to my old life, afraid to speak up for myself, happy to go along with whatever direction my parents guide me into, too scared of failure.

I can't go back.

"Yes," I whisper, and I'm taken once again by the light.

—

There's a heaviness on my thigh. On the leg without the cast. I blink and I see an elbow, a ponytail. Tina. There's another blurry figure in the distance, looking like she's reading. I squint.

"Ma?" I manage to call out.

"Ruby!" She rushes to the other side, grabbing my hand. "Ruby... you're finally awake."

"Can you...can you get me my glasses?" She grabs them from the side table and slides them on my face, the world slipping into clarity once again. Ma looks tired, heavy bags under her eyes.

"What happened?" I ask, tentative. Not knowing how much she knows.

"There was a gas leak at the mall during the performance," Ma says, brow furrowing, the way it usually does when she's angry. "It caused everyone to get sick. Lose consciousness. There was a terrible accident."

She shakes her head, remembering whatever the guardians must have imprinted in her mind.

"The stage collapsed," Ma continues, frowning. "When we came to, the ambulance had already taken the injured away, so we didn't see much of what happened. Part of the metal structure fell on you and broke your leg. Your friends from the bubble tea café? They...dragged you out before the...secondary explosion and saved your life."

"The...explosion?"

"The gas leak was caused by a broken pipe, in one of the storage rooms underground. Everything burned...." The broken skylight. The bodies. The fire below.

"Wait." I catch on, my mind still too slow from waking up. "My friends? What happened to them?"

"Yes, that boy who does the paintings, Shen? And Delia, the other girl that works there too. She says she knows you."

There's so much I want to tell them. Shen. Delia. And another part of me is simply happy Delia's alive. That they made the exception, like she said. Mazu's divine intervention. They must have spoken with the guardians too, if my mother has seen Delia since. Do they know what happened to Shu-Ling? Is Hope alive too?

Ma's cell phone rings and she answers, standing up. I can hear Baba on the other end, and I'm assuming Denny too, safe at home. I lean back with a sigh, exhausted.

"You're awake!" Tina is suddenly on top of me, squeezing me so hard that I feel like I might pop from the inside out.

"Hey! Hey!" I'm half protesting, half laughing. "It hurts! You're hurting me."

"I'm so sorry, big sis," Tina says, letting go. She looks up at me, all apology in her eyes. I know what she's apologizing for. Even she if she doesn't quite remember. I can see the remorse on her face.

"That's okay," I tell her, squeezing her hand tight. My heart is so unbearably full, happy she's back and here with me. "You didn't know."

尾聲

(Epilogue)

The recital is held at the Annex downtown. An intimate theatre with plush seats and a beautiful natural wood stage. The evening opened with a string quartet, playing some chamber music selections. I barely heard most of it, nervous as I was to play right after the intermission.

I step onto the stage with my flats, not quite ready to perform in heels like my favorite virtuoso, but I am wearing a gown I love. One that I picked out for myself. The blue dress shimmers around my body like a waterfall, silky against my skin.

I turn toward the audience. It's hot up here, under all the lights. I can only make out vague faces in the distance, but I don't pay attention to them. I settle on the cool piano bench, raise my hands, and begin to play.

My nervousness dissipates as soon as I play the first stretch of notes. I fly through my ARCT program, knowing already that this will be one of my best performances. I feel utterly confident in my treatment of the music, in my knowledge that I played the best that I could, even if I did falter very slightly on one of the runs of the Fantaisie-Impromptu.

My left leg still aches very slightly when I put weight on it or turn it a certain way, an occasional reminder of what happened last year at the mall. But my piano playing remained intact.

I bow to the applause of the audience, my face stretching wide into a grin. The electric feeling of performance still dancing over my shoulders and down to my fingertips. Piano is a lot less daunting once you've survived supernatural attacks by demons and ghosts.

After it's all done, Mrs. Nguyen is the first to hand me a bouquet of yellow roses.

"Fantastic performance, Ruby!" She beams at me. "I knew you could do it!" All that's left is to attend my diploma exam at the end of this month, and then I'll be done.

Arms wrap around my legs, and I'm squeezed from another direction as Denny and Tina both hug me at the same time. I laugh, trying to tug my dress out from under Denny's shoes as they chatter around me excitedly.

"You did it!" Tina looks so happy for me, because she knew how nervous I was leading up to this. I give her another hug, just because I can.

"Ruby! Come here." Ma gestures for me to join her and Baba in talking to another couple.

"You must be so proud." I recognize the woman as an engineer at Baba's firm, but I don't know the man.

"We are, we are!" Baba says, smiling at me.

"She took first place in two of her Kiwanis Festival entries this year!" Ma is eager to brag about my accomplishments. I know indirectly they are proud of me, their way of keeping me humble by never telling it to my face.

"Ruby! Ruby!" Another voice calls out for my attention, and this time it's Mrs. Sui. She thrusts a bouquet of lilies into my arms. "You were wonderful! Absolutely wonderful!" I can see the other members of the Chorus of Aunties a few steps away, talking with Dawn, and it makes me happy they were all able to come.

"These are my favorite! Thank you!" I breathe in the scent of the flowers.

"Well, who do you think got them? I'm here to steal his thunder!" Mrs. Sui cackles, turning to look at Shen behind her.

"You can take all the credit, 姑婆." Shen laughs.

"Let me take over as your chauffeur." Delia appears with a wink, taking the wheelchair from Shen. "Leave the lovebirds to chat."

"Delia!" I exclaim, looking around to see if my parents heard. As far as they're concerned, Shen and I are "good friends," and they're more lenient about him because they believe he saved my life.

Delia sticks her tongue out at me, already pushing Mrs. Sui toward the other aunties. "Oh and, Hope says hi. She'll meet up with you and Tina next week like she promised when she's back in town."

After the horrifying events that reconnected Hope and Delia, we found out the true story behind what happened with her family. When the guardians saved them, Hope was taken in for safety. But when the split in the temple occurred, the malevolent spirit inside Hope made a bargain with Mrs. Tsai. To let her use her daughter as a vessel, help her grow in power, and she would grant her everything her heart desires. It was convenient then that there was a disgruntled disciple who knew a little too much about the workings of the guardians, who had knowledge of the dark rituals that would make all of this possible. Mr. Lee, Shen's uncle.

Hope lived a nightmare as a vessel for a demon for two years, having someone else operate her body, alive and yet never in control. She's only starting to unravel all the ramifications of that on her mind and body. I shudder every time I think about it.

I lead Shen to the little room in the back where performers can prepare for their sessions—more a closet really—where I can drop the flowers on the floor next to my things. When the door shuts behind us, I finally feel like I can breathe. Away from all the noise.

"Come here," Shen says, voice low. I step into his embrace, enveloped by his body and his familiar warmth. The past few months have been nice. Getting to know each other better, even as we are dealing with our new . . . responsibilities.

"You're freezing," he murmurs, rubbing my bare arms. I rest my head on his shoulder, close my eyes.

But it's also been a lot. Training with the guardians. Trying to catch up to him with all that he knows about the Sight, about talismans, about the gods and the magic that surrounds us. Delia moving in with him now that Shu-Ling is gone, the three of us preparing for what is coming. Pretending to be normal the rest of the time. Hiding it from my family. It takes a toll.

With Shen though, I can be myself. He understands the burden, the responsibility, the weight of everything.

"Can you just hold me for a little while?" I whisper.

And he does.

A Note from Judy

Dear Readers,

I identify as a 1.5 generation immigrant, having immigrated to Canada from Taiwan when I was eight years old. Old enough to remember what it was like to live in Taiwan and carry around an ache for my previous life there, but I didn't live there long enough to be fluent in Mandarin or Taiwanese. The longing for a home that will never be mine followed me all throughout my life.

I used books and movies as a way to bridge that gap, and a fascination with folklore and urban legends is something that stayed with me and deepened in the years since. This story is inspired by the way Taiwanese folk beliefs is woven intimately into the day-to-day, as evident in the temples that are present on almost every city block in my hometown of Kaohsiung, and I have added my own interpretations for the sake of the story.

A few points of consideration:

This story cannot be set in Vancouver, BC, without acknowledging its location on the shared traditional territory of the Coast Salish Peoples, specifically the xʷməθkʷəy̓əm (Musqueam), Sḵwx̱wú7mesh (Squamish), and sel̓íl̓witulh (Tsleil-Waututh) Nations.

I wish I could have delved deeper into the rich history of Vancouver's Chinatown and the Chinese, Cantonese, and Taiwanese communities in the Greater Vancouver area and Richmond. I encourage anyone who has their interest piqued by what is mentioned in *The Dark Becomes Her* to visit the Chinatown Storytelling Centre and the Chinese Canadian Museum located in Vancouver's Chinatown to learn from the exhibits there.

I have drawn from the many branches of Taiwanese folk religion to craft the "magic" in this story, especially Taoist practices, and it's important to point out what may be viewed as supernatural are common beliefs held today by others. In particular, the guardians are inspired by the 八家將 (a Taiwanese folk belief of minor gods who are able to capture evil spirits), but they are not supposed to represent real gods.

I want to note especially that **the spiritual practices in this story are embellished and fictional details are added and this book is not meant to be educational material on how Taiwanese folk religion is currently practiced or utilized in Taiwan and in overseas Taiwanese communities today.**

Glossary

Note: Traditional Chinese characters are used within the text as purposeful representations of the thought patterns of my personal experience of speaking multiple languages. The glossary is provided for the reader who has an interest in pronunciations of character names and certain terms and phrases. I have chosen Hanyu Pinyin for Mandarin and Taiwanese is represented in italics in Tâi-lô.

Character Name Pronunciation Guide

Name	Chinese Name	Pronunciation
Ruby Jing-Xian Chen	陳靜嫻	Chén jìng xián
"Shen" Kai-Shen Chang	張凱聖	Zhāng kǎi shèng
Shu-Ling Chang	張淑霖	Zhāng shū lín
Delia Xin-Di Sun	孫馨笛	Sūn xīn dí
Juyan	鋸豔	Jù yàn

Terms and Phrases

Type	English	Chinese	Pronunciation	Alternative/ Specific Meaning
Family	Older sister	姊姊	jiě jiě	
	Great-aunt	姑婆	gū pó	Grandfather's sister (on the father's side)
Religion	Hanged Spirit	吊死鬼	diào sǐ guǐ	A spirit who died by hanging, characterized by their long tongue
	Split-Faced Spirit	石榴鬼	shí liú guǐ	A spirit that constantly grins with a mouth filled with bloody teeth that looks like pomegranate seeds
	The Wardens	七爺八爺	qī yé bā yé	Help spirits go to the underworld; also known as Lord Seven and Lord Eight
	The Sight	陰陽眼	yīn yang yǎn	The ability to see spirits (Yin-Yang Eyes)
	Dark Temple	陰廟	yīn miào	A temple that does not worship a recognized god
	Earth God	土地公	tǔ dì gōng	A minor god that protects businesses, farms, and travelers
	King Yanluo	閻羅王	yán luó wáng	King of the Underworld
Phrases	Ugly one	醜八怪	chou bā guài	Insult for an ugly person
	"Don't put your warm face against a cold butt."	熱臉貼冷屁股	rè liǎn tiē lěng pì gǔ	Don't keep trying to impress someone who doesn't care about you.
	"Work hard before you can win."	愛拼才會贏	*ài piànn tsiah ē iânn*	You have to put in effort before you can be successful.
	Shut your mouth	閉嘴	bì zuǐ	Shut up.
	All brawn, no brains	頭腦簡單, 四肢發達	tóu nǎo jiǎn dān, sì zhī fā dá	An insult for someone who is physically strong but mentally weak

Type	English	Chinese	Pronunciation	Alternative/ Specific Meaning
Phrases (cont'd)	"If you avoid dark roads, then you won't attract ghosts."	若無行暗路,袂去拄著鬼	*nā-bô kiânn-àm-lōo bē-khì tú-tiȯh kuí*	You don't have anything to be afraid of if you don't do bad things.
	Guilty things	虧心事	kuī xīn shì	Activities that could be shameful
	"When you mention Cao-cao, then Cao-cao will appear."	說曹操,曹操就到	shuō cáo cāo, cáo cāo jiù dào	Speak of the devil
	Foolish child	戇囡仔	*gong gín á*	Taiwanese term for children who are not listening

Acknowledgments

Thank you first and foremost to Rick Riordan for selecting my book to be part of this amazing imprint and for writing such a wonderful introduction. It made me cry when I first read it. I am so deeply grateful that I get to share this particular story with readers, one filled with Taiwanese legends and folklore, as well as food and traditions.

To my editor, Rebecca Kuss: Thank you for understanding from the start the type of story that I wanted to tell and for helping me shape Ruby's book into a much better one. I could not imagine a more perfect editor to work with on this project.

Thank you to Rachel Brooks, for continuing to be my agent extraordinaire, and supporting my many random ideas and concepts, whatever they may be.

So much appreciation to the Rick Riordan Presents team for all your work on bringing this book to life. Thank you to Assistant Editor

Ash I. Fields, Managing Editors Sara Liebling and Iris Chen. Thank you to Guy Cunningham for copyediting. The sales team: Andrea Rosen, Vicki Korlishin, Michael Freeman, Lebria Casher. The marketing team: Holly Nagel, Danielle DiMartino. The School and Library team: Dina Sherman, Bekka Mills, Maddie Hughes. Publicity: Crystal McCoy and Daniela Escobar. Many, many thanks to ZIPCY for making such a stunningly terrifying cover, as well as Zareen Johnson for the cover design and working with me to perfect the interiors and the Chinese text.

This book would not be possible without the inspirations of the Taiwanese authors that I greatly admire: 笭菁 (linea) and 星子 (teensy).

I'm thankful to Kat Cho, Axie Oh, and Janella Angeles, who I will always consider to be my mentors. For seeing something in my summer camp horror story, and for encouraging me to keep going. And to Rebecca Schaeffer, who told me to never give up on my horror dreams.

Thank you to Kate Alice Marshall and Ava Reid for your kind words. I continue to be huge fans of your work.

Many thanks to Bob of A Wok Around Chinatown and the guides of Chinatown Wonders at the Heart of the City Festival for sharing your vast knowledge of Chinatown's history, buildings, and food.

Thank you to the Chinatown Together team for your collaboration and for working hard toward the goal of an accessible and welcoming Chinatown. Thank you to Queenie Choo of S.U.C.C.E.S.S. and Beverly Ho of Yarrow Society for the generosity of your time and knowledge.

Thank you to Yilin Wang for wandering around Vancouver with me. May we discover more secret temples and hidden realms!

I'm grateful to have my writing friends—Nafiza Azad and Roselle Lim, for always having words of encouragement and inspiration.

To Mimi, for always being there to listen to my late-night rants, for putting up with my horror movie sessions, and for teaching me about sisterhood (fine, I guess the next bubble tea is on me).

And so much love to my beloved family: my husband, Aaron, and my daughters, Lyra and Lydia. I do it all for you.

Coming soon: more exciting, exhilarating horror from Judy I. Lin and Rick Riordan Presents!